The Pack

Crystal Bittel

First edition

Editing by Nicole Kralis

Agent: Nicole Kralis

Cover art by Zoe Tmax

To Mayla, Lillianna and Everleigh, my real life Everelle, may you never stop reaching for your dreams, and following your hearts wherever they may lead. I love you three so much.

Love, Mom.

Trigger Warnings

This book contains some scenes that may be triggering or upsetting to some readers. Reader discretion is advised. Please take your mental health seriously.

Examples of these triggers are:

Violence

Loss of a loved one

Grief

Sexually Explicit Scenes

Torture

Abuse

Sexual Assault

Explicit Language

Pronunciations

When I first started this series, the places and names went through a few different changes. I thought for sure my editor, my friend, would fire me after the first set. However, she loved them. Being that the novel surrounds itself with wolves and lions, I felt the innate need to honor them as beings, not just characters, and that meant honoring their ancestry.

Wolves can be dated to historic times in Northern Scotland and Ireland, with the last wild wolf being killed in Ireland in the 18th century. I felt the need to honor them by being represented by the Scottish and Irish Gaelic community. So, each of the villages and locations on the map of Siochan are all representative of these heritages.

Siochan- Means peace in Scottish Gaelic. Pronounced she-ukh-awn.

Tuathanas- Means farm in Scottish Gaelic. Pronounced two-hon-us.

Seoid- Means gem or Jewel in Irish Gaelic. Pronounced show-ed.

Mac tíre- Means wolf or son of the land in Irish Gaelic. Pronounced Mac-tee-reh.

Lyall- Means wolf in Scottish Gaelic. Pronounced Lie-ull.

Cailleach- Means old woman in Scottish Gaelic. Pronounced Ky-yuch.

Draiocht- Means magic in Scottish Galelic. Pronounced DREE-uct

Just as the wolves are significant, so are the lions and their prides. It only made sense to take them back to their rightful homeland. I incorporated an homage to Africa, with most of the words coming from Swahili, a Bantu language widely used in East African countries.

Nyumbani- Home in Swahili. Pronounced New-ban-ee.

Sahara- After the Sahara desert. Pronounced Suh-hair-uh

Lusaka- The Capital of Zambia. Pronounced Loo-saa-kuh.

Folasade- Honor or one whom wears the crown. Pronounced four-lah-shar-day.

Baraka- Blessings in Swahili. Pronounced ba-ra-ka.

Xolani- Peace in Swahili. Pronounced kso-l-ani.

Mbali- Away in Swahili. Pronounced mol-lee.

Askari- Solider in Swahili. Pronounced as-ka-ri.

Pollsmoor- An actual prison in Cape Town, South Africa. *(This author has no affiliation, experience, or allegiances to this prison. It was strictly used for its name.)*

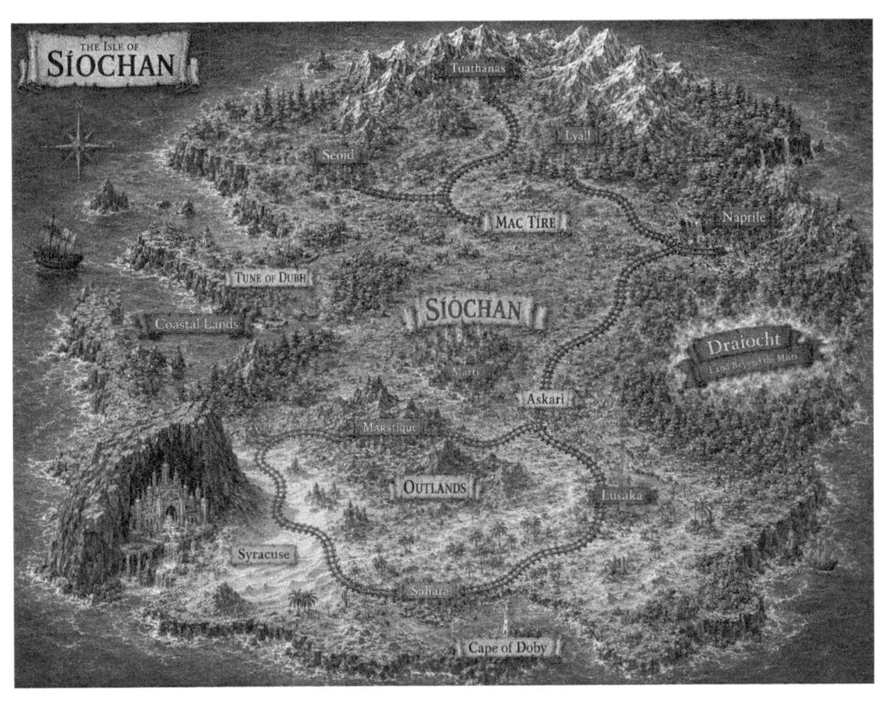
THE ISLE OF
SÍOCHAN
N
Tuathanas
Seoid
Lyall
MAC TÍRE
Naprile
TUNE OF DUBH
Coastal Lands
SÍOCHAN
Draíocht
Land Beyond the Mists
Marti
Askari
Marstique
OUTLANDS
Lusaka
Syracuse
Sahara
Cape of Doby

1. Don't Blame Me- Taylor Swift
2. Reasons To- JP Kennedy
3. Start a Riot- BANNERS
4. Always Something With You- Mitchell Tenpenny
5. Sleeping Alone- Mitchell Tenpenny
6. Believe it- Jared Benjamin
7. How Could I not?- Spencer Crandall
8. Femmeine Energy- Alexandra Kay
9. All Out Of Me- Callum Kerr
10. Till I Can't, I Will- Dylan Scott
11. Whirlwind- Lainey Wilson
12. Turn This Truck Around- Jordan Davis
13. Hope It's Hot Out- Kyle Clark
14. MIGHT BE DANGEROUS- Tyler Braden, Kaitlin Butts
15. Haunted- Kane Brown, Jelly Roll
16. Start a Fire- Kane Brown
17. Body Talk- Kane Brown, Katelyn Brown
18. I Had Some Help(Feat. Moran Wallen)- Post Malone, Morgan Wallen
19. Carry You Home- Alex Warren
20. Save You a Seat- Alex Warren
21. Durning Down- Alex Warren
22. Lose Control- Teddy Swims
23. Losers(Feat. Jelly Roll)- Post Malone, Jelly Roll
24. Nosedive(Feat. Lainey Wilson)- Post Malone, Lainey Wilson
25. I Am Not Okay- Jelly Roll
26. Ain't How It Ends- Post Malone
27. What Don't Belong To Me- Post Malone
28. Ain't My Fault- Zara Larsson
29. Confident- Demi Lovato
30. Sorry Not Sorry- Demi Lovato
31. You're The Only Reason- Gabby Barrett
32. Hills of Connemara- Gaelic Storm
33. Johnny Jump Up/Morrison's Jig- Gaelic Storm
34. Rocky Road To Dublin/Kid On The Mountain- Gaelic Storm
35. The Leaving of Liverpool- Gaelic Storm

Prologue

"EVERELLE!!!" screamed a booming voice. My eyes shot open, but the room didn't become clearer. The scent of decaying humid earth infiltrated my nostrils and stole what little breath I had. My heartbeat was rapidly increasing to an almost deadly rate, and every nerve felt as if it were on fire.

Rolling over, I felt the floor quickly, running my hands in sweeping motions across the stone. Heart pounding, I frantically crawled, making my way toward anything that I could use as a weapon or hiding spot.

"EVERELLE, YOU COME OUT RIGHT NOW!" The voice berated my head with its power, ricocheting off nearby walls as if it were tangible. I could feel the urgency, the pure hatred that its tone inflicted.

I had to get up; I had to clear my head of the disorienting room and focus. If I failed, I wouldn't be able to save them or myself. I couldn't lie here like a damn damsel in distress. It's not who I was, at least, that's what I liked to remind myself of. From what little I've learned about who I truly am, I know I don't end in this shit hole.

I began maneuvering around the room, urgently searching for some sort of escape. Something or someone was looking for me, and I had a sinking feeling, it was to finish what it had started. Finally, after what seemed like an eternity, I felt it. My salvation. I had discovered a slit in the wall just slim enough for my fingers to slide through. I dragged them upwards until I met the ceiling. Finding nothing, I dragged them back down to waist level before I found what I was searching for, a latch. I removed my fingers and inserted them again blindly into the crevice just below where I had met the smooth metal and flicked my fingers upwards. I heard the snick of the latch at the same time the booming voice again echoed my name, taunting me to come out of hiding, as if I'd chosen to be here.

I knew I had just minutes to figure out where I was if I was going to save anyone and survive. I shoved the heavy stone door with what little energy I had left, gritting my teeth through the pain I felt. I found myself in a sunken hallway, dimly lit by flickering candles. I paused in the doorway, looking for movement in the flame, willing it to indicate a source of air travel. I looked to my right and saw a sliver of light beaming down from the ceiling at the end of the corridor, and I frantically made my way toward it. I felt a burning in my chest begin. Subconsciously, I began to massage my sternum as I ran crouching up the dirt path. Come hell or high water, I was getting out of here, and no one else would suffer. The thought, however, was fleeting as I was immediately tossed into darkness. A moment later, I felt a hot, sticky rush of air blow past my face with incredible force. I was screwed, and nothing I did was going to fix it.

Chapter One

6 months earlier...

Everelle

What do you mean I have to go?" I asked, with what I'm only certain was a level of sheer disgust. "I hardly think it's fair for you to expect me to just drop everything and board a train because 'some man' said that I needed to." I was currently sitting on the bottom step in the foyer of our home, watching my mother as she checked the entry way table for her keys.

"Ever, for once stop making everything a crisis," my mother said, rolling her eyes into the mirror. At fifty-one she was, what you could say, "done with my drama" at this point. She was a hair stylist at the local salon, married to my father for thirty of her years and led a low-key life. If I had to sum her up, those would be the most characteristically interesting things about her... depressing.

Living in Tuathanas wasn't the most exciting place on the continent, but it was home to her, and she'd never seen reason to live elsewhere.

"I just don't see why I can't stay here and run the shop with you, or farm with dad. That has always been what I thought were my next steps. Why do they get to decide what it is I do?" I countered, as I rose to face her. The "they" in this equation were an elite group of societal members that made up The Sector. This reigning form of government maintained that we would all live respectfully and follow orders, be obedient when asked to perform duties we didn't understand and swear an oath of allegiance. Political discussions in the Monica house were strictly forbidden. My father never spoke of political nuances nor stated his opinion, not that I'd ever witnessed anyway. My mother pretended to be oblivious to all things of unrest or injustices on the continent of Siochan where we lived. Between the two of them I'm surprised I'd even been summoned to the capital at all.

"I don't make the rules, I just simply abide by them," she said as she kissed my head and grabbed my bags off the floor in the foyer. I'd been up most of the night packing, unpacking, then packing again. How do you pack for something you knew nothing about?

At the end of your nineteenth year, you're put through an assessment from the Sector which should point you in the direction of your future, but I feared they got mine wrong when they reviewed my scores. Every Tuathanas student that took the assessment, to my knowledge, always received a farming position on one of the many farms in our village or some other trade in town. I was still grappling with the idea that the Sector believed I was fit for Askari Military Academy. Me, all five foot two inches and one hundred and twenty pounds of me. It was unfathomable.

The Siochan continent was a symbiotic culture of distribution of products dependent upon the village you reside. Each of the nine major villages produced goods for the masses throughout the continent. The Sector always decided your level of contribution to the village production goals on Siochan. Most of the resources always seemed to end up in the capital known as Marti, despite Nyumbani, a village in the far West, twice the size of Marti, being the most heavily populated.

Tuathanas was a farming village. Over six hundred different families lived here, each specializing in different products to grow. My father owned the farm which produced the largest grain distribution for Siochan. Other families grew grapes to make wine, some grew exotic fruits, and other farms yet harvested the most exquisite vegetables. We had all the bases covered in Tuathanas.

I'd assumed the assessment would point me in a position on a farm like my father and neighbors despite my size and lack of strength. Those attributes could be conditioned over time. The other direction I'd hoped for was to take over my mother's hair salon. My mother was a magician, therapist, artist and informant. I spent more time in her salon in the last three years than anywhere else. I learned as much as I could from her, and I thoroughly enjoyed sitting in the front window seat, reading a novel, and listening to the town's gossip.

I aspired to be just like her. The Sector, however, believed I was fit for the Askari Military Academy. I rolled my eyes, huffed, slung my backpack on and started out the door.

The Academy, also known as Askari, was a militaristic college where the toughest, strongest and most loyal members of Siochan went to learn how to defend her if anything should ever happen that would result in the need to take swift action. I couldn't be farther from any of those things. I was below average in height compared to the people I'd grown up with in Tuathanas and my strength was laughable.

I could distinctly remember the last time my father had asked me to help him load up the trucks to head to town for export. I was thirteen, barely over five feet and had little to no body mass. I'd begun to struggle while lifting a fifty-pound sack of grain. I watched him as he stared at me with sympathy. My heart sank, feeling more heaviness in my chest from the disappointment of my father than the weight of the bag in my weak arms. He shook his head as he walked over to me and easily snatched it from my hands. "You're dismissed," he curtly said to me, never turning around. I knew then I'd failed him in more ways than one... the first being born the wrong gender. He and my mother had tried again for years to have a son. I was the only child she'd ever carried to term, and I could tell the inability to carry on our familial line weighed greatly on him. I also was far from his favorite person to go fishing, hunting or gathering with. He took me for educational purposes more than loving affection.

"Where exactly am I going?" I demanded as I slammed the front door to our home. Stepping down the small walkway, I turned and admired it. It wasn't the largest house on the block, in other words, it was a modest two floor colonial with a front covered porch. It was white with years of weathered paint and one or two black shutters missing. The front swing, wide enough for three, rocked in the slight breeze. I'd helped my dad, every spring, plant a bed of flowers along the porch and down the walkway. Who would do that this year if I was gone? It's the minuscule things like that, which reminded me this was all a joke.

"To the train station, then you'll get on platform three, train D to the city. We've been over this Ever, I just wish you'd stop fighting it." She looked frustrated and worn down. Wearing her same distressed blue jeans that hugged "all the best places," and faded soft pink button up, she was still pretty. Even now when she was tired and wrestling her own demons, she was pretty. Soft brown curls laid off her shoulders and hit mid back. She wore just the right amount of soft make up that made her green eyes pop. She had the natural beauty that seemed to have skipped right over me. I got my father's looks and as a child, I'd secretly look in the mirror and beg God to make me look like her. I mean after all, what girl wants to look like their father? Unlike her, I had strawberry blonde hair, freckles and pale pasty skin that got sunburned just thinking about going outside. Where her eyes sparkled like emeralds, mine just looked like blue blobs with yellow flecks in them. They held no shape and were considered "too large" by most standards. It was pointless. I was not a looker.

"But I've never even left Tuathanas! How will I know when I get there, or where to go once I've left the train? You didn't prepare me well enough for my adult life," I huffed, rolling my eyes at her. This wasn't her fault, It truly wasn't, but I felt better knowing I could squeeze the guilt in where I could. Truth be told, I was nervous to leave home.

"Ever! Just stop!" She slammed my bags into the bed of the truck and looked at me exacerbated. I'd pissed her off. Whoops. "They'll announce on the damn train when you depart, and I'm sure there will be God forsaken signs! Have I raised you to be so self-involved that you'd think you're the only person in this position?" She brought her hands to her face, wiping her eyes then, and it was me who felt guilt. "I'm not trying to make this harder on you, Everelle, I'm not. The Sector called for you yesterday, and that's all there is to it," she finalized as she walked toward the front of the truck to get in.

"You don't even find that remotely suspicious? I mean come on, some man whom you claim to have never met, showed up here yesterday and informed you I'm needed in the city, and you don't even question it?" It was by far one of the most bizarre things I'd ever heard. What I knew she wanted to say was that we were not allowed to question it. If the Sector shows up on your doorstep and asks you to do something, you do it. The fear of the repercussions was too great. If I'd learned anything from my parents, it was that. This was not the norm for people in Tuathanas, however. Tuathanans weren't chosen by the Sector, none of the citizens here that I know had been asked to be trained by the Askari Military Academy.

Askari was one of the long-standing training programs for the continent. Created upon the declaration of independence from Baroque, our continent officials created the Sector, Askari and a universal system of compliance and obedience. A set of laws and regulations, if you will. Checks and balances to keep everything running smoothly. Primary school was the only time in my life I'd ever learned about Siochan and its creation. We were taught the basics of that time period. My parents never bothered to fill in any missing pieces or gaps. The Sector only trained the best of the best in combat fighting, security and protection at its illustrious college. Again, I scoffed at the thought that I'd been selected to attend Askari for training.

Siochan was the continent that was a perfect balance of almost any terrain and provided plenty of diverse biomes to give its citizens the perfect living spaces. Tuathanas was a farming, grain, and food supply village in the far North. Our people didn't fight; we raced through woods, hiked, fished, planted, harvested and lived happily. Tuathana's citizens were the lovers of Siochan. We were far from the protection detail. I still struggled to understand how I got chosen.

"Ever, you're nineteen damn near twenty years old, why do you feel like I even get a say in what you do anymore? Most women your age would be well into their second rebellious streak," she said as she walked back over to me, still standing firmly on the sidewalk.

We were both standing on the front sidewalk now, the sun ducked behind a cloud as she pulled me into her embrace. "I wish you so much success and good fortune, I do. I hope you understand this is what they've decided, not your father and me. It's been fated. Try and give it a fair go and give your family a good name in Marti." She kissed my forehead and turned toward the truck. "Let's go," she called over her shoulder, "You'll miss your train if you keep stalling."

I turned and gave one last look to the home that held me for almost two decades. I began wishing life had been different, but chided myself that she was right; there were no choices, only orders. When members of The Sector spoke, you didn't fight it out of fear they'd raise your taxes, raise the number of exports that you're mandated to supply or worse, take your home for provocation of disobedience to the Sector and Prime Minister of Siochan. From what little I'd managed to hear over the years, the Sector was more feared than respected.

Lucky me, for whatever reason, they'd chosen me to be a cadet at Askari, and my parents found no reason to fight it, reminding me that my expectation was to get on the train. I hoped that while on the train, I might meet someone I could talk to about this process. I felt so naive for going blindly into the capital with only knowing the basics of who made up the Sector and even less about Askari, because it'd never mattered to me. Askari was mythical to me, almost like the fae. I'd never seen it, but I'd heard the rumors. I never dreamed one day I'd ever attend.

What bothered me even more was that my father wasn't here to see me off this morning. To my knowledge, he had no idea this was even happening. He'd been gone for three days traveling with an export shipment to Seoid, the next village over from Tuathanas. One of the men that typically assisted with the monthly transports became ill, requiring my father to step up and fulfill the order to Seoid, lest my father's production rates rise for a missed deadline. Would he even miss me when he returned and learned that I'd been summoned?

I looked across the fields, toward the mountains that were covered in pines. I spent years of my life running through them, building forts, playing and hiking. I learned to hunt deer and build fire in those woods. Who knew when I'd be back? I sighed and shook my head. I'd make the best of it. Or, even more hopeful, they'd get one look at me in Marti and ship me back. "There's been a mistake, you're not needed at The Academy, our apologies," I hoped they'd say. They just had to see me first.

I got into mom's beat up old truck and we backed out of the driveway. Slowly making our way to the center of Tuathanas, I whispered a prayer that I'd get a sign that I was making a mistake, but no sign came. Watching out the window I saw the people I've come to love and emulate most of my life. Hardworking farmers in and out of the supply chain, wives with their kids in strollers headed toward the coffee shop, pre-teens walking home for their school lunch break, laughing as if they had a million lifetimes to live. The slow hustle and bustle are all I've ever known. I've never left Tuathanas. This would be a first.

Approaching the train station, I blew out a sigh and looked toward my mother. She was driving intently, a small furrow on her brow. She hadn't spoken since we'd left the house, and I began searching for the right words to ease the worries she tried hard to keep silent. What do you say to someone who has spent her life raising and protecting you and now has no say in what else happens to you? I reached for her hand and squeezed it three times, our secret form of saying, "I love you." She smiled and squeezed back. What else was there to say?

As she pulled in front of the small, wooden station, Mom finally let out her breath with a sigh. Once she threw it into park, I climbed out of the truck. I walked a few steps down the side of the blue truck's bed and collected my two bags. That was all I had, two leather-bound cranberry-colored bags. Enough space for a few outfits and a collection of my favorite stories. That is all I could afford to take. I walked back to the window which was now rolled down. I leaned in as my mother began to speak.

"Make sure you take care of yourself, Ever. You're the greatest thing I've ever made from scratch, and I'm so proud." Tears welled in her eyes as she reached over to squeeze my hand again. She then pulled it away and I stepped back. I waved as she pulled away, kicking up some dust and I knew she would cry the entire way home, it's how she was. After watching her turn out of the makeshift parking lot, I headed up into the old wooden building that resembled more of a dilapidated barn, than a station. I swung the door open, and a bell chimed as I stepped inside.

Adjusting my eyes, I looked around. It was a small room, with old wooden slabs for floors. To my left stood a ticket counter with a large bay window. A stout woman with blonde hair staffed the desk, and to my right were just two wooden benches. They looked as if they were stolen from the church in town. Across the back wall were maps of the different villages, plastered with a layer of dust and peeling corners. Mail, packages and bags were waiting to be placed on a delivery truck or on the train, to which I was uncertain. In the back corner were two bathrooms and a large clock on the wall telling me it was quarter to noon. I had fifteen minutes until my train was due and it didn't appear as if I'd have a problem making it. *Shit.*

Slowly, I made my way to the ticket counter and cleared my throat. Apparently approaching alone wasn't enough to signify to the woman that I would need her assistance. "Hi, umm, I..." I began before being cut off.

"What is it honey. Speak up, I don't have all day," she gruffly said.

"Oh sorry, I just need to board the train for Marti." I answered, this time with a little more pep in my voice.

The woman looked at me as if I had completely interrupted her morning crossword and caused her an inconvenience to do her job. "Alright, well I suppose I can help with that. Have you ever traveled with us before?"

"No ma'am, this will be my first time," I said, showing her my ID and the card the Sector had given to my mother. She took both, inspected them, and began tapping on her keyboard. A few moments later she was printing a ticket and sliding my documents back to me.

"Have a good trip. Platform three, train D. Oh, piece of advice for you," she said earnestly as if I was someone in need of the intel. "It would suit you to keep your nose down on the train, lots of people you may not want to be associatin' with," she said, while she closed the window.

Left alone, I began making my way to the platforms on the other side of the ticket counter. It was a warm day for spring, and for once, I didn't mind being alone with my thoughts. I found a bench against the train station wall once on my platform. It wasn't occupied so I took a seat to wait for the train.

The sun was out, and very few clouds were in the sky. I looked out across the tracks to see the tree line of the mountains that made their way to our land. Very few people spent as much time on them as my father and I did. There were rumors of course of wild beings and unfriendly people living in them, but in my nineteen years, never have I come across any of the things people spoke of.

I breathed out and stretched my legs. I was in my normal outfit with skinny jeans and a coral-colored hoodie. I wore sneakers most of the time and truly little make up as it never did anything for me. I was shorter than most people my age and didn't get along well with the popular crowd. I just found more peace by myself or with my family. I'd much rather spend a night at home reading or helping my mom sew some of my dad's ripped coveralls than meet the kids my age at the meet shack downtown.

Sitting back, I closed my eyes to contemplate whether I could jump off the platform and make a break for the woods before the train came, when the bench jostled. Startled, I opened my eyes and sat up. I'd been joined by someone who appeared to be annoyed. Adjusting his bag next to me, was a muscular boy about my age. Let me rephrase that, a man my age. As I scanned him up and down with my eyes, I noted he too seemed to be headed somewhere he didn't want to be. He was tall, with silver hair and olive skin. He had permanent reminders of his past etched deeply onto his forearm and jaw. His black leather pants and black linen shirt fit him snugly resting on his massive biceps, and opened exposing a very well-toned set of pecs. I continued down and noticed his boots looked like he'd gone to war in them.

"Damn it!" he said to no one as he tossed his bag to the floor and brought his hands up to his face, rubbing it before raking them through his hair and slapping them to his thighs. Still looking at him, he turned, almost startled that I was there. I get that. I'm invisible to most people. No offense taken, sir. But then something in his eyes sent goosebumps down my arms. I felt him, as if I knew him prior. Looking at him now, into his deep warm golden eyes, with flecks of blue in them, I felt like I was looking at him again, instead of for the first time. If the feeling was mutual, he didn't show it.

"Hey, I'm Ever..." I got cut off as the steam engine blew a loud blast alerting us as it was entering the station. His head jerked back to watch as it made its way slowly to the platform.

Made of dark blue and golden steel, I watched as this magnificent iron horse rolled past us and came to a jerking stop. It had five cars in total, and tons of gleaming windows. The conductor, dressed in a captain's uniform of pressed blue and gold cotton, stepped out of the now caboose and blew his whistle, signaling the opening of the car doors. At once, the man next to me got up, grabbed his bag and walked in the direction of one of the cars. "Tough crowd," I said to myself, although aloud.

As if appearing out of nowhere a girl was standing next to me."Oh that's just Kolter, he's always like that. You won't find too often where he gives a shit. Hi, I'm Priya," she said while sticking her hand out to me.

"Everelle, but my family just calls me Ever."

"Nice to meet you, you're headed to The Academy, right?" she asked as she adjusted her bag on her shoulders. She was tall, around five foot eleven inches and she was lean and toned. She also wore black leathers and worn boots. Her hair was jet black, and her orange eyes warmed with excitement. Immediately, she put me at ease, erasing the butterflies that fluttered in my belly.

"I am, I just can't for the life of me figure out why. I'm the daughter of a farmer and hair stylist. What could I have to offer?" I blanched as I picked up my things and secured my ticket in my hand. I was in car four and had a sleeping quarter unit.

"They must have seen something because it's been said forever that they only pick the best. Some from our village never get called to go, so they make it by teaching the next generation. The adage, those who can't do... teach." She chuckled.

We made our way to the conductor and presented our tickets. Lucky for me, Priya was also traveling in a sleeping quarter in car 4. "Hey, Ever, you coming?" she asked, looking back at me from the car. She had already climbed aboard, and I had yet to take my ticket back from the conductor. I smiled meekly and climbed onto the train. *Here goes nothing*, I thought as a deep sigh left my lips.

Chapter Two

Everelle

Stepping up into the car, I was taken aback by how small it appeared on the outside, but how sprawling inside looked. I chided myself for thinking it was magic, it couldn't possibly be... I must have miscounted the cars and misjudged their size.

It was the beauty of the train that held my attention most. The floors were brilliant white and gray marble, gleaming with the reflections of what surrounded it. The walls were flanked with large windows with large plush blue velour seating. Round cedar tables sat between sets of four chairs, a large bookcase was positioned on the far wall bursting with volumes I could only have dreamed of reading, and a hallway that continued down the far-right side of the car. The excitement in the car was electrifying. Some in the car had been riding the train for a bit and had made themselves at home with a book or a drink, chit-chatting with their neighbor, or looking out the windows. However, as I approached, the air thickened and the mood changed. Men and women alike stopped talking as I walked by and stared with looks of disgust, as if I were somehow misaligned with the car's other occupants. *Yeah, I know, the feeling's mutual,* I thought as I refused to walk further into the room. Priya had gone on ahead and put her stuff into a sleeping quarter and was already making her way back.

When she saw me standing idly in the doorway, she rolled her eyes with a silent chuckle. She quickly floated over to me, as if air and she occupied the same space, grabbed my arm, and pulled me back toward the hallway.

"Here, you can stay in my sleeping quarters; I don't foresee Lisbeth having an issue with it. I'm sure she would *love* to share sleeping quarters with Baldur if you catch my drift."

I didn't, but I didn't want to let on. I had no idea who these people were or why they had a sudden disgust in me, but I was glad Priya was unaware of it. Priya brought me to the second-to-last sleeping quarter in the car. It was spacious, dimly lit, and adorned with a private bath. As we walked into the room, I noticed both sides of the quarters had full-sized beds with plush blue velvet down comforters and silk golden sheets. It mimicked the furniture in the common room of the car and the exterior of the train. The floor had a soft white rug, which felt as if I were walking on a cloud, and the ceiling was made entirely to replicate the sky. It left a feeling that we were going to be sleeping outside under the night sky instead of in a locomotive at full speed. Two large windows, with cobalt blue drapes, hung at the head of the beds. One small desk and chair sat at the front of the room, and a large bathroom was on the other side.

Inside the bathroom, the same white and gray marble flooring continued. A golden freestanding claw tub, large enough for two, was sitting below the windows. It was something I could only dream of. Bathing as we traveled, watching the world fade away, seemed like peace, if only we weren't headed toward my entire brutal future.

On the right side of the bathroom was a large glass shower. The marble climbed up the wall until it was met with a massive golden rain shower head, large enough for half the train to all stand in it at once. As I ran my eyes down the back wall, I saw four jets that offered up the ideal amount of relaxation. It was mesmerizing.

A small door to the left of the entrance housed a single toilet. To the right, sat a linen closet that, when I opened it, I saw contained shelves of what seemed like every hair and body product known to man. "Sheesh, if my mom could only see this now..." I said, amazed at the sights.

"Oh yeah, this is my second year; this was all new to me last year too. I recommend not getting too used to it; the Academy is nothing like this. I feel like they send us on here to remind us to behave and show us what we could have in the future if we play by the rules, pffft. As if it would work on some of the pack animals out there," Priya said, with a curt bob of her head.

I left the bathroom and headed back into the main sleeping quarters. Priya flopped onto the right bed and began brushing her hair. "I chose this one; hope that's ok?" she remarked.

"Yeah, that's fine by me. So, what do we do now? How far is it to Marti?" Marti was the capital of Siochan. It held the Academy, most of the officials, and the president. It was an industrial capital from everything we had read in school, but I'd never been, so figuring distance on a train wasn't my strongest suit.

"About three days give or take. We will pick up a few other villages along the way. They start with the furthest village out and make their way in. Tuathanas, as you know, is the last of the villages from Marti. So, we should be there by Friday morning." She said while putting her brush back in her bag and stashing it in the closet.

I sat on the bed and stared out the window. I watched as the countryside slipped by and the sun moved across the sky. Priya and I chatted a bit about my life growing up, and then hers. She was one of eight children and the fourth in her family to go to the Academy. She has enjoyed it, but it's not very different from how she was raised. For her, it was nothing new; for me... It was about to be a wake-up call.

"Who was that man at the train station? The one who sat next to me?" I asked nonchalantly, trying to sound unfazed. I secretly wanted to know why we felt connected.

"Ha! Kolter? Oh, he's something. He is a first-year student, but I've known him my whole life. He's the type to act first and ask questions later. If he asks questions at all. He is strong, keeps to himself, but is worshiped by all the ladies, if you catch my drift," she said with a wink in her eye. Sitting up straighter on her bed, she added, "He's someone you'd want on your side, but it's up to him if he even allows that. Just don't waste your time trying to impress him, he's not worth it. He breaks hearts more than bones," she quipped.

"I'm not interested in him like that! I was just wondering. He looked almost pissed that he had to be here, not to mention that I was an inconvenience to him when he sat on my bench."

"That's Kolter; he probably didn't even see you, to be honest," she shrugged. "He has a lot on his plate as the alpha of Highland pack, but don't worry, you two will get along just fine. I just know it!" she was beaming now.

As if wishing the conversation to an end, the train made a loud whistle, signaling a new station being entered. "Looks like we made it to our second stop of Lyall. Why don't we head to the common room? Have you eaten today?" Priya asked as she sat up and put her boots back on. She then stood, and I nodded. I was still unsure as to what the others would say when I stepped out. My welcome aboard didn't go over that well, and since then I've stayed in the room. If I were going to make something of myself at Askari, I may as well start by making a few friends. How hard could it be?

We left the room and began our progression down the hallway toward the common room. The sun had since gone down, and outside was as black as I'd ever seen. It looked like no homes or villages were for miles. Stars twinkled in the sky, and the lights in the dimly lit hallway all had to light our way forward. Passing by one of the sleeping quarters, noises could be heard that brought heat to my cheeks.

"Looks like Lisbeth was perfectly fine bunking with Baldur," Priya said with a laugh. She banged twice on the door as we passed by. "Keep it down in there! We got cubs out here!" she shouted, sarcastically.

Cubs? Were new cadets considered cubs at Askari? Interesting.

Back in the common room, there were fewer people than before. Dinner would be served within the hour, and the car was filled with a savory aroma of garlic, onion, and butter. It was truly droolworthy. Despite what I'd told Priya, I hadn't eaten today, and the loud growl from my stomach let me know I was pissing it off.

"We usually eat around 6. It's buffet style, or you can have it delivered to your rooms. Please, whatever you do, don't do that. It'll make our room smell for the rest of the trip. This is all we have for luxury until Christmas break," she begged.

I nodded to let her know I understood and made my way over to the bookshelf. If we had three days, I may as well pick something worthwhile to read. Glancing at the spines of the books, I took note of the titles. Some were the history of villages, some were fantasy novels, and others were novels about urban legends of Siochan. I remembered these from when my mother had read them to me when I was little. A particular novel piqued my interest, but just as I reached for it, I heard a loud squeal.

"Ooh my God, Priya!! That was so embarrassing!" Lisbeth, I'm assuming, made her way into the common room, dragging by the hand who I also could only assume was Baldur. Lisbeth was very tall; she had to be over six feet, and her body was proportionally muscular. She had beautiful long black hair that was in a long, thick plait down her back. She too had black leathers and fiery orange eyes. Baldur was a similar build, only he stood at least six foot five. The depiction on his leathers told me he was a second year. His slightly darker skin complimented his orange eyes. He couldn't remove the wide shit-eating grin plastered across his face as he was dragged across the room.

"Oh, come on, Lissy, it was funny. I'd never heard you squeal like that," he teased her as he pulled her in for a kiss.

"Don't call me that!" Lisbeth hissed as she shoved Baldur away from her. "You know that's just *our* name." She rolled her eyes and turned her back to him. Priya was still just shaking her head as the pair sat across from her at the table.

"So, how was your break?" Baldur asked Priya.

The Academy, like the other traditional schools across Siochan, worked on a calendar schedule that allowed for the most time off over winter to adjust for colder climates. The course year ran from April until December.

"Took as many showers as I could, ate a lot, and ran the courses. With four of us now in The Academy, I swear it gets my mom even more worked up. How did you guys fare?" She asked just as she made eye contact for me to come sit down.

Making my way over to the table, something caught my eye in the reflection of the floor. A pair of black boots stood, blocking me from moving further. I drew my eyes up and noticed for the first time just how tall Kolter was. He stood before me at six foot eight, give or take an inch. His body appeared to be toned and chiseled in his black linen shirt that stretched across broad shoulders and sat snugly on his pectoral muscles I'd caught a glimpse of earlier. My eyes traveled down his body, scanning him with a silent appreciation. I sweepingly traced his body back up to his glowing yellow and blue eyes, and he gave me the impression I was an inconvenience again.

"I'm sor-sorry. I was making my way there, over there, to that table," I stuttered. Oh my God, what is wrong with me? Internally I smacked myself in the face. Kolter looked me up and down, as if really seeing me for the first time. I caught something in his expression, a softening around his eyes, just for a moment, and then it went back up.

"See to it that you stay out of my way. Got it?" He didn't wait for an answer before he passed by. As if I were frozen in time, I stood, unsure if I was allowed to move. Priya, sensing my discomfort, appeared at my side.

"Told you. Just let it go; he can go brood by himself. Come! I want you to meet part of the pack." She quickly steered me into the seat at the window, across from Lisbeth.

"And you are?" Lisbeth asked curtly, rolling her eyes and sneering.

"Put your damn claws away; she doesn't want your man. God Lis, you can be a real bitch sometimes," Priya scolded. "This is Everelle, Ever for short. She's a first year from Tuathanas; she will be joining our pack, got it?" Priya leaned over, daring anyone to disagree.

Pack? I was part of their pack now? I'd never so much as had a true friend in my entire school career. Two hours on this train with Priya and I were now part of her pack? I refused to let the happiness that bubbled inside of me show on my face. If I'd remembered anything from my school days, it's that awkward things like celebrating friendship was a quick way to commit social suicide.

"Tuathanas? I'm confused; I didn't know any..." Baldur was cut off by the announcement of dinner being served in the main compartment.

"Oooh, let's go, Ever! You've never lived until you've dined on the train!" Priya grabbed my arm and brought me with her toward the front of the train.

Halfway down the hall the aroma became too much for my empty stomach. It growled with hunger unlike anything else. Entering the dining compartment, I was taken aback by the expansive room. Long tables of rich cedar, high back blue velvet chairs and rich golden table runners. Crystal chandeliers glistened from the mirrored ceiling and the lights dimmed to set the mood. Golden goblets of wine, water and spirits flooded the tables, and the party was already underway. The far end of the car had three double sided buffet lines. Each table seemed to be magically filled to the brim inside deep golden dishes.

Entering the line behind Priya and ahead of Lisbeth and Baldur, I grabbed my large, white porcelain plate the size of my mother's roast platters at home. The first table was filled with all the fixings of a salad. Crisp green lettuce, sweet chopped tomatoes, cool cucumbers, and more. I hadn't seen a spread this nice since my aunt's wedding. We may be the crop and grain village, but eating what we grow is very discouraged. Other villages come before us. That was the motto. I'd have been lucky to have a salad this good on my birthday, let alone on a train. I began to assemble my salad when Baldur leaned over.

"Trust me, you don't want to waste your stomach on that; wait till you see the real food."

"Oh my God, Baldy, not everyone thinks with their tank first; leave her alone," Lisbeth said as she rolled her eyes.

I kept my salad small and moved to the next table. Silently, I chuckled to myself at their bantering relationship while I heeded Baldur's advice. Looking toward the next section of the buffet, my jaw hit the floor at once. This table had dishes filled with pasta, dishes with seafood, chicken dishes, potatoes au gratin, mashed potatoes with gravy, and rice. From behind me I heard Baldur say, "She still doesn't know." Choosing to ignore him, I again placed a little bit of pasta and potatoes on my plate. Moving to the third table, I finally understood what he meant. There were carving platters filled with ham, turkey, and roast beef. Porcelain dishes filled with clams, lobsters, and tuna steaks. I swear, if an animal walked this continent, it was dead on this table. I sampled some things and walked toward Priya. She delicately placed a cloth napkin in her lap and bowed her head. She said a silent prayer while waiting for Lisbeth and Baldur.

"So, what did you think?" Priya asked.

"I think I am being set up, like stuffed full just to have it taken away. There must be a catch." I looked down toward the end of the table and again noticed Kolter. He had an air of mystery and conveyed an aura of confidence and slight arrogance.

"Would you like wine or water?" Priya interrupted my thoughts and drew my attention back.

"Honestly, I'll stick with water for now, thank you," I said while I gladly accepted the pitcher.

"It's not like they don't feed us at Askari, but you will go through some of the hardest moments of your life there, and lessons you probably have never even thought of. You'll do great. There isn't a catch," she said solemnly. "It's just, you're taking a new direction in life, and the capital has everything in it, so sometimes you'll be introduced to some higher quality of living."

Contemplating what she said, I began to eat. Feeling for the first time in a while, strength and warmth. I never fit in at home. People just didn't get me, and I didn't seem to align with their interests. Priya was the first person in my life, aside from Mom and Dad, to look at me and see me. It felt nice.

We continued to feast as we traveled along the route to the capital. The feast transitioned to coffee, desserts, and snacks. As the night wore on and more cadets ran into friends, the celebrations erupted loudly each time. Backs were slapped, hands clapped, and faces beamed with excitement for those returning to Askari. Fresh faces introduced themselves as first years. I found myself in the minority of welcomed cadets. I knew it would be a tough climb. Most surrounding me seemed to have a bond of sorts already, as if they'd known each other previously or traveled with them prior. I also seemed to be the least knowledgeable or trained to come. Most, if not all, the cadets, new and returning, had been trained their entire lives to go to the academy. It left me again wondering if the Sector had somehow gotten it wrong.

As I crawled into bed that night, I couldn't believe how someone like me got brought into such a unique way of life. I was a small-town girl. I worked in dirt, climbed trees, and hunted deer. My hobbies included sewing and reading. I spent my time between my mother's hair salon and learning to hunt and survive in the woods with my father when he'd take me.

I didn't spend my time in rooms like this. I felt out of place. I felt homesick. I felt... exhausted. What was I headed for and how would I survive it?

Rolling over, I glanced out the traveling window, still seeing nothing but dark. Until...as if waiting for me to look, a pack of wild dogs appeared from the shadows. Sitting up, I adjusted the curtain a little further and looked out the window. Out into the night, almost as if they were racing the train, were wolves. Large wolves, with orange eyes. I gasped and held my hand to cover my mouth, just as the largest, a silver wolf, looked directly into my soul. It was like he was urging me to see him. I looked over next to me to wake up Priya, but she wasn't there. I never even heard her sneak out. Then, as I glanced back, they were gone as if they'd never appeared at all. I was left feeling like this couldn't have been real. Wolves aren't that big. Wolves can't run as fast as a steam engine...right? I must be more tired than I thought. Turning over, I milled over my thoughts until sleep finally pulled me under.

Chapter Three

Kolter

I didn't want to ride the damn train. My brothers all rode it and said it was a three-day shit show, orgy fest. I had zero interest in being part of that. I just wanted to get to Askari and get it over with. It's damn pointless that I must attend, but I drew the short straw. I had to be the chosen one this year. Walking into the train station, I had a sinking feeling I had left my rubix, a small yellow stone that I used to center my power and keep me levelheaded, at home. I usually kept it in my pocket, but it wasn't there. As I dropped on the bench, I began to dig inside my bag. "Damn it!" I snarled; I fucking lost it. Great. Now my younger brother will most likely take to using it to try to dominate over his bullshit friends. Honestly, it's more psychological than practical. He wouldn't be able to channel his abilities with it, nor control his powers, whenever he finally was awarded them, but it was important to me.

"Hi, I'm Ever..." I looked up and completely choked. Those eyes... I know those eyes... I've seen those eyes. No? I don't know. I must be mistaken; she doesn't look like us, she emitted meekness and fragility. Her coloring wasn't that of any of the packs that I'd seen. Then again, who am I to judge? I don't match my own pack, the result I'm told of early shifting.

Just then the whistle of the train blew and entered the station, allowing me the perfect opportunity to break contact and get the hell out of here. Looking quickly over my shoulder to see if she was watching me leave, like all the girls do, I saw Priya catch her attention. Great. Just what that girl needs, Priya Jones, the pack cheerleader and Ms. Fix-it. I shook my head and tossed my ticket to the conductor. I didn't even let him punch it and give it back. I just climbed on board the train and found my sleeping quarters. It would be three long days.

An hour into the train ride, we stopped at Seoid, my home, and one of the more safely guarded villages. Its prize possessions were those its people dug far into the caverns to carry back out. Mainly Seoid exported rubix and other priceless gems continent-wide. Let's be real though, the only people that got those prizes were the elite in the capital. Slave labor for pennies had never sat well with me.

My rubix had been gifted to me on my seventh birthday. I'd had a rough year, and my mom gave it to me to symbolize a new beginning. She said it was infused with powers to help calm me and keep me level-headed. I never went without it, until today, apparently.

Within minutes people boarded and entered our car. The knock on my sleeping quarters is the last thing I needed or wanted. "Yeah?" I barked at the stranger on the other side of the door.

"Open up, prick. I know it's you," demanded the voice from the hallway.

Sighing deeply, I got up and undid the deadbolt on the door. Victor Ulrich was standing at the door, a bag slung over his shoulder. He nodded and checked me as he pushed in. "I'm bunking with you because I damn sure am not bunking with those two horn dogs. They'll keep me up all night." He was talking about Baldur and Lisbeth. They had started dating last semester after taking advantage of a lack of an alpha. They consequentially bonded and now were apparently insatiable. I clapped hands with Victor and patted his back. He and I were both first years. He was my height, black-haired, and had orange eyes, much like everyone else who made up our family, aside from me, that is. I was the odd ball. I had been born into a family just as everyone else had. Tall, broad shoulders, muscular build, that made working out come easy. I used to have jet black hair and bright orange eyes. The photographs of me as a child prove this. However, around six the change began. My mom liked to say it's because I'm pure at heart. I would hate to burst her heart into flames by letting her know how utterly wrong she is.

Victor lived in Seoid, though his part of the family was more nomadic. His dad was the general and was moved from village to village on two-year rotations. He never seemed to know where he would be needed next. By default, Victor and his kin were also moved. I'd known him since we were four when his family received orders to help the borders of Tuathanas. Protecting their citizens seemed to cause the least amount of hostility and, therefore, was the perfect location for his growing family in their younger years. No one wanted to expose young people to this kind of lifestyle; at least the general had a heart.

"I hope we get to choose our room assignments like years past. I don't want to room with him either. God, they're insufferable," Victor muttered.

Victor and Baldur had a rocky past, one I knew little about as I chose to stay impartial. Being a leader means sometimes you let the flanks fight their own battles, stepping in only when it became too much of a risk for the other members. Killing themselves would alleviate only the problem at hand. The mark it would leave would devastate the pack if carried out. Both men seemed to understand that, so they kept their distaste at a superficial level.

Victor complained about the late boarding this year as he unpacked and made his way toward the shower. "I'm kind of jealous you get to get on board in Tuathanas; I wish I could. My mother made the last few hours unbearable, making me promise not to do anything stupid when I arrived at Askari."

I ignored his bitching and went back to my bed. Seconds later, the dread- ed sounds of Victor singing off-key to some boorish trash he called music, had me closing the door to our room and walking down the hallway to the common rooms. Dinner would be served soon anyway; I needed a book and a drink.

When I stepped into the common room, electricity pulled me toward the girl I'd met earlier. The girl from the platform. Her eyes were on the ground as she was making her way to the table. She would damn near run into me if I didn't interject, but I didn't make any attempts to move. I wondered if she felt it too. If she felt the electric hum that was currently racing down my arms and into my fingertips. If she felt it, she made no reaction as she picked her head up and locked her wide eyes with mine.

"I'm sor- I'm sorry," she muttered. She didn't even have the confidence to stand in a room of strangers, and yet she got on the train to face three years at the Academy? The toughest, grueling course you could have chosen... It wasn't meant for girls like her. Shit, she was still talking, and I missed it in my irritation. "See to it that you stay out of my way. Got it?" I snarled as I rolled my eyes and pushed past her. I almost at once regretted my tone. Fuck! Why was I such an asshole? I really needed a drink and to chill the fuck down.

Sitting at a table in the corner were Brandt Mason, Flynn Mason, and Kentaro Bridges. My right hands. We grew up in Seoid, hunting the same pass and earning our stripes together. Twins Brandt and Flynn were born the exact same day as I; our mothers sat together pushing through the agony of producing the pack's largest of men. The women were trauma-bonded or some shit. Members of our pack would call us the triplets. With my life I trusted them.

Kentaro was my older brother's age. Same class, same distinction, just didn't end the same. While my brother never made it back from his first year at the Academy, Kentaro did. He swore an oath to my mother that he wouldn't let anything happen to me here. Protecting the line of succession and all that bullshit. It had little to do with me and more to do with supporting pack dynamics. Kentaro shared the role of beta with Priya in the pack. The two of them had been destined. It wasn't like Baldur and Lisbeth, who had the free will to choose.

Between the seven of us, we were a solid group. Talent and finesse came naturally with our pack. So why Priya was associating herself with a novice, and a naive one at that was beyond me. But charity runs deep in her line.

"Kolter," a hand in the air rose in a come-hither motion. The hand was attached to Nikita McNabb. She was a second year from back home. She was the tallest of the females in our pack, standing at six foot three. She too had jet black hair, although hers was shaved on the right side of her head with a lightning bolt pattern and her left side had hair cut in a blunt bob ending at her jaw. With heavy dark make up accentuating her orange eyes, she looked like someone pissed her off by just breathing. She was leaning over the bar, wearing a skintight black leather suit which hugged her body as if it were painted on. Most of the pack drooled over her, especially now that she was "available."

My mother would want nothing more than to see Nikita on my arm, but I could never stomach the thought. She had been destined for my brother, not me. The fact that my brother and I were somehow interchangeable to her and Nikita until bonded was something that wasn't sitting right in my stomach.

"We need to decide what positions we want our pack in, and how we will fill out formations," she said while handing me a drink. She knew my drink because it was the same as every alpha in my line. Crown neat. Simple, smooth and hit the mark. The way she said, "we," instantly boiled my blood.

"I'm going to go out on a damn limb here and say, I don't really think what I want matters in the grand plans of the Sector," I said and swirled my whiskey before meeting her paled expression.

"I'm going to need you to run that back on me slowly. Did you bump your head this morning? You're the alpha. Kasen didn't return. End of discussion," she said with a burning in her eyes and flat expression. "What did you think Kentaro would boost up rank because he's spent 9 months at a bullshit school?" She threw her head back scoffing. "Listen, learning about the inner workings of shit that doesn't apply to real life, doesn't do dick for the lineage. He's a beta. He makes no rules," she said matter of factually as she looked me square in the face.

"And what? You think you're just going to sit here with some bullshit pep talk to enforce rank, as if your intentions aren't also pinning for that alpha spot?" I taunted and got closer to eye level to look her dead in the face, I wanted to make sure my next words hit so she could stop the entitlement she presented. "You lost your alpha; you don't get to have a fucking do over with the next in line as if the first was a practice round," I said, without blinking. "They have names for that, don't you know?" I shot the whiskey back and slammed the glass down on the cedar bar. "I'm headed to the dining car. I don't have time for this bullshit right now." I turned my back on her, glanced in the direction of the girl that electrified my skin, and walked out of the room.

Heading into the dining car I found it overwhelming. I didn't have the stomach for food but knew I needed the protein. I couldn't suffer and pout because I was dealt the cards I had. We had been told by the sector that my brother died protecting a first-year student, whose name I can't even remember. That was Kasen. He knew how to lead. He had planned for it his entire life. He knew what his next steps were. It was as natural as breathing for him. I never had that dream, nor did I plan for this. It was thrust upon me, and though I didn't want it, I couldn't let people in my pack down. So, regardless of my feelings, or lack of them for Nikita, she was right. I had to plan positions, and preferably before arriving at the Academy.

"Aren't you going to let us know our positions?" Brandt asked me as we all sat down to eat. *Oh, for fucks sake. Is this all I'm going to hear until they're dished out?* I ignored his question as Flynn sat down. Flynn was the second born of the twins. Smaller in stature, but stood at a whopping six foot four. He was the pack's aerial analytics guy. He could be counted on to know exactly what we were doing, where we were going, and have an alternate plan if needed. He was the brains. Nerdy, but still identical in looks to his brother Brandt.

Brandt was a different story. If you looked up the average jacked up body builder, you'd see someone who paled in comparison to Brandt. I think he made it his personal mission to compete for bigger biceps than anyone else in the pack. Anyone on the damn continent for that matter. Where his brother excelled in brains, Brandt made up for with brawn. Not saying Flynn didn't have brawn; he'd take your average person and still make them feel weak any day, but Brandt just had a slightly bigger edge.

While in my own self-absorption, I'd missed the conversation, but what Flynn was saying piqued my interest.

"Shouldn't we check the roster with the conductor? No one knows who the girl next to Priya is, or why she's here. I've asked around," Flynn said. As he said it, subconsciously our entire table turned to look at her as one.

"Do we even know her name?" I asked, curiously.

"Her name is Everelle; she's a farmer from Tuathanas. That's all I've managed to learn. Priya is quite tight-lipped," Flynn said irritated. "It's not like I want to date her... but we still have two more days locked in this titanium dick-shaped engine; might as well get a romp under my belt." Of course he went there. He always overcompensates, partially because he never has romped in the sheets.

"I'll call a run," I said, now going back to Brandt's previous question on positions. I wasn't going to sit here and listen as Flynn degraded some meek fresh meat; it turned my stomach. "Be ready by 10pm," I snarled, as I snatched my plate and rose to leave the table before everyone else had even turned back. I needed to be alone. I had to do an assessment and put everyone in their ranks. It wouldn't be a light discussion. I had a feeling that tonight would show exactly what they were made of.

Later that evening, I made my way to the end of the train. It was dark out on the gangway. The train was hurtling at around sixty miles per hour. I held on to the railing, looking down at the coupling, and wondered what I was going to make of myself. "Kase, bro, you gotta help me here. Send me something," I said out loud. In frustration, I hit the rail and looked up at the sky blowing by.

I was going to have to be the leader, and I had to suck it the fuck up. Midway through my pity party, the vestibule door slid open, and Nikita sauntered out.

"Are you about done with your fake masculinity yet?" she asked while she drilled her eyes into me with a smirk. "What are you thinking for positions?"

It was a quarter to ten. I'd been thinking about it since dinner, and the only thing I could come up with that I felt was remotely fair, was a face-off. My flanks against my brothers in a race for beta. From there, the rank would move down the line with positioning as I saw fit. I'd put them through the ringer tonight, and maybe, just maybe, by morning, we would have a solid pack. One that was ready to work and put our noses down. Nikita would be my biggest problem. She had a lot of pull with Kasen; he was pussy-whipped. I wouldn't be. She wouldn't be that problem for me, so therefore it was a leg of control I could keep.

"I'm putting you all through the course. You'll face off and your rank will be decided based on how you all fall in line," I said curtly. She could be pissed all she wanted. I wanted things in this pack to be fair and unbiased. She wouldn't influence my choices.

Her eyes grew wide as she looked at me with worry and pain. "What? And should Baldur outpace Kentaro? Does that..."

"Push Priya out of beta positioning?" I finished for her. "It does. If you guys want it, you'll earn it. I don't plan to do favors in this pack. Kasen may have run it differently in the past, but it's my future. We are leveling the playing field." I refused to break our gaze first. If I did, she'd no doubt see it as a sign of weakness. While Nikita may be a lot of things, her need to overly dominating was one of them that I could break.

"You're really going to step on the train and open a whole can of crazy on the first day?" She shook her head as if unable to fathom my decision. This further proved to me she couldn't be trusted as my partner. If she was already in disagreement about fairness, she wasn't someone I wanted to run a pack with.

"I'm going to give everyone a shot; everyone deserves a chance to prove their strengths. Nepotism only works for the first in line. I don't make the rules in that regard, but I damn sure make the rest," I barked, inflicting the perfect amount of bite and confidence she'd need to hopefully back down.

As if we ended our conversation on a perfect note, the door to the vestibule slid open, and stepping into the light came my pack, Victor, Kentaro, Baldur, Priya, Lisbeth, Flynn, and Brandt. Most nodded and filled in the tiny space we had on the gangway. Each of them acknowledging the other members of the group. Anxiety became palpable on the gangway; I knew we'd need to get started, lest the anxiety spark aggression and unwarranted attacks. I lifted my head to address the group when the door to the train opened again, and we snapped our heads toward the door, confused, as two more female cadets piled out.

"I heard this is where we're meeting for Highland Pack positions... are we late?" said a heavier-set busty woman with a perfectly placed jet-black bun in her hair. Her orange eyes shifted to her friend; she too was of the same coloring, although her stature resembled that of Lisbeth. Tall and built. "I'm Flavia, Flavia Indelicato, and this is Assata Bitt," she said, gesturing her thumb toward the taller female. "We're here from Lyall," she said, standing strong and confident. Each village in the Mac Tíre had representatives of the Highland Pack as ambassadors. They represented our pack in all things governmental, from war and protection down to food and allocation. These two ladies must have come from our representative's line. "We don't feel like waiting until we're at the academy to fight for a position. We'd like to remain together, and my father has the most respect for your pack, so here we are."

"Alright," I said while nodding in agreement. I hadn't known their father, but if my father was appreciated by theirs, then they'd be welcome here. I looked over toward Brandt and Flynn, and I knew they needed partners. How the two new females measured up, would ideally tell me which counter of the men to put them with as a partner. In most packs, there is always a male and female in the same position linked and bonded together. No one would have your back more than your bonded mate and partner. While it was frowned upon to officially bond while at the academy for plenty of unforeseen reasons, we still operated as if our pairs were bonded. Linking Brandt and Flynn was one of my higher priorities.

Nikita shot me a look. "Can I have a word? In private?" She made no effort to hide her disapproval.

"No," I said flatly and turned back to the group. "Alright, I'm not expecting any others tonight. So, we're going to go ahead and get started."

"Wait, what about Ever?" Lisbeth said, stepping forward, looking curious. "Didn't you say she was Highland? Shouldn't she be here too?"

"Absolutely not. Are you out of your mind?" I looked at her as if she'd absolutely lost it. Until the general hands me her orders, she can stay her scrawny little ass in her room."

"She hasn't shifted yet. She'd be of no use here tonight. She knows nothing of our kind..." Priya began, and I cut her off with just a look, this conversation was over. The girl couldn't shift? If she truly knew nothing of our kind, it would explain why she appears meek and naive. I didn't have time to think about her right now.

Shaking my head, I wished again I'd brought my rubix.

"In the past it's always been the alpha male's obligation to assign the rank and position of those in the pack. Tonight, we change things." There was a collective gasp from some of the females and nods from the men. "I've decided we will run a course. I'll put you through a few challenges, and by morning, whatever place you come in, your rank follows suit," I announced.

"Alright!!" Victor nodded excitedly and cracked his knuckles. "That's what I'm talking about. Let's do this, men!" he finished.

"Excuse me, asshole," Priya said with disgust. "We happen to be standing here, and last I checked, I can outrun you any day, so keep the gloating to your damn self." She threw an elbow directly into his stomach, which made him bend with the blow, wincing.

"Alright, alright. Enough showboating," I said, as I tried to regain a sliver of order. "Tonight, I understand it will be different for some of you. I'm letting you know right now, your partners could and probably will change. None of you were supposed to have bonded yet. It's time we make a stronger pack, and that doesn't always mean we take that word to its exact definition." This seemed to get their attention. Where Brandt seemed excited, Lisbeth and Baldur held hands, quietly looking into each other's eyes with pained expressions. There's never an outcome where I split them up. It was more a lashing to scare the newer members not to bond. Lisbeth and Baldur were better suited together than apart. It's the only thing that will save them from the consequences they should be receiving for breaking orders.

"Shit's about to get reallllll weird," Flynn whispered to Nikita and winced at the look she shot at him. "Alright then... dibs on anyone except Nikita." Flynn quipped, scooting away to stand near the newbies. He pretended to claw like a cat and hissed at her.

"Can we focus please?" I started again. This was the part no one warned me about. That there would be a need to corral a bunch of unhinged duos. "We will start with running formations. If you want your spot, you keep it. This isn't going to be a quick jaunt. I'm looking for stability and endurance. Keep up." I looked at the group, and so far, they seemed to follow. "Once I've felt you've made sufficient effort, I will then run you through a series of hunt maneuvers. I'll ask that you assemble in two small groups, both fitted to track and hunt each other. Only I will decide the completion of this task," I said, with heat behind it. I didn't need them to be in charge out there. "Being that this is a practice run, please refrain from attacking your fellow opponents." I needed to emphasize this, as I know some of those in my pack will intentionally disadvantage a competitor for a spot. While in theory it would be beneficial to see what they could do, I didn't need any less members by dawn.

"Once we have successfully hunted and practiced maneuvers, I'll ask that you bring me a valuable item. Something worth hunting, gathering, and protecting," I instructed, as a hand shot up.

"Ummm, clarification on that broad-ass request of an item?" questioned Flynn, "I mean, could you be any vaguer?"

"You'll know it when you find it," I barked. "Now, we've spent enough time discussing the course. Let's get moving. I want this completed by dawn."

Watching as the group nodded and shook hands, it gave me hope that this new course could be beneficial to learn our strengths; however, there was a sinking feeling inside of me that this was about to get ugly. I sent a silent prayer up to Kasen and signaled the pack. As quickly as we arrived on the gangway, we were gone into the night. Only a loud howl could be heard among the hum of the trains' flanging rims on the steel rails.

Chapter Four

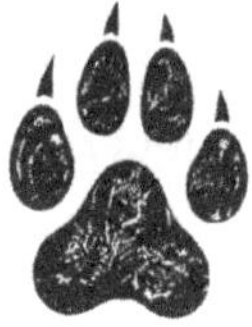

Kolter

Racing the train, I was filled with a kind of adrenaline I'd never felt. I knew just how hard I was pushing myself, and it was a wonder I could still feel the power sitting low in my chest. I looked to my left and was happy to see my ride-or-dies. The twins were flanking me as always. It felt good to know that our rhythm hadn't faltered with my new position in the pack. I perked my ears and waited for the others to come into focus. I was the head of a pyramid formation. As the pacesetter, it was my job to go at a reasonable and realistic rate of speed.

To my left shoulder was Brandt; he was always in tune with the pack's surroundings, always scanning for threats as we made our way through the cold spring night. To my right shoulder, I saw Flynn pacing me. His orange eyes met mine, and he gave a slight nod. He was letting me know we were still on course. I'd push the rest of them for another hour before breaking into smaller packs. They needed to wear themselves out a bit before they would end up fighting over fictional mini pack alpha positions.

In my mind I saw that my six was covered by Nikita, trailing about five yards. She was keeping pace with Kentaro and Assata. I was pleasantly impressed at the rate at which Assata was moving. I reached the connected line between us and felt her strength. She was running at a perfect rhythm. She didn't seem to be weakening, nor accelerating to make a point. She was keeping just two steps ahead of Nikita, as if letting her know, she was just that bit stronger. She was also respectful of my leadership, and if chosen as a beta, she would be perfect. Nikita could learn something from her, if only she'd get her head out of her ass and quit the ego bullshit.

I looked further down the line and saw Victor, Priya, and Flavia were trailing in the gamma positions. They were running their jobs as if by nature rather than by desire to compete. That would work for me. I didn't need any more rank jumpers. They seemed content with direction and following orders. They didn't push the status quo and, in turn, earned silent praise from me. I gave them a smile of appreciation down the line.

Closing out the pack in the delta positions were Baldur and Lisbeth. They were not there because they weren't as strong as the others. They were there for each other and the pack's best interest. I knew in my heart the second I announced that partners could change, that Baldur and Lisbeth would end up in delta positioning. There was no way Baldur would look for a new partner; officially bonded, Lisbeth was his mate, and he would be wherever she was. The back of the pack was an excellent spot for the two of them. They were able to scan the terrain with precision and were strong enough to protect the pack from any advancing threats from behind.

Pleased with the way the pack was performing, I sent a signal down the line that we would hold positions until further notice. At once, I received nine nods of approval.

Approaching the train, electricity surged through my body, tickling my senses and directing my vision to a precise window. As if drawn like a moth to a flame, my eyes met another set in the window. Two round blue eyes with flecks of gold looked out at my team, as if she had never seen a pack run. I could all but feel curiosity piquing, as if I too were seeing our greatness for the first time. The feeling had begun to heat my blood, with every push forward. Never breaking eye contact, I felt her, Everelle's heartbeat race as she met my eyes. Only when she broke eye contact did I pull away from the train. I was eager to have my own senses in check, worried that she too could sense me as I had her.

The pack raced along the mountain side, distancing us further from the train. I knew we would catch back to it later as it slowed to pull into the station in Naprile. The stop was scheduled for 9 am, and that would be when my pack would have completed rank positions.

What the hell was that? I heard Victor say down the line.

Ohhh, that was just our alpha, making eyes at his new pup, Flynn said, mockingly. Sometimes I wanted to beat his ass.

There will be no alpha female in this pack, I barked, without caring if Nikita was hurt in this decision or not.

Yeah. Ok sir, you let me know when your little heart stops pattering like that. The line is a two-way street, Flynn mocked; I didn't have to see him to know he was rolling his eyes. I'd make him pay for his little jab. I pushed harder, forcing the pack to keep a new pace. As if to say, "challenge me again."

We ran in silence for the better part of the night, before I slowed them to a clearing. Once all had drunk from the creek nearby, they met and sat diligently awaiting my next orders. I paced in the center of the circle and gave them their next course.

I'd like you to break yourselves into two packs. One with five and one with four, which will include myself. Nominate an alpha. This doesn't give you more points toward final rank if you are your team's alpha, I said down the line with enough force, making sure they heard it. Being an alpha isn't all it's cracked up to be, and I didn't need some feeling slighted. *Understand this, the pack is only as successful as its weakest link, not on its ability to have a dominating alpha.*

I'd like to take this moment and really congratulate our new alpha, began a highly sarcastic Brandt. *I mean, not every day does one get this thrust upon him and just decide to be all fair and shit,* he cracked with a grin.

Oh, give it a rest, fleabag, Nikita quipped. *You're not making beta because you enjoy licking his ass. We alllll know who he will choose, and it's clearly not...*

Enough! I bellowed toward both of them. I was done with the bickering between the ranks. If we were going to work together, we would have to stop breaking the seams apart. *I want formations, and I want them now,* I barked, baring my teeth at them. I gave them a few minutes of quiet while they arranged themselves. Victor stepped forward as alpha of mini pack A; his pack included Nikita, Baldur, Lisbeth, Priya, and Kentaro. Brandt stepped forward as alpha of mini pack B, which consisted of Flynn, Assata, Flavia, and me. I already knew this would be a showdown in their eyes. Both men coveted the beta position.

Alright, pack A, please make your plans. The line will temporarily go down now. We don't want an unfair advantage with plans being set. If anyone needs anything at any point, the line can be reengaged. You have forty minutes.

Watching as pack A slumped off into the woods; we in mini-pack B made our plans to spread out. "We need to hurry this along," I said, looking up. A quick assessment of the sky and moon determined it to be closer to five am. We had been running most of the night, and to be honest, I was kind of over this mission. For reasons I could not explain, my body wanted to be back on the train. I wanted to be sure Everelle was safe. Shaking my head, I tried tossing the feelings away and concentrating on the task at hand. After all, during this course, I wasn't alpha, Brandt was, and it was a good trial run to see if he could truly be my beta. It was assumed because of his long-running stance as my flank, that he would just continue, however, for me there were more serious prospects, and I didn't want that to interfere with our friendship or the camaraderie of this pack.

A signal from Brandt came through, and stalking slowly through the trees, he made a motion that at his three o'clock a shadow was lingering. We paused as everything surrounding us stilled. Crouching forward and sniffing the air for any trace of what the shadow was, I picked up on a smoky mixture of black cardamom, bergamot, and cedar. I knew we had a trace on Kentaro. He always had a habit of overcompensating with his cologne, as if any of us could truly mask what we were.

Stealthily, we began to stalk forward through the pines. The snapping of twigs and rustle of leaves were at a minimum under our weighted feet. The air was hovering above forty degrees, but we could still see the steam escaping our controlled breaths. Brandt looked back at me, checking to see if I silently agreed with his approach. I gave him a look as if saying, "This is your rodeo, I'm just the bull." He nodded and then met eyes with Flynn, tossing his head to the left, and turning to the right, he signaled Assata that she should head to the right through the tall pines, but she paused and threw a glance over her shoulder, her eyes darting back toward Brandt. He paid her no regard. *Strike.*

Brandt held steady, waiting as they all got in positions surrounding the shadows of Kentaro. Then all at once, he signaled, and they were on the move. Full force toward black shadows. I held my breath in anticipation of what was to come next. The three of them had Kentaro surrounded in what felt like an intake of breath. However, all except Assata had failed to sense the whole picture in their rush. They missed what she and I didn't. Kentaro was an intentional sitting duck; he was the decoy. No one noticed I had hung back. I stayed hidden among the full pines. The three who thought they had one were now surrounded by four. From the depths of the trees stalked Victor, Nikita, Lisbeth, and Baldur.

With the hunt complete, I called it. The five on mini pack A celebrated with joyous yells, and the remaining members of mini pack B sulked. They hadn't paid enough attention, and as a result, their mission was a failure. This would be a lesson we came back to. We couldn't have this happening again if it were a real hunt.

We ran hunting drills for at least another hour, switching pack members back and forth. It truly was eye-opening to see different strengths and strategies become known.

Finally, as dawn broke and we raced back to the train, I reminded my pack down the line of their final task before positions would be revealed. I felt the eagerness each had and thoughts racing through their minds. I could also see the night had been long, and as tired as I seemed, the reflection of each set of eyes I looked in seemed even worse. We all needed food and a deep sleep.

We made it back to the train just as it began its deceleration into Naprile, the last village in the Mac Tíre. Mac Tíre was the name of the North; it separated our villages from the Outlands. Naprile was the last stop before the long final trek to Askari. It was a good first night together, and I couldn't be more proud of my pack. I was first to hit the shower in our room. I pulled rank. I'm not too ashamed to admit it. I also knew Victor showered before dinner, so the justification was solid in my opinion. When I was done, I dressed quickly. Brunch would be served soon, and I had a feeling I didn't want to miss out on it.

Chapter Five

Everelle

The early light filtering through the train windows painted everything with a soft, golden hue. I blinked against the gentle brightness, adjusting to the sense of peace that seemed almost foreign after the adrenaline of the night. For a moment, I lingered in my bed, stretching as I took in the muffled sounds of the train and the distant laughter from the dining car. My mind wandered to the events of the night before, replaying quick flashes of running feet, orange eyes, and the sensation that I'd missed something important, though I couldn't put a finger on it. It irritated me and left me feeling unsettled.

While shuffling to the bathroom, I passed Priya's bed, noting she was not in it but at least it looked as if she did come back in the night. She must have left early for breakfast. I shrugged and relished in the peace and privacy I had.

Turning on the shower, I waited for the heat to rise and steam the glass before I dropped a eucalyptus tablet onto the floor and stepped in.

I tilted my head back and relaxed in the heavenly scent. I began to stretch my limbs. I had never experienced a shower this luxurious. The pressure of the water bursting through the jets in the wall hit all the right areas. Albeit I wish I were about a foot taller, but if I ducked under one of the jets, it wouldn't hit me in the face. I laughed at myself as I reached for the shampoo. For the first time in my life, I didn't feel rushed or guilty using the hot water. I savored the feel of the smooth body wash that smelled of citrus. I then exfoliated with a sugar scrub of clementines. Just as I was contemplating moving permanently onto the train, Priya was back shouting my name with her singing voice.

"Just a sec! I'm in the shower!! Be right out," I called as I rinsed my body. Turning around I jumped with fright, noticing that she had now joined me in the bathroom.

"Oh, it's fine, I don't mind coming in. I have a question!" she said, in complete oblivion to the social norms that this was not acceptable. I quickly used my hands to cover my small body, grateful for the first time that my lanky arms were of use.

"What? Girl... stop," she said, as she dropped her face. "I'm flattered, but you're not my type. I'm not here to sneak a peek at material I'm already working with," she said while shaking her head.

I'm not sure that made me feel any better at all. I quickly reached for the soft white bathrobe and threw it over my shoulders, cinching it at the waist. While gathering my hair into a towel I asked, "What can I do for you, Priya?"

"I'm hoping you'll help me out. You see, I'm trying to figure out an item that will win me a higher position in rank, one that's decent enough to get me standing next to Kentaro," she said meekly, looking at me with big puppy dog eyes of orange.

"Okkk, are you going to tell me more? Kind of needing more details here," I said, trying to get her to spit it out.

"Well, you see, I want *you* to be my item..." she looked at me directly now, blinking a little rapidly and tilting her head to gauge my reaction. Seeing that I must have had a "What in the fuck?" expression plastered across my face, she divulged more information. "We were tasked to find something valuable, that we could hunt, gather, and protect," she began, slowly but then picked up speed with excitement. "I think that's you! No one understands why you're here, and you *surely* will be hunted, and I kind of like having you around, so I feel it's in my best interest to protect you. See what I did there? Heavy emphasis on the *protect*," she concluded and threw herself onto my bed.

"Alright, well now I don't know if I should be scared of you or everyone else out there!" I whined in confusion and disinterest. I walked toward my side of the bedroom and reached for my closet door.

"Oh, get it together, no one likes a weak bitch. You need to stop thinking you're the weakest in the room. They wouldn't have called you to Askari if you didn't have value. It's time you started loving yourself," she said, tossing a pillow at me. I just rolled my eyes and opened my closet, shutting it again quickly after realizing it only had black leathers in it. "Sorry, I thought when you said the right side of the room, it meant you'd use the right closet, I didn't mean to open your stuff," I said, turning around.

"What? That is your closet?" Priya said, looking blankly. "I already showered and dressed while you were sleeping. My stuff is in here." She hopped off her bed and opened her closet. She was right; her Academy jacket with insignia was there.

"Well, then, where is my stuff?" I asked when I turned back to my closet.

"That *is* your stuff," she said. "You're going to Askari now, and for whatever reason, you're in The Highland pack, so we wear black leathers, which means you also wear black leathers," she finished as if not understanding my confusion.

"But how did I get them? Where did these come from?" I began pulling out the leathers. Inside the closet hung a slim pair of black matte-leather pants, appearing about eight sizes too small, accompanied by a corseted black top. The top was adorned with black leather twine that tied on the sides, a low-cut sweetheart neckline, and a delicately sewn black matte rose down the front. It was beautiful. I'd never worn anything like this in my life.

"Askari always equips our wardrobe. Leathers are required, but each piece is custom to the person. It's one of the more fun ways we get to express ourselves. Each pack has an insignia, which the Academy adorns onto the leathers they pick out for you. See?" she said, standing up and spinning. "These are my leathers." The small mountain range was also sewn into her black leathers at the bottom of her high-collared corset with flowing long sleeves. We had black leathers with matching mountain ranges, but that's where the similarities stopped. Her top had a choker-like neckline with a large slit, opening just enough to expose her budding chest. The slit ended just between her breasts. I had never noticed any of the other sets of leathers on the train. Do all packs have different designs or colors? I'd never bothered to get out of my head long enough to pay attention to the nuances that were evidently surrounding me on this train. My naivety was beginning to infuriate me. Never had I wished for a different upbringing before, but now, standing in this room and realizing just how much I didn't understand about the world I was about to enter, I silently chided my parents' ignorance.

I ran my hand over the smooth leather, and I had to admit, it was beautiful. I headed to the bathroom to put it on. I began by stepping into the pants and said a prayer to the powers above that they'd fit. Shockingly, they did. I adjusted the top with a shaky breath and stood to look at myself in front of the mirror. Looking back at me was someone I hardly recognized. I turned to one side and then the other, and I took my image in. I was...

"Smokin! Damnnn, girl, okay!!" Priya gleamed with excitement. "I may have lied when I said you weren't my type... or when I said I was working with the same parts, because..." She dropped her finger to my chest and tilted her head, smiling smugly, "I wasn't blessed to have those perky beauties." She did a pass around me, checking me out. "Yeah, sorry to say it, but you're definitely going to be needing my protection."

We both started giggling like schoolgirls again. "Well, thanks, I'm glad I have someone to show me the ropes," I said genuinely.

"No problem. I can't promise the men won't drool though; they do stupid shit around hot women." She shrugged. "Let's go. Lunch will be served in a minute." Hot women? Never had I been labeled as such. I smiled to myself as we left our quarters, with a little more confidence in my steps.

Priya led the way to the dining car we had dinner in last night. It was the same basic layout, but instead of a heavy meal being served, we chose between platters of sandwiches, salads, and soups. Walking back to the table, I felt him before I saw him. I knew Kolter had entered the room, I just don't understand why I felt his presence so strongly. I looked up just in time to see him do a triple take. His eyes met mine and narrowed to half their size. He looked...pissed? What the hell did I do? Kolter's face hardened as he dropped his eyes and headed to the buffet line.

"Alright, either I'm crazy, or that man wants me dead," I whispered to Priya, never removing my eyes from Kolter as he filled his plate.

"He has a lot of pressure on him right now; I wouldn't let him bother you too much. You're a newbie, he's probably trying to figure out where to put you," she said nonchalantly as she shrugged her muscular shoulders and continued to eat.

"Why would he have to put me anywhere? Who is he?" I looked at her, letting her know she was leaving out some key pieces of information.

"Do you seriously mean to tell me you have no idea where you're headed or what you've signed up for?" She spoke as if she thought I had been lying all this time and it baffled me further.

"No, I seriously have zero clue. A man showed up at our house two days ago and informed my parents and me that my scores on the assessment showed I was to be trained at Askari. He said the train left the next morning and to be on it. That is all I have to go on." I pushed my plate away just as Kolter sat across from me.

"You're in for a real rude awakening if that is the case," Priya shrugged as she began to fix a piece of my corset. "So Kolt, have you officially met my item? This here is Ever, and I'm going to protect her." The smug look on her face made me nervous.

"We've met," he said curtly, dropping his fork to the table. "Priya, I don't think that's how the course works. You can't just go picking up random people, even if they are meek and weak. The task was to find an object." He began to slather butter on his roll as if I didn't have ears to hear all his insults. I'd had about enough of this little, all right, big, ok, yes, he's big, weasel.

"Mphm," chortled Kolter, never raising his eyes to meet mine, a smirk played on his lips. Why the hell was he so arrogant?

"I beg your finest fucking pardon?" I looked at him with what I could only hope was a challenging look and not something he'd feel sorry for. He looked at me with just the smallest hint of shock. He had tried to mask it, but it was there. "When do you suppose *we met*?" I asked, with heat. "Are you referring to the platform when I tried to introduce myself and you rudely walked away? Or how about when I was headed to my friend's table and you stepped in front of me, and told *me* to stay out of your way? Which of those times do you feel was sufficient enough to claim as a meeting?" I was fuming.

His eyebrows rose almost an inch, and he sat back, bringing his folded arms into his chest and cocking a smile. "I didn't..." I cut him off completely; no one was going to insult me and then gaslight me anymore.

"I'm not meek or weak! I'm respectful to most people, just don't take now as an example of that, because let's be real, this is not my best light. I like to think I'm kind, and I have strengths, albeit analytical ones, but still..." I was rambling, I knew that, but I couldn't stop myself. He was egotistical, and my blood was boiling. It didn't stop me from thinking he was irresistibly sexy when his confidence showed as it did now.

"Are you finished?" he asked, appearing so unbelievably bored. He got up from the table and began walking out. He slammed his food into the garbage bin by the door and left.

"UGH," I snarled. "He is infuriating." I picked up my fork and began mercilessly stabbing my chicken breast. Suddenly, a whistle began to interrupt my self-loathing, and into the seat recently vacated by Kolter, slid Flynn.

"Mmm mmm, do I love some fresh meat?" Flynn remarked, staring blatantly at my chest. The unease of the attention made me cower just a little, covering my chest with my arms.

"Oh my God, someone give me a trash bag?" Brandt said as he slid into the seat next to Flynn.

"He only does it because it pisses you off so much. I don't know when you'll learn," Nikita said as he saddled up next to me on my left. "He's a flirt with everyone, don't take it as a compliment." She glanced over my outfit and gave a small, approving smirk as she picked up her sandwich. "Then again, maybe with you he actually means it."

"I honestly don't understand how he's not bonded with anyone yet... oh wait. Yes, I do," Brandt said, rolling his eyes. He dropped his arm around Flavia as she scooted in with her plate. She rolled her eyes, letting out an exacerbated huff as she shoved his arm back off her, making him chuckle.

"You two are cut from the same damn cloth, Brandt," Assata clucked.

I glared at Flynn, but his grin only grew wider and he puckered his lips into a kiss, unfazed by my annoyance. Despite myself, I couldn't help but notice the way the others seemed to relax around him—maybe it was his irreverent humor, or just the fact that he didn't take anything too seriously. For a fleeting moment, the tension at our table eased, and I caught myself almost smiling.

"Listen, someone must stake a claim! You two always get first dibs at mates," he said, pointing his knife at Brandt and Victor. "I need to work with what I got." Flynn shrugged.

I was thankful that Priya had thought to give me a run-down last night of who each member was that made up our pack. She laid out in detail how to tell Flynn and Brandt apart, how to get on Nikita's good side, and that Victor was a quiet and solid pack mate. While he did exude that air about him, to me, I could see that he was also kind. Priya let me know the nitty-gritty details of last year's horrendous journey of Lisbeth and Baldur becoming mated, and that Kasen had been a solid alpha. It made my heart yearn for that level of friendship, and hopeful that I could someday become a real part of their pack.

My worry was still prevalent that the Sector had chosen wrong. I had little hope that this assignment would stick; however, I'd make the best of it while here.

"Did you all get your items?" Victor asked. I hadn't even seen him sit, but there he and Kentaro were, wearing shit-eating grins as if they were privy to some inside joke I clearly wasn't a part of. I looked around, suddenly suspicious.

"What are your items?" I asked, my voice cautious and wary. I prayed they too wouldn't try and collect me under the guise of protection to win points in this hypothetical conquest.

Flynn waggled his eyebrows, grinning mischievously. "You'll see," he said, and the rest of the table burst into laughter. I glanced at Nikita, who just shrugged, so I tried to ignore the sinking feeling in my chest and forced myself to take another bite of chicken I'd murdered with earlier frustrations.

"You're looking at mine," Priya announced while thrusting her thumb in my direction. "You can't tell me she's not a perfect item." I watched in embarrassed horror as she began ticking off her justifications while pointing at her fingers. "She's a new cadet and has zero clue what she's getting into." She ticked off one finger. "She's blonde... Eh eh, we know Kolter has a thing for blondes; they're the only bitches he takes to bed." She swished her hair, then reached around me, grabbing Nikita's ponytail, and was swatted away. Priya pointed at every other member of the group, and it dawned on me they all had jet black hair. She put down another finger and continued. "She's smaller than the rest of us." Another finger dropped. "And most importantly, Kolter seems to have something for her." She imitated a mic drop and smugly leaned back and crossed her arms over her petite chest. I was mortified, noticing again just how oblivious I'd been to this entire pack. My stomach sank. Somehow being an item in some sort of show and tell scheme didn't feel like a win in my column on this pack's roster.

The group looked contemplative, as if Priya had swayed their opinions.

"I found his rubix," shrugged Nikita, still picking at her sandwich. "I thought for sure that was a win."

"You mean, you stole his rubix before leaving Tuathanas. The thought never occurred to you to give it back until this challenge," Kentaro corrected, dismissing her as competition. "You know he will see right through it."

Challenge. I was part of their challenge. I looked around at them all tossing around their items. Each trying to outshine the other, and bring forward enough evidence to prove their merit. It dawned on me then, that what I'd missed was that this was in an effort to win some sort of respect from Kolter, not for the academy... they were presenting items to Kolter, and I was one of them. I didn't think I could have felt more embarrassed, but again, I was proved wrong.

"Wait a minute," I snapped, slapping my hands down on the table and looking at the lot of them. "You're presenting these items to Kolter? Why?" It didn't make sense to me. Why would they all be competing in some sort of collection competition for Kolter?

"You really don't understand any of this, do you?" Assata asked me, her eyes softening as reality set in for her. Assata began again, nicer this time. "He's our alpha...you're on the Highland Pack. We all fall under Kolter. He's like our boss for lack of a more appropriate word. We're competing for rank and position assignments," she concluded, setting her item down in front of her, a small black wooden box with a sword carved into it.

"What does any of that even mean? When Priya front-loaded me this morning, I thought it was some sort of school hazing thing to get credit. I hadn't realized I'd be put on display as a weakling again to Kolter." I was no more informed now than I had been before she made that statement. I felt as if I were drowning in a conversation that everyone else seemed to understand, except for me. My mind raced, trying to string together the bits and pieces they'd tossed out, but nothing seemed to fit. The room felt smaller suddenly; the laughter and easy banter only made me feel more like an outsider.

"Excuse me, I'm feeling a little tired," I said as I stood up and gathered my things. "I think I'm going to go lie down." Everyone seemed to nod or smile as I retreated.

I had to find out what was happening, and fast. My only hope was that when I arrived at Askari tomorrow, someone would tell me this had all been a misunderstanding and I'd go home. For now, I quickly grabbed a tome, *Siochan History: A Political Debacle Indeed,* off the shelf in the common car, and headed toward our sleeping quarters.

Tomorrow. Tomorrow, everything will work itself out, I thought as I slipped into my room and closed the door behind me.

Chapter Six

Everelle

The sun had barely begun to rise over the train when I awoke, my mind still tangled in the confusion from the day before. Frustrated with feeling like a naive outsider, I stayed in bed the rest of the day and read the book I'd brought. I didn't even stomach coming out for dinner. Priya was explicit in her request to not order food to the room, but after she'd embarrassed me without my knowledge, she could suffer through the smell of calamari.

Shadows stretched long across the floor, and for a moment, I wondered if I'd dreamed about the entire conversation with the pack. But the uneasy feeling in my chest told me it was all real. Why would a school allow another first-year student to be the alpha or boss of the rest of his pack?

Rising from the bed, I stretched as I looked out the window. The train had begun to slow, indicating that we would soon be arriving in Marti. I made moves to shower and dress quickly.

Upon leaving my room, I felt a strong hand grasp my elbow and direct me back into the room without a single word said. Kolter's grip was firm—too familiar and unyielding for someone I barely knew. My heart pounded as I searched his face for an explanation, but his expression remained unreadable, shadowed by the early morning light. "What are you doing?" I demanded, my voice caught between fear and indignation. He hesitated for a moment, then finally spoke, his tone low and urgent.

"There's something you need to know before we arrive at Marti. You can't trust everything you see," he quipped. He was so close to me I could smell remnants of a run on him, weakened slightly by the scent of a shower with an oceanic, clean-air-type scent. I hated the way the scent of him made me feel. Warm and tingly, like I was amongst comfort rather than a stranger.

His audacity struck me next. I tugged my arm from his grip and watched as he dragged his fingers through his silver hair, then back down over his face before crossing them over his chest, as if protecting himself. It struck me that he was different from the others in the pack. Priya had noticeably pointed out that they all shared jet black hair and orange eyes, but his features were completely different. His silver hair made him appear much more mature for his age. His eyes were honey-colored with flecks of blue. It was truly mesmerizing how he could exude so much confidence and appeal. I wouldn't let it cloud my judgment.

"Who do you think you are? You're going to push me in here and give me some half-assed warning, as if you haven't been a complete narcissistic asshole since we've been on this train?" I was hot; I wasn't some dainty flower. I could handle myself.

His face twitched, and he leaned in to meet my gaze. "I have done what I felt was best. As the alpha, I have obligations and expectations. You'd benefit greatly if you'd take notes and follow my lead," he challenged, lowering his face to bore his eyes deep into my soul. I get it, this intimidation tactic probably worked on the rest of the pack, but at this point, he wasn't going to intimidate me. "Fix your face, it doesn't suit you to scowl," he sniped as if he even knew who I was.

He turned to leave, and I caught his arm; electricity again began pulsing through my fingers and rushing to my core. I broke the connection and pulled my arm back, looking at my fingers as if they'd burst into flames. He looked at me as if he knew what I was experiencing, but said nothing. "I will try my best," I added curtly, as I reached around him for the door. I swiftly opened it and gestured for him to leave.

Shaking his head, he sighed, "Just take my advice. Keep your nose down; trust is earned, and minimally at that." He quickly left the room, and I slammed the door, forgetting momentarily that I was headed out. The nerve of him. Does he seriously think he can just waltz in here with some bullshit macho-ism and think I'll just fall at his knees? Please. He doesn't understand. I've been on my own my whole life. I've never fit in. I've taken everything I've ever met at face value. I won't crumble now.

Left alone, I leaned against the door and exhaled, trying to steady myself. The morning light flickered on the walls, chasing shadows from the corners, but not dispelling the lingering uncertainty. I couldn't ignore the warning, even if it came wrapped in arrogance; something in his eyes had told me this was more than just a power play. Whatever waited for me in Marti, I would have to be ready.

An hour later, I was packed and headed out into the common room, returning the book I'd borrowed. If nothing else, it provided me with some knowledge as to the colonization of Siochan and the ways of politics in which it was run. As we made our final pull into the station. The room was buzzing with conversations about packs, ranks, and Askari. I noticed for the first time that all the different packs had different colored leathers. There were some that were chestnut brown, and more of pure white. It was an interesting tidbit I thought I'd stow away for later.

A crackle of the speaker alerted everyone's attention to the space above the backdoor. A soft melody began, followed by the boom of a gruff male voice. "I'd like to be the first to welcome those of you first years to Askari Military Academy. I am the commanding General Ulrich." A sudden surprise outburst behind me from Victor stole my attention away from the speaker.

"That lyin' son of a bitch!" growled Victor. I looked over in time to see Kolter grab him by the collar and drag him toward the sleeping quarters' hallway and out of sight. I turned my attention back to the speaker in the front, scanning the crowd as I drew my eyes back up to the box above the door.

"...I will be leading you through your education and training here for the next three years. Returning cadets, thank you for your continued dedication to the course. Soon, you will arrive through the gates of Askari, and you will be briefed. This is not a time to wander, but a time to remain silent, diligently listen, and follow your instructions. As in years past, we will be dividing you by pack, requesting your rank and positions from your alphas, and directing you to your dens. Please be warned, this is not the time for challenges, we will get to that when a cadet has submitted a grievance, and your commanding officer has approved your request for a duel on the field. We will reconvene at eighteen hundred hours in the quad. That is all." With that, the speaker cut off, and the doors to the train opened onto the platforms.

Priya appeared at my side as we tunneled through the doors, following the stream of cadets out onto the platform outside, where a blur of movement and color took over my senses—cadets lugging bags, voices echoing, the crisp morning air thick with anticipation. For a brief second, I hesitated at the threshold, wondering if Askari would finally offer answers, or just more questions I wasn't prepared to face. Shouldering my bag, I took a steady breath and stepped out, determined to meet whatever awaited me with my head held high.

"We need to meet with..." Priya began but was cut off by a curt voice.

“Everelle Monica? Come with me, please.” I turned to see a thin man in a mustard yellow uniform. He was wearing a hat, and thick dark sunglasses. He didn’t wait for my response, just turned abruptly and began walking toward a large stone building up ahead.

“Catch up with you later. Don’t worry, everything is going to be fine. Give me your bag, I’ll put it in our room,” Priya said, reaching out and taking my bag before I could argue. She put me in a tight squeeze.

“I’ve enjoyed getting to know you so much. Thank you for being so kind and supportive to me,” I said, releasing her. Part of me was still worried the jig was up. That the Sector caught on to me that I wasn’t supposed to be here. Part of me was saddened because for the first time in my life I felt like I’d finally made a friend.

Turning away from Priya, I began to scurry up the stone steps after the man who’d summoned me. I’d been right after all, I thought. They probably figured out by now this was a mistake. I’m surprised it took so long.

Walking between two of the eight large columns, which created the face of the massive building ahead of me, the sun slowly seeped away, allowing my eyes to adjust. “Admissions Office,” was carved into the large stone wall of the building. Stepping forward the man grabbed the massive windowless wooden door and swung it open with ease. I shuffled to the side as he held it for me.

Stepping through the door, I stood off to the side as I waited for him to lead me further. Upon entering, the building opened to a large oval room. Two massive twin staircases opposed each other on the back wall. Directly in front of me, however, was a majestic fountain. It depicted a lion standing proudly on top of a large boulder, as if looking down on the rest of the world, its kingdom. It was a magnificent piece of art. Interrupting my admiration, the man gently ushered me forward toward the left staircase.

"Please follow me, the General is waiting," he added curtly, his eyes never meeting mine.

The General? What could the General want with me? I nodded politely and followed the man up the stairs. With each step, the anticipation and anxiety scratched at my throat. Maybe this was a good meeting? Perhaps the General would take care of the mix up, though I'd assumed that would have been an admissions issue. Clearing my throat, I asked the man what the meeting was about. He treated my question as if I'd never spoken. Apparently, in the capital, they don't have to answer your questions if they don't find any point in it.

Once at the top of the stairs, I made a point to commit to memory how stunning the architecture in this building truly was. Everything was made of stone. It was polished until gleaming. I drew my eyes up toward the light that showed brightly through a large dome made of glass. In my nearly two decades of life, I'd never seen anything so wonderful.

"Ahem," the obviously irritated man clearing his throat interrupted my appreciation, and put a pep in my step. I rushed forward through the next door labeled "General Ulrich," into an office of grand design. It was large, with warm-toned furniture. A desk large enough to sit ten people, stood proudly in the center of the room. A wide black and brown leather chair sat behind it. Just beyond the desk was a huge floor to ceiling window, allowing The General visibility to what I could only assume was the quad of Askari. On each wall were massive bookcases. There were so many bookshelves that a ladder on wheels was attached, allowing for someone to move effortlessly from shelf to shelf. It truly was a wonder to behold.

"Please take a seat, General Ulrich will be with you shortly," the man quipped as he turned on his heels and left the room, closing the door behind him. Instead of sitting, I walked over to the large windows to see the place

I'd read about briefly on the train. Looking out, I could see a large rectangular quad, sandwiched between what appeared to be lecture halls. I could already see packs of people moving about in one direction or another. Beyond the walls of the lecture halls, I could see mountains like those back home, filled with tall pine trees. Tracing my path back toward the school, I saw large fields that looked like they held different adventure course equipment and large rock piles. Odd to be placed there, but the entire campus was breathtaking to see.

The door behind me suddenly opened and I made my way back around the desk toward the chairs.

"Everelle?" This must be the General. He walked toward me with his arm outstretched, coming in for a handshake. He looked about my father's age. He was tall with long sandy blonde hair. It had sprigs of gray intermixed to give him a look of distinction and was fashioned into a low pony tail down his back. The General had a goatee under his bottom lip that looked intentional. His eyes were warm chocolate brown, and he held a genuine smile. "I'm sorry to keep you waiting. Day one is always a hectic one. Please be seated," he said, gesturing toward the chair. "Impressive, isn't it?" he asked, referencing the view as he rounded the desk.

"It truly is, sir," I began, and hated the way my voice came out meek. Perhaps Kolter had been right about a few things. "The last three days have truly been eye opening for me. Until now, I'd never left Tuathanas."

The General nodded as if he had expected as much. "I'm sure you're wondering why you're here, and we will get to that in time. For now, though, I'd love to hear a little more about you. Tell me about yourself." He said it with such a calm and genuine presence that I immediately felt like I was speaking with Victor. He had the same mannerisms as Victor, though, I had to say, the vast differences in appearances between the two, left me wondering if they were kin.

I spoke slowly, mindful not to be hasty. I was always chastised in school by my professors for speaking too quickly. It was a deterrent for them. A professor I was fond of told me once, “If you continue to talk as if someone won’t listen to you, so you have to get all the words out, it’s a sure-fire way to get them to not listen to you at all, Everelle. You have to be intentional with your speech, and assert yourself.” So, I slowly filled the General in on the mundane pieces of my life.

“I’m glad to have you, Everelle,” The General began after I’d concluded my makeshift biography. He began adjusting his desk mat in front of him, and placing a pen back in the cup holder. Opening the desk drawer next to him, he pulled out a standard cream-colored folder. Flipping it open, he scanned it quickly and began, “I’m sure you have tons of questions. Mainly, how you were selected. As you know, yearly we send out placement assessments for all citizens turning twenty in Siochan, and although it determined you to be a member of the Highland pack, I wanted to see you for myself, see if that was the proper placement for you.” He eyed me now, suspiciously, as if I were holding on to a secret that he wanted answered. When the best I could do was nod, he rolled his eyes and continued. “Upon review of these assessments the Sector determines whether someone is destined for the fields, a trade, or amongst us here at Marti. You, my dear, scored exceedingly high. It appears you were able to provide them with enough confidence that being a cadet was best suited for your future. Have you heard anything at all about Askari?” he asked. Again, I felt this overwhelming sense that he thought I knew more than I let on. With both of his brows raised, he began flipping through slips of paper from the file in front of him.

I shook my head. “Not much, sir. Only whispers back home—stories about how Askari is the heart of Siochan, where cadets are shaped into the leaders of tomorrow. But most details were vague, and no one I knew had ever been here before.” I hesitated, glancing around at the impressive room, then added, “I’m both excited and a little nervous to finally see it for myself.”

“Indeed,” he smiled coyly, as if not believing a word I’d said. He continued, “well, that’s all right. Here at Askari, we train packs and prides to be the best they can be. These very walls have forged the greatest of fighters and unsung heroes of protection. You were called because you exhibit attributes of pack mentality and perseverance. The Sector registered you under the Highland pack." He paused again, waiting for me to rebut. Seeing that I didn't say anything or move, he again continued. "How have you adapted the last three days to them?"

"I like them, each seems so strong and like-minded. I'm sorry, I just have to ask, why am I here? What part of me makes the Sector, makes you, believe I'm like you all. The strongest part of me is my father, and he's a farmer; he works in Tuathanas. He produces 83% of the grain distribution throughout the continent. Monica Farms? Perhaps you've heard of it?" I watched the General's face for any indication that he was disappointed in my answer. If there was any, I was missing it. The General leaned back in his chair, considering my words with a thoughtful nod.

"Monica Farms, of course. Your family's contribution to Siochan hasn't gone unnoticed," he said. "I'm going to fill you in on a little secret, Everelle, you're more like the other cadets at this school than you are a... a farmer." The way he said the word was in pure disgust, and I immediately despised him. "I'll see to it that you meet with Kolter, your alpha. He will put you into a rank and position based upon your strengths. From there, you will attend courses in history, physical strength combat, and survival skills. Courses begin on Monday; however, the weekend is for your pack to become one unit that operates as if it were one soul and body. Please take the weekend to adjust and I'll add weekly check-ins with you to ensure you're adjusting to your new pack." I nodded and felt a sense of relief. I ached for the chance to have a notebook so I could have written some of the information down, but felt it would make me appear even more naive than I already came across.

"Here at Askari we have three main pack families, they include The Highland, The Hadlick and The Mazza packs, but this doesn't discount the other packs you'll see here." He waited to see if I was following along so far. This time, I could nod with confidence. "In just the same formation we have three main prides: The Ade, The Nkosana, and The Molti. Again, we have other prides, but these are the oldest families. Each of the packs here has ten positions. Each pride has fourteen." He waited, brushing the invisible lint off the desk. "Other packs and prides will be seen throughout campus learning other aspects of military education. These tend to be returning students we've personally selected for specialized training and operations."

Anticipating that he was looking for a sign of understanding, I repeated, "Three packs of ten, three prides of fourteen. Oldest families. Specialized operations of packs and prides, Got it." Nodding, he continued.

"Each pack and pride will work together, run courses, complete training, and combat. All strictly monitored by your professors. At the end of each term, you will be challenged on retention and mastery of skills. You'll be given a competence grade, and it will determine your ranking for next year." I silently wondered what would happen if an alpha weren't able to score well enough for their competency. Remembering the conversations about Kasen on the train, I couldn't help feeling like his premature death wasn't the result of heroism. "I'm excited to see your progression this year, Everelle. You'll be a great asset to your pack, but if issues arise, do not hesitate to file a grievance to your commanding officer."

His tone was reassuring, yet there was an intensity behind his gaze that suggested he saw more in me than just a farmer's daughter. "Here at Askari, heritage might shape your roots, but it's your actions that define your path. We'll help you discover which branch best aligns with your strengths." With that, he rose to shake my hand, signaling this meeting was over for now.

As I followed him out of the office, my mind raced with everything I had just learned. The weight of new expectations and possibilities pressed against my nerves, and yet a spark of determination began to grow inside me. I glanced back once more at the grand room, knowing it marked the beginning of something entirely unknown, but deeply significant. With each step, I felt myself slowly accepting the challenge, ready to discover the person I could become at Askari.

Chapter Seven

Everelle

After my meeting with the General, I had no clue where to find my pack, or my den for that matter, so I began to aimlessly walk around the campus. I found the library and was enthralled at its impressive size. I could have spent hours in there alone. I continued my self-guided tour around campus for the remainder of the afternoon while waiting for the general's assembly.

A few hours later, the quad was so silent you could hear a pin drop. Standing tall and still, I allowed my eyes to wander. Across the stone courtyard were rows of cadets. All in line, quietly waiting. No one was moving. No one was speaking. In front of me stood Priya, behind me, Baldur. I released a pent-up breath into the frosty evening sky. Flood lamps illuminated the square, and I was able to see we were surrounded by tall walls, mostly solid with a few windows scattered seemingly in random places. I was able to quickly locate the General's office in which I stood this afternoon. Looking up into the night sky, I began to wonder if by next year at this time, I'd feel a sense of home, or if I'd always feel this sense of worry and dread.

It was freezing. The sun had set about an hour ago, taking with it what little heat the day brought. Spring in Siochan was still hovering around fifty degrees most days. Our breaths all joined into streams of evaporated steam as the clock slowly ticked toward the top of the hour. I looked to my left and immediately regretted it. I was met with the fiercest eyes I'd ever witnessed. The woman looked to be around my age, but taller, and had dirty blonde hair desperately in need of a brushing. She had warm tan colored leathers that were strikingly designed with cut outs that resembled a scratch of a big cat around her rib cage, accentuating her thin waist and hourglass shape. Her low-cut top did little to conceal her engorged chest. She had similar pants to mine, but what set her apart, even from her own crew, were her exceedingly tall, heeled boots. It added a solid four inches to her already impressive height. She gave me a menacing look and cracked her knuckles. I didn't break eye contact until the stage in front of us had lit up, indicating that the assembly would soon begin. I never wanted to show my fears or anxiety to these people. Kolter had warned me not to trust half of what I saw, and I didn't intend to forget it. I struggled with inner demons of wanting to impress him and wanting to completely piss him off as he did so effortlessly to me.

My hands trembled slightly, tucked tightly into my sleeves, as I fought to keep my posture straight. The anticipation in the air was almost tangible, everyone seemed to be holding their breath for what would come next. I could hear the faint shuffling of boots, as they ascended the stairs to the dais. Despite the cold, a flush of adrenaline kept my senses sharp, and I kept my eyes glued to the people crossing the dais and taking seats as if assigned. A podium was fashioned at the center of the dais, equipped with a singular black microphone. The Askari crest, a massive golden shield depicting the head of a wolf, holding two intersecting arrows in its mouth, over a lion standing in a fighting pose, was proudly hung at its front.

Once the group was seated, General Ulrich approached the podium and tapped it twice. "Good evening cadets," he began and a chorus around me in unison responded, "good evening."

Silence filled the quad again as General Ulrich gave a polite nod, "I'm pleased that you all were able to make it and find your dens easily today. This evening I'd like to take the time to introduce the professors you will have this year. Some, you may know as returners, a few are brand new to all. As many of you may know, you will have six educational courses while you are here at Askari. This will include the following: Siochan History taught by Professor DeMarcus." He raised his right arm and motioned for her to raise. To the far left of the dais a kind looking woman rose from her seat. She had long brown hair that hung in loose waves with strips of blonde through it. She dressed in an understated yet elegant brown tweed jacket paired with brown pleated trousers. She looked friendly as she held a warm expression.

"It's my pleasure to teach all of you this year," she began. "History has a way of catapulting you into a future of success or dooming you to repeat your past. I encourage you all to take advantage of the lessons you will be taught this year. You never truly know when you may need to use that knowledge." She kindly shook General Ulrich's hand and headed back to her seat.

As Professor DeMarcus took her seat, a ripple of anticipation moved through the rows. I found myself glancing nervously at the cadets around me, wondering which of them would become rivals, and which might someday be friends. The solemnity of the setting pressed in, but I tried to let the professor's words—about the importance of learning from the past—steady my nerves. I reminded myself that everyone here was starting fresh, all equally untested, all with something to prove.

"Thank you my dear, it's always a pleasure to see you." The General motioned for the next professor. The man that rose from the chair next to Professor DeMarcus was in similar attire to the general in that he wore a mustard yellow militaristic uniform. He too had long blonde hair, although his was kept pulled back in a neat elastic tie. That is where the similarities ended. This professor had a stern look that didn't falter and he kept his posture rigid as he accepted his turn at the podium.

"I am Professor Monaghan." He looked out at the crowd and scrutinized the lot. "I will be teaching those willing to learn about war tactics and survival. This will not be for the faint of heart. I do not tolerate tardiness or interruption." He paused now, scanning the crowd with his icy gaze. If anyone else was intimidated, they didn't show it. My eyes crept again to the left and the woman from earlier met my sight. Her scowl was more fixed, and I quickly returned my eyes forward.

"I will push you to the brink, but not far enough to require a stay in the hospital wing. Please see to it that you are continuing the training of your minds and bodies for my class in your free time." He suddenly moved closer to the General, shook his hand, and then returned to his seat without so much as another word.

Introductions to the four other courses and professors continued, and I became more aware of how little I was prepared for this academic year with each new introduction.

Once the last professor reclaimed his seat, General Ulrich stepped to the podium to address the crowd. "Now, let us remind you, assessments are due by mid-June. All cadets are required to finish and turn in their evaluations by the deadline. These assessments are an important part of your academic progress at Askari and will be reviewed carefully by your instructors. Be sure to manage your time wisely and seek guidance if you have questions or concerns about the requirements. Your alphas will be of service to you throughout your courses. If for any reason, you don't feel comfortable with your alpha or they cannot help you, please see your commanding officer. Remember, timely and thorough completion of your assessments will contribute to your overall success in the program," he said as he looked out over the packs and prides of cadets. All lines were stoic and rigid. "We anticipate the first of the courses to be run in May. This too will be a testing point as to who will make the cut and who may be returning home with no prospect of accreditation. Study hard, train hard, and you will succeed. There is nothing more tragic in life than failure. Here at Askari, we don't fail," General Ulrich stated pointedly while looking down toward his golden pocket watch that he released from his breast pocket. Swallowing hard, I noted that there were other first years and I wouldn't be alone in this. I had a pack, and they had me. I just prayed they'd give me grace. "Enjoy the festivities of the evening, Monday begins your work here. Cadets, you are dismissed." With that, he gave a curt nod while raising his hand to say goodbye. The General and professors dismissed themselves in the same way that they had entered.

Askari was clearly meant to train us for the future in military careers. Protecting and serving the borders of Siochan. It was evident that we all had signed our oath to the Prime Minister and the Sector the day we got on the train to come here. I prayed I'd be strong enough to pull my share of the responsibilities in the pack.

Before I could truly let the realizations sink in, I felt a hard push from the left. "What? You have a damn staring problem, mutt?" came a gravelly voice from the eyes that haunted me throughout the assembly.

Turning back toward her, I countered her gaze. "I beg your pardon?" I narrowed my gaze as I looked up at her.

"I said..." the younger girl made a move to shove her hand into my chest, but I swatted it down. "Do you have a damn problem?"

"There is one thing for sure, and two things for certain," came a voice from beside me. "She most definitely doesn't have a problem with a puss like you, and if she were to, *believe me,* she would handle it, or we would for her," Flynn retorted. He had my back, and looking around me now, my pack had surrounded me. Most with arms crossed over their chests and looks like they wouldn't mind taking one for the team and knocking this woman into better manners.

Her eyes narrowed, “You won’t always have bodyguards, and I assure you, when they’re gone, I won’t be. Enjoy your night, fresh meat,” she threatened. Then, as if finally realizing they were outnumbered, she and two others who flanked her took a few steps back into their line.

“Sheesh, Ever, I have to hand it to you, you really know how to make a first impression,” Flynn said, shaking his head with a grin. “The Princess of Ade pride, really? That’s who you decided to size up? Ballsy,” he whistled, shaking his head. “I’m here for it, don’t get me wrong. Just, wait just a second, I need to stretch.” He began mockingly doing lunges, hands on his hips.

“What the hell is wrong with you?” Nikita snapped as she grabbed me by my arm and spun me toward her. “Are you seriously trying to start a war? They aren’t on our team this year, we have Molti pride as our course mates. We really don’t need any of this bullshit started. Get it together, then go apologize for whatever the fuck you did that pissed her off!” Nikita was glaring at me, as if her eyes alone could eviscerate me.

“First,” Kolter’s voice echoed over Victor and Brandt who until now had blocked him from my view. “I run this pack, and I decide what members do and what they don’t. Stop putting your nose where it doesn’t have authority,” he asserted.

Kolter began sizing Nikita up as he spoke. “Second, we have no idea why Folasade pushed weight around. It could be to show rank, it could be to intimidate since she’s also a first year, we don’t know. But what I do know is that you will not talk to Ever as if you have out ranked her,” he snarled at her now.

I swallowed deeply. He had stood up for me. I was instantly humbled, and just the idea of him standing up for me was doing strange things to my body that left me feeling things I had to push away for now. I didn’t have time to be growing soft for the man who yesterday called me meek and weak. “For now, let’s get back to the den. We don’t need a scene displayed for other packs and prides; it makes it look like we already don’t have our shit together.” Kolter swirled his hand in a circle, gesturing to the others to head out and he tossed his hand over my head and pointed toward the exit of the quad.

The walk back to our den was a blur of tense silence and sidelong glances. The echoes of the confrontation still rung in my ears. I replayed back the altercation with Folasade, trying in vain to connect with something that I'd done to piss her off in any way.

You're just her newest target, stop reading into it, you're driving me nuts. Kolter's voice stole me from my inner turmoil.

I looked startled. His eyes were stoic and forward facing as he walked beside me. His voice was in my mind as if it were said aloud.

"What the hell," I stopped walking and looked at him. "How did you just..."

Talk to you in your mind? he interrupted, again speaking through my mind. This time he stopped turning to face me. *We're a pack, we have a line of communication. It connects us all. Depending on your desire, you can share your feelings, thoughts, and words down the line to any one of us or all at the same time.* His eyes were kind and relaxed. This was the first time since meeting me that he didn't seem angry while looking at me.

"But forgive me for my ignorance, how do you do it?" I asked him, puzzled and excited at the same time. Was this something that strictly happened here at Askari? Or could they always communicate this way? His answer would help explain a lot of the missing pieces I'd witnessed on the train from the group of them. It seemed like they were always aware of what was happening, and I was always two steps behind.

He rolled his eyes and shook his head, turning away from me to continue the journey back to the den. There it was. The feeling that I'd irritated him by my obliviousness. How could he expect me to know things I'd never experienced? I'm not like him. I'm not like any of them. I'm just a girl from Tuathanas.

He stopped again suddenly, turning to look at me, and making sure we were out of ear shot. "No, you're not," he said aloud, looking directly into my eyes. "You're more than that, you've always been more than that. It's why you're here. Stop constantly decreasing your value to make yourself smaller when you're meant for so much more." He stunned me. My heart figuratively somersaulted in my chest and a warmth grew slightly for the man I thought hated me. He watched me then, as a look of shock appeared across my face. It was apparent that he didn't want to continue this conversation, so he turned and began walking again toward our den.

"Come on Ever, you've obviously got so much to learn."

Chapter Eight

Kolter

Everelle was electrifying, terrifying, and oh so naive; but I was drawn to her, and I couldn't stop myself from interrupting her spiral of self-deprecation. She had, until now, been undetectable to any of us. No one had so much as been able to penetrate her mind or feel her.

As we were walking away from the quad, I was suddenly drawn to her, like the tug from a fishing line. Invisible to the naked eye, the feeling began blooming in the center of my chest, a dull thudding. Almost as if my heart had secured a second rhythm all on its own. The pull encouraged me to slow my fast pace so that I could allow others to pass me on the path, drawing myself closer to her. If anyone noticed what I was doing, they neither said nor thought it. As she approached me, Everelle's face was clouded with worry and anxiety. She wasn't much of a concealer. She wore every emotion as if it were intentional. I could tell she was running through the scenario from the quad again, without even having to enter her mind. It was evident she was struggling.

I began to reach out toward her in my mind. I could see the menagerie of pathway's that represented my pack clearly in my head. Each path winding and twisting in a different direction, in a different color, like neural channels, each representing a different member of our pack. I pressed on down the center path in my mind and slowly approached a new direction entirely. It was hazy at first, as if appearing from the fog as my brain, a long lost connection that had always been there, just hidden from my view, slightly out of reach. I hesitated as I processed the revelation of another member. Her path, I noted was vibrantly yellow, like a warm sunny day. My chest tingled at the thought that she would want to be depicted that way. Part of me wondered if she even knew this was plausible. From what little I'd learned of her, Everelle was either exceptionally good at lying, or she truly was a novice to our customs.

I reached for her then, in my mind, witnessing myself begin to walk down her little yellow path, that would allow me the privilege to bridge the door of her mind. I paused, momentarily. Instinctively self conscience that she wouldn't want me there. I was about to step into the very intricacies of her mind, would she be ok with that? Did I want full access to her every whim and thought? Probably not on both accounts, but I was more intrigued than ever before. Stepping forward I twisted the ornate brass door knob that detailed a floral vine and humming bird, and cracked her mind's door wide open. Immediately, I was overrun with an onset of stress, worry, confusion, tumultuous ramblings of her thoughts and lastly I felt her irritation. Pausing, I made sure that the other lines of communication to the rest of the pack were sealed. I didn't need them barging in on her insecurities. It seemed she was already causing unrest in some of the pack. The last thing she or I needed was more ammunition.

I heard her then, her quivering words to herself, the full throttled spiraling had becoming more self-deprecating with every step. Without thinking, I interrupted her thoughts. She needed to know it wasn't her fault. She needed to know what she was feeling was wrong. She wasn't to blame, no one was mad or upset with her. Well...maybe Nikita but she would have to get over it.

"How did you just..." Her face was of sheer shock as she stopped on the trail and stared at me, Her eyes were wet, a tell that she was on the edge of tears. We would have to work on that. She was too readable. Again, I pushed my way into her mind down her ever growing brighter yellow path, our connection was growing. Pride filled me, burning my chest with each crumb she gave me in her mind.

Talk in your mind? I asked her again, telepathically.

Our connection was weaker than the others in my pack. I could sense everything each member always felt, right down to their most embarrassing thoughts. I, unlike some alphas in our past, would be respectful of their privacy. I wasn't going to reach into them and humiliate them just to assert dominance or maintain order. Their feelings, unless given freely, were safe. Everelle's feelings, however, were infiltrating my head at a rapid speed.

She couldn't control her thoughts when she didn't know this connection existed, so I was showing her grace, something that none of my alpha's had ever exhibited. I wanted to look at her; I wanted to see her in my true raw and honest view. I didn't want an image in my mind clouded with misjudgments. I wanted her in HD. I explained to her what I was doing, leaving out that the others couldn't sense her yet. Maybe that would come with time.

She was completely captivating me with her inexplicable ability to jump from self-doubt and worry, to worrying about me. I'd never felt anyone worry about my opinion more rawly, it warmed the pit of my stomach and softened me.

She was staring at me now and the pull I had from her was all consuming. I had to keep walking, so I didn't put my tingling hands on her. I had never felt this intensity from another soul. The feeling of urgency to be next to her, the complete sinking worry when we weren't together, it was all too much. It brought me guilt because of how I'd been treating her until now. I turned away, closing her door in my mind, and focusing on the coolness of the night, and the bright stars that lit the pathway to our den. The paths to the rest of the pack were lighter now, and relief washed over me. The members ahead of me were teasing one another and discussing topics other than the incident in the quad. It brought me back to a feeling of ease. I loved watching them tease each other. It was the only time they could truly relax and be carefree.

Unwarranted, my mind became clouded with Everelle's worry again. She unknowingly followed me through the yellow door and brought her feelings right to my door in her mind. I felt her self-deprecation again like a full force. It irritated me that she viewed herself with such low standards. Why didn't she see this for what it was, rather than just a mistake? How could she not sense she was made for more? This time I would make it a point that she understood she was worth it. I stopped again, turning to face her. I got close and I looked deep into her soft blue eyes flecked with spots of honey yellows. I wanted her to feel what I was going to say, and maybe then she would begin to believe it.

Her pull was intoxicating my senses, over running my own emotions with lust and desire. I wanted to graze my fingers over her cheek and tuck the loose strands of her golden hair behind her small pierced ear. I wanted to breathe in her sweet scent and let it warm my soul. I shook my head trying to regain a semblance of control. Instead of doing the things I desired, I kept my hands clenched at my sides. She had so much to learn and I couldn't get distracted from being the alpha. I had a job to do and a team to look out for. I wasn't as free as Victor, Baldur, Flynn or Kentaro. I didn't get the choice to put my feelings first and thoughts second.

Turning away from her, I followed the pack up the long gravel path into the mountainside. The night was becoming crisper as it dragged on. The moon was full and other than the quiet banter of my pack, the night was silent. We rounded another bend in the woods and then the den slowly came into sight. It was made of dark obsidian stones, gleaming in the moonlight. The stones that made up the outer face of our den were so smooth, they reflected what surrounded them, masking the den to anyone who didn't know it was here.

One by one we began slipping inside a gap no bigger than a bookcase. Quietly we all wound down the slim spiral path into the depths of the den. While the door to our den may have been carved into a mountain side, our common rooms and sleeping quarters were meters below the continent's surface. This again aided in our protection.

Small pieces of calcite, fluorite, and aggregate made up the walls as we descended. Naturally occurring luminous rocks that aided us in sight, keeping the pathways softly lit as we traveled. It was a beautiful sight of blues, greens, and vivid reds. The smell of damp, musty ground began to fade away to a warm scent of garlic, butter, and spicy peppers. We were getting closer now, and it seemed that the den's caretaker had already delivered our celebratory dinner. I heard Flynn whooping up ahead as we completed our last turn down and came into a clearing.

The small passage opened wide into a dimly lit corridor flanked with large white dripping candles mounted to the walls. Walls which were carved into the obsidian stones, resembled more of a home and less of a cave. Once through the corridor, I found warmly lit hallways to my left and right. These, led to sleeping quarters. Ahead opened into a large common room. At its center stood a large black fireplace, its flames licking upward as the wooden logs crackled and snapped, making the room feel warm in contrast to the long walk we just faced.

The room was adorned with large soft black leather oversize armchairs, black leather couches and bookcases exploding with volumes of our pack's history. It was the perfect combination of masculine energy and touches of soft femininity woven into the monochromatic designs. Above the mantel of the fireplace, the crest of Highland, the same one that had hung in my own living room back home, hung proudly. The large brass shield depicted that of a wolf, howling toward a crescent moon. Its background was the very mountain range of Tuathanas, which was sewn into all of our leathers, tying us together. I wondered if Everelle knew that. She'd seen those mountains her entire life. Would she recognize them?

Running my eyes down to the mantle, I noticed photographs of alpha pairings as far back as could be documented sat proudly. To the far right, my photo now sat in a simple golden frame. Turning my gaze, I found my brother and Nikita's photos next. They were a handsome pair, that was for certain. My mother's and father's photos sat next. Oddly, theirs gave me chills, reminding me that they once roamed these same woods.

Turning away from the mantel, I saw Everelle walk in. She was smiling and whispering with Priya, again. Had I been a dick, I could have easily eavesdropped on their conversation so I could know just what was making her face light up. It gave me warmth seeing her like this. I wished if nothing else, that she could always find simple joys here. Jealousy coursed through me after in a sharp wave. Irrationally I felt that I should be the only person making her smile like that, my words being what caused her head to toss back into a singsong laugh.

I tore my eyes from her as I watched everyone make their way back into the common room. I guess now was a better time than any to announce their ranks and positions. I should have done it earlier as promised, but I didn't want to handle diffusing what I'm sure was about to be a shocking blow to egos in a very public space. The privacy of our den was best suited for this conversation.

"Can I have everyone's attention please?" I watched as they all took their seats around the room, my back to the fireplace and eleven pairs of eyes all locked onto me at once. " I know dinner is waiting in the mess hall, but I would like to make a quick announcement first." I watched as they all turned their attention to me, invested in what I had to say. The immediate burn of anxiety caused my throat to tighten. I breathed out forcefully before I continued. "As you know, ranks and positions haven't been distributed. The reason being, I felt it best to wait until we were all present, and in a secluded location." Immediately, eyes began to wander, checking themselves with others in the group, then slowly making their way back to mine. "As alpha, this is one of the hardest decisions I must make, and I want you all to know, it's not a personal vendetta. We will be the only pack with twelve members, so a little finesse was needed to assure everyone had a position that worked for the pack's best interests. I have witnessed magnificent work over the last three days, and positions have come almost naturally to some. With that said, when I announce your positions and thus, partners, I need you to have an open mind and take it to heart. I want us to run as if from this moment on, we are bonded. No fighting, no name calling. Accept that I have the pack's best interests at heart." I looked out over the group and could see Nikita picking at her nails as if already bored of this conversation. Ever was doe eyed and holding Priya's hand.

Brandt had a shit eating grin, "well, rip the band aid off Kolt, what are we doing?"

I cleared my throat and brought my hands together with a small clap, and briskly began rubbing them together. "In beta male position, can I please have Victor Ulrich," I said, still holding Brandt's eyes, gesturing for Victor to step forward. Brandt's wide grin slowly faded, his face changing to depict how I'd wounded him, his eyes dropped to the floor, as he shook his head. I knew he'd take it hard, however for the sake of the pack, I had to choose someone that wasn't as likely to rush into bullheaded situations. I needed someone to counter balance my position in a way that strengthened the pack. Brandt had been my beta for as long as I could remember back at Seoid Primary School. They ran a similar program to Askari for us, in which we were broken off into packs. Brandt and Flynn were always on my side. Until this week, I thought that would have continued, but Victor had surprised me. Brandt knew his position was on borrowed time. Hell, Victor's beta position may be on borrowed time because Kameron comes to Askari next year. I didn't let Brandt's hurt stop the flow of position announcements. There was still another announcement I was sure would be taken far worse.

"Beta Female position, I've awarded to Assata Bitt," I said again, motioning for her to step forward, a gasp was heard around the group as all eyes flew to Assata who nervously stood and walked toward the front. I chose not to acknowledge it. "These two will be your beta's. If ever I am not around, understand, you answer to them. Please respect their leadership and follow orders as directed." The group nodded in agreement, and I continued. "In gamma male position, at my six in formation, can I please have Brandt Mason, with his gamma female being Nikita McNabb." No sooner had the words left my lips did I feel the sharp stab of anger of Nikita down the line. Her anger was hot and raging. The look on her face screamed murderously. Brandt looked at Nikita, his face matching the wounds she too felt, and reached for her hand. Nikita took it and they rose, eyes never ceasing to eviscerate me as she stepped forward, falling in line after Victor and Assata. Handshakes and nods were given as they took their positions in line, facing the remaining members of the group.

"As you know, gamma has two male and two female positions. I'd like to call Flynn Mason and Flavia Indelicato." Flynn pounced up ready and scooted over to Flavia, extending his hand. She just laughed and watched as she put her hand in his and he brought it to his lips.

"My lady, might I have this chance at life beside you?" Flynn bowed before her in mock regal like gestures.

"You may!" Flavia gasped, feigning a love-struck girl, as she beamed back at him, before jumping to land in his outstretched arms. He carried her to their positions in line and set her down gently. Everyone chuckled and congratulated them. Shaking my head, I just smiled. I knew they'd be a good fit. Each seemed to have a solid sense of humor and a fresh outlook on life. They each hid their insecurities I'd noticed, in humor.

"Next, we need our final two hunting duos. In delta positions, we have Kentaro Bridges and Priya Jones followed by Baldur Goncalves and Lisbeth Erichs."

As they stood smiling and began walking to their formative positions, Nikita's growl came so loud and strong that she blew out the candles on the wall beside her.

"So, she's our alpha!!!!!" Nikita bellowed, stepping toward me now, thrusting her outstretched hand, forcing my attention toward Everelle who was beginning to sink into the couch she was sitting on..

"Yikes. Anyone else in here hungry?" Flynn said blanching while looking around the group. "Victor? Come on man, I know you could always take down a buffalo." He gestured for the door, when Kolter's eyes met him harshly, making him drop his hand. "Then again, staying here is great. I love being witness to all the crazy," Flynn chirped as he rolled his eyes and tossed his hand.

"Are you out of your damn mind Kolter? What is this? The girl doesn't even know her own name, and you make her alpha of the Highland Pack? You have got to be joking!" Nikita was absolutely fuming. She tore her gaze from me and began pacing, throwing her arms in the air before stopping and swiveling back toward me. Her anger was singeing the neural pathway in my brain that led to her door. It gave me an immediate headache.

The room went silent, and glances were exchanged between Brandt and me. He nodded in agreement before turning toward Nikita.

"Alright, here we go," Brandt said as he picked her up and slung her over his shoulder. "We're just going to go for a quick run... maybe kill a few deer. Alright with you cupcake?" Brandt joked as he slapped Nikita's ass.

"Put me down, you jackass! I'm not going *anywhere*!" Nikita hollered at him, she began throwing her fists into his back and kicking her legs, trying in vain to be released. Luckily for the rest of us, Brandt was able to outweigh her strength and keep her pinned.

"We'll be back, Kolt, don't wait up," Brandt said winking as they left the room. You could hear Nikita screaming the entire way up the passage.

Silence again over took the room, and I sighed as I brought my attention back to the task at hand. Looking back toward the couch, I made the strides to Everelle quickly, and reached my hand out toward her. As if she didn't know what to do, she sat there wide eyed looking at me. I looked back toward the group, and back to Everelle.

"This is the part where you join me, at the head of the line." I whispered, reaching again for her hand. Slowly she sheepishly nodded and stood. She, however, didn't take my hand. She gave me a wide berth as she moved to stand next to Victor. He patted her on the back, and replaced his hands behind his back. They all stood now, staring back at me.

"Alright, that went about as well as anticipated. How about we go eat?" I suggested.

Nods and cheers went through the line, when suddenly, a sickly loud howl came from above. It emulated notes of pain and suffering, more than anger and hurt. Nikita, I thought. She would have to get over it. She was my brother's alpha; she wouldn't be mine. Her attitude is why I couldn't make her a beta. She'd always be one step behind me, chirping her disapproval, she would for sure override and intimidate Everelle. Solely because of her own actions, she was made a gamma. I waited as the pack left from the room, hanging back to talk with Everelle about what had just transpired.

"I guess I should thank you, but I don't really know if that would be genuine," she softly spoke first, her eyes dropping to the floor, never meeting mine.

I crouched slightly in front of her, forcing her to look at me. Once her eyes finally met mine, I could see her worries and doubts etched so deeply across her smooth forehead. I didn't need our pack line to know she was intimidated and for good reason.

I chose Everelle as the alpha for a multitude of reasons, none of which had to do with the yearning my body felt every time she was in my presence. As of now, I was the only one who could hear or feel her in the pack, that I was aware of anyway. I had nonchalantly asked prior to the muster in the quad. When all had shrugged and said they couldn't hear her, it told me she was a liability to the pack, because she wouldn't be able to communicate with anyone unless spoken to aloud and vice versa. That meant anyone could know our plans, and to me, that was a weakness only I could swallow. If she were close, I could communicate what our plans were through our smaller line, therefore alleviating some issues.

"You will. Thank me, I mean," I said, gesturing for her to follow me. "Your rank in this pack is vital to how it operates, and I expect that you will treat it with the utmost respect and responsibility."

I led her down the dimly lit hallway to my sleeping quarters. I didn't want to be overheard, and it wasn't uncommon for duos to meet in privacy. I just wasn't sure any of them met in privacy when they didn't truly know one another. I was just following orders. The General had pulled me aside just before the muster in the quad and told me I needed a private meeting with Everelle, just to fill her in on her missing pieces in her understanding of our world. He never alluded to more. I wasn't sure what he truly needed to be filled in.

Opening the wrought iron carved door, I stepped aside letting her into my room first. The inside of my room was large. Similar in size to the trains' sleeping quarters, but not nearly as bright and welcoming. I had one king-size bed against the far wall. It was adorned with a black bear pelt used as a blanket and starchy white sheets. To the bed's immediate left, there was a singular nightstand with adorning brass lamp. Across the room, a large mahogany desk sat beneath a shelf filled with the only possessions I had left. No one tells you when you become alpha of your pack, it means you leave everything behind in the notion that something greater was coming. You get whisked away to a school you had no interest in and then have massive amounts of responsibility thrust upon you. I didn't ask for this. I wished to God Kasen was still here, then he could handle the tyranny of the pack.

I watched Everelle as she took in my minimalist surroundings. She stood in the center of the room, thoughtfully taking in my room before meeting my eyes again.

"So, can you finally tell me what is going on? I'm sick of feeling like I'm walking on eggshells or everyone is coddling me," she stated curtly. Her eyes were bright but inquisitive and untrusting, as if she were studying me truly for the first time.

I blew out my breath as I walked to my bed, taking a seat, I motioned for her to take the desk chair. This would be a lengthy conversation, and I didn't think it would be appropriate to have her sitting on my bed. Just because I had determined her to be my alpha, didn't mean she was accepting of what that truly meant, or if she even had a clue. There was so much about her I still didn't know or understand.

"Let's start with this, tell me what it is you do know, and I'll do my best to fill in the rest." I waited for her to take her seat and braced myself against the magnetic pull she still had to me.

"I don't suppose there is a whole lot that I do know. I woke up Monday being a farmer's daughter. Now it's Friday and I'm at a military college, far from home, in a city I've never been to," her brow began to furrow, and a snarky look crossed her face. "Oh, and I was named alpha for a pack, and I have absolutely no idea what it means or how I was even chosen. Looking at me compared to everyone on this campus, you'd think I was brought here by mistake," her eyes widened now, her expression becoming more animated. " I assure you, I thought so too. I thought that when General Ulrich met with me, he was signing my papers to go back home..." She paused now, as if noticing she was beginning to spiral again. It took everything I had not to pull her to me. She was captivating. "Jokes on me though, because he in fact did not send me home, but rather wants me meeting with him weekly and also you too," she shrugged her shoulders and looked at me with sympathy before continuing her tirade. "Sorry, he thinks you need to personally train me. Is that why you made me alpha?" ***Surely it must be. The shortest of you giants still stands about a foot taller than I do. I've yet to meet anyone below six foot here! What did they feed you all growing up? Fertilizer? Sheesh. This is all too much sometimes.*** She blew a breath out, a strand of her red hair blowing away from her eyes as she picked them up to meet mine. I fought every instinct to not laugh at her. She was mentally unloading on me, and had not even realized it. I was impressed and intrigued. Instead of calling it out, I spoke to her. I wanted to ease her mind, but my fears seemed to be correct.

She had no idea what I was, what any of her pack was, what SHE was. She was about to have her life changed, and I could only hope it was in a positive way, and she didn't drop dead on my floor from a heart attack.

"Do you know what I am?" I asked, my voice coming out more gravely and ominous than I'd wanted. I would ask the most basic question. I watched as her eyes drifted slowly over my body, her gaze scorching my skin as it raked up my chest, then met my eyes.

"No." Her answer was simple. I reached toward the brightly lit yellow line between us, to read her feelings like I had just moments before. I wanted to know if she feared me at this moment. At this last second before I was sure she would fear me for the rest of her life. No emotions were there. Our connection was unreachable. Like she had shut me out somehow. The door in my mind at the end of her yellow path was locked. This had never happened before and now I was more curious.

With a steadying breath, I began to ruin her entire image of me, of her pack. "We are known as the Highland Pack." She nodded, as if annoyed. Like she had already known this and was waiting for the next piece of the puzzle she'd been trying to put together.

"When you look at me now, you see I'm human...but that's not at all what I am... that's not what we are. We are shapeshifters, shifting from the human form we project into the northern giant wolf." I paused again, less for emphasis and more to read her reaction to what I'd just said. Looking at her now, her face was stoic, eyes wide and staring back at me unblinking. Abruptly, she began laughing. Slowly at first, then in a complete breakdown of laughter, tears streamed from her eyes, and she bent over hugging her stomach.

"Oh, that's good," she said between belts of laughter as she wiped the tears from her eyes. "That's wonderful. I didn't know I needed that laugh. I suppose next, you'll tell me I'm one too." She sat up, wiping the rest of her face, but the minute her eyes met mine she stopped laughing, her voice caught in her throat. "Wait, you're serious?" Her eyes dried almost instantly and she looked at me with an intensity I'd yet to witness from her. "Answer me, Kolter," she screamed. "Are you serious?"

As a heart attack. I growled through her mind, this time finding she'd left the door wide open to our connection.

"Stop!" she yelled standing up, throwing her hands up over her ears. "You stay out of my damn head! How are you doing that?"

"OK, I'm going to need you to take a breath. I'm not here to hurt you, and the last thing I want is to freak you out." I began to rise from the bed, my hands raised up in a defensive stance.

"Well mission fucking failed, alpha! This is me freaking out," she said, gesturing at herself. "What in the hell? How was I brought here? How could I have been mistaken for one of... one of you?" She said it in such a way that my skin down my back began to prickle. she was pacing the floor now, making laps around my bedroom. I needed to calm myself or I'd shift right here, and then we'd really have a problem.

"Ever..." I started, but she cut me off. This wasn't going well. I grossly underestimated how she'd react.

"Don't call me that!" she snapped, stopping abruptly swiveling in my direction she glared at me with a face of disgust.

"That nickname is reserved for my family...the people who love me. Oh my God! My mother! What will she say? This will surely kill her." She began pacing the small room again. If this weren't such an important discussion, I'd find her reaction almost cute. This helped to calm my nerves partially.

I let out a slow exhale, steadying myself before I spoke again. My words came softer this time, measured, like I was afraid the truth itself might break her further. "Your mother is safe. No harm has come to her, and I promise you; she probably has no idea what's happened here." I judged that based on her own knowledge of what we were. Just how much she was in the dark, led me to believe her family must be in part, human. I watched her closely, searching for any sign she might believe me, hoping my reassurance would ease her panic, even if only a little.

I watched as she took a sharp intake of breath. She rung her hands out at her sides, as she paced back and forth in front of me. I rose and slowly, with my hands up, as if showing I meant no harm, I urged her to take a seat. "Stop pacing, you're making me nervous," I said as she rolled her eyes at me, huffing while she took the seat at my desk.

She blew out the breath she'd been holding in for too long, and I slowly backed away, hands still in the air. "I'd like to answer your questions, and help you through this, but I'm going to need your cooperation first." I paused. As if she knew I was looking for understanding, she nodded and I continued.

"I'm from Tuathanas. We are the pack of Highland wolves that reside between Tuathanas and Seoid," She made a motion to interject, but I held my hands up to stop her. This would be a long night if she interrupted me after every statement. "Just let me get through this, and I swear I'll answer all your questions." I waited as she looked at me skeptically, but she nodded at me, pulling her legs up to her chest. Everelle then swiped a zipper motion across her mouth and turned an invisible key, held up her 'key' and threw it. She then motioned for me to continue. This little action made me chuckle, and I instantly felt more at ease. Seeing humor coming from her made me hopeful she would do better with this than I thought.

"Shape shifting is a form of physically taking on another form. It can be done with all sorts of animals. In some cases, shapeshifters have also been known to shift human to human, those however, are the most powerful and deadly. None that we are aware of live on Siochan," I paused here, expecting her to have a question, but she behaved and sat quietly allowing me to continue. "Lycanthrope is the shapeshifting form my family takes," I gestured from myself and moved my arms out to indicate those in the den, as I spoke. "Becoming a wolf is like second nature. Most often we turn around fifteen. Some rare occurrences have happened, however, where the person has turned as late as twenty-one. I, changed at six." I paused waiting for her to absorb all I was telling her. She seemed OK with me continuing, so I steam rolled through it.

"Now, not only are we Lycanthropes, but most of us also have powers based on the type of wolf we originate. You can tell the distinction between the groups of wolves by their coloring first. Highland wolves are the largest breed of wolf, hence your views on us being giants. We tend to be jet black in color with orange eyes. You may begin to realize now; they all have black hair and orange eyes out there. It's a clear indication of our breed. Our breed can also outrun any of the other packs. Our speed and strength are unmatched. This coupled with our individual powers and the line of internal communication, are the manifesting powers we possess." Looking over at Ever, she had softened, and sat with a piqued curiosity, as if she were hanging on my every word. She raised her hand as if we were in class, making me smile. "Questions already?" I grinned; I couldn't help it. A tougher man wouldn't have I'm sure, but she, I was finding out, was my weakness.

Smiling, she dropped her legs. "So, being that there are mainly three packs here, are they the different species of wolves?" Damn she was smart. Pride filled my chest that she had been able to connect that.

"Yes, but that doesn't mean there are only three species of wolves on the continent. At Askari, the three oldest pack families are trained in WAG or Weapons and Artillery Ground Force, however, there are other wolf packs from around the Mac Tíre that are in other branches of the military. Their packs are attending other 'schools' of Askari. Highland will be running courses with the Hadlick and Mazza packs," I answered and waited a breath to see if she was struggling to follow what I'd said. When no indication came that she needed clarification, I continued. "Hadlick wolves are characterized by chestnut brown coloring, and they're slightly smaller and less muscular than we are. However, they can naturally heal the wounded. Moreover, they can sense when someone needs healing. They are the empaths of the wolves. The last elder family set of wolves are the Mazza wolves; they are light gray in nature. They have soft gray fur and light purple eyes. For their extra attribute, they can warp vision and time. Think of the times in your life you've been running late, and you'd just wished for five more minutes, they can do that.

It's one of the most impressive traits in the wolf lineage; however, they're also bound by strict order and expectations of when and how their powers can be used. We wouldn't be able to function in a society that was constantly jumping in time." I was impressed by her interest, and pleased that she wasn't making a beeline for the door.

"So, are you saying I somehow am a Highland wolf? How could I know? I mean, I have strawberry blonde hair, I'm small, and I have freckles. I don't think I match any of the elder families in characterization. When will I shift? I don't think I've ever felt any signs that this is my fate," she rambled mostly to herself. I had to admit, she was a tough case. Her coloring confused me also. None of the elder families matched her. She was also right in shifting. In history, I don't think anyone had ever been admitted to Askari sans shifting. I hadn't met late shifters, so this was unfamiliar territory.

"There would usually be a triggering event when shifting happens for the first time. Something takes you and puts you under extreme duress and your body naturally shifts to protect itself from the threat."

"How will I know when that happens?" she asked, innocently.

"Oh, you'll know," I said. It'd been fourteen years since I'd first shifted. I couldn't even tell her the event that made me shift for the first time, or how I'd felt. I could only give experiences of those around me that I'd witnessed.

"Are you telling me then, that everyone out there," she gestured over her shoulder and dropped her voice lower almost whispering. "Is a wolf?! I've been hanging out with wolves all week?" She looked stunned. I had to admit it made me laugh. Her innocence was refreshing. It'd been years since I'd been around an unchanged. She made my life feel more fulfilled, and she didn't even know it.

The stride in which she was absorbing this news, made my heart warm. If she adjusted this quickly to life altering news, she would be a perfect alpha. We just needed to work on her ability to conceal.

After minutes of quietly processing, she looked up at me and whispered, "will you help me, that is, will you be there for my first time?" The complexity behind her eyes brought me to my feet. I made quick work of closing the distance between us. Kneeling in front of her now, so we would be eye level, I took her hands in mine. "I'd be damned if someone else gets to put their hands on you." My eyes filled with rage. "You are my partner. I alone will protect you. Whether it be my mind, my reputation or my physical body, you will be protected. You have my word." She nodded and dropped her eyes to our interlocked hands.

"Then I'll say it. Thank you for making me alpha." She smirked looking back into my eyes. If I hadn't already begun to suspect, my chest just confirmed that she was my mate.

Chapter Nine

Everelle

The next morning, I finally allowed myself to creep from my bed as the five o'clock hour ticked to a close. I'd slept fitfully after processing my conversation with Kolter. Realizing what I was, and the implied liability I presented as an unchanged, it left me missing out on quality hours of REM sleep.

Walking out of the den into the fresh air, I noted the sun had just broken across the sky. I closed my eyes and breathed in the heavenly scent of the pine trees, damp soil and was that...coffee? I popped my eyes open and standing in front of me, holding out a cup, was Nikita. '*Shit*,' I thought. "Should I wonder if this was laced in poison?" I asked, before accepting it.

"If I wanted you dead, you would already be buried in the ground. You should be more aware of your surroundings," she said, snidely. Nikita wasn't wrong. "Let's take a walk. There are things we need to discuss." She turned from me and stared down the winding, wooden path. I nodded and gestured for her to lead the way.

"I want to start by apologizing. Brandt made me realize my anger was misplaced, and for that, I'm sorry," she said as we began walking through the woods. This was not what I was expecting would happen this morning, but I was willing to hear her out. Noting her statement warranted a reply, I cleared my throat.

"No offense was taken. I can understand that it was probably hurtful to see your position taken, by a wolf who hasn't even shifted."

Nikita stopped walking, turned her head to face me, and asked, "You know?"

"Kolter." I nodded my head and continued, "he filled me in last night. I admit it was a shock, but now I'm filled with worry that I'll be a liability to the pack since I haven't shifted yet."

"You will. I was talking it over with Brandt. He suggests that the reason you haven't shifted was merely because of the fact that our pack protected Tuathanas, and you weren't needed. You lived a cushy life in town. What was there to protect?"

Walking forward through the densely wooded trail, I silently milled over what she said. "That makes sense. I just don't know how we will start classes Monday when I've yet to shift. I don't know the first thing about it. I feel like I should be strapped to a chair until my body gives up and forces me into a wolf."

"Couldn't hurt," she said, smiling. Her eyes were dancing with the thought of inflicting some stress on me. Nikita would be my biggest ally or would ruin me. I was sure of it.

"When did you first shift?" I asked as we continued the path through the woods.

Nikita cleared her throat and tightened the grip on her coffee mug. I watched as she kicked a few of the left over fallen leaves on the ground before she finally began. "I was fourteen. My little sister and I were walking through the woods on the way home from school. My sister would run up ahead and hide, waiting until I just about passed her before she popped out to scare me.

She had done this a handful of times, but the last time, she ran further ahead of me than before. I heard her giggling at first. Then eerily it went silent. That's when I heard her let out a blood curdling scream. I remember fear fueled me. Panic-stricken, I began running along the path in the direction I'd last seen her. I frantically remember scanning all the trees and rock walls that had surrounded us and couldn't find her. I was in misery. My body was reacting solely on instinct rather than awareness. It was only after rounding the bend, that I saw it." Nikita got quiet now and had slowed her walking a bit. She took a sip of her coffee, holding the cup with both of her hands, as she swallowed.

"I was so enraged. One of the older boys from town held my sister in the air by her throat, high against a tree. His grip was so firm, her face was turning purple; fear in her tear-soaked eyes. She had her little legs kicking but they never connected with him. I knew I only had moments before he would end her life. I felt it then. The burning rip across my chest. Anger fueled by fright. I raced forward, lunging at him, and just before I reached him, I shifted. I used my force to knock him over. He dropped my sister, and she hit the ground with a sickening thud. I didn't move again until I heard her gasp for air. Knowing that she would be OK, I turned on him. His eyes were locked in fear as he slowly began to turn and run, his head kept turning to look over his shoulder. I hung back for a few seconds, allowing him to think he could get away. I was fourteen when I took my first life. I scared myself but more than that, I scared my sister. After he breathed his last breath, I spit on him. I turned walking back to my sister while I silently cried my stomach heavy with remorse. I hadn't meant to kill him, just scare him a bit. The damage was done, though. My sister held on to me as we cried. I made sure she was calmed down enough to continue our journey home. It wasn't until then that I had noticed I'd shifted back to my human form. Pulling away from her, I noticed I was naked. Upon shifting, I shredded clothes. It was embarrassing walking the rest of the way home with not so much as a towel to cover myself. It's why we wear leathers. The material our clothes are sewn with mimics the skin of a wolf; as such, we can stretch and grow in them, and they don't tear."

I was impressed and in awe of Nikita. She was right, nothing in my life had ever been so terrifying that I would have needed to respond in that manner. Part of me felt sorry that she had to have something so awful happen to her. We began walking again and she continued.

"I'm sorry for the way I acted about Folasade yesterday. It wasn't my place. I was using my misplaced anger as an excuse again," she shrugged. "She's always been a bitch."

"She's in a pride, right? Do prides shift?" I asked as we approached the base of the mountain we lived on. Stepping into the clearing of the woods, I noticed a large lake sat in front of it. The morning air was cooler than the warmth of the water, resulting in steam like fog hovering the lake's surface. We made our way over to a bench that rested at the water's edge and took a seat.

"Prides are shape shifters, yes," she answered before sipping her coffee again, "We are Lycanthropes, meaning wolves. Prides are made of Manticores, or lions."

"Folasade is a lion?" I asked, hoping the shock I felt wasn't obvious.

"Yes, just as there are three elder packs, there are also three elder prides. Each represents one form of their kind. But it doesn't discount the other prides in the Outlands," she said, looking out toward the water.

"Do the Manticore also have powers?" I wondered mainly out of fear. I needed to know if this woman who had already threatened my life, could wield any exotic powers. I needed to know what I was up against.

"To be honest, if they do, they don't act like it. They function as if their shift alone is a power. But I wouldn't put it past the elder prides to conceal their powers." Nikita turned her head quickly back toward the mountain. I didn't need a line to know who she was looking for. I felt the electricity in my blood before he even stepped into the clearing.

"Well, this is nice to see," Kolter said, while approaching the bench. He also had two cups of coffee, which made me smile. He returned the smile as he sat next to me. "What are you all doing out here?" He asked, while he smoothly took the coffee Nikita had given me out of my hand, set it on the ground and handed me a new cup.

"Discussing a coup. How to overthrow our current alpha and live victoriously with a solo female alpha." Nikita quipped as he drank, rolling his eyes.

"She was telling me about her first time shifting. I'm impressed by her ability to look fear in the face and charge full steam ahead anyway." He began nodding his head in agreement.

"Nikita has always been that kind of girl." He smiled, "She may have a fierce bark, but her bite is worse. I'm honored to have her in our pack."

"How did you first shift?" I asked, drinking from the cup Kolter had brought for me.

"I don't know." He looked down at the ground, dragging the toe of his boot in an infinity sign. "No one would tell me, I woke one morning, wrapped in bandages around my arms, and lying in bed. My mother... She looked beaten down. When I spoke, her eyes flew up to mine and tears welled in them. She called for my father, frantically. They must have been going through hell. I was six at the time. Neither of them looked like they'd slept in days. I tried to move and my mother shushed me and tucked me back in. That night, while pretending to sleep, I overheard them saying we had to move. Mom was worried about my health while traveling, but dad made it seem like it wouldn't be a problem. The next day we packed up and moved away from Tuathanas. We moved to the foothills in Seoid. It's how I know Victor, Brandt, Flynn and this pain in the ass," he said while reaching around me to shove Nikita's arm. "We never went back to Tuathanas. The only reason I boarded the train there, was because I was born in Tuathanas. The Sector likes to document where cadets originate, and it's the easiest way for them to take roll call. I'm still registered, as are my brothers, in Tuathanas."

"That's probably why I didn't know you then," I said. "I know everyone back home, my dad is the distributor for grain."

"You wouldn't have known us, just as you didn't know Priya or Kentaro. Wolves and humans don't intermingle. We would have gone to separate schools and stayed mainly in the woods on the mountain," Nikita said. Rising, she reached forward and picked my abandoned mug up off the ground, noting it hadn't been drunk from, and rolled her eyes.

"I'm going to head in; I want to catch up with Brandt and see if he has any decent ideas for our position. Later."

Kolter and I both nodded and watched as she walked away. I was first to break the silence. "So, I really must be a drop off from the back stoop of my mother's salon."

Kolter began to laugh, knocking his coffee back, "No, that's not how that works. I have a feeling we will find out more about you as time goes by. For now, I want you to focus your energy on our line of communication. I've never met a wolf who can close it down like you can."

"Close down communication? What, like kick you out of my head?" I asked, turning on the bench to face him. Sitting this close to him made my spine tingle. My hands ached to touch any part of him. My body betrayed me by feeling this way.

"Precisely," he said, mimicking my movements. We were both now sitting sideways on the bench facing one another. "I want to try something," he said, moving his hand forward. He reached out and tucked a piece of my blonde hair behind my ear. I immediately felt the rush of blood to my cheeks. After all I'd learned in the last twelve hours, you'd think I'd shy away from moments like this, but I didn't, I craved them. It continued to baffle me that I even developed connections with my pack so quickly. I'd gone most of my life as a recluse. To find that my body craved this level of yearning was boggling. "I want you to sit here, with your eyes closed and think of anything that comes to mind. I want to see if I can penetrate your mind."

I shot him a questioning look. "Ok, ok, perhaps horrible choice in words, just do what I ask, please." He laughed. The sound of his laughter vibrated through my body and warmed me again. I prayed he couldn't enter my mind yet, because I didn't need him seeing how I was feeling at that moment. He didn't need a false sense of who I was.

I relaxed, listening to the soft sounds of the wind rustling the pines. I could feel his warm and calloused hands holding mine. It felt too intimate for someone who until last night, I could have sworn, wanted me dead. He breathed a frustrated sigh out. "I can't get in. Are you purposely blocking me?" he challenged me.

"Nope, but now I kind of wish I was. You're being an ass," I said, snatching my hands back from his. I made a motion to get up, and he caught me.

"Sit down. We're not done." Something in the way his voice ticked made me obey him. "Give me your hands," he continued in his gravelly voice. Again, I obeyed him. "Now, clear your mind, allow me to see you."

"Hold on... If I clear my mind, how are you seeing anything?" I challenged him.

"Just close your eyes, Everelle." He was exacerbated.

"Ugh how long do I have to do this, my coffee is cold, and the leather does absolutely nothing to warm my ass on this cold bench." I thought to myself, ***If he wants to play fortune teller, maybe he should consider a damn booth at the local fair.***

"Shut up. A fortune teller, really Ever?" His face held a glint of smugness. Realizing before I did, that he was listening to me ramble in my mind. *Now, you try,* he said to me in my mind. *I want you to speak to me, as if I'm in your head, not sitting next to you.*

Oh, that won't be a problem, I thought, *even if you weren't sitting next to me, I'd smell you.* I made a motion with my hand waving over my nose.

*You're an ass, h*e said in my mind.

Ditto, I challenged him, grinning now.

*I want you to try now, to reach down and see if you can feel or sense any other members of our pack, h*e said to me now. The way he asked made me sense he knew I couldn't be reached by them.

Sitting still, I closed my eyes. I tried to sense Priya. I wanted to tell her she left the damn bathroom light on when she left this morning, and it irritatingly woke me. I couldn't feel her though. Intrigued that I couldn't sense her, I tried to sense Nikita but ended with the same result. I grew frustrated now, blowing out my breath and sighing. Sagging my shoulders, I whined.

"It's fine," Kolter said, rubbing my hand, and sending goosebumps up my arms. "You did great for your first time. I don't recall if I've ever known a shifter to be able to communicate before shifting, so you're already ahead of the game." He dropped my hands and patted my leg. "Let's go in, you should probably eat and we can evaluate the line with others later."

Agreeing, I got up and began to follow him in. "Did your parents never tell you about your first time shifting?" I asked as we made our way across the clearing. "That seems crazy to me that they'd never tell you."

"I was young. Younger than anyone who'd shifted before. I think they were more afraid that if they'd told me what made me shift, that I'd do it more frequently. Children shouldn't be shifting; bones are too vulnerable at that time. The smaller the stature, the more likely you are to suffer severe consequences."

"Should I be worried then?" I couldn't help but state the obvious, again that my size was significantly smaller than the others.

He shrugged but continued as we walked into the tree line. " I think your size, while small, is different. Your bones and muscles are matured," he calmed my nerves as if he knew I'd been worried.

"You also don't want a kid walking around with that strong of a power. Imagine you as a child. Someone steals your purple crayon in school, and it pisses you off to the point you shift in class. You could do considerable damage and have no restraint."

"I'm more of a pink crayon kind of girl," I teased him, nudging him with my shoulder as we walked on. "But that makes sense. So did you shift again around that time, or were you able to wait?"

"I was able to maintain my childhood. I didn't shift again until fifteen. By then my parents were okay with it and less stressed."

"Do you think the move helped you?" I asked, still unsure about his trigger.

"I'm sure it did. Seoid is a much larger village than Tuathanas. My dad made a comment once that maybe if Tuathanas had more adult shifters, I wouldn't have been needed. But that was the most I ever got out of him."

We continued the walk up the mountain in silence. I was still curious about the process of shifting and was becoming more aware of the liability I brought the pack, especially when I couldn't even control my line of communication. Stepping inside the entrance of our den, I sent up a silent prayer that though Kasen may not know me, may he protect me.

Chapter Ten

Everelle

Monday came too quickly, and I was a nervous ball of fear. We woke early because Kolter wanted the pack to get in the habit of doing a five-mile run before breakfast each morning. Because I hadn't shifted yet, I sat on a slick piece of obsidian reading a course book on Siochan as I waited for my pack to return. The morning held a warm breeze, as if a promise to us all that the cold spring months would soon end. It was peaceful.

"I knew I'd find you alone, sooner or later," purred a voice from behind me. *For fucks' sake*, I thought rolling my eyes, I really needed to get better at observing my environment. "What? Can't run like your pack?" Folasade stepped into view with the same two women who flanked her in the quad after the muster.

"I prefer to start my mornings with coffee and not cardio," I quipped, willing that now was good as any for Kolter to sense me down our line.

"Eh, Ok," Folasade scoffed, coming closer. "You peg me as the damsel in distress type, just waiting on her prince charming to rescue her from the mean, old villain," She cracked, tossing a fit of giggles to her minions.

"Mean? Old? Sheesh... I'd really hate to talk about myself like that," I said feigning a wince.

"What did you just say?" she snarled at me. Her face narrowed and she looked pissed, shooting daggers toward her groupies, stopping their laughter immediately. I'd struck a nerve, good.

"I mean, you said it, not me. I'm just checking in with your mental health. Tell me, Folasade, do you have some unresolved daddy issues? Is that why you call yourself mean? Old? I mean, I couldn't tell you were a day over.... forty-seven," I batted my eyes coyly. Obviously playing into her insecurities.

"I swear to God, you'll regret speaking to me like that," she snarled, now closing the distance quickly between us.

"I'm sorry, it must be really hard knowing you'll never be the leader... and that I already am an alpha," I bit back. Suddenly, there was a sharp blow to my left cheek. Folasade had slapped me across the face with her eyes glowing, she began to back up, shaking. Snarls and screams erupted throughout the little cove where we stood. My eyes widened as I watched the shift in slow motion. Where once a girl stood, a massive strawberry golden lion now crouched, lowering her face to the ground, readying a pounce. A deep throaty growl erupted as her friends also shifted.

Fuck. What was I supposed to do now? Glancing around, I took in my surroundings, my thoughts cut off by Folasade.

"They're not coming. They're too far now to protect you," she purred, stalking forward toward me, narrowing the gap in an attempt to box me in. "What are you going to do, Mutt?" The way the word rolled off her tongue as she winced, led me to believe it had left a bitter after taste in her mouth. Like I was something dirty to her. Her female companions also crouched as they stalked forward, their deep throaty growls reverberating through my stomach.

Thinking quickly, I ran. I raced through the woods, zig zagging as I went. I had to get to the rocky cliff that I saw earlier. While lions could climb trees, I'm not sure they could dig into the obsidian with their claws.

The pounding in my chest ached excruciatingly. I refused to turn around. I could hear their thunderous paws stampeding behind me, crushing leaves and snapping twigs. I ducked under branches, holding them in my hands long after I'd passed under them, in an effort to let go last minute, allowing the branch to whip back, connecting with one of their faces. The growl that emitted further told me they were gaining on me and pissed. If I'd learned anything from school, it's that when you're being chased, you don't turn around. Their roars echoed in my ears and continued to echo as my feet flew across the needle-covered forest floor.

Finally, I could see the obsidian wall ahead. Fifteen feet, I just had to run fifteen feet. The snarls and snapping of the women's jowls felt far too close. Eight feet. I was now eight feet from the wall when I slipped on the silky pine needles that blanketed the freshly thawed forest floor. I began to curse myself for not working out in any past life. Picking myself up, I ducked to the right as the first lion jumped over me, blocking my path to the wall. Looking up, I said my final words to my mother, father, and Kolter.

Closing my eyes, I braced for the impact, but one never came. "What the hell are you doing, Malaika?" screeched Folasade from behind me. "Don't just stand there, get her!"

I heard the snapping of twigs and crackling of leaves beneath their behemoth bodies. A cold sweat began to dribble down my spine, and my heart felt like it was going to burst. I opened my eyes just in time to catch sight of Malaika being thrown from her position and skidding across the ground. She landed with a thunderous thud against the base of a tall pine tree.

I quickly snapped my head back in the direction she'd once stood and saw a large, dark golden, male lion was now in her place. He wore a face that challenged anyone to move. "Mbali and Malaika," he shouted, as their heads snapped in his direction, and began immediately dropping their cowering bodies to the floor. "I'd have expected more from you three. Apologize at once and head back to your den. There was no grievance filed, and this damn sure isn't how you orchestrate a duel." His words cut them as if they were a whip that lashed out.

"Sorry, Everelle, this won't happen again," the two women said and slinked off. They got about five yards before shifting back to their human form, looking over their shoulders once more. I watched as they gave worried looks for their friend.

"Folasade, step forward, NOW!" bellowed the lion. She did as she was asked, head still lowered to the ground, not making eye contact of any kind. "What happens when a cadet is found in violation of the duel guidelines?" His eyes bore down into her. "Speak!"

"You are at the mercy of the victim," she responded meekly, eyes still on the ground. Part of me felt bad for her then. To watch someone get reprimanded in front of their peers was humiliating.

"Quite right," purred the lion in a deep ominous voice. He turned toward me then, and I too dropped my eyes to the floor, more out of fear than respect. "What do you say, Everelle? What punishment should you deal Folasade?" I snapped my eyes up to meet his intense, familiar chocolate brown eyes. Confusion must have riddled my face because he was staring at me, urging me to come out with something.

"Oh, umm, I don't..." I stuttered. He's asking me what punishment I think she should have? How was I going to dish out a punishment to someone, when I had no clue what a punishment even was? Wasn't the embarrassment of all of this enough? Mid spiral my thoughts were interrupted.

"Two days in Pollsmoor," came from a deep voice behind me. I turned to witness my pack, circling around me, out of breath and sweating. They had taken their human forms. A shirtless, very sweaty Kolter reached my side and rested his hand on my lower back. I flinched at the feel of his fingers scorching my skin in such an intimate place.

The lion studied Kolter for a moment with a stern look, then nodded in agreement before continuing. “Two days in Pollsmoor, noted. Folasade, head there now. I will meet you when I’m finished.” Folasade bowed and turned to leave. Watching her go, she never shifted back, just kept her head down as she was walking.

“I apologize for her behavior and applaud you for not retaliating. Please accept my sincerest promise that she will be taken care of,” the lion said, looking at me. I nodded, still stunned at what had just transpired. I was seconds away from becoming her breakfast. With nothing left to address, the lion bid farewell to the pack and vanished as quickly and quietly as he’d arrived.

“Ever, are you alright?” shouted Priya. She raced toward me and picked up my arms, holding them out as she circled me, checking for signs of damage.

“She’s fine. She’s tough, aren’t you, kid?” Flynn retorted. “What’s *more* intriguing,” he said, “was the look on Folasade’s face as she left. Oooh ooh, I don’t want to be a part of that.”

“Shut the hell up, Flynn. God, you always have to start,” Nikita said, rolling her eyes. “You good?” she asked me as she approached.

I nodded and gave a slight smile, to show I was ok.

“Pollsmoor for two days? That’s all? Jeeze Kolter, I thought you were tougher than that,” Victor poked.

“I want an example set, but not a target,” He interrupted. “I want her to know that coming for her,” he said , pointing at me, “means she’s coming for us all. She shouldn’t be feeling so comfortable thinking she has the upper paw.”

Accepting this, the group started the walk back to the den. “If that didn’t make her shift, I don’t know what we have to do to get her to,” I overheard Nikita say to Brandt.

Brandt shrugged, “beat’s me, but if it gets out that she hasn’t shifted yet, we will have a lot more to worry about than just Folasade.”

A sickening feeling settled in my stomach. The last thing I wanted was to be a liability, but here again, I was finding myself in that position. "You guys," I called out, getting their attention as we approached the den. Everyone stopped and turned to look at me. Each of them was a glistening sight in black leathers. "I'm sorry," I began. "For the risks I'm asking you to take. I wish it weren't the case, but it is. I appreciate you all. Thank you for sticking with me."

"Girlll stop. You don't think we have all been there before?" shrugged Assata. "It's what family does."

With that, they turned and headed into the den.

"I'm sorry," I said without turning around. I knew Kolter was behind me. I also knew because he'd made me his alpha partner, he wouldn't leave me now, not after what just happened. We were bound or some other sort of cosmic, astral, fated, wolf thing.

"Why are you sorry?" he asked, joining me his voice husky and low. "I should be the one who is sorry, I shouldn't have left you alone, especially after she threatened you at the assembly. I was stupid," he said, shaking his head as he punched his fist into his other hand. This made me feel worse. He was beating himself up for the fact that I was the liability, and it didn't seem fair.

"I don't want to constantly feel like I need help, or that I need someone watching over me. Do you think other first years have this much of a disadvantage? Probably not. I'm going to be prey if I'm projected as weak." He nodded, agreeing with the direction I was headed. "If we stick together, constantly walking with me wrapped in a plastic bubble, I'm going to get picked off. I think it would be best if we functioned as if I don't shift, because I'm choosing not to, not the other way around." Wrapping my arms over my chest I blew a breath out. How long would I have to wait for my shift to happen? How long could I go before it became an issue that I couldn't shift?

"I agree for now, we project that you're simply choosing not to shift," he began slowly, his eyes facing the lake through the trees. "I think during classes, we should observe. We aren't going to participate until you shift. Once you've started shifting, not if you start, but once you start, you will be put through a crash course with myself and Victor. We will have you up to speed in no time. Luck is on your side that you're Highland. We are the biggest and strongest breed, and as such, a certain level of intimidation comes into play. Even more if you are not showing your shifted form."

It sounded like a solid plan; I just needed to figure out how I could fast track myself into shifting. Like Nikita said, if Folasade hadn't forced me to shift, I don't know what would.

"For now, I want you to arm yourself with these," he said, taking a hold of his shirt and lifting it slightly. Strapped to his chest was a long leather-bound sheath, holding dozens of blades. When the hell had those gotten there? He selected three of them from the middle, and presented them back to me. They were delicately made, small enough for my hands to grasp, and heavy enough to inflict damage if needed. My eyes turned from the blades to him.

"Where am I supposed to put them?" I asked, looking myself over to see if I'd missed a spot.

Slowly, he stepped forward, taking the knives out of my hand and running his hand along my side. I held my breath at his touch, again, hating the sensation that a simple touch could do. He made quick work, sliding the blades into my corset until they were nestled in, discreetly snug against the lower part of my breasts. Being that I'd never used a weapon, I'd have had no idea that they were even there.

"We will practice with them during your sparring time, and I'll have more commissioned for you," he said, sliding the last dagger into place and slowly pulling away from me. I released a breath I hadn't noticed I was holding, when he stepped closer to me.

"While Nikita may be the best in combat, Priya is the best with a blade. She's your perfect partner for sparring," he said, removing his hands from my side. I immediately missed the warmth and pressure from his hands, but felt such relief knowing I'd have a small form of defense should I find myself in this situation again.

Chapter Eleven

Everelle

Siochan History was my first scheduled class. Thank God for small blessings. I knew in here I wouldn't be expected to shift. I could survive this. "Good morning class, I hope the weekend found you in good regards." Professor DeMarcus was in front of the lecture hall. Colosseum-like rows of desks with cadets at each of them wrapped around her in a semi-circle. We sat bracing ourselves for the morning's lesson. Professor DeMarcus was wearing a rendition of the same outfit she wore Friday. She had a coarse beige jacket made of tweed, a white flowing blouse which was tucked into her beige pencil skirt. Her brown hair was placed back in a simple twist, and she looked up addressing the room with a small plastered smile.

"Who can tell me what year Siochan dissected from the mainlands of Baroque?" Looking around the room, she waited as a few cadets eagerly raised their hands. "Yes, you there," She said pointing to a girl wearing soft tan leathers. This indicated to me that she was a pride member, not a pack member.

"1286." The girl said, proudly. ***Good for you,*** I thought. ***It's nice to be recognized for your intelligence.***

A snort came from my side, and I dragged my eyes from the professor to a grinning Kolter, who wouldn't meet my eyes. ***Mhmm, keep paying attention,*** I thought, rolling my eyes at him as I refocused on Professor DeMarcus.

"Very good," the professor beamed in approval. "Now, who can tell me why we dissected?" She began walking around the room and I noted that a pack member from Hadlick raised their hand. "You my dear, what is your name?"

"Paloma, Ma'am," she said softly. "Siochan, previously, Martichora, was an island state, and part of the country of Baroque. In 1286 war broke out between the shifters of the country over the proper run of the government and desire for fair and equal representation of its constituents. Meaning Baroque, then and still, only wants the governing body consisting of the Chosen shifters. Not all shifters are equally represented. The Manticore and Lycanthropes disbanded from the country of Baroque and worked together to push those that reflected ideals of the Chosen off the island of Martichora, thus enabling our independence and the chance for us to create our own governmental structure that allowed acceptance and representations of both sets of shifters equally."

Chosen? I looked toward Priya with a quizzical look. I quickly scrawled out on my paper asking who the Chosen were. She scratched back without even looking at the paper... Human/Human. It clicked then. The Chosen weren't a body of government made up of selected shifters; they must be the category of shifters that Kolter was talking about in his room that night. They were the most powerful...and dangerous of all shifters. The idea of them wanting sole power of the countries in Baroque, terrified me.

"Excellent!" Professor DeMarcus said, again floating around the room. "Why did we change our name when independence was won?" I remembered this from the book on the train, and for once at this school, I felt like I fit in. I looked up in time for her eyes to meet mine with kindness and warmth, "Yes, you, Everelle, is it? Can you elaborate on the name change for the class?"

I anxiously took a breath, swallowing deeply. Public speaking had never been my expertise. "When the Chosen were removed, they swore they'd find legislation that proved they didn't need to be evacuated but would fight for their right to property and land in this nation. Knowing we didn't have issue with the Chosen themselves, we wanted a fresh name that would allow us to keep parts of our past but face the future with more "Siochan," or peace. Honoring our past, we named our capital Marti, and the country was changed to Siochan," I concluded. When I'd read this in the book on the train, I'd thought the Chosen had just meant those who had been selected for government. I hadn't put together that the Chosen were actual a dangerous sub species of shifters.

"Brilliant. You are most right, Everelle." She gave me a warm smile and continued with her lecture. "The power hungry are doomed to repeat their mistakes with every passing era. It is a constant battle between the weak-minded and the educated scholar. When we choose our paths for the greater good, we find we live a more docile life."

"Teacher's pet," Flynn winked at me while biting his pen.

"But who is to say which side is right? I mean isn't that the very foundation of our country? Allowing peaceful existence and freedom to live by choice?" The voice came from the front, a male from the pride of Ade.

"Always the kittens who have to play devil's advocate," Flynn said while slamming his pen down. "Wake me when class is over, ok?" Shaking my head, I just smirked, returning my attention to Professor DeMarcus.

"You are quite right, Xolani, indeed. However, what shapes our future isn't necessarily the freedom of choice, but the right of acceptance and mutual respect. When one Pack, Pride or Chosen, fights for just their rights and not those of the greater good, we revert to a Baroquian standard of living."

The room was silent as we considered her words, the weight of history pressing around us. I glanced at the intricate murals lining the walls, each one depicting moments of resistance and unity from Siochan's storied past. For a moment, I felt connected to generations of shifters who had fought and hoped within these very halls, all striving for a place where every voice could finally be heard.

Once class had ended, I pulled Kolter aside. “I think I’d like to head to the library; maybe I can find some information on shifting late and if something could speed the process.” I could see him internally wrestling as he mulled it over in his mind.

“I can’t see how it could hurt. Try and keep yourself out of trouble, would you? I’d hate for my alpha to depart prematurely because she couldn’t escape falling shelves or something,” he teased me, giving me a hint of a smile as he headed down the steps of the lecture hall with Victor and Kentaro. I watched him walk away, feeling the electricity fizzle and fall with each step he took further away. Is that the connection?

Hey, I thought toward him in my head, testing out our bond.

Hey, he said, turning around and walking backwards. *Good job.* He smiled and turned back toward Victor, as he walked out of sight.

Warmth filled my chest as I gathered my bag and began walking down the steps and out into the hall. The corridors were quieter now, the earlier rush of students faded, and my footsteps sounded unusually loud against the ancient stone floors. I made my way toward the library, determination settling in. If answers about shifting late existed anywhere, surely, they would be hidden within the library’s towering shelves and dust-laden tomes

Hours later, I slammed another tome closed. Rubbing my forehead, I tried in vain to ease the onset of a headache. *Ugh, damn it.* Frustration was taking over. I'd been through at least half a dozen tomes and couldn't find one mention of late shifting. I was doomed. Leaning over the long cedar table, I placed my head in my hands. I was no closer to finding out why I hadn't shifted yet, as I was yesterday. Professor Monaghan's class began shortly, and I was wondering how long I could prolong shifting. Hopefully, it wouldn't be needed today.

A gentle cough brought me out of my spiraling thoughts. The librarian, Cailleach, with silver streaks in her hair and keen eyes, approached quietly. "Looking for something in particular?" she asked, her voice low but not unkind. I hesitated, embarrassed, but nodded.

"Information on late shifting," I admitted. If she were to share my secret, at least, I'd have asked for help. She regarded me for a moment, then gestured for me to follow.

"Not everything worth knowing is found on these shelves," she murmured. "Sometimes you have to look between the lines." Intrigued, I gathered my scattered notes and trailed after her, hope flickering anew in my chest.

She led me to the far end of the library, passing rows of tables and shelves brimming with books. Once we turned the corner, I met a darkly lit hallway with two doors to each side. She waved her hand and instructed me to follow.

"Down here is where we keep the diaries and manuscripts of past leaders, scholars, and shifters with stories worth telling. I think you'll find what you seek in here," Cailleach said as she opened the last door on the right.

Entering the room, the air lingered, cool and stale. The large room provided no natural light in an effort to preserve the tomes in which it held. I made my way toward a rack against the back wall.

"I'll leave you to it then. Please let me know if I can be of any more assistance," she said. I nodded in response.

Scanning the journals, I found myself unsure where or with whom to start. The brittle marked bindings showed the passage of time, and I allowed myself to sit with the gravity of the space. Each manuscript was the copulation of struggle, triumph, secrets, and perseverance. I hoped that one day, I could make a future cadet intrigued by my life.

Staring at the rows of diaries and tomes on a shelf, I ran my fingertips over a few older journals. While I was drawn here for the idea that I could read someone's journey through the same steps I was walking now, the sheer age they appeared to be had me worried that I would damage them. I refused to select one of them. Instead, I continued along the shelf and came across a somewhat newer section of journals. I found myself selecting a small black leather-bound simple diary. I began to flip the parchment to the beginning of their record. It followed the life of a Hadlick pack member that was worried for her son. She spoke with urgency and dread. Discussing prayers of making him better and wondering what would happen to him.

Titillated, I brought the journal to the table and began to read her entries.

January 8th,

It is the height of winter now, but the mountain hadn't fully covered in snow yet. K2 has been running a fever and has yet to awake. I worry about him as it's been three days since the incident occurred. Sitting in the chair next to him, watching his shallow breaths, I send up prayers to my elders that somehow, he will regain consciousness and be ok. I chide myself every day, knowing I should have been with him, I should have taken better precautions to warn him. You can't save anyone, you're taking your father's course, not mine. I find myself foolish then, knowing that he is strong and independent. He would make a good alpha, but he's third in line. Not often do members of a pack that far removed become alpha. He cares for people; he has a sweet heart. I just wish he would awaken. His father feels I'm to blame, had I not shown him the nature of healing, he wouldn't have tried it himself. I agree with that. Especially because he tried to heal a lion mix breed.

Maybe I am to blame, but only time will tell if he will be alright. Until then, I'll sit silently holding his power in my hands.

Entranced in this mother's pain, I wiped the tears that escaped my eyes and continued to read her next passage.

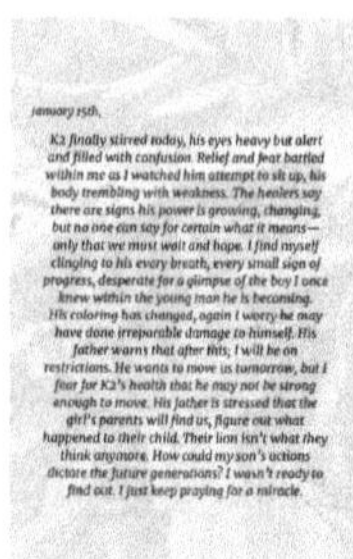

January 15th,

K2 finally stirred today, his eyes heavy but alert and filled with confusion. Relief and fear battled within me as I watched him attempt to sit up, his body trembling with weakness. The healers say there are signs his power is growing, changing, but no one can say for certain what it means—only that we must wait and hope. I find myself clinging to his every breath, every small sign of progress, desperate for a glimpse of the boy I once knew within the young man he is becoming. His coloring has changed, again I worry he may have done irreparable damage to himself. His father warns that after this; I will be on restrictions. He wants to move us tomorrow, but I fear for K2's health that he may not be strong enough to move. His father is stressed that the girl's parents will find us, figure out what happened to their child. Their lion isn't what they think anymore. How could my son's actions dictate the future generations? I wasn't ready to find out. I just keep praying for a miracle.

Heartbroken, I closed the journal. Her story resembles that of Kolter, but it could just be me grasping at straws, especially because the packs aren't the same. I swear I turn every thought to him lately. Noting the time, I quickly gathered the journal and my things. Professor Monaghan was explicit; tardiness was not something he took lightly. I wouldn't allow myself to find out what happened if I were late.

Chapter Twelve

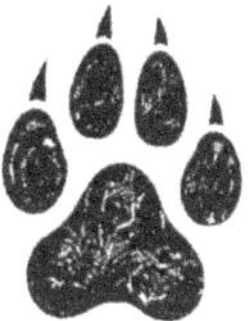

Everelle

Stepping out onto the practice fields, I rejoined my pack. Priya and Assata were stretching when I approached.

"Hey, how was the library?" Priya asked, standing back up and dusting off her pants. I found myself scanning her body to see if I could see her daggers hidden away. A slight ripple in the material at her thigh told me they were probably stashed there.

"No dice. There doesn't seem to be any mention of late term shifting in the tomes," I said discouraged. I joined them on the ground and began my own set of stretches. Though to be honest, I'm not even sure if what I'm doing could count as stretching. I've never worked out before.

"I wonder if any of our parents or bloodlines would have insight," Assata said thoughtfully as she stood up. "You aren't the only person I'm sure to be a later shifter. Someone must know something."

The sun was high now, warming my bones. It felt good to be outside. I began mimicking little stretches I saw others do around me, and it helped relieve the aching I felt from being hunched over a book for the better part of the morning at the library.

The guys returned from their run, sweat dripping off their bodies. Kolter was shirtless, and the sunlight was glistening off his fully toned abs. His pants rode low on his hips, highlighting a very defined v section of his body. My fingers ached to trail the deep set lines. I had to turn away, the burning it brought to my cheeks would give away my thoughts, even with the line down.

"How'd the library go?" Kolter asked, stopping in front of me. He began using a towel he pulled from his bag to wipe his face and chest. I was mesmerized. Taking a second to drag my eyes back to his face, I noted his grin was splitting his face in two.

I rolled my eyes. "It was about as helpful as you standing here shirtless." I huffed, "My god, do you have to flaunt that?"

Seeing his grin spread wider, his eyes challenged mine. "Something wrong, Ever?"

"No, just put your damn shirt on, you're making Flynn feel insecure."

I heard the offended gasp and saw as Flynn raised his arms quickly and slapped them hard to his thighs. The sound cracked my ears. "Ooh, here we go." He began walking toward me angrily, throwing his shirt over his head. "Excuse me? Ma'am, I have zero reason to feel insecure. Have you seen this body?" He swung his hand from the top of his head, sweeping down to his feet. "If I were you, I'd get working on your own sorry excuse of muscle and tone and stop drooling over my alpha."

"You've got plenty to feel insecure about," Nikita said, joining the group. "You can start by clearing our air of your body odor." She waved her hand in front of her face as she pinched her nose. "Do you ever shower?"

"I know, my pheromones really drive you all crazy. Sorry to disappoint, ladies, I'm off the market. Good ol' Flavia here made an honest man of me." He slung his arm over her shoulders as he spoke.

"Keep dreaming." She shoved his arm off her shoulder and stepped toward Nikita, wiping the sweat he'd left behind from her arms, the slight blush to her cheeks didn't go unnoticed however.

The banter of the group kept my spirits up after what little I'd found in the library.

"Good afternoon, cadets." Professor Monaghan voice boomed inside my chest, forcing adrenaline through my body. "I appreciate the efforts made to be on time." He stepped onto the fields accompanied by two men in similar uniforms. Each of the men wore matching scowls, one checking his watch, another assessing the cadets lined up in ranks.

Anticipation rose as we silently stood awaiting our orders from the professor. Next to me, Kolter slowed his breathing. I felt a warm tingling sensation begin to crawl up my spine, a soft caress stroked over my shoulders, calming my nerves; he was soothing me down our line without even moving. I relaxed at the sensation, and found myself mimicking his breaths. The sensation slowly dissipated off my body, and I missed it at once. I craved his touch, as if it were the very water I'd drink on a sweltering summer day. He alone was my salvation. This was unfortunate because all I'd ever be was a risk to him and his pack. All of these feelings baffled me. Never had I so much as looked at a classmate back in Tuathanas with the same biological urge that presented itself when I looked at Kolter. It made me feel weaker, this uncanny feminine urge to drool over a good looking male. *Ugh.*

Are you alright? Kolter was looking at me now, a worried scowl pained his face making me feel like I'd distracted him. ***Liability,*** again screaming in the forefront of my brain.

I'm fine. I forced a fake smile across my face and directed our attention back to the sparring circle where our professor was speaking. I saw him sigh and shake his head toward me.

"Today, we will begin sparring techniques while cross-shifting. We have already assigned pack and pride team combinations for the entirety of your academic year. This class instruction is not to be taken as a course in attacking your opposing shifters. Instead, we hope you'll learn better ways to enhance each strength, not vilify weakness. My men will be around to instruct you should you need adjusting, as well as maintaining fairness throughout the trials. Please be sure to use them should you find yourself in need of assistance." The two men at the professor's side didn't make any attempt to introduce themselves nor look as if they'd be willing to help if needed. Swallowing a lump in my throat, I looked to Kolter and instinctively I thought, *What do I do if I'm required to shift today?*

You won't, I'll make sure to it. He had an air of confidence that made me envious. *Fix your face*, he grunted at me, and I cracked a smile.

"Now, you will begin by breaking into your shifting teams. I'll be asking each Pack and Pride to shift one member of like rank at a time. All others will remain unshifted to prevent grappling and allow for clearer vision on our behalf. We don't need a bunch of untrained animals peacocking. You may begin." The stern look on his face, seemed permanent.

With corps of cadets breaking up, we stayed rooted. Surrounded by my pack, I took notice of the striking differences Kolter and I shared with the rest of our pack. It was as if you took black paint and diluted it once to make Kolter, and twice to make me. Observing the rest of the packs on the field, this variation in coloring didn't seem to be repeated.

Approaching our pack silently was the Molti Pride led by Neo, their King. Stepping forward, Kolter extended his arm like an olive branch.

"Ah Kolter, it's a pleasure." The king had a snarl on his face, deep and dark. He was a little shorter than Kolter, but similar in build. A long-since-healed gash separated parts of his eyebrow down to his cheek, and his eyes were a cool chocolate brown, not at all inviting. His blonde hair was long and choppy, as if it had been caught in bubble gum and someone cut it out. Unlike most of the cadets, Neo had a full rough beard, which was unusual for someone his age. He struck me as someone far too old to be a student at Askari.

The tension in the air was palpable. Standing next to Kolter, I wondered if my place would always be here. He winked at me, as if he just heard my thoughts. This did little to steady my nerves. The pride and pack of our team had stood in a silent divide, gathered around a sparring circle in anticipation of the first match-up. I was unsure if this training exercise would end in rivalry or an uneasy shared alliance. Respective parties glanced forward, meeting the eyes of their counterparts. Neo and Kolter shook hands. "Likewise, Your Grace. I hope we can all maintain an air of civility?"

"But of course," Neo growled. "Otherwise, we'd be pressed to end up in prison alongside Folasade. Or did I hear wrong this morning?"

Tension began growing amongst the groups. "That isn't entirely inaccurate. Stay away from what's mine," Kolter said, stepping forward, creating a visible shadow over Neo's face with his height. "I'll make sure to stay away from what's yours. Fair is fair." The gulp Neo swallowed was visible. He scanned the eyes of Kolter before proceeding.

"Understood. Are we in agreement?" he asked his pride, without removing his stare from Kolter. A loud grumbling echoed across the mass. The vibrations penetrated my chest with its power. "Looks like we have a deal." Neo broke eye contact first and met mine with a burning fire. "Is this the 'mine' in question? It's a pleasure...?" Neo asked smugly, looking at me with sheer disapproval.

"Everelle, si..." I started.

"She is my alpha," Kolter, said as he grabbed my arm and started walking us away from Neo. "We will watch today's match-ups. Select anyone else first."

Kolter dropped my arm as we stepped out of the circle and onto the side of our practice ring. Both sides disbanded and formed their lines on opposite sides of the circle carved in the sand. My fingers began to tremble as I watched with pure adrenaline as the groups tossed around names to duel.

"Prison? Pollsmoor is a prison? Why didn't you tell me you sent Folasade to prison for two days?" I met Kolter's eyes with a fire behind mine. "You don't get to fight all my battles for me. God, you'll make it worse." Shaking my head, I moved to stand beside him. His arms were crossed over his chest, legs spread, dispersing the weight of his body equally, as he bore his gaze forward.

"Victor, step forward." Kolter called, signally the end to our conversation. Yeah, that wasn't going to work for me.

"So that's it? You're not even going to dignify me with a response?" I was pissed.

Kolter continued to ignore me, but I felt an invisible tug at my head, almost like a pair of hands was turning my head for me to face the ring. ***Whatever. Be an asshole then,*** I thought, rolling my eyes and shaking the invisible pressure of my face. Out of the corner of my eye, I saw Kolter's jaw tick, leaving the faintest smile across his lips. He was irritating to say the least.

I watched as Victor stepped forward, adjusting his belt. He began swinging his arms as if to stretch while thrusting his head from one side to the other. He brought his hands forward and clapped once as he walked into the middle of the circle. I watched him intently. I was holding my breath as he crouched to the ground, closed his eyes, and sighed deeply, releasing all of his emotions into the ground. Then, he thrust, calculated, and concise, forward, leaping high into the air, fully shifting into a massive jet-black wolf before his paws even touched the ground. *Holy shit.* A loud growl escaped him, as he opened and slammed his jowls closed. I'd never seen them shift before, just Folasade and her crew. They...my pack...they were the wolves I saw that night from the train. I couldn't believe it. I forced my face to school, bringing my attention back to the ring.

Victor was an impressive beast. Standing on all four legs, his back reached upwards of eight feet from ground to shoulder blade. His paws, larger than a truck tire, flexed into the soft sand. I released my breath at the same time he let out a howl, deep and long, casting his head toward the afternoon sky.

"I can't believe what I'm seeing," I said, staring at Victor as he paced back and forth awaiting his sparring partner to meet him in the circle.

"You think that's impressive," Flynn began, hovering over my shoulder, "You'll be really excited when you see who you're bonded to, ruff ruff." He winked.

"What happens now?" Before any of my pack had a chance to answer I heard the whoosh in the air, and the crack as four paws pounded onto the sand. Standing a full head shorter than Victor, a lion now crouched, baring his teeth as he growled. This lion was much different from Folasade. He was taller, with a full mane and was more muscular, though he didn't have to use his words to intimidate his prey.

"Oh honey, we sit back and watch these two very bad men play a game of patty cake, then when that's all over, we go home and make friendship bracelets."

"Flynn!" shouted Brandt. "Enough, it's time to pay attention." With that, everyone's eyes faced forward. Brandt never lost his cool, so when he addressed someone in the pack, usually Flynn, we all paid attention and followed. I took it as years of being a beta. He had an air of confidence that demanded respect. Old habits die hard.

The crowd fell silent as the two shifted creatures faced off, every eye locked on the inner circle in which they danced. The late afternoon sun glinted off the sleek fur and carved muscle, casting long shadows on the sand. The air smelled heavy and wet from the sweat dripping off the bodies in front of me. It felt electric as each of us silently cheered for our pack mate. The first sickening sound of a heavy blow came from Victor; he swiped his long front paw, and it connected hard with the young lion's face. The force was incapacitating as it caused him to lose his footing and skid across the sand, as if a round pebble was tossed against a still lake. We all watched on as a shower of sand flew out of the ring and rained over the pride of onlookers. They continued as if their sparring was a captivating movie playing before our eyes and not our family members. Each time the lion lunged toward Victor's throat, he misjudged and came up empty or misdirected. Victor had the wherewithal to anticipate his movements and become just one step out of reach. The lion became increasingly agitated, noted by the panic-driven movements he made while advancing on Victor. This gave credit to my previous inquiries as to whether lions had powers. If he had any, he wasn't showing his cards.

Once bored of his prey, Victor made a final lunge and grabbed the lion directly under his neck, sinking his dangerously large white teeth into his soft flesh, just deep enough to release a trickle of blood that began beading at the surface. In one swift motion, Victor tossed the lion up, releasing him just in time to watch him fall with a nauseating thud. Victor stalked forward, slowly placing his paw on the unconscious lion's chest. The match was over. Pride filled my chest as I watched Victor bow to his opponent. He may have defeated him, but he still respected him. Turning back toward our group, Victor delivered a small nod. He closed his eyes as he walked, crouching slightly, and leapt into the air, shifting back into his human form before ever hitting the ground. It was inspiring to watch. I prayed silently that when my time finally came to shift, I could have an ounce of his finesse.

"Impressive as always," Kolter said, clapping him on the back and pulling him in for a hug. The young lion stirred on the sand. Rising to his feet, he shook out his mane and turned in our direction. Narrowing his eyes at me, I saw a molten lava look form in his eyes. Without warning, he lunged in my direction. Landing at my feet, his massive face was so close that the strands of his mane burned my skin as they licked my face. I didn't flinch. I didn't cower. I refused to show weakness again. Luckily for me, I didn't have much time to wait before the lion turned around and soared back through the air to where he came from. Bewildered, I began scanning my surroundings. I was now standing between two giant, silver paws. I gulped as I drew my eyes up his front legs, bracing my beating heart with my hand, as if it alone could ease the trepidation it felt. Above me was a mass of silky silver strands, intertwined amongst themselves as they traced his enormous chest. I felt his deep growl rumble in my chest as if at a concert next to a loudspeaker. The deep possessive tone captivated my attention. I didn't need to see his face to know it was Kolter, and he was pissed.

The lion hit the ground with such force that the sand sprayed the crowd of observers, whose attention was now unwavering and focused on Kolter. They watched in shock as their pride mate struggled to get back up. He had the wind knocked out of him twice in as many minutes. This wouldn't end well for him if he kept going. Shaking off the aftershock of the hit, the lion rose to his feet. His stare was murderous toward Kolter as he stalked forward. In my head, I heard Kolter's voice, louder and more direct than ever. *Get the hell back; we will take it from here.*

Hesitantly, I began stepping backwards, careful not to awaken any more feelings of ill intent. With a swift rush of air, Kolter was on the lion again, pinning him to the ground easily with his paw, thick like the trunk of a willow tree. Beside me, Priya wrapped her arms around me, steadying me as we watched the two men grapple on the dirt in front of us.

"You really know how to piss everyone off; I'll give you that," Nikita said without removing her eyes from the pounds of fur before us. Suddenly, two more lions entered the circle. Kolter, now outnumbered, stepped back and began to slowly lower himself to a crouch. His lips were pulled back, showing his large, pearly, sharp teeth. The growl he released was enough to make Victor, Baldur, Flynn, and Brandt leap forward into the circle. The lions, previously in control, noticed the change; odds no longer in their favor, they began to cower and slink out of the circle, baring their teeth and smacking their jaws loudly as if that were enough of a threat. It was not. Our men began flanking Kolter, making sure he was protected and setting the standard of the future matches.

"Enough, Neo, tell your men to stand down. You know better than to challenge an unshifted teammate," Kolter barked.

"He doesn't speak for me," the lion who started it all said, rising taller now. "I am the rightful King of Molti. *I* make the rules."

"The rules are you don't come after an unshifted teammate, regardless, Baraka." Kolter was still crouched, face lowered to meet the young lion's eyes, making sure no words would be misconstrued.

"So let her shift; I'll challenge the traitor any day!" Baraka let out a powerfully loud growl. Birds in a nearby tree flew away in search of a safer resting point.

"She isn't fighting today!" Kolter bellowed, "I make the rules for my pack. I said she was off limits, and I meant it. You want to fight? Come for me!"

"I'd rather expend my energy into a fight worth the accolades," Baraka scoffed as he turned away from the wolves.

"You won't get another chance, Baraka, I can assure you that," Kolter fired off at his back.

"You have no idea the number of chances I'll have," he tossed over his shoulder. The rest of the lion pride began walking out of the circle, shifting back to human form as they touched grass on the other side, signaling to all that the fight was over.

I watched with anxiety as Kolter and the men walked back toward us, shifting back into their human forms only after exiting the ring.

"I'm really sorry, I don't..." I was cut off by a sharp hand in the air. Kolter didn't even bother to look at me as he walked past. Dropping his hand only after he'd gotten far from me.

"I don't know what I did, I don't know what I keep doing. What the hell is going on?" I began spiraling, asking anyone who would listen.

"It's not you, it's testosterone," Flynn said, grabbing my shoulders. "Believe it or not, not everything is about you." He looked me squarely in the eyes and said, "It's awfully narcissistic to think of yourself so highly. Tell those demons in your head to take a nap." He tapped my cheek as he retracted his arms.

"But he tried to step back to challenge me. How can I not think it's about me?" I said, following Flynn, who was making his way back down the path.

"Honey, it's because you're the female alpha and you project weakness. You really need to pull your shit together. I wasn't kidding earlier when I said it."

"Well, don't sugarcoat it or anything," I said, rolling my eyes at him and crossing my arms.

"Stop pouting. This is exactly what I'm talking about." He motioned toward my posture. "If you want to be taken seriously and not like a weak link, you need to pull yourself together. I think you haven't shifted yet because you're too content with other people fighting your damn battles for you. You've been spoon-fed your whole damn life! Read a damn room, Ever. Not everyone grew up living where the worst thing that could happen to you is your coffee order was made wrong or their mommy cut their bangs too short. We lived real lives, hard lives, and we are still living them. Stop whining so much and be a badass alpha, or no one will follow your lead." His eyes met mine and softened before continuing. "I'm not saying it's a bad thing to always have people in your corner to count on. I'm just saying it would be nice to have you in ours without feeling like you're a liability." He then began jogging forward to rejoin the group, leaving me alone with my thoughts.

A liability, those words haunted my every moment. I can't keep being the weak link in this pack. I just wish I could find the answers I needed before it was too late. There were so many secrets here at Askari, and I needed to figure them out. I was tired of sitting in the dark just waiting. Until I stepped on this campus, I'd never even met a lion or a wolf. I didn't choose this life. I couldn't understand why every lion was pissed at me.

Chapter Thirteen

Everelle

The remainder of the week was much of the same. Morning runs for the pack, while I sat drinking coffee on a boulder waiting for them to return, or sitting at the lake, while contemplating why God hated me. Classes in history, tactics, sparring, and then waking up to do it all over again the next day. I was no closer now to shifting than I had been, and each day, the lions became more and more resentful.

Sitting in the library for my daily research, I reached for the diary of the Hadlick wolf again. Perhaps I'd find some strength in her words.

January 20th,

It's cold today, much colder than the previous days. K2 is coughing more than usual, his color still fading. Where he used to be as jet black as the night sky, now his hair is the coloring of liquid mercury. I keep praying that he will pull through, but I think the journey to Seold may have made him weaker. I've found myself reading anything I can to see if what happened to him in the woods would have an adverse effect on either the lion child or him, and so far, I've found nothing.

As of yet, I don't think there has ever been a solitary wolf who has selflessly gifted his blood to save a lion. My poor boy, he had no idea what he was even doing. His father say's it's my fault. I knew he'd made a friend in the woods, I knew he and the girl played. I never saw any reason to worry. They're young! Negative biases hadn't been bestowed yet. No one was telling him or her they couldn't trust in the other. They simply found joy playing.

At the end of the day, it's a moot point. If he had not given his blood, she would have died. He is a hero and I refuse to let him or anyone else see him as anything less. He has alpha traits, and I'm proud of him.

February 1st,

I know it's been some time since I've written, but so much has happened! K2 is healed! It took longer than expected, but he seems to be fine! He hasn't shifted again since that day, but his line is still intact. His color has stopped weakening. Albeit his hair isn't black, but its not white either. We try and keep him grounded and happy. We decided we will not tell him about his shifting. I think it's best he doesn't remember. If he remembers, then he'll remember her, and I can't have him running off to Tuathanas in search of the girl. I worry the effects his blood will have on her, or if he was infected with hers and perhaps that's why it took him so long to recover. Only time will tell what the future holds for either of them.

I went to her home last night. In the cloak of nightfall. I had to see if she was alright. I watched through the window as she slept. She was beautiful, lying there in her tiny bed. Her breaths were shallow and even as her eyes roamed free behind closed lids. Her dreams were peaceful. While watching her, I heard her whisper his name! She began to giggle and rolled over in her sleep, snuggling her pillow tighter.

My breath caught in my throat. This wasn't good. I couldn't allow her to remember my son. I know I shouldn't have, but I crept inside. Gently, with my hands on her head, I closed my eyes and entered her mind. I found the same images from K2. I grabbed them, and as if taking scissors to paper, I cut them out of her memory.

I told myself I was doing this for the betterment of both their lives. I just hope I don't live to regret it. I watched her sleep a little longer, then as quietly as I'd come, I left.

Now our family and hers are protected from what lies ahead.

Closing the diary, I took a deep breath and held it. This Hadlick wolf was a mother. Her son saved a lion cub with his very own blood, and his mother feared it would only cause pain for him. I wonder if any of the others know the back history of the Hadlick wolves. I'd love to get their take on the story and see if some truth can be found in the middle. I remember Kolter saying Hadlick wolves had the ability to heal, but it seemed this mother had the added ability to erase memories. I wondered then if Highland wolves had more powers than just brute strength.

I collected my belongings and quietly exited the library into the main passageways. I wasn't sure of the schedule that Hadlick wolves kept or even where their den was. I walked silently toward the lake, assuming that if they were around it somewhere, they would be bound to run by. I would just wait for them to stumble upon me.

“What are you doing out here, again, alone?” I heard the deep timbre of Kolter’s voice, carrying a hint of disappointment and irritation. Turning to meet Kolter’s angry eyes, I sighed.

“I’m waiting for a member of the Hadlick pack to run by. I’d like to talk to them in regards to a journal of a Hadlick mother I found.”

“You’ll be waiting forever. Each pack and pride has a different section of campus, each with its own resources. The only reason they’d be here would be to look for us,” he said, sitting down on the bench. “What is the journal about?” he asked, curiously. “Did it mention late shifting?”

“No, it followed a mother. Her son had become ill or wounded after saving a lion cub. He had gifted her his blood, and the mother was fearful of the outcome. She erased their memories, the lion cub and her son’s, I mean. I was wondering if they all had the power to erase memories or if any of them knew who the journal was written by. It’s just her initial’s.” Watching Kolter, he made no indication he needed to speak, so I continued. “I’d just like to see if any of the Hadlick pack members recognize the story or can elaborate on it. It may be pointless, but it’s the only interesting thing I’ve read in the tomes so far.” I shrugged.

“You will find that the Hadlick’s won’t have any knowledge of that story. It’s a waste of time.”

“Why? What’s the harm in even asking them? You know, you don’t know everything. It’s ok to not know something sometimes!” I was at the end of my rope with him. I was annoyed that he thought he knew more, and he hadn’t even read it.

“I’m just saying,” Kolter said, taking it from me for a minute. “I’ve never heard this story, so I doubt others would have heard it.”

"It's not just a story! It's someone's life. This is someone's struggle, Kolter. It wouldn't kill you to let me give her some consideration. You're not even an Hadlick, so why would you know about it?" I felt the anger behind my words, my annoyance bubbling over like a pot of boiling water.

Kolter rose to leave but turned to look down at me. "Head inside; it's not safe for a woman like you to be out here alone." He turned to leave. "Let's go, Princess."

"Just who do you think you are?" This made him turn back. "I'm serious. Who do you think you are? You're always mad at me, always making me feel like I'm doing the wrong thing..." My rant was cut short with his sharp growl.

"Because you are! Even now, you infuriate me because you know you're a risk to yourself and the pack, and yet you sit idly in the open. You may as well have strapped a damn neon sign to your chest that says, 'Attack now! I can't shift yet!'" he said, face turning red and his eyes narrowing into mine. "You were attacked last time you were out here!" He gestured to our surroundings. "I don't know how many more times we can fight for you! You're reckless and..."

"Oh, so the little mutt can't shift yet? That's why she ran in human form! Ooooh, this is good," came a cackling voice from just beyond the tree line. Both Kolter and I snapped our attention in its direction. "Is that why you stepped to Baraka, too? To protect your alpha mate? Tell me, Kolter, how could you have picked an alpha mate when she hasn't even shown you she can be a shifter yet?" The look she gave Kolter was enough to send his blood to the boiling point. I could feel it burning in my veins. He took a step to the right, putting a barrier between Folasade and me.

"It would be in your best interest to back up and go on home, Folasade. This isn't your side of Askari." His voice dropped lower, with a gravelly growl.

"Or what? Ulrich isn't out here to save her ass this time. You put me in prison for two long days, and now you want to give me ultimatums. Hehe," she scoffed, narrowing her lava-filled eyes at him.

Ulrich? Ulrich didn't save me last time; her pride's King did. This girl wasn't firing with all neurons.

It happened in seconds. Too quickly for my brain to even begin to process, she'd moved. Folasade lunged at Kolter, catching him with her teeth before he'd had a chance to shift. Her jowls slammed closed around his right shoulder and arm, crushing it with a nauseating crunch. I felt his pain, burning my veins as it coursed through us both. I felt him go dark down the line in my head as he began to drift unconscious. *Oh no!! This can't be happening, Kolter! Wake up, wake up!* I shouted down the line, trying in vain to get Kolter to show signs of life. I looked up, and Folasade was feet away, laughing. She...was...laughing!! She crushed his arm and shoulder and rendered him unconscious, and she was LAUGHING! That bitch.

The anger inside me exponentially grew. I was fuming; fire was reaching down my spine, and I was suddenly aware of how pliable it was. I felt my arms and legs scorch down to my fingers and toes. Every fiber of my being was red hot. I closed my eyes and breathed fire. I couldn't believe how fueled by hatred I was. Opening my eyes, I searched hers, seeing the terror hit her. It felt like crossing the finish line of a marathon. I was ravenous in vengeance. I watched her hesitantly cower back.

You're not...wait, what is going on... what is happening? She was tripping over her thoughts. I could feel fear in her as if it were palpable. I saw the terror in her eyes as she watched me grow before her. Her head shook side to side, and her eyes brimmed with wetness as she began dragging them skyward. Taking me in, the pure terror she felt coursed through her body and made her limbs tremble. My body lifted from the ground, slowly being transformed. My once lean and frail limbs burst forth, thick and muscular. I would no longer be a weak link in our pack. I would be feared. I shook my giant white body, awakening the demon that had been trapped inside of me, and it felt exhilarating. Continuing to absorb the pain of the stretch, I groaned with each passing second until the transformation was complete, and I landed softly on the ground, hovering over a still unconscious Kolter.

"I am not what? WEAK? SMALL?" I snarled, snapping my jaw in her face as she cowered. I stepped toward her until our faces met. "I'd say get the fuck out of here, but then, how would they feel if I allowed you to walk away, knowing you hurt our alpha?" I shifted my gaze, directing her to look behind her. My pack members, in all their glory, stood motionless on the rocky ledge, overlooking the tree line we had just fronted, their mouths agape. I leaned forward, my eyes meeting hers again, inches from her face, and made a show of breathing in her fear. "Run! Go home, lest you end up in the ground."

Her eyes widened as she nodded. Then, without a second thought, she turned and took off in the direction of her den. After watching her go for a few moments, I dropped my attention to Kolter. I wanted to make sure he was ok. As if reading my thoughts, Nikita, Victor, Baldur, Lisbeth, and Kentaro raced down the ridge line.

They looked at me as if looking for an understanding of what happened. I realized I still couldn't communicate with them, despite being a wolf, despite being in their pack, I still couldn't talk to them nonverbally. Sensing this, Kentaro was the first to speak. "How long has he been out?"

"About 3 minutes. I couldn't stop her. He never even saw it coming. It's all my fault!" I howled at the sky, frustrated that I'd shifted too late. They all stared at me as if I'd not been speaking. What was going on?

"It'll be ok. We need to get him to the hospital wing. They can assess him there." Nikita said to the group. She then turned to me and said, "you didn't do anything wrong, don't let the voices win." Nikita shifted into her wolf form, bent over, and gingerly picked up Kolter in her mouth. She stood then, with me towering over her. She gave me a nod, then turned and jetted toward the hospital wing of Askari.

"This is not at all how I pictured my first week here," I said to myself.

"We're going to head in and figure this out. Why don't you go for a run?" Brandt suggested, nodding toward the others.

"I'm going to head up toward the hospital wing; I'll catch up with you all later," I said, without even waiting for them to try and respond before taking off. I needed to clear my head.

Racing through the woods, I felt alive. I'd never felt this kind of freedom. Air was rushing over my sleek white fur. My muscles groaned and stretched with every stride I made forward. My senses were strengthening. I was now smelling, feeling, and seeing things at a much stronger rate. The air was fresh, cool, and damp; the undertones of pine and fresh water infiltrated my nostrils. I could smell a hint of burning wood, though no fires could be seen in my far-reaching sight. Until now, the furthest I could see would be twenty feet with clarity. Now, I could zero in on things miles away. The sounds of babbling streams coursing over the obsidian stones were mesmerizing. I shook my head, trying to concentrate on one thing at a time, but it was all so overwhelming.

Suddenly, a surge of fear, worry, and warmth burned through my chest. Pain was throbbing in my shoulder, bringing me to a stop. I jumped, bucking my hind legs and biting for a nonexistent threat on my shoulder. The pain was insufferable, bringing a stinging sensation to my eyes. On instinct I headed toward the pull of pain.

I reached the hospital wing just as Nikita was walking out with Kolter, his arm wrapped in a sling. His beautiful golden and blue flecked eyes were brimmed with a crimson color. He winced, rotating his shoulder. With his left arm, he reached up to untie the sling, dropping it to the ground. Taking a step forward, I lowered my head to him and Nikita. His eyes shot open, as if seeing me for the first time with recognition and wonder.

Hey, I said, through the line.

His eyes softened. *Hey.* I'd never quite felt relief like this.

Just then, across the yard, rushed our pack, eager to find Kolter.

The group joined us, hugging Kolter and patting him on the back. The relief on everyone's faces was mirrored over and over again.

"EVERELLE! KOLTER!" bellowed a voice from behind us, breaking the high of celebratory relief we we're riding. Turning toward the source, I noticed a very red, sweaty General Ulrich quickly approaching.

"I'm going to need answers to quite a few questions, starting with, WHAT THE HELL IS WRONG WITH YOU?" he snapped.

"It wasn't her fault. If you want someone to be your punching bag, you overshot your target by at least 3 miles. Her den is that way." Kolter gestured to the East. "You have a problem with how we handled it; you may want to rethink why we had to handle it to begin with." He stepped forward, staring down the general with no regard for his rank.

"I want Everelle in my office, within the hour," Ulrich sneered. Noticing he would get no further response from Kolter, he turned and left much the same way he came, in a huff.

"Over or under, we see Ever naked today," I heard Flynn say to someone behind me, again breaking the tension with humor, but I didn't care. My thoughts remained entirely on Kolter. I wanted to crawl out of my skin with anxiety, the thoughts reeling that I caused him to become wounded. It was again my fault that he was put in a position to protect me, this time ending in him getting a shoulder wound. His gaze met mine, and his eyes widened again.

"I'm going to need you not to panic," began Kolter.

"I'm totally winning this bet; there's no chance she isn't shifting back naked," Flynn said, stroking his chin with an eager grin.

"Shut uppp Flynn," Priya shouted, exacerbated. "You're such a dick." She turned to me, looking up with watering eyes. "It's FINE, you're going to be FINE!!!" she shouted while shooting a look that could kill towards Flynn. She was shouting as if I weren't right next to her.

Flynn was now sitting crossed-legged, leaned back with his arms stretched out behind him, his smile only growing. "I wish I had some popcorn."

"We've all been there!! Take your time and slowly release your muscles!" Priya continued coaching me, shouting.

"Oh, for the love of God," Nikita pushed through, reaching me and looking up. "Close your eyes and visualize yourself human again. That's all you need to do...don't forget to visualize yourself with your clothes still on, or I'll owe this douche bag twenty dollars."

"Douche bag?" Flynn said, tossing his hand to his chest and pretending to be offended, "It's not a win if you tell her how to do it!" He sat back up, rolling his eyes.

"Ever, look at me," came a voice that soothed my soul. I could feel Kolter. I could feel his emotions coursing through my bloodstream, sending shivers down my spine. Nothing, I swear, could ever top this feeling. I closed my eyes, relishing the feel of him silently caressing me with his words, scratching an itch I didn't know existed. *I said, look at me.* His voice caressed my brain and sent goosebumps down my body. I did as I was told. I'd spend my life obeying his every word if it felt like this. I looked him in the eyes, and slowly, without knowing how exactly it happened, our eyes came closer together. I was no longer towering down on him but admiringly looking up. *There you go. That's perfect,* he said soothingly. I blinked rapidly looking down at my body, now in my black leathers and boots. I returned my gaze to his and felt a pull like never before. He was pleased. I sensed it; he didn't need the words to tell me that I'd figured it out. My rapid heartbeat was slowly returning to baseline, but he still stood there watching me intently, trying to focus me before setting me loose. Our connection was coursing through my body, delivering coolness to my scalded nerves.

"Welp, I'm turned on. How about you?" Flynn said, nudging Nikita and bringing into reality that we weren't alone. They were all still there, watching us.

Can they... I swallowed nervously, looking around the group at their pleased expressions.

No, they can't. For some reason, it's just you and me. Our line is just for us two. He finished my incoherent thoughts before I could finish speaking them. He gave me a soft smile before releasing me.

"You're white. Huge and white," Nikita looked even more confused. "How is she white, Kolter?"

"Maybe they got it wrong? She could be Mazza, she is lighter than us, perhaps that's why we can't hear or feel her," Flavia acknowledged with a shrug.

"Oooh no, I definitely felt allllll of that." Flynn gestured, waving his hand around us in a circular motion, bringing the other hand to his collar and fanning it as if he were overheating.

"So, am I not a Highland then?" Saddened, I looked over at Kolter, who was deep in thought.

"If you weren't, I couldn't feel or speak with you down our line. You're Highland; there is no doubt in my mind. Your coloring though, is most definitely odd. I briefly wondered about it when I noticed your human form. Then again, I'm also not black colored. The second day on the train, when you stepped out in black leathers, I thought maybe it was a mistake, and you were wearing Priya's to get under my skin. But when I felt you for the first time, I knew you were where you were meant to be."

"Are you thinking she may be a crossbreed?" Baldur stepped forward to ask the question I'd just been thinking.

"I honestly don't know. It's atypical for a pack not to be able to have a line with one of its own. We will have to do nightly library time to see if something is written there about wolves like her," Kolter finalized.

"She can't go to my father's office without one of us. We can't trust him." Victor stepped to the side of me, as if protecting me from an unknown threat. "You can't trust that he would have our pack's best interest or hers."

With that, they all turned to look at me. I hadn't felt this confused and hopeless in a long time. Where most shifters celebrate their first time, I found myself questioning if I had prayed too hard and if a mistake was made again.

"Let's get this over with then," Kolter said, holding his hand out for me to take it. "I'll take her in. You all head to the library and see what you can dig up."

"You still owe me twenty dollars." Nikita smirked at Flynn. "Cough it up." She stood with her hand held out.

"Double or nothing, these two fuck within the week," Flynn said as he dangled the bill in front of her face, tempting her with a second bet.

I nearly choked. "Flynn!! I will not be doing that!" I said, mocking his circular motion from earlier. "I know for damn sure I am not losing my virginity to my alpha!" Immediately, the words left my mouth with regret as all widened eyes turned on me again. "UGH! Ok fine! Yes, virgin," I said, motioning up and down my body. "Happy now?" I reached out and snatched the money out of Flynn's held-up hand. "Stop looking at me like that!" I scowled at them all. Each looked like they were about to burst with laughter.

To his credit, Kolter kept a flat look on his face. "We about done here?" he gruffly asked the group. Getting no response, he nodded. Kolter ordered our pack to get to the library before taking my hand and leading me up the gravel path toward the admissions building.

Chapter Fourteen

Kolter

There was a pounding in my head, and fire was ripping through my shoulder as I shot my eyes open. Looking around, I noted I was on a hospital bed, a boiling liquid was being poured into my shoulder wound, and did I mention I had a massive headache? I had no recollection of what brought me here. Dizzy, I began to roll my head. To the left, I saw Nikita, standing behind the nurse with a pained expression. The nurse was now wiping away the excess liquid that was running down my chest and onto the bed.

"There there, just a few more minutes and you'll be right as rain if I do say so myself." She turned and gathered some linen that she fastened over my neck to secure my arm and create a sling. "I don't have to tell you not to shift for at least twenty-four hours, do I?" The nurse resembled my grandmother. She had a touch of silver in her hair, lines protruding from her eyes, signaling years of smiles and laughter. It was comforting.

"I think I'll be just fine, thank you for helping me. And you," I looked at Nikita now so she would accept my thanks. "Thank you for bringing me in."

"Such a beautiful girl you got yourself here," the Cailleach said, patting Nikita's shoulders as she excused herself.

I shook my head, smiling. Women always seemed to think that if a man was with a woman, she must be his. Bracing myself, I stood up to prepare to leave.

"Wait," Nikita's hands pressed firmly on my good arm. "There's something you need to know." I felt it, right then, like a thirty-foot wave beating the shore. I felt...her. Everelle. She was in my body, her emotions a colossal torment of fear, worry, stress... and she was running. I looked down her bright yellow line in my mind and saw her vision, saw what she saw. She was just about here. She was so strong. I could see the contours of her solid-toned body. Human form be damned. This version of her was to be a force to be reckoned with.

"You don't need to finish," I said, looking at Nikita. "I already know." Longingly, she looked at me, then, as if knowing no matter what she said nothing was going to change my feelings, she reached out her hand to help me up.

Stepping outside onto the pathway, I waited for Everelle's approach, holding my breath. I could feel the agitation in my bones. Between the shoulder that Folasade fucked up and the realization that I missed Everelle shifting for the first time, I was ready to punch a wall. I promised her I'd be there, that I'd help her through it, and I fucking passed out? How heroic.

I felt Everelle approaching before I saw her. I felt the strong stride of her legs, the heaviness in her chest as her heart pounded, the sounds of the twigs snapping under her weight. I felt the physical distortion of the ground as she pounded my way. Then, she was there. She slid onto the gravel path, sending rocks ricocheting off the walls and windows of the hospital wing. Dust floated in the air, and my breath was stolen completely.

In front of me stood this wondrous, beautiful, magical being and I was captivated. She stood with her back at nine feet. Her fur glistened like flecks of glitter, the color matching that of freshly fallen snow. Her eyes were composed of the purest blue with orange around the pupil, resembling that of an island lost at sea. Had her eyes always been so enticing? Looking at her now, my heart was ready to burst. I staggered. I missed her shift, but I would not miss her return. I ached to hold her. My body, completely entranced by hers. I could feel her, all the power, the longing, the emotional turmoil. I felt her inside me at that moment as if she were composed of me. *Hey,* came the voice in my head. The things it did for me. To hear her voice inside my head. I felt myself go rock hard. I wanted her. I wanted every piece of her, selfishly. I needed it. It was a need so primal, stronger than anything I'd ever felt. She would be mine, not just by the luck of the draw but destined by blood, we were fated mates.

Chapter Fifteen

Everelle

Walking side by side up the path to the academic building, I felt his confliction radiating down the line, so I stopped us. “I’m so sorry. I didn’t mean for any of this to happen.”

Kolter stopped and stared at me, his jaw tightened, indicating he was wrestling with his own inner demons. Looking at me now, he shook his head.

“You did nothing wrong.” His voice was raw, full of emotions, and it was breaking me. “I worry that if we don’t get this figured out, I could lose you long before I’ve had the chance to...”

“The chance to what?” I asked, wanting him to let me in. I didn’t like how badly this was tearing him up. Between the attack today and shifting, I couldn’t handle another misstep.

“To keep you.” The pure vulnerability he showed was heartbreaking. I didn’t know whether to reach for him or let him be. To everyone else, he was dangerous, but to me, he was my protection.

"You want to keep me?" I asked, looking deep into his eyes, sharing my hope that he felt all the electricity and warmth too.

"Since the day I first felt you." He answered honestly. This was as raw as it could be, and I never wanted to lose this part of him. Reaching for him now, he met me with open arms, and I melted into his embrace. He felt like coming home, like a piece of my soul had been missing, and suddenly it found where it belonged. Looking up into his eyes, I saw hope.

"I'm yours then, until the day you no longer need me, and even after," I concluded with sincerity.

I reached my fingers up to trace the deep-set scar just below his cheek. I locked eyes with him, seeing his eyes reflect mine; before I could change my mind, I stood on my tiptoes and reached my lips to find his. I'd make the first move; I didn't care. All I could think was that I wanted him. He captivated me at once with his hunger. In an instant, the burning took hold. I was enthralled as I opened my mouth wider for his tongue to take ownership of mine. I felt his growl in my mouth, a deep-throated call to me.

"Ever, we can't do this. You just shifted; you don't want this. You're not thinking straight." He started pulling away, pressing his forehead to mine and closing his eyes.

My arms, draped around his neck, as I still hovered inches from his mouth. I bit my lower lip, and his eyes greedily darted to it, burning with hunger.

"I don't think I've ever thought straighter... When Folasade took you in her jowls, and I heard the snapping of your bones and saw as she spit you out lifeless..." I shook my head, pulling away from him as I relived the moment. "I knew in my heart there would never be anyone I'd protect more, or would kill for, other than you."

I've never wanted anyone with every part of my being. Every part of me burned with certainty; there was no confusion. I wanted all of this, and I refused to deny it. If being reckless meant letting myself fall for the alpha, then I'd gladly submit as long as he wanted me.

He grabbed hold of me, walking me backwards until my back was pressed into the smooth stone of the building. No one could see us here; there were no windows or doors. I let myself go. Wrapping my legs around his waist, he moaned in my mouth. His hard length pressed against me, burning my core as he shifted his hips. "Ever, we need to stop. We can't do this right now."

"Make me believe it, make me believe you don't want me, and I'll stop." I challenged myself, moving my hips back and forth. In seconds, his mouth was back on mine, and my hands slid up to his hair, twisting strands around my fingers and pulling gently. His hands traced my body. His moan caused my body to arch into him, as it throbbed in places where I've never felt heat. He pulled away from me suddenly. Adjusting himself and running his fingers through his hair, he looked back at me and wiped his mouth. He gestured for me to fix my corset. I looked down and saw I was all but popping out.

"We need to hurry; the general will send someone if we don't go now." He stalked toward me, moving in a way that only predators do when they narrow in on their prey. My breath caught in my chest. God, this man, the things he did to me are precisely why I couldn't be trusted. I was reckless and foolish in his presence. My heart was beating entirely too fast for a normal human heart, stretching my chest cavity, filling me with anticipation. Closing my eyes as he drew near, I breathed in his deep, warm scent of leather and soft jasmine. He was everything I'd ever craved. I felt him leaning against me, cautiously, placing a soft kiss on my forehead. I burst, my heart burst, my blood turned into rivers of hot lava as they coursed through my body.

Kolter pulled away again and began walking up the path toward the back of the administration building. Once he reached the door, he looked back, giving me a smirk. "Let's go, princess."

Until then, I hadn't realized my body had forgotten how to move. He had ruined me at nineteen. I would never find another man more capable of handling me than Kolter was. I was screwed.

Chapter Sixteen

Everelle

The general's office was dimly lit. The sun was setting outside the massive windows, and I looked hesitantly around as we sat in the oversized chairs awaiting Ulrich. My eyes met Kolter's, and he gave me a slight frown. *It'll be fine. Stop worrying* and *fix your face.*

Youuu stop worrying. I can feel you too, you know, I chided rolling my eyes at him, then adjusting my head back toward the windows. Annoyingly, he was in my head again. *Stop pouting and fix your face, now, or I'll fix it for you.*

The tone in his voice made me pop my head back toward his irritatingly handsome smug face. I snarled at him, making him look forward with a fixed grin. *That's better.* As if preventing me from saying anything further, the doors were thrown open against the stone wall with a startlingly loud thud. The sheer magnitude of vibrations the doors caused when being slammed against the wall sent paintings falling. Sitting up straighter, I prepared myself for the wrath. I didn't need a crystal ball to know what was coming.

"I hadn't realized an invitation had been extended to you as well, Highland." His words inflicted a sharp blow to my confidence that this meeting would in fact be "fine." The general stalked toward us, sneering as he made his way around his enormous desk.

Adjusting his chair slightly before sitting, his little movements led me to think he suffered with some form of obsessive-compulsive disorder. Like everything had to be just so, or his brain might short circuit. I wanted nothing more than to dump his cup of pens over and tilt the delicate golden frames of photos that resided on the desk.

"I hadn't realized you offered private reprimands without seniority present," Kolter quipped back, slouching into the general's chair, draping his leg over the arm of it. Kolter was really looking for trouble. This wasn't going to go well, not with both men so fueled by arrogance; maybe I could help soften the issue at hand. If I could just apologize, maybe he'd offer me a pass and chalk it up to a naive girl who knew nothing of these customs. Anything was worth a try.

"I apologize, sir..." I began but was again cut off by Kolter.

"She apologizes for nothing. Unless you're here to apologize to her, I expect this meeting to be short." His cockiness, still amplified by his posture. He began to pick his nails with a dagger he'd pulled from his belt. The sight of him made the general's face tick. Little beads of sweat began to form, and his face turned a faint hue of pink.

"I will do nothing of the sort. Ms. Monica, you've overstepped your rank and violated protocol by shifting without professors present to incite an unauthorized duel, in which time you also used intimidation with threats of pack-on-pride violence. As such, you will spend three days in Pollsmoor." The general threw the student handbook at me, literally and figuratively, and nausea crept up my throat as I caught the large book he'd tossed. What? I was going to prison for three days for defending myself and Kolter? How? How was this justified? I began to fret. There had to be some way out of this, right?

Kolter stood immediately, so fast in fact that he knocked the small table that was between us over. "You can't throw her in Pollsmoor for protecting her alpha, who was rendered injured during a high-ranking pride attack! You're lucky she doesn't come after you for the inability to keep her safe! This is twice now, unprovoked, in our own quadrant of Askari, that she has been threatened by Folasade." The veins in his neck bulged. He snatched the book from my lap and tossed it back toward the general before he leaned over the general's desk; hands pressed so firmly the tips of his fingers began to whiten. "You talk of intimidation. Why don't you look in the fucking mirror?"

"You're out of line, alpha. I can do whatever the fuck I want. I am general of this school, and as such, when rules regarding safety and protocol are violated, on a Pride Princess no less, we take matters seriously. She will spend three days in Pollsmoor, and if you keep talking, you'll be there also." Ulrich wasn't backing down. The sneer etched across his face rendered me breathless. I was going to prison. If for nothing else, then to send a direct message to Kolter. "Tell me, Highland, who will maintain your pack then?" Ulrich's eyes narrowed. He was snarling. Spit flying from his mouth as he hammered down threats. This had turned into a glorified pissing match, and I was the prize to be won. I knew Folasade's prison sentence would come back to haunt me.

"If you can dish out prison sentences, you can take them. Your time starts now. Guards," he motioned over our shoulders for the two large men that I hadn't even seen enter the room to assist him. "Why don't you show our lovely female alpha of Highland what happens when we violate major safety protocol? Disarm her and hand the daggers to her alpha." He smirked. "And I am warning you, Highland, any interference from you or your pack will not result in positive outcomes for anyone." He looked up at the men again. "Take her," was all he said as he again began to organize invisible threats to his sanity on his desk.

Looking toward the two men, I began to sweat down my back. The fear bubbling inside of me. The first guard to approach me was quite oversize and out of shape to be a guard, I'd suspected. He had scarring on his face and a weak attempt at a beard. It was full of patches and thinning. He stepped forward, sneering at me as he reached toward my ribs. Roughly, he ripped the daggers Kolter had gifted me out of my corset. One by one, I was disarmed ten times. The guard didn't miss a single blade as he sliced through the material on my corset. The guard never took his eyes off of me as he dropped the blades into the leaner, more gangly guard's outstretched hands. He at least appeared to have kind eyes. They met mine with a note of apology. Once I'd been disarmed, I noticed they were preparing to cuff me. Anxiety again crept in as I quickly spouted, "Is that really necessary? I'll go willingly." I rolled my eyes at Ulrich, trying to present a little confidence. I needed Kolter to not worry about me.

"Oh, indeed, Madam, it is. You never know what may happen. It's safety for both parties," he countered, mocking ignorance.

The men were not gentle by any means. One of them wrenched my arms forcibly behind my back, forcing the backs of my hands to come together in an unnaturally straight way, while the other locked the cuffs around my wrists, binding me tightly. The guards exchanged a quick glance, confirming my compliance, while Ulrich watched with a steely satisfaction in his eyes.

As they readied themselves to lead me out, I fixed my gaze forward. I wouldn't show Kolter the fear that was creeping up inside me. I couldn't face him. I didn't want him to feel responsible for my actions. If he thought for one minute I was worried or hurt, he'd do something foolish. I violated protocol, and I would serve my time. Folasade didn't seem to be overly phased by Pollsmoor, so I would be fine as well. That's what I told myself on repeat, the entire three-mile hike to Pollsmoor.

Shortly after nightfall, we reached the ancient walls of prison. Prison… I was headed toward a prison. Looking up toward the medieval giant slowly appearing from depths of the dark forest, I blanched. For all intents and purposes, it met its goal. Large stone block walls fortified the structure. Rows of sharp barbed wire laced the top, and armed guards sat at the outposts on the wall. It smelled of rotten flesh and spilled blood. The overall experience walking into the building was nauseating.

The men led me over the creaking old wooden bridge. Looking down through the open slats, I could only see dark water. Lord knew what hid below its surface. I tried not to think about what awaited me as I swallowed deeply and let out a sigh. It was the only way I could keep a semblance of control. At this point, I couldn't tell if it was Kolter's emotions or mine radiating through me, because no matter how hard I tried to mentally talk myself into being calm, I couldn't settle the nerves bubbling up in my chest.

The interior of the prison was dark, moist, and decrepit. Clearly no resources had been spared for the maintenance of the prison in quite some time. It wasn't a shock; what should a prisoner expect after all? You're not here on vacation.

As I made my way through the dark, slim halls of my personal hell for the next three days, I noted that several times the other officers made crude jokes toward me as we passed by. I'd never been accused of being anything more than ordinary in the looks department, so hearing this threw me off. Either these men hadn't seen a decent woman in their lifetimes, or they used this as a form of torture.

Hallway after hallway, we continued on. Each time we entered a new area of the prison, doors were unlocked and locked again; the snicking of locks became a more appealing sound considering all that surrounded me. Behind me, another lock snicked as we made our way further down into the depths of the world. The only source of light came from candles with varying degrees of life left in them, this further proving to me that there would be no escape. I was sealing my fate for seventy-two more hours. The men's boots clapped the solid wet stones, their echoes reverberating through the dimly lit corridor. Every step forward felt heavier, the weight of my actions pressing down on me. I steeled myself, determined not to show any sign of weakness; survival here depended on maintaining both resolve and pride.

At last, we made it to a singular cell. Opening the large wrought iron door, the guards roughly shoved me in, tripping me over his foot and throwing my body against the floor. He slammed the door once I was inside, the sound so loud it caused my ears to ring long after the sound dissipated.

"Get the fuck up," the gruff guard screamed at me. "Back yourself to the hole in the door, and place your hands through it."

Quickly, I did what was told. Fear and anxiousness taking root in my stomach. Once I was at the door, he yanked my arms with such force through the hole that my shoulder dislocated, causing me blinding pain. Twisting my fingers, he wrenched them over, letting me know without any words that for the next three days, I wasn't in control of what happened here. He forced my hands down until they were on his hard cock, laughing at me as I looked away, repulsed.

"You're not so tough now, are you, bitch?" The brute of a guard twisted my wrist the other direction now, forcing my fingers to stroke his dick through his pants. In my mind, I was gagging, disgusted, and thanking God that Kolter didn't feel so small. The second guard told him to cut it out as he removed my hand from the guard's tootsie roll of a member. Out of retaliation, the first guard twisted my hand backward until I felt it break. I was then shoved back through the hole. The state of my arm and hands did little in the way of bracing my fall as I again met the cold hard stones of the cell's floor.

"When you fuck with our pride princess, we fuck with you. Welcome to hell," the leaner guard roared.

I don't know how long I sat in the dark, crying to myself, but it had to have been hours. Sometime after I hit the floor I must have blacked out. I awoke to more pain than I had ever felt before. My wrist and fingers of my right hand were broken; my left wrist was severely sprained at a minimum. My shoulder was hanging still out of socket. I needed to get up the nerve to force it back in, but it was hard to talk yourself into more pain when you've already had enough to send you under.

However, deciding to lessen one load of pain, I decided I needed to fix my arm. If I didn't, shifting would be impossible in the future. Only God knew if the damage already inflicted would become a disability to my new form.

I'd shifted. I thought then, bubbling in me a small sense of pride. It had been a freeing feeling. Shifting was my only semblance of hope. If I had come to this shit hole before shifting, I don't think I'd have the courage to get up and pop my shoulder back into place. I'd most certainly not have the hope that was now bubbling in my chest. I wasn't a liability to my pack any more. Well, I guess I wouldn't go that far, but it felt good to finally have one answer to my problems solved.

I stood, getting off the floor. I knew I couldn't leave my shoulder hanging out of the socket for three days. Steadying myself against the stone, I crouched, letting my shoulder fall freely, and rotated my arm slightly in preparation. I was going to thrust my shoulder upwards into the wall beneath a makeshift window with its sill protruding. I could do this. I slowed my breathing and counted, one... two... I bolted, smashing my shoulder directly into the underside of the window sill, forcing my shoulder back into place. The pain was so unbelievably excruciating that darkness consumed me at once.

Sometime later, I awoke to the guards, taunting me from the door of my cell. "Come here, bitch. Your food is ready." They snickered to themselves. I don't care what it was, there was no chance in hell I was eating whatever they planned to give me. "Let's go! Now! Move!" They banged on the cell doors with batons, hurting my ears as the bars rung out. I wouldn't look at them. I refused to give them the satisfaction of so much as a tear. I continued my quest to ignore them.

The snick of a lock echoed off the cell walls. "If you won't come to us, we will come to you," the larger man growled. "It's time for you to learn some fucking manners." Yanking me upward by my hair, I was forced off the ground as if I weighed nothing. The blow came directly to my face, cracking my cheekbone and splitting my lips open. I tasted warm iron like blood as I felt the explosion of pain burst across my face.

"You hungry yet, bitch?" the leaner guard mocked. The third blow came to my back, forcing me to the floor while his hands still clung to my hair. "How about now?" He shoved something cold and slimy into my mouth, and I began to gag. I couldn't tell what it was he was trying to force-feed me, but I didn't care. I just hardened with each blow I received. Finally, when they were bored of their abuse, they threw me to the cold stone floor and took turns pissing on my limp body before they left me writhing in pain and the darkness took me once again.

Hours later, I awoke to the screams of someone else finding out just how awful Pollsmoor truly was. I fucked up. I'm not saying I wouldn't protect Kolter again, but the next time I would make sure the person wouldn't have a voice to repeat back what I'd done. The next time I'd fucking make them pay for this torture.

Then it hit me... Kolter. What would he do when he saw me? I sent a prayer up to God, or Kasen, whoever the fuck was failing at looking out for me, and asked that they watch over him. They needed to prepare him for what he would surely witness when, no, if I finally walked out of here. I knew he'd blame himself. I thought about Folasade and how she must have felt during her abuse here. I felt sick to my stomach knowing I inflicted this kind of torture onto someone else. I passed out again from the guilt and pain I was enduring.

Waking yet again hours later, I realized I wasn't offered food again. Though I could hear other screams, I was given a reprieve from the beatings. The men must have found my lack of emotion not worth the effort when other people were clearly livelier. Lying on my back, I tried my best to talk myself into thinking I was ok. Though I missed feeling Kolter through the bond we shared, I was glad that it meant he couldn't feel me. I didn't need him knowing just how bad this was. Internally I was a mess thinking about how he'd respond when he picked me up from wherever the hell I was being let go.

How long is three days? Time seemed to never move down here, but we had to be getting close, I would imagine. Being down here proved to be worse than expected. The beatings aside, the entire cell was dark. A makeshift window in the corner proved to be just a hole, an opening to another cell, not a window at all. It's where I heard the screams of the other inmates being abused and heard other inmates taunting one another. I think that's what tortured me most.

Just when I was certain all hope was lost, the grim reaper appeared to inflict his ugly spin on torture. He walked in, fully cloaked in black, and hovered over my body on the cold, wet ground. With one clean sweep, he raised his sickle and brought it down through my ankle. Pain blinded me. I began my positive self-talk to keep my screams down and my emotions limited. Seeing that his strike inflicted no reaction, he moved forward and started his wrath. Again, my shoulder was dislocated, my face was pummeled, and my fingers were broken, one by one. I cracked a rib on the way to the floor the last time he struck me. I focused on the tangibles as he assaulted me. With each blow I repeated, *stone wall, dark corner, cracked brick.* The smell in here was putrid, acidic with a tang of death. I continued to hold myself together. When I'd refused the grim reaper a reaction, he snarled and left. Darkness enveloped me as I floated out of consciousness once again.

Awakening, I heard the snick of the lock. This time a woman entered the cell. Great. What kind of holy hell would I face now?

"Here you are, deary... that's it," she spoke softly as she gently sat me up. I had no life left to me. No energy. "This will help; I will need you to drink it up before I can clear you to leave." Leave? I was here for three days? Relief flooded me at once. I began to sob into her arms, praying this wasn't just another form of torture and that I truly would be leaving this fucking place.

She forced into my mouth a liquid that tasted worse than goblin piss. The burning coursed through my body, and I writhed in pain, internalizing the screams that I so desperately wanted to escape my mouth. I knew this was a sick joke. I knew I shouldn't have shown emotion. I forced myself to stop reacting. I forced all my walls back up and plastered the stoic look back to my face. I couldn't let them know they were winning. If this was another test in prison, I'd take it the same way as I had the beatings. No one would say they bested me.

"There you go. Now it's working. You'll be good as new in a moment. Just sit still while it does its work." She caressed my hair as I faded in and out of consciousness. The liquid she gave me coursed through my veins. Scorching a trail of lava and embers as it made its way throughout my body. My bones rebuilt themselves, my face regained its shape, and the hole in my stomach filled with some semblance of hydration. She'd given me a cure to erase the beatings I'd endured. This must be why Folasade looked untouched or unphased. I had long come to the conclusion that she hadn't received the beatings I had, but if she did, they erased them. Guilt began to swell once more.

"Ok, let's get you up and dusted off, shall we?" she asked, with a slight giggle. Was she seriously joyous? She saw me, she knew the damage that had been inflicted on me, and she was happy to go about fixing me. As if it mentally repaired me as well. It took a special sick twist...

Blinking rapidly, I looked around. A woman stood beside me holding my hand, patting it as I took in my awful surroundings. "Who are you?" I asked her, confused. "Where am I?" Frantic, I began to spiral. Where was I? Where was Kolter? Where was my pack? My body was blindingly sore. My head throbbed and I began to feel dizzy as she made me stand. Assisting me to prevent me from falling. "Where am I?"

"Come along darling. Let us get you back to your den. You'll want to sleep for a bit. Come, come." She began to walk me through the twists and turns of a dark, dimly lit hallway while my mind reeled in a million different ways of how I got here and what was happening to me. The last thing I remembered was the soft giggle of the woman that healed me as I drifted out of consciousness.

Regaining consciousness, I saw the woman again, clinging to me, holding my frail body upright. For a small woman, she had brute strength, I thought. After what seemed like hours, but was in all actuality closer to five minutes, we were breathing the light of day. Fresh air hit me, cool and clean. Closing my eyes, I breathed in deeply, allowing the air to settle my nausea.

"Ever! Are you alright?" I heard the frantic and desperate call from Kolter. He was racing down the bridge toward the woman and me.

"Is she ok?" a panic-stricken Kolter asked the woman as he began reaching his arms out for me.

"Quite alright, dear, just see to it that she gets plenty of rest today and tomorrow. They did a number on her, but I fixed her right up good as new. She won't remember anything." If looks could kill, she would be six feet under with a gravestone already by Kolter.

"What did you give her? What will she remember?" he demanded, snarling his words.

"Curefix. It should kick in at any moment. She suffered a couple of broken ribs, a fractured cheek, a cracked jaw, a dislocated shoulder, two broken wrists, eight broken fingers, and a torn achilles. She's one of the lucky ones. She will remember nothing of this week's extended stay." I was fading fast; whatever she'd given me was making me extremely tired. "Make sure she doesn't shift for at least twenty-four hours." Everything went dark, but at least, I was with Kolter. Nothing ever seemed as bad when I was with Kolter.

Chapter Seventeen

Everelle

My mind came to before my eyes even opened. I was innately aware of Kolter's scent engulfing me. I wasn't in my own bed, and I froze, panic-stricken. Cracking open my eyes, I peered around. *OH MY GOD*. I sat up, frightened. I was in Kolter's bed. Slamming my hand to my face, I frantically scanned my brain and tried to remember any reason as to why I'd be in his bed! *Oh no no no no no, please please no*. I lifted the covers slowly, closing my eyes. I sent a silent prayer to God that I'd have clothes on. Opening one eye, I peeked down at myself, and I was mortified. *OOH MYYYY GODD!* I was in my panties. Only panties... in Kolter's bed. *Fuck*... I had a feeling I was going to owe Flynn forty dollars. I looked around the room but saw no one. I rolled over, still holding his silky white sheets to my chest, and I began searching for my leathers. Looking around the room, I saw them on a chair that sat next to the desk, neatly folded.

Moving as quietly and quickly as possible, I dragged the sheet and myself to the side of the bed and stretched my foot down in search of the cold floor, but I misjudged the fact that his bed sat on a slightly elevated platform, and

I face-planted onto the floor. *Shit. That's going to leave a mark.* As if sensing I was awake, or hearing my commotion, the door opened, and in walked a devilishly handsome, smirking Kolter with cups of coffee. "Well, hello there," He said, looking down. "How'd you sleep?" He set the cups down on the desk then made quick work of crossing the room before he reached an extended hand down to me to help me up.

"Mmmmmmmhmm" I groaned in embarrassment. "Look, I'm sorry, whatever we did last night, I'm sure it was wonderful," I said. I looked around to make sure I was covered, twisting in the sheets with each step I took toward the chair with my clothes on it. "It was amazing in fact. I just, uh, I just need a moment to reflect on it," I continued in my rambles. Looking down at my clothes, I silently debated putting them on or just doing the walk of shame into the hallway in his bedsheet. "I mean, I'm sure you were great, rock-hard abs and perfect body and all." I stopped and stared at him standing there, imagining his abs. "It's not you," I said, shaking my head and picking up my clothes, determined to just do the walk of shame. "It's me. I tend to do stupid shit..." ***like fuck my alpha one week into knowing him.*** I finally looked up to meet his eyes, and he was grinning like a fool, arms crossed, sipping coffee as he leaned up against his desk.

"You finished?" he asked smugly, setting his cup down.

"Yep, I think that about wraps it up here. I'll just make my way back to my room. I'll bring this back," I muttered, gesturing to his sheets that were still wrapped around me. "Or I'll just burn it. Probably should burn it, I mean... memories, right?" I said, shrugging my shoulders.

Kolter sighed, shaking his head. Standing up, he walked over to me, stealing my breath as he drew near. Taking my hand in his, he made sure to look me square in the face, his smoldering eyes reaching into my soul.

"Nothing happened last night, I promise you," he began, bringing my hand to his soft lips and brushing them against my knuckles. "And I assure you, if it had, you would *most definitely* remember it, and you'd be leaving with a limp." He emphasized his words by dropping my hand and running his fingers slowly over the silky fabric of the sheet wrapped around my thighs. "Your legs wouldn't walk straight." He pulled his hand away and brought it up to my hair where he tucked a loosened strand innocently behind my ear. "Why don't I give you five minutes to get dressed, and I'll meet you in the common room." He leaned in to kiss my forehead.

"Yeah... uh huh, ok..." I said as he exited the room. I did not fully release the breath in my chest until the door latched closed.

Oh my god... I think I just came.

You didn't... trust me, everyone *would know if you did. Get dressed.* I heard his chuckle in my head as his husky voice penetrated my thoughts.

Holy shit...

"Well, good morning, inmate. How was it being someone's bitch this week?" Flynn mocked, sitting in one of the leather-bound chairs next to the fireplace in the common room as I walked in a little later.

The room immediately went dark, and Kolter was up before Flynn had even adjusted his crooked smile. The sounds that erupted in the room thereafter were deafening as the men began to grapple on the floor. Kolter was landing punches directly to Flynn's head as he was pinned to the floor.

"Alright, knock it off you two!" Nikita said, forcing herself in between them. "I swear you two are worse than children," she said, tugging at Kolter's arm unsuccessfully. She lost her temper then. "For fuck's sake, STOP!" she shouted, shoving them apart. "Seriously, what the fuck is wrong with you two?"

The men looked at each other, one cocky and the other raging in venom. "He can't handle a little joke," Flynn said, spitting blood from his mouth, his lip cracked. "You both better fuck soon. I'm tired of this insanity." His words came out with a slight whistle, his mouth and brow scrunching.

I swallowed hard. What would that have to do with anything? Heat flushed my cheeks as embarrassment crept in. The last thing I needed was to be holed up in some room like Lisbeth and Baldur or Priya and Kentaro. I swear, they didn't even eat sometimes, going days before emerging from their rooms. Nothing about that sounded the slightest bit fun. My attention was brought back to the room when Kolter raised his voice.

"Sometimes, Flynn, your joking doesn't read a damn room!" Kolter barked, stepping in the direction of Nikita's outstretched hands. "I wouldn't mind teaching you how to become literate."

"Oh, because I joke, I'm somehow stupid now? Fuck you, Kolt." Flynn shook his head in disgust.

"Prove me wrong, bro." Kolter threw his hands out wide, as if challenging Flynn to present evidence of the contrary. Ugh, this was going so horribly wrong. Kolter was our alpha. He was supposed to be role modeling better behaviors; however, when it came to me, he took our partnership seriously and defended me without a second thought.

"What happened?" Priya asked curiously, as she and Kentaro entered the room, looking disheveled and out of breath. Oh, so they can come out. I grinned at myself and quickly removed it. The situation was much too serious for my quips. Priya and I would revisit this later.

"See!" Flynn yelled, thrusting his arms out toward them. "At least they know the key to fitting together is working on your bond. I know, hard concept for you since you're so damn used to women throwing themselves at you. It sucks having to work for it, doesn't it? Welcome to the other side, asshole."

The punch flew with enough force to throw Flynn into the wrought iron hearth tools. The clatter of them knocking against the stone was muffled under Flynn's massive weight as he fell to the floor. Kolter stood over him now, fuming. "Stop talking about shit you know nothing about."

"Right," Flynn said with defeat as he picked himself up off the floor. "Because I'm stupid?" He spit blood and a tooth out into his hand, stared at it, then his eyes shot to me; a look of disgust plastered his face as he, without looking at me, threw his tooth into the fire. Guilt crept up like bile into my throat. These two were my favorite men, and at each other's throats because of me.

"Well, bud, you said it." Kolter retorted, his eyes never so much as blinking.

"I'll have you know, Kolter, I'm quite educated," Flynn began, bringing his attention back to the alpha. "I know that for a wolf pair to sync, mating is important. More so, when you've chosen your alpha. As you fight the natural urge, you cause a disconnection that can leech into the damn pack's line. In case *you* can't read a room, we have yet to hear or feel her down the fucking line! I'm tired of this pack not taking me seriously because I crack jokes. It's a trauma response. Look it up." Flynn shoved through Kolter and Nikita and stormed out of the room. Moments later, the slamming of a door shook photos off the obsidian walls.

"He's right, you know?" Priya began. "Not necessarily about the mating thing, although it's pretty damn great." She shot me a look of satisfaction accompanied by lifted eyebrows. "I'm just saying, there is a definite disconnect happening. At this point, we should be able to feel her and talk to her, at the very least in shifted form... yet we can't. All the research I've been looking into in the library has come up short. You two either need to roll in the sheets, or we need to start asking other packs. Someone must know something."

"Moreover, we're not going to figure it out fighting amongst ourselves either," Kentaro barked. "Nothing good comes from a weakened pack. Look what was able to happen just this week. You two fought in public, and privileged information was used against you. Everelle landed in the brink, and now you two are fighting." He gestured from Kolter across the invisible line to Flynn down the hall. "You need to get this under control as the alpha. No one respects someone who falls apart and can't accept help to pull themselves back together."

With that, they all began exiting the room, leaving Kolter and I alone.

"I should go talk to him," I began. "Flynn, I mean. I feel like he deserves my apology. It never feels good to feel like you're the butt of everyone's joke, and I think he truly does do it as a defense mechanism. What kind of friend would I be to let him fall?"

I rose and stepped toward where Kolter was. "Thank you for whatever it is you're shielding me from. I know it must be hard. I can feel you doubting yourself and beating yourself up," I said softly, reaching for his face to gently cup it. "Stop doing that. Nothing is that bad that it can't be fixed." I kissed him softly on the cheek and walked out of the room, leaving him with his thoughts.

I knocked on Flynn's door but heard no answer. I knew he was in there, so instead of knocking again or leaving, I twisted the knob in my hand and pushed the door open. Stepping into Flynn's room was like stepping into his mind. While he had the standard furniture that came with the room, he had also adorned it with books and words of affirmation written in neat handwriting on index cards, that were stuck above his bed among photos from home. He was well organized and neat, and it continued to show how deep he truly was.

"Flynn, can I come in?" I asked from the doorway. I could see he was lying on his bed, tossing a ball into the air.

"Looks to me like you already are. I could be wrong though; after all, I can't read a room, and would you look at that..." He sat up gesturing around him, "Yep, by God, this is a room." He shook his head and lied back down, resuming his solo game of catch.

I stepped further into the room and closed the door. Walking over toward his desk, I pulled his old wooden chair out and twisted it around so it faced his bed. It was cool in here, and the smell of lemongrass was pleasing. "I wanted to apologize. I feel like this was my fault."

"Oh, here we go again. Do me a favor. Skip the part where you whine and play the ignorant fool that somehow wants to do better. Spoiler alert, I don't care enough, and you won't change. I've read this story before."

Well, shit, that hurt my feelings. I tried again. "I'm not apologizing for being ignorant. I'm apologizing because I was reckless and foolish, and as such, the pack and you were affected."

He caught the ball one last time before sitting up and swinging his legs over the side of the bed so he could face me. "No, Everelle Marie," he said mockingly, "that's not why I'm upset. I don't give a fuck that Kolt and I threw punches. Hell, I don't even care that he called me stupid. I don't expect you to know everything about this pack, Christ; I don't even expect you to know 50%. But what I do expect is for you to fucking try. Just try! Stop pretending you're weak, or vulnerable, or you can't do something because you never have. That's exactly how we learn! We attempt something, and guess what? One of two things happens. Either we're really fucking lucky and we succeed the first time, in which case we truly didn't learn anything, or two, we fail and now we're forced to try again, approaching the situation differently." He was looking at me now, truly looking at me. I swallowed the mass that was forming in my throat. I felt the sting at the tips of my eyes, threatening tears if I didn't get my shit together. I wasn't going to allow him to see me cry. "The problem I have with you is you're so complacent. You let everyone step in for you and fight your battles. It started with Priya, then Nikita, and now Kolt. When are you going to step up and protect your damn self? I meant what I said last week. We need to be able to rely on you, especially because you're an alpha. Currently, not one person, including yourself, thinks of you as an asset."

Blood was boiling through my body. The more he talked, the angrier I got. *You're pissing me the fuck off.*

"Good!! You should be pissed! You should be angry, for fuck's sake; it shows you care!" He stopped suddenly and sat back, holding up his hands. "Wait... you didn't say that out loud... Ever, do it again!" He was standing now, excitedly. "Seriously, try again. I heard you!"

"I... I don't know what I did..." I said, searching my mind for answers.

"Everelle Marie Monica, don't sit here and make excuses again after I just dressed you down and made you finally open the line. TRY AGAIN!" The regret that I had for telling Priya my name, immediately plagued me, but I pushed it away. I needed to focus.

This time I closed my eyes. I looked deep into my mind. When I thought of Kolter, I saw him, clear as day. Sitting here in Flynn's room, I could feel Kolter in the next room. His path in my mind was royal blue, buzzing and humming. Looking down the path, I saw Kolter was pacing. His heart was hurting, and so was his hand. Realizing that path was only for Kolter, I shoved it out of my mind as if were tangible and tried again. This time I focused hard on creating a path just for just Flynn. Then slowly, appearing through the fog of my mind, an evergreen road appeared, and I could see a door developing at the end of the road. In my mind I visualized myself stepping forward, only this time, visualizing Flynn's path and door. I reached for his doorknob, and twisted. It glowed then, opening a connection to Flynn in my mind as if he weren't in the same room, but was standing on the evergreen street in my mind. In front of me, just out of reach was a glowing ball of hope. I stretched my mind, reaching for the ball. It grew brighter, bigger and stronger the closer I got to it. Slowly at first, then all at once, I felt him, Flynn... I felt his pride beaming down this new line. I felt Flynn breathe out relaxing, as if I'd finally won him over. I kept reaching then, turning away from the evergreen path. Appearing before me was now a pink sandy path that opened to Priya and Kentaro. They were...Ooops, that's embarrassing. I quickly turned my attention back to Flynn's evergreen path, as if locking Priya's so that they could be in a room alone.

"HAHAHAHAHA," Flynn laughed and clapped his hands together. "You'll get used to that. They're worse than Lisbeth and Baldur, I swear, ugh."

I tried again. Flynn sat back, getting comfortable. He wasn't going to rush me. I appreciated that. I closed my eyes again, trying to create new connections in my mind.

Another half hour would go by before I opened my eyes, feeling successful. I could feel them. All of them. Each somehow buzzing individually and together in my mind. Like little bees in a hive. My eyes began to sting again, this time with gratification that I finally did something right.

"Yes, you did... and it's because you tried. You stopped making excuses, and you tried! That's all I want from you, every day. Do you understand? Stop making excuses. You're not a weak bitch. Ever, you're a fucking alpha... It's time you started acting like it." He reached for my hand and pulled me up from the chair. As he wrapped me in a hug, kissing my forehead. I'd never felt more accomplished, supported, and loved. Flynn was like the brother I'd never had. I needed him in my life, more than either of us realized. Tears welled in my eyes as I hugged him. Knowing that I'd taken him for granted, I hugged him tighter. He would never be disappointed in me again. I'd make sure of it.

"Well, let's not go overboard. I'm sure you'll still disappoint me plenty," he said, kissing the top of my head. Tears were streaming down my face now, and I chuckled at his humor.

"You know, you don't always have to break the tension with humor. We'd still love you without it," I said, pulling away and meeting his eyes.

“Yes, but how ever would I love you?” he said, wiping the stray tears from my cheeks. A smile stretched across his face, and for the first time I noted his missing tooth, and I couldn’t keep a straight face. I lost it; all of my built-up anxiety released in waves of hysteria as I fell back onto his bed, giggling.

“You know, it’s awfully rude to receive someone’s help and then make fun of them as payment.” He stuck his tongue through the hole of his missing tooth, and new wave of bellyaching laughs escaped my mouth, tears rolling down my cheeks.

There was a loud, urgent knock on Flynn’s door, and he rolled his eyes, breaking away from me and crossing the room. “For fuck’s sake Kolt, just look down the line...I didn’t hurt her,” he said, swinging the door wide open and gesturing toward me. Standing in the doorway was a worry-stricken Kolter. He pushed his way in, pulled me up from the bed and wrapped me in his arms, burying his face in my hair.

“Great, you two made up. We made up. This is all great, but your rooms are that way,” he said, gesturing behind him. “Find one of them and maybe practice rolling around, playing; I don’t know, how about you try bobbing for some damn carrots, if you know what I mean. At least she can be felt now.”

I couldn’t hold it in any longer. I laughed so hard my stomach hurt and I couldn’t catch my breath. Happy tears streamed down my face as I turned away from Kolter and embraced Flynn again.

“Ugh, I love you too,” he said, closing our embrace. In my mind, I saw Flynn stick his tongue out at Kolter, rubbing salt in the wound.

“Alright, enough of that. Your fronts should never be pressed that hard against each other,” Kolter said, making his way across the room and pulling us apart.

“I don’t know man. Seems to me like she likes this hard body against hers... you may have some competition.” Flynn flexed, showing off his biceps, then brought his arms in front of him, flexing his shoulders. “Maybe she’ll bob for my carrot.”

"Doubtful." With that, Kolter picked me up and rested me on his shoulder. "We're out of here."

I could still feel Flynn's laughter from three rooms away as Kolter set me down on his bed.

He backed away from me slowly, sitting down in his desk chair, and then he began to roll backwards toward me. He studied me, my features, and then the soul behind my eyes. It was like he was taking inventory of my body to make sure I was alright.

"He didn't hurt me," I teased him, trying to lift the tension I now felt wrapping around us. It was hot, sticky, and tight.

"What are you talking about?" he asked me as he met my eyes again, obviously done scanning my body.

"Flynn, he didn't hurt me. I was crying happy tears."

"You think I'm worried about whether Flynn hurt you?" He clenched his jaw. "It's not Flynn that I visualize grabbing you by your throat or beating you with batons. Flynn is far from my worries. They may have erased your mind and mended you with a potion, but they didn't erase mine. That punishment Ulrich gave was just as much a lesson to me as it was to you." He swallowed now, so hard I saw his adams apple bounce. Worry and sadness began creeping up in my chest. I pushed back at it, trying to be there for Kolter. "I had to watch every strike, every vile thing they said while torturing you. I witnessed your strength while feeling your jaw shatter. I watched in horror as your eye swelled shut. Because of me!" He was volatile now, clenching and releasing his fists. The torment on his face broke me in ways I didn't know I'd been capable. "I listened to you pray for my soul, while yours was attacked mercilessly. He was warning me, he was sending me a message, and it was done through you." I swallowed as the bile crept up from my throat and he jerked his face from mine. He stood now, pacing the floor. "It took all I had not to completely lose myself, going on a ravenous, murdering spree. Anyone who so much as looked at you wrong or thought something indecent is permanently etched into my brain as a reminder to me. When the day comes, when we seek our retribution, they will all pay for what they've done to you. There is no fight too large that I won't battle for you in." He looked at me now, a shell of his former self in my eyes. He was a victim just as I had been, only much worse. He was right. Where I got to escape the pain and mental anguish, he continued to relive it, countless times.

I rose to stand in front of him, reaching up, I felt my breath hitch as I traced his jaw with my fingers. "I am so incredibly sorry for the pain I've caused you. I never meant for any of this to happen."

"You don't get it. It's I who should apologize. The lion baited me that day in the forest. He asked you what Folasade's punishment should be, knowing you had no clue, and I'd step in. I sentenced a pride princess to prison. *ME.* Ulrich had me. He was just waiting for an opportunity to arise when he could return the favor." He looked defeated. Staring back at me, he hung his head with the shame he felt. Seeing this all for what it was made me sick.

Looking deep into his eyes, I held his gaze until he was paying attention. He needed to hear what I felt. He had to know what I knew in my heart. "They can't win this, Kolter. They won't break us down. They won't break you. I refuse to let them."

Chapter Eighteen

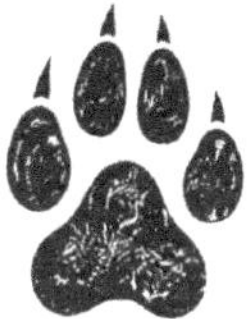

Six days ago...

Kolter

I watched her go; the men, with grips too tight, shoved Everelle into the hallway and slammed the door, leaving me alone with Ulrich. Eyes remaining on the door, I felt the heat rise in my blood. "You will pay for this," I said now, turning to face him. I gripped her blades that the guard had thrust into my hands. I wanted Ulrich to hear my words and let them sink in. "If she as much as loses one strand of hair or gets one tiny scratch, I will come for you, and you won't..."

"Shut the hell up! You act as if you're somehow in control. Take a lesson from your brother's failed attempt at alpha... You keep your fucking nose down, and you don't fight the hand that feeds you. She is receiving her punishment for threats toward a royal. What should yours be for threats toward a general?" He shot me a long, fiery look while he stood perched over his desk. "I'm doubling her sentence due to your continued insubordination. Get the fuck out of my office, or I'll have you locked up next to her." In fury I watched as he straightened items on his desk. His eyes looked back up, an image of fury and hatred, reflecting my own. I was the first to break the contact.

Fuck!! I'd added more time to her punishment. Ulrich knew he had me. I turned away. All I wanted to do was beat the living fuck out of him, but I knew it wouldn't do a single ounce of good. He had me and my pack by our balls, and there was absolutely nothing I could do about it. Walking out of the general's office and into the night sky, I looked up and asked Kasen to have her back in there. "No matter where you are, or what you're doing up there, nothing is more important than she is. Watch over her. Please."

In a moment, a tidal wave of pain hit me all at once. A burning, excruciating pain radiated throughout my wrists and fingers. It was blinding. I dropped to the ground, gasping for air. I knew in my heart that I was experiencing Ever's pain during her walk to the prison. Regaining my footing, I stood just to be debilitated again. This time, my shoulder felt as if it was ripped from my body. Panting now, I crawled across the cold stone of the quad, just as a searing pain radiated down my back. Flopping over onto my back, I looked at the night sky, pain echoing in my mind, and I heard her voice. She was reciting a mantra to herself repeatedly, telling herself to remain calm, to not show emotion... She was stronger than I was. It seemed the beatings had stopped for now, but the pain still lingered. My heart hurt for her. Feeling both useless and hopeless, I staggered back to the den. Whatever I was feeling, I knew for her, it was exponentially worse.

I stumbled into the common room and fell into a chair. Fear-filled eyes around the room all looked onto mine, and at once everyone was talking.

"What happened?"

"Where is Everelle?"

"Are you ok? Where is she?"

Attacks began again; I felt every single blow. My mouth and eyes watered with the depiction of what she was feeling. It was then, while picking myself up off the floor with Priya's help, that I heard her. I heard her pray for me. She was asking my brother or God to look out for me and help me through this. What kind of soul could be facing near-deathly blows and still pray for someone else? Looking up, my eyes locked with Victor's, and he nodded. I was thankful for my bond with him; otherwise, he wouldn't be leaving right now headed to his father. He knew exactly what I needed. He alone could do more than I ever could.

I needed to get off this floor. One final blow to the back of my head caused the darkness to take over.

I woke up sometime later with excruciating pain in my heel. Everelle was suffering. I couldn't even get out of bed. I'd been in and out of consciousness for days. My body would writhe in burning agony, only a drop of what she had to be feeling and going through. Despite it, I didn't hear from her. Either our verbal bond had been severed, or she was remaining quiet. I wasn't sure if it impressed me or hurt me more to know my partner, my alpha, my mate had to endure this level of pain. For at least three days they'd left her alone. I'd hoped that Victor's talk with his dad had done some sort of good for her. For three days I didn't have to feel the blows of pain or the stabs of heartache. But I worried that it was because the line to our bond had been severed. I couldn't stand not feeling her. I stood in my room, stretching through the sore agony of my muscles and bones, each a reflection of hers, and it was enough to tell me she was still there. Still wounded. I'd make all the dirt bags who touched her pay. I'd make sure anyone who so much as looked at her indecently paid. No one, and I meant no one, touched my mate and lived to breathe after.

While pacing my room, I felt it then. I was crumpled on the floor, a blinding, scorching pain directly to my ankle. I screamed out in agony, my bedroom door flying open, Victor and Brandt rushing in to help as I was again assaulted with blows to the face, head, and chest. The last thing I remember, was Victor getting up and leaving the room before I again lost all consciousness and the line to Everelle.

Two days later, I woke, a burning in my chest. The desire to no longer sit idly by while she was tortured became too much. I needed to get her. The sheer need to find her was overwhelming enough to pull me out of my room and into the hallway. I would go stand outside the fucking prison and wait for her. It had been six days. I'd silently prayed Victor could have gotten his father to release her at the original three days, but it didn't work out. He refused and taunted that if we tried to interfere again, he'd add more time or worse. I didn't want to know what worse would be.

I'd wait out her remaining days outside of Pollsmoor. She wouldn't be with these fucking assholes any longer than she had to be. I was going to collect what belonged to me, and I didn't care if I had to burn the whole fucking place to ashes to do it. The men, whose faces I could see so clearly, had no idea they just signed their own death warrants. She would be their last torment. I would be their last vision. Make no mistake.

Chapter Nineteen

Everelle

The next few months flew by. I kept my nose down and wouldn't so much as look at the pride members unless in class. If I wasn't in the library researching, I was sparring with my pack. They've been trying to help me get into shape, while strengthening our pack line and running fight maneuvers. I had gotten pretty decent with a blade too, thanks to Priya.

Since shifting had become easier and easier, I'd been able to join the pack for the five-mile runs each morning before classes. With each of us in our running positions and Kolter and me side by side, it had felt so freeing. I could sense everything while we ran. The smell of wood, grass, streams, and other animals ignited my senses. It was pure animalistic rushes of adrenaline that fueled me. I learned to match Kolter, stride for stride. At first, I had a tough time making it long distances at the speed at which he tore through the woods. However, over the last few weeks, we've extended my reach through runs and strength training.

Fight maneuvers were a slow progression. At first, every move I made was wrong. The way I stalked prey, somehow always ended with me stepping on a twig or branch and the noise it caused diverted attention to my presence, and we'd have to start again. Or better yet, I'd slip on the smooth obsidian stones and we would have to restart, yet again. It took me weeks just to get enough strength in my hind legs to crouch for more than a few minutes at a time.

Luckily, I wasn't the only wolf who needed extra support. Lisbeth seemed to be struggling with her new position. While previously she had been a hunter, she was now a rear guard. It was hard for her to break her instincts and stay back when she wanted to follow her racing thoughts forward. I could tell she was not my biggest fan. It seemed I found ways to piss her off the most.

"Everelle, why is this such an issue for you?" Lisbeth screamed at me after another failed attempt to silently approach my target, her. "I mean seriously, are you even trying? It's not that fucking hard! Stay low, step lightly, make sure your weight is fully pressed before placing your next step forward, and repeat. Stop fucking rushing it!!" she snarled at me.

"Well shit, sweetie, tell us you haven't been getting laid without telling us..." Flynn snipped while rolling his eyes at Lisbeth. "How fucking quickly, you forget you were young once and needed practice. Oooooh wait, that's now. Are you not also struggling with your position?" he taunted her, his eyes deepening their gaze toward her. "Why don't you go slog a hog, and I'll work with her, mmmkay?" He waved at her to signal she was no longer needed in our presence. I watched as she snarled at him, then slinked off.

"Thanks, but she's not wrong. It shouldn't be this hard. I'm trying my best." I plopped my wolf body on to the ground with a thud.

"Get your ass up. You don't need that beautiful white fur of yours getting all dirty, and I didn't interfere for your benefit. I interfered for the pack's benefit. She doesn't get to mess with you, only I do. Now, get up," he said, pointing at the pile of mud I just landed in. I scowled and lifted my body from the mud, stepping away from him. I shook out my fur and flung mud everywhere. Once cleaned off, I rejoined him.

“If this came easy, it wouldn’t be taught at a military school as its own year long course. Stop beating yourself up.” He looked me in the eyes then, seriousness and love emitting from them. “Maybe the problem is you’re trying too hard; you’re fighting natural instincts and trying to force something that should be like breathing. How about this... you hunt me for a while, and we will see how it goes.”

Three hours later, I finally succeeded. I pounced on Flynn as if he were my real prey. He had no clue which direction I was even stalking from. “YESSSS, Queen! We will make a hunter out of you yet!” It was the happiest I’d felt in a long time.

“Excellent,” I heard a husky male voice, ricocheting off the trees that surrounded us. Kolter, in all his smug handsome-faced glory, clapped as he stepped forward in his human form. “Now, if you can do that every time, we would have a successful female alpha to be proud of.” I know it wasn’t intended, but the words stung when they hit. All I wanted was to not be a liability and make them all proud of me.

Later that morning, as we were approaching the start of the trail for our run, Kolter began speaking. “Hey guys, our first course test out is in two weeks. I want to start training harder for that. Ever, you’ve been doing better keeping up on the run and working diligently on stealth hunting, so keep working hard. Lisbeth, I know how rocky it was for you to confront your natural instincts when the positions changed. You've come so far, and I'm so proud of you for doing so gracefully." He made his way around the group, stopping to give us feedback on the most important aspects of our training. It was nice to hear that he'd taken notice on our improvements.

"The course this year consists of three parts," Kolter continued. "One part is the timed five-mile run. We have that down, I'm sure of it. I'm confident no matter what time they give us to complete it in, we will succeed. We're faster than the other packs and prides. They have to make the time limit achievable for everyone," he said, as he walked around our group filling us in.

It was midday now and the sun was peeking through the trees. The warmth of summer was just starting to warm our fur as we all listened to Kolter explain our trial.

"The second part is the hunt. We will be given our chance to track the Molti pride, and we will need to hunt them for a period of time determined by the professors. If we lose contact with them and are unsuccessful at capturing their pride, we lose the course, no matter how well we would have done at any of the other parts. The third part is evasion. We will need to try and evade the Molti pride and remain hidden. I'd like today to break into two groups. One group will hunt, the other will evade. We will go back and forth as many times as we can between now and Professor DeMarcus's class. Understood?" The pack seemed to appreciate the change in pace. We began tracking skills labs in Professor Monaghan's class two weeks ago, so getting hands-on experience should help me solidify the techniques.

"You got a second?" Assata asked me, stepping away from the group. I nodded and followed her a little further down the path. "Cailleach asked that I give you this." She was holding a small, sealed envelope. Intriguing.

"Did she say what it was for or what it was in regard to?" I asked softly.

She shrugged. "Your guess is as good as mine." She turned around and headed back up the hill, rejoining the pack. I looked back down to the envelope in my hand and saw no markings on the outside. Looking up to make sure I had a moment of privacy; I opened the envelope to find a small white index card. The only thing on it appeared in the top right corner. *Keep reading.* I flipped the card over to scan it. Nothing was written there. Opening the envelope again, I scanned it and found it empty. Stumped, I put the index card back inside the envelope and tucked it into my bag. As I went to close the bag, my eyes caught on the journal of the Hadlick woman. Perhaps the librarian felt there was something in the journal that could help answer some of my unsolved questions.

I rejoined the pack at the top of the hill. Kolter took a moment and broke us into two equal groups, and we began the process of testing each other's strengths and weaknesses. For hours we ran the drills until it was time to head in for class. Hunting and evading was an enjoyable experience all around. I think the pack really found a stride toward the end on all accounts. I knew I shouldn't say it was fun; we were supposed to be learning tactical ways to survive and capture, but when it's done as practice with your new family, it isn't that bad.

An hour later, I found myself seated in my normal seat between Priya and Flynn in Professor DeMarcus' class. "Good morning class. I'd like to start by saying the assessments that you took earlier this week were quite extraordinary! I'm incredibly pleased to see you have taken a serious approach to your education," the professor raved as she stood behind her desk at the head of the classroom. "Today, we begin to shift our focus to what we know about the differences between Lycanthropy, Manticopy, and of course, Therianthropy. Who can tell me these words and how they correlate?"

Looking around the room, everyone seemed uninterested, or as if they didn't know the answer to Professor DeMarcus' question, so against better judgment, I found myself raising my hand. I'd been working hard these past months to absorb as much knowledge as I could about my new environment and the ways of the continent. I wanted to prove to myself I'd learned.

"Yes! Everelle, please enlighten the class on the topics of Lycanthropy, Manitcopy, and Therianthropy."

"Lycanthropy is the study of the human ability to shape shift into a wolf; some people also refer to us as werewolves, but that's historically a different species. Manticopy is the study of how a human can shift into a lion, thus the prides here in this room, and then lastly, Therianthropy is the study of how humans can shift... into whatever they'd like. Human to human is the most common for that type and also the most dangerous," I said, eyes dropping to my paper.

"You are absolutely right, Everelle. Human-to-Human shifting is against the law in Siochan. Why is that, Xolani?" she asked, turning the classroom's attention to the young lion and king of the Ade pride up front. He cleared his throat. "Because, if a human can walk in another human's skin, there is no determining which person, the true human or the one who presented itself as that human, was present during specific occurrences."

"Indeed, and has there been a specific occurrence that transpired to make this law come into effect?" She was baiting the classroom. She wanted us to know.

"Yes, the prime minister in 1286, ma'am." Xolani said.

"Exactly. Please continue." She gave him the floor to finish the lesson for her. All eyes were attentive and pinned to him. I could feel his stress as he looked at Professor DeMarcus. He began speaking, stuttering slightly on his words. Little beads of sweat speckled across his brow.

"In 1286 the Prime Minister of Baroque passed a law by executive order that stated only those with the chosen ability of Therianthropy could serve in the government and run for the position of Prime Minister. This caused unrest amongst the other shifters in the country. They thought that the prime minster must have passed this executive order under duress or that he himself was being mimicked, thus creating a fraudulent law. The citizens of Baroque were convinced he had been captured and a Therianthrope must have taken his place. No such claim has ever been substantiated, nor was the law overturned. Once the news that Baroque would turn to a more dictatorial-style governmental system, an uprising happened in Martichora, causing it to dismantle and assert its independence from Baroque, thus creating Siochan. To this day, we still live in a democratic form of government, and there are no documented Therianthropes among the other shifters on this continent."

"Thank you. Xolani, you are most helpful." She concluded the lesson with that and dismissed us.

"You really think there have been no signs of Therianthropes on the continent since 1286?" I leaned over to Priya, whispering.

"That's what's been said," she shrugged. "In my short lifetime I've never so much as heard that name, much less seen any. The Chosen, as we call them, stick to themselves across the ocean."

She stood then, packing her bag. Following suit, I began packing my bag when I felt Kolter through the line, *Fix your face. I don't like it when you worry.* I looked up to see him grinning at me from the door of the classroom. My heart erratically raced. It wasn't fair that he was so damn good-looking. The other men had to feel like it was an unfair advantage from God above.

At least he is nice to look at. I chuckled to myself as I began trudging down the stairs.

That's my girl, also not bad to look at. I heard him say with a slight chuckle as he looped his arm over my shoulder, preparing to leave the classroom. I stopped for a second, curious to know if I'd sent that down the line. I hadn't thought I did... I guess I must have. I was *his* girl... he'd said. My heart beamed with pride, the smile never falling from my face as I gathered my belongings to leave.

Later, I found myself sitting in the sun on the sparring fields. I stretched my legs and leaned back on my arms. I was watching some of the men grapple among themselves in the circle. Since the first day of sparring when Baraka had taken issue with my presence, there hadn't been any issues. It seemed that the Molti pride had remained civil and heeded Kolter's warnings.

"Everelle, you're up," Professor Monaghan called out. Hesitantly, as my heart pounded in my chest, I stood and began walking toward the circle. I hadn't been in a match-up with an actual lion yet. Since I'd shifted, I'd only practiced with our pack. I'd watched the other men and women spar while in class, but today would be my first time. Closing my eyes, I envisioned myself shifting. I'd gotten better and faster at shifting, but I still wasn't as quick as the others. I unfortunately had to still visualize it. Kolter promised it would become like second nature soon enough.

I began to soften my body, to allow it slack to reform itself. Hyper focused on my limbs, I imagined them strong and powerful, with the paws of a wolf. Within seconds, I was now standing tall and strong on four large white paws. I entered the circle and zeroed in on Kolter's voice down the line.

You're up against Nalea. She's a tough competitor, but she is a first-year like you, so experience could be an equalizer. Stick to basic maneuvers until the time is right and you've worn her down. I nodded, listening to the feedback and advice he gave me from the sidelines. *Keep focused and you'll do great. Prides are made typically of one male lion as the sole king. All the others under him are female, so the odds of you fighting a female, if ever it came to that, are higher than a male.*

Nalea entered the ring and exploded forward, shifting midair and landing swiftly on her four paws. She gave me a loud snarl, mashing her teeth together as she growled.

Alright... another kitty with a bad attitude, I can do this... I just have to wear her down.

Ha, as if! You're not getting me anywhere on my back, you filthy mutt. Eyes glued forward, I slinked lower, cowering mere feet above the ground. A pull toward Nalea began to stretch across the vast space between us in the circle. A slight tug of internal urgency. I didn't have the time to analyze that right now; I needed my mind clear and to be focused on this match. She mimicked my movements as we danced around the circle... Staring her directly in the eyes, I could sense her unease with my vision locked on her, and for just a moment she adjusted her eyes, looking toward her pride. That was all it took. I swung full force, hard and fast. The impact at which my paw hit the left side of her face radiated through my body, and I felt the gasps from across the circle. Her head went with the force of my swing, resulting in her feet tripping on themselves as she was carried with the momentum of my power. Shaking her head, she growled loudly and pounced without even waiting to make sure her target was calculated right. She landed inches short of me, her target. She'd managed to bite my ear upon her faulted approach, ripping the top half of it off of my head, leaving what remained hanging in pieces. The pain became blinding, but I didn't let her best me. I took off, lunging for her back. Upon impact, we tussled to the ground. We became a dust cloud of claws and teeth. Both of us growled deep and throaty as we refused to let the other succeed in pinning their prey. Soaked in my own blood, a fuse was lit. I wasn't allowing this woman to think she had the upper hand. My pack would see my strength. The blind swipes of my paws connected in succession. The power, rendered her unconscious, and she fell to the floor. I looked up in that moment to see proud expressions plastered across my pack's faces, Flynn's the largest, as he clapped.

I'd competed in my first sparring match with a lion...and won. Pride didn't even begin to describe my euphoria. No longer feeling like a weak link, I began exiting the circle so I could re-shift, when someone grabbed my hindquarters.

Sharp claws penetrated deeply into my muscle and tissue and threw my body backward. *You don't get to turn your back on a pride royal, get the fuck back here!*

You were down, fair and square... I don't owe you anything. In this circle, it's fair, or not at all! I snarled. We began pacing each other again. Our eyes were locked on each other, both of us determined to outlast each other and not break.

"That's time!" announced Professor Monaghan. "For those who were victorious today, excellent work. For those that landed on your back, practice more. Nalea, for future reference, please refrain from attacking once you're pinned and your opponent is leaving the circle," his voice radiated toward us, falling flat as if unimpressed by her behavior.

With the crowds breaking up, Nalea and I refused to leave the circle. I wouldn't turn my back on her again. Not out of respect, but for my own protection. She played dirty, and I wouldn't let her get me again.

"You need to drop it, ladies. Now," Kolter's voice came through the circle.

Neo and Baraka stepped forward. "Nalea, come!" At this, her head dropped and she turned her body to begin her exit. The deep growl she emitted told me she wasn't happy about it either.

"You ok?" Kolter asked as I stepped out of the circle, shifting effortlessly, holding on to my ear, to make sure it would return to its proper place. "That may need to be seen by medical," he said, reaching up to examine my ear.

"I hate that she bested me. I should take it as a lesson to never turn my back on a 'teammate'," I scoffed.

"You should never turn your back on anyone," Victor said. "That's a hard pill to swallow. However, you still pinned her honestly first. Excellent job overall for your first match."

Evening fell, and I was pissed I'd spent the better part of the afternoon in the hospital wing getting my ear sewn back on.

I wanted to be alone with my thoughts. Sitting at my desk, I picked up the journal and my bag and headed outside for fresh air. Sitting by the lake on my favorite bench, I reopened the Hadlick mother's journal. After the note from the librarian, I couldn't shake that I was missing something, but I only had four more entries. Opening the journal, I flipped toward the back of the book to find the dates in question.

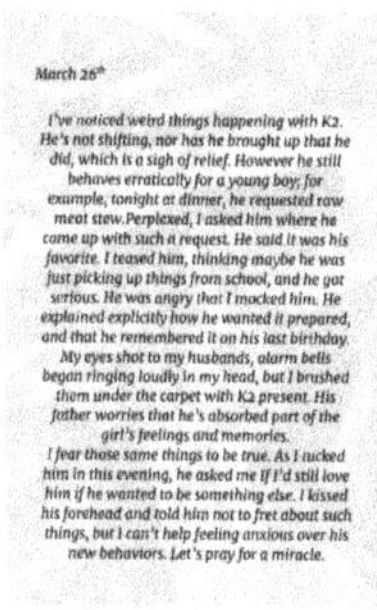

March 26th

I've noticed weird things happening with K2. He's not shifting, nor has he brought up that he did, which is a sigh of relief. However he still behaves erratically for a young boy; for example, tonight at dinner, he requested raw meat stew.Perplexed, I asked him where he come up with such a request. He said it was his favorite. I teased him, thinking maybe he was just picking up things from school, and he got serious. He was angry that I mocked him. He explained explicitly how he wanted it prepared, and that he remembered it on his last birthday. My eyes shot to my husbands, alarm bells began ringing loudly in my head, but I brushed them under the carpet with K2 present. His father worries that he's absorbed part of the girl's feelings and memories.

I fear those same things to be true. As I tucked him in this evening, he asked me if I'd still love him if he wanted to be something else. I kissed his forehead and told him not to fret about such things, but I can't help feeling anxious over his new behaviors. Let's pray for a miracle.

April 8th,

K2 got sent home from school today... It's the first week of school, and he was sent home. Someone in class called lions a disgusting race, and K2 beat him bloody. He screamed that the child shouldn't talk about his family like that. I don't understand. We are wolves. I worry that when her blood mixed with his, it caused a horrible reaction. I will need to go back to the farm to see if the girl is doing as well as can be. I can only hope for signs that she isn't regressing and will be ok.

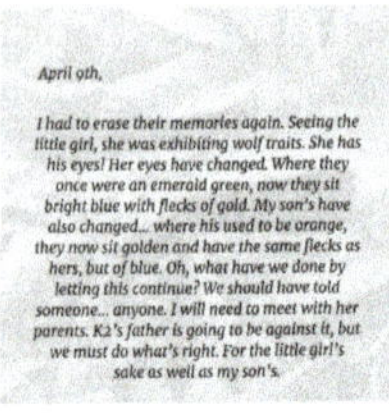

April 9th,

I had to erase their memories again. Seeing the little girl, she was exhibiting wolf traits. She has his eyes! Her eyes have changed. Where they once were an emerald green, now they sit bright blue with flecks of gold. My son's have also changed… where his used to be orange, they now sit golden and have the same flecks as hers, but of blue. Oh, what have we done by letting this continue? We should have told someone… anyone. I will need to meet with her parents. K2's father is going to be against it, but we must do what's right. For the little girl's sake as well as my son's.

April 10th,

We met with the little girl's father just outside of Tuathanas, while he rode a large red plow over the grain fields. He now knows who we are and why we wanted to meet with him and his wife. He refused us. He didn't take what we had to say well. He told us to get the hell off his property. He considers us liars. He behaved as if we were crazy by saying his daughter was a hybrid child. He accused us of slander and provocation. I pleaded with him to help his daughter see what she truly was, and to keep in contact should she develop worsening symptoms, but he refused. He chased us away with a pitchfork. My husband said we did all we could, but our priority was to our son. I hope God watches over that little one. She needs it.

Closing the journal, I froze. My father was the only grain farmer on the edge of Tuathanas. He was the only farmer in Tuathanas with a plow of that depiction. *Oh my God, that child couldn't be me, could it?* Quickly, I gathered the journal and raced back inside the den. Fueled with anxiety and unease, I rushed through the maze of illuminating minerals and halted in front of Kolter's room. Frantically I began banging on the door, begging him to open it.

Nikita opened the door, looking irritated, like I'd interrupted something. Looking over her shoulder, Kolter was getting up off the bed. *Oh, this was too much.* I turned and ran back out of the den, ignoring their calls for me to wait. I ran back up into the fresh air. Seeing the stars and moon, I knew I could breathe again. Taking in a deep breath, I smelled the forest coming to life. Pine, water from the lake, moss growing on the decaying stumps— I saw it all. My ears pricked to the left, and the snapping of twigs under heavy feet alerted me that I wasn't alone.

I shifted, on the spot, for the first time, and I was able to shift in the blink of an eye without thinking about it. Looking toward the East, I bolted without looking back. I ran forward, pushing my legs at full speed. I raced up the mountainside watching as the black obsidian turned to sediment. I kept running down into valleys, meeting up with a brook that matriculated into a lake. Despite not knowing where I was going, I pressed on, allowing instinct to take me where I'd find enough clarity to work through what I'd just witnessed. I ran until I couldn't feel the lines of my pack anymore. I ran until I couldn't sense the school anymore, and even then, I continued to run. Morning broke the skyline before I finally stopped. Exhaustion was taking over me completely. I began to walk forward, toward a small river through the woods. I bent over to drink the water and revel in its refreshment. I felt its coolness wash over my broken, burnt nerves. Once I was sated, I found a small cove hidden amongst the branches of a fallen tree, gingerly I crawled in and collapsed. Only then did I start crying. I'd done exactly what Flynn had accused me of. Exactly what I'm known for. I gave up. I didn't even stop to fight or get clarification. I wasn't worthy of the alpha title, clearly. Nikita had always wanted it; she should have it now. I wallowed in self-pity, there beneath the roots of the fallen tree on the water's edge a day's run from my new life. I couldn't help feeling like my entire world just crashed on me in one fell swoop.

Chapter Twenty

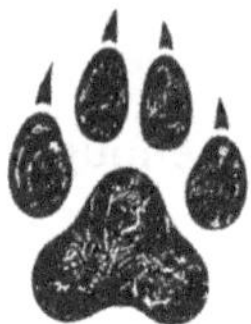

Kolter

Son of a fucking bitch!!! I punched the side of the rock wall we were facing. I turned, shaking my hand out, and kicked at a large dead stump. "What the fuck do we do now?" I pleaded, my voice raw and fueled with hurt. I was out of ideas. Nikita, Victor and I'd been running all night, and we still hadn't found Everelle or caught so much as her scent. In hindsight, should I have allowed my beta to follow my emotional ass though the woods in the middle of the night in search of my alpha female? Sure, as shit not. But we were hours from the den, and smack dab in the middle of bum fuck.

"I suggested that we head back, three times now, but your stubborn ass won't head my mental clarity. We should head back and send the next party out to look. Who knows, maybe she just doesn't want to be found by *you,*" Victor said, shrugging his shoulders. His eyes were bloodshot. He'd been pushing himself all night for something that quite literally had nothing to do with him, but he couldn't help it. It's just who Victor was. He was a fixer and he didn't like the thoughts of Nikita and I going alone, not after we were the reason she left to begin with, and Flynn is much too callous in these types of situations, he would surely make it worse. *Fuck you and your stupid fucking ideas Nikita!*

She stopped walking and cocked her head back at me. "I can still hear you, dumb fuck." She barred her teeth at me in a growl. "In case you forgot, it was *you* who asked for help in there. Not me! I agreed to help you, not make her think I fucked you!" Nikita now stood with a face of pure disgust.

"Why were you in your room anyway?" Victor asked. "You quite literally could have been anywhere else. It's like you were using a neon sign directing her to see you. Seems like you were just asking for it to blow up miserably in your face." He shook his head, then stretched his hind legs and plopped down for a rest.

"You all don't think I know that? You don't think I've been kicking myself in the ass all night for how fucking stupid I looked. I'm in deep, and I need help fixing it. I've never cared for anyone, the way I care for her, and I'll be damned if I lose her now." I was too; I was hurting. I'd successfully made it twenty years without so much as liking a female for more than just a night or two. Everelle has been the only person to make me feel this...shitty and happy all at once.

"Then I suggest we head back. Who knows, maybe she's already back, and we're too far from the others for them to communicate," Nikita said. "For what it's worth, I am sorry. I didn't know she was so sensitive, or I wouldn't even have agreed to help." She looked genuine.

"UGH!" Screaming into the vast forest was doing no amount of good. They were right; we should turn back. I just don't understand how we found no trace on her at all. We were mere steps behind her... then she was gone without any scent lingering. She had to be out here somewhere!

"Alright, let's head back. The sooner we get home, the sooner I can come back to find her," I sighed in defeat. Shifting back to my wolf form, I took the lead, racing through the woods, back to a place I knew she wasn't going to be, quite literally running with my tail between my legs. I was done.

Chapter Twenty-One

Everelle

It was midday before I finally felt the sun warm my nose. I'd been asleep for hours tucked into the little canopy of branches and leaves. Stretching out, I yawned and shook my head, looking down. Jumping backwards, with my heart pounding in my chest, I closed my eyes and opened them again. Looking at my paws, I noticed they weren't the right shape... I was still white... But where I used to have paws as big as a truck tire, shaped like a diamond, I now looked at softer, more rounded paws, smaller than they'd previously been.

What the fuck? I thought as I walked carefully back down to the river. I closed my eyes, pointed my face toward the sky, and prayed to God that this was a crazy dream. I then turned my face back down to the water and slowly opened my eyes. *HOLY SHIT.* This could not be happening right now. I tapped the water, erasing the image, then waited on bated breath for it to slowly still. Looking again, I winced. *It was totally happening.* I now adorned the face of the animal I'd grown to despise. How in the absolute...

I heard voices then. My ears perking up, I began crouching by the water, heart racing, panic rising in my throat. I turned my head and listened. *Damn, this hearing is TERRIBLE.* Still crouching, I began stepping slowly and quietly forward, trying to calm myself with each small breath I allowed my lungs to pull in. I inched toward the direction of the voices. I was careful not to pick my head up too far, to not lift it over the tree I'd slept inside just moments ago, lest they see me.

"I'm telling you; another lion was here. I smell it." *Oh God, oh God... What do I do?* Slowly, I began backing away, softly retracing my steps back down the small hill that separated me and whomever was on the other side. I was a white lion; there's no chance I'd blend in with anything. Looking around, there was nowhere at all to hide. If I bolted, they may hear me, and I'd be in trouble. If I stayed, they could round the hillside and find me still.

Why did I act so foolishly last night? I couldn't just stay outside, throw my pity party by the lake, and then return inside the nice, safe den... Nope, that would have been too easy. Instead of me slamming my door in Kolter's face and ignoring him like a petty bitch, I decided the best course of action was to run away, like a whiny schoolgirl, and somehow change into a fucking LION. I was screwed. *UGH* I was about to be a dead bitch if I didn't stop spiraling. *What's worse is that right now, I'm not even a bitch. I'm a pussy... Ugh fuck you, Flynn.* He was to blame for this newfound inappropriately timed sense of humor.

Looking around again, I saw a large tree had been knocked over some time ago. Noticing the fallen branches and over grown moss and rocks, I thought it would be as good as any place d to hide me. I began to slowly back further away from the hill in the direction of the stump, just as the voices carried clearer over the hill.

"See!! I knew I was right, there it is!!" came the voice of a younger man. "She's white too!!" Frozen in shock, I didn't know what to do. I was caught in the wide-open clearing of the forest. Baring my teeth, I began to crouch forward slightly, never taking my eyes from the two men that crested the hill, staring at me in awe. A deep growl hung in my throat, elongating the threat I was trying to convey.

"I don't think she's one of them. She doesn't look like any of the lions we've ever tracked," a second voice piped in. The way in which he spoke was as if he didn't think I had ears to hear his queries.

"Let me see!" came the third voice. This time, I saw a young woman come into focus as she appeared over the hill, her eyes a deep emerald green, her hair soft, curly, and brown. She looked so much like my mother that it hurt. "Oh, she's beautiful. I agree, I've never seen a kind like her. Her fur is atypical for the prides we have in this area."

"Should we tag her?" the older of the two men asked. Tag me? I didn't know what that meant, and I most certainly didn't want to stick around to find out. I crouched lower, my eyes narrowing to make myself understood that my deep growl meant I would ruin them if they so much as approached me.

"No," she looked me deeply in the eyes, as if reading my soul. I was still standing there, crouching in fear. "I know she will be missed very much by someone if she doesn't go home. I just hope she knows how truly rare and special she is. Not even The Chosen can choose to mimic an animal with white fur. Only the highest in the magical clans are born with it, and though she looks like one, her confidence isn't there. Who knows, maybe someday we will hear of an amazingly talented white lion. The sector doesn't need to be tracking her." She winked at me, something neither of the men caught. Feeling an overwhelming sense of gratitude for the woman, I nodded my head to her, my attempt at showing gratitude for sparing me, before turning and bolting back toward Askari. The woman had given me so much more to think about, and I needed to get clarity from the only people I could trust. My pack.

The journey back took less time than the previous day. I spent the entire time replaying the conversation I overheard and the journal entries in my head. I was unsure how my pack would take it when I expressed that I could change into a manticore or what would even happen to me once they knew. I shook the thoughts from my mind. In the meantime, I knew, once back, Kolter and I would have to go see the pack of Hadlick wolves in Seoid. I was certain they would be the only people who could shed some light on what I was going through.

Dusk was settling in when I finally found myself stepping onto the mountain that housed our den. I shifted back to my human form and began the final ascent to the entrance, just as Kolter, Baldur, and Flynn were exiting. Kolter's eyes were on the ground, then, as if he smelled me, they flew up and met mine with a burning passion. He stopped walking and just stared at me. We were so close we could reach out and touch each other, but yet so far that no one knew what to say first.

"So, how was your pity party?" Flynn asked, stepping forward. "Get a good cry out?"

I slugged him directly into his jaw, breaking both the tension and my hand. "FUCK FLYNN! That hurt!!" I bent over, holding my hand between my legs.

"Well shit, babe, that just sucks, doesn't it? You know, come to think of it, it just TICKLED me," he quipped, motioning toward his face, his mouth agape.

Staring at him now, as he spit out a tooth, I laughed. I laughed so hard tears escaped my eyes and continued until the hysterics took over. All three men just stood there watching me, unsure exactly what to do or say. They nodded and gestured between each other, silently urging each other to do something. When that didn't work, the idiots began a round of rock, paper, scissors.

"Stop trying to figure out who is going to pacify me." I shot them a scowl. "You! I'm pissed at you," I said, pointing to Flynn. "For always saying the wrong shit at the wrong time. You've practically rewired my brain to immediately say and think the wrong shit. People literally think I'm crazy because I can't pull it off like you can!" I was steaming now. I heard a snicker from behind me, and my blood boiled. I snapped to the side, and my eyes and nostrils flared with a fury I'd expected to feel toward him. "And you! I'm hurt by you!" I said, looking directly into Kolter's eyes. "You said you'd always be there for me... And you weren't. You're an asshole. It's always something with you, and I'm tired of it. Stop being a prick." I saw in the corner of my eye the movement in which Baldur tried to slowly creep away from my wrath. "And you!" I said, finally rotating to Baldur. He waved his hand, cutting me off before I could think of why I was mad at him.

"Whoa, whoa, whoa," he said, holding up his hands and beginning to back away. "I didn't do anything. In fact, I hardly do anything at all. I was dragged from my bed to be out here!"

"Fine... I guess you're safe," I huffed, rolling my eyes.

"But I'm guessing I'm not?" My head whipped toward the mouth of the den. Nikita was walking out, looking smug. Suddenly the way she wore such a tight, revealing shirt and too-high heeled boots made me want to throw her off the closest bridge. No wonder Kolter fell for her. How can a girl like me compete with the looks of that? "Glad to see you're back in one piece. Where did you go? We couldn't track you." *Oh, because you truly cared about me, whatever,* I thought to myself, my anger rising even further. I wanted to rip her throat out.

"You're a fucking bitch! I trusted you. I thought you had my back. I thought you were my friend!!" I snarled, walking briskly toward her.

"Oh honey, but I am." She said extravagantly. Making a show of it as she mocked bowing to me. Her smug smile never left her face. I was going to hit her.

"A friend doesn't sleep with another friend's mate!" I gritted my teeth; I was seconds away from shifting and ripping her half-shaved head clearly off her shoulders. "He's MINE!" I screamed inches from her face. It took all I had not to punch her.

"Stop, you're embarrassing yourself." She said, stepping backward, away from me, "I don't want him... trust me. You can have his dopey ass."

"Oh, I can have him? Like you won the fucking right to gift him to me?" The slap both caught her off guard and turned her gaze sickly at me. She deserved worse.

I watched as her face ticked, turning back toward me. Stalking now. Her words turned to venom as she tried to hold it together. "I am only going to say this once, and I'll forgive the slap, because if roles were reversed, you'd be on the ground missing some hair by now." She stepped back into my bubble, and I had to admit, my anger began to subside, only to be replaced with a little bit of fear. "I was helping Kolter! Last night, in his room, I was helping him!" The way she screamed it made me instantly regret everything from the last eighteen hours. I dropped my eyes to the ground, then to Kolter, then finally back to Nikita. Her eyes were softening now, but her face still had a pretty significant red mark. My stomach churned as she continued. "The idiot was trying to infuse his rubix into something for your ungrateful ass as a gift and couldn't get it to stick." She must have felt the blood begin to trickle down from her nose, because she brought her fingers to it. Pulling them away, she dropped her eyes to them, then back to mine, her anger still very much present. "Make no mistake, that slap will be the only hit you get on me. Ever." She reached into her pocket, revealing a necklace with a rough-cut yellow stone encrusted onto a white gold chain. It was set inside a beautiful oval, woven with diamonds. "I expect you want the whine ass to have this still?" she said, glancing at Kolter. In her hand swung the necklace. I felt like the biggest asshole. How had I misconstrued the situation so badly?

"I'll take it," Kolter said, reaching out and snatching it from her hand. His sunken eyes still bore heat as he stared into the depths of mine.

Noticing she had nothing left to say, Nikita headed back inside without a second glance.

"Well... would you just look at the time? Baldur, I do think it's time for some tea, wouldn't you agree?" Flynn asked, his wide eyes blinking rapidly toward Baldur.

"Oh yeah... tea," he agreed, then leaned in closer to Flynn, dropping his voice lower, but not low enough for me not to hear. "That's just code for us leaving, though, right? I don't have to actually drink tea?"

With a heavy sigh, Flynn dropped his head into his hands. "You're sooo lucky you found a mate already. Good lord, sir." He faced Baldur and thrust his hands in the direction of the den. "Come on, come on, let's go." Baldur, finally getting the hint, turned and headed back toward the den door. "Ugh, and you think I need to learn to read a room." Rolling his eyes, Flynn left the two of us alone.

The woods were quiet, the sun slowly rimming the edges of the tree line as it began its daily descent from the sky. I sighed deeply. How had I read the situation so wrong?

"You didn't trust me. It's not that you read it wrong," Kolter began, throwing weight behind his words. "You just didn't trust me enough to not expect the worst. I don't know if I'm more hurt that you feel that way or pissed at myself, because obviously I've given you reasons to doubt my loyalty to you."

"It's not that. While the situation was compromising, I had enough uncertainty rolling around in my head that I couldn't think straight. It's easier for me to run from my fear than face it." I was a coward. Flynn had warned me that I do this, and I'd felt attacked and offended, and yet, I still did it. I ran the first chance I had.

"I'm going to need you to trust me. If we are to ever work as a bonded pair, we have to rely on the fact that we each will have one another's back over anyone else. Fuck, we have to have each other's backs over our own pack. You don't bond with a pack, you bond with a mate, and wolves bond for life. So, whatever you are struggling with, whatever doubt you have, we have to work through it. I can't spend another night chasing you through the woods, begging for you to stop, to turn around, to face me and listen to me... not again. It was hell." I could see it then, him staring at me, his shoulders dropped and face looking full of misery. He wouldn't hurt me. Not intentionally at least.

"What does it truly mean to be a bonded pair? No one has really told me," I asked nervously, my eyes failing to meet his. I didn't want him to think I was asking out of insecurity based on the events that led us to this discussion.

He sighed, rubbing his face before sliding them back through his hair. "Look at me, Everelle. I need to make sure you hear this and understand it," he said softly. My heart began to beat rapidly again.

I looked up slowly, meeting his eyes that were brimmed with red from a combination of not sleeping and worry. The pain I caused him caused my stomach to flip.

"It means I choose you. Over anyone in my entire life. Parents, friends, pack mates, future children, anyone. I. Choose. You." He emphasized the last few words with a fist that he tapped against his other hand. "When you're given your positions in the pack, the alpha takes personality and qualifications into account when making the pairs. Most of the time you're never given an option. You get what you get, and you don't throw a fit. If you don't like your mate, well, you sure as hell better figure it out, because most alphas won't rotate a pack once they've been selected. Once you've received your mate, a shift happens. It's usually after your first physical mating session. A connection so strong and powerful links you together. It's more powerful than a piece of paper humans get when they marry. It's biologically engineered to link the two wolves together for eternity. If one of the wolves happens to pass, the other will never have another mate. It's fated. It's why having sex for us is so strong and powerful. It's not something to take lightly. Nikita and my brother thankfully never bonded physically. Otherwise, she'd be struggling more than ever right now. It's why Baldur and Lisbeth couldn't be broken up. They're bonded from last year. It's why I haven't... I just worry you're..."

"You worried about me?" I asked, cautiously. "Why? I've shifted; I can handle myself now. I'm no longer as much of a liability." Although I didn't know if that was entirely true. I'd run at first instinct. If something like this happens outside of Askari, how could I be trusted? How could anyone trust me to be their alpha if I was always thinking the worst and reacting before getting all the information?

"You think I worry about you solely because of a physicality? Like you're just another pack member, and it's my job to?" He shook his head and walked toward me; the frustration was emitting from him as if steam was coming off a hot body on a chilly morning. "I don't just worry about you because you're my pack mate, Ever, I worry about you because you're *mine*. I feel you as clearly as I feel myself. Whether we've physically bonded or not, the very blood rushing through my veins *feels* like you. Fuck, my bed *smells* like you. Your hair is on my pillowcase, and I've refused to move it for three nights because it's where you slept." He was close now, close enough to wrap me in his arms and never let me go, but he didn't. He didn't bridge the gap. He just dropped his body, so he was directly in front of me, eye to eye. "Maybe I'll stop worrying about you when I've run out of reasons to." At that moment, he reached for me, grabbing the back of my neck and back, and pulling me against his body. I looked up, and he began gently caressing my neck with the pad of his thumb. "You have completely captivated me, Everelle, and I'll be damned if I lose you." His lips met mine then, gently at first, soft light kisses, that melted my core. Running my hands up his strong back, I dug my nails in gently, causing him to arch his back and release a deep moan, breaking our kiss. He looked down at me now, eyes emitting more than just hunger.

"I had this made for you. You both kind of spoiled it, but nonetheless, it's yours, and I'd love nothing more than for you to wear it," He reached back into his pocket and pulled out the necklace. Hanging it in front of me, I saw a yellow and blue speckled stone, about the size of a large coin. It sat embedded in twisted white gold strands, cradling smaller diamond stones, creating a teardrop shape. It hung on a delicate looking white gold chain. It was beautiful. I felt my eyes well with tears. "This is my rubix. It's an infused stone that helps calm my nerves. I've never been without it. In fourteen years, it's never left my person. Well, until Nikita stole it, but she gave it back the next day. Now, it's yours. I want you to feel the calming nature of it when you need it most."

"What about you? What if you need it?" He began putting it around my neck. Tenderly brushing his fingers over my collarbone, he followed the chain back down to the rubix, which sat gently nestled into my bust.

"I have you. I don't need this anymore, not when I have you." Without hesitation, I leaned up on my toes and kissed him. This time, with passion and power. I fully took his mouth to mine, ravenous. Opening my mouth, I relished his tongue as it darted from his mouth, stroking mine with just the right amount of pressure to make my knees buckle. Heat began to fill my core, pulsing as if it alone was where my heart lived. I gripped the front of his opened shirt tighter and felt him push me gently up against the large pine behind me.

Hunger and need took control as he dragged his fingers up my corset onto my breasts, leaving a tingling burning sensation as he went. Moans escaped my mouth, and he flicked his tongue deeper into my mouth. I lifted my legs to wrap around his firm waist and immediately gasped into his mouth. His thick shaft was hard and was pressed directly into my core. Releasing my mouth, he traveled his lips softly down, stopping first at my neck, sucking softly on it sending goosebumps and chills down my body. Little moans of ecstasy escaped my mouth as he continued forward, trailing the tip of his tongue over the tops of my bulging breasts. The pad of his thumb began to softly stroke my erect nipple budding against the leather of my corset. With bated breath, I released my legs from his waist, so I was standing in front of him. I began to run my fingers just under the waist band of his pants, gently at first, then with more urgency. Kolter threw his head back toward the sky as he growled.

"Wait...wait. I don't want you to rush into this. Bonding is a serious thing, and I don't want you to regret being chained to me for eternity," he said, huskily.

"There will never be a time in my life I'd ever regret being bonded to you," I said sincerely.

Moving my hand further, I popped his button, and with one swift motion, his zipper was pulled apart next, exposing his bulging cock inside his boxers, stretched to their capacity. I ran my fingers through the band around his hard, warm pelvis. He groaned, louder this time. Dropping his mouth again to mine, he devoured me completely, sweeping his tongue fast and hard over mine, the strokes mimicking what I began doing to him with my hand. I could feel the urgency beginning to rise with every breath he took. Now more certainly than ever, I needed to break our kiss and dropped to a squat.

Squatting in front of him, I stared up at him; his eyes burned back at me, and his hard dripping dick was inches from my face. I grinned and slowly slid him into my mouth, never breaking eye contact. He stiffened and rolled his eyes back in pure ecstasy. I began running my tongue down his vein-filled shaft. I began sucking with light pressure, then tightening my mouth as I finally reached the base of him. He was breathing raggedly, and with his hands threaded through my hair, he began to thrust with every pull I made with my mouth. His fingers tightened in my hair, and his thighs flexed under my hands as I used them for support. I was completely devouring him. His groans became louder. "Oh my God, Ever...oh my God." He looked down at me again, and it was all it took. In an instant a hot, thick liquid filled my mouth. I knew I'd won this round. I sucked every last bit of him out until he stopped moving and went slightly limp in my mouth.

Only then did I wipe my mouth and chin and stand to face him. The hunger continued to burn as I looked into his eyes. Reaching for my face, he traced my chin with his thumb. "You are the most incredible woman I've ever met." He dropped his hands then, to my waist, flicking open my leather pants and slowly began to drag them down my slim hips. Realizing what he was doing, I stopped him.

"Wait...we can't do this out here!" I looked around hoping we were alone. "You never know who is out here. We could get caught."

"Ever, you just quite literally blew me away with complete disregard to your surroundings, and now that I want to reward you, you want to stop?" He chuckled in disbelief.

"I just don't want my first time to be on display." I burned with embarrassment.

He considered this for a moment. Then nodding, he slowly adjusted my pants. Then he moved to my corset, placing delicate kisses over my breasts as he made sure they were tucked in tightly. Lastly, he adjusted his rubix, making sure it was front and center, like it was an official marking of his territory.

"You are the most brilliant woman I've ever had the pleasure of knowing, and I'm thankful you're my alpha."

"Does this mean I'm your girlfriend now?" I asked coyly. Almost immediately I regretted how insecure I sounded. Asking to be his girlfriend would have been one thing, but this? I internally slapped my hand to my face.

"Princess, you're so much more than that, but if that's the label you want for it, I'm ok with it," he said, now kissing me gently on my forehead. I melted. Pulling back from me, he redressed himself, then held his hand out. "Come on, we should eat, and then you can tell me why you were excitedly banging on my door last night."

Oh! I had completely forgotten. Like a wave, all the memories from yesterday flooded back to me. "I don't think you're going to want to wait to hear what I have to say," I said, stopping on the trail back toward the den. "I learned quite a bit about myself, and once you hear it, I hope you'll agree that the best place for us to be is headed to Seoid. He nodded, and I began to fill him in.

I explained to him about the journal. Connecting it back to me as a lion cub. Letting him know that my father would have been the only farmer in Tuathanas on that particular plot of land, on the outskirts of the village near the mountains. He also was the only grain farmer with that big red plow and had a daughter—me.

"But you're a wolf, you're not a lion. So, it doesn't make a lot of sense." Kolter was pacing, back and forth, as he had been throughout most of my confession.

"Unless... I'm a lion...who can change into a wolf," I said quietly. My eyes met his with apprehension.

He stopped pacing and looked down upon me, sitting on the rocks. "Ever, whatever you read in that journal, you're latching on to as if it were you. You're trying to force connections where there aren't any, just hoping it sticks and you'll have the answers you need. Honestly, we can stop researching now that you've shifted and your access to the line has strengthened." He began, dropping into a squat as he reached for my face. "You aren't a lion, babe."

"There's more...I think you were the wolf child who shifted to save me..." He cocked his head to the side with a quizzical expression, as if he were holding onto a laugh.

"Because you and I have the same eyes." I reached into my bag then and pulled out the journal, reciting word for word what the Hadlick wolf's mother said. "You also said your mother told you that you had shifted when you were young and you got sick. The stories match." I watched his face register what I was saying with disbelief. There was a storm brewing behind his eyes.

"Regardless if that's true, you aren't a lion... you're a wolf. So, it's a moot point."

I figured I'd have to do this. Running this scenario through my head this afternoon, I came to this exact conclusion. He wouldn't take the story connection to me for what it was. He'd need to see me shift to believe it. Part of me is glad we didn't fully mate... I wouldn't want to trap him into having sex with a lion.

"I'm going to need you to remain as calm as you can and to shut the line to the pack off. Can you do that for me?" I asked him, rising and placing my bag down beside him.

"What are you doing now, Ever?" he said, looking lost.

Closing my eyes, I asked him again to close the line down before I reached inside of me like I normally did when shifting, only this time I could see in my mind two paths before me, like being in the woods and seeing the path fork up ahead. To the left, I could choose to be a lion, to the right... a pack mate, his alpha. Knowing this would be the moment to change everything, I breathed a huge sigh and raced in my mind down the left path. Without even moving from my spot, I shifted effortlessly into a lion's form.

The sheer shock on Kolter's face registered at the same time as his gasp. He was now backing away from me, shaking his head in disbelief.

"What the hell?! When did that happen?" he asked, throwing his hands up at my now shifted form. He looked sick.

Yesterday. After leaving your room, I ran into the clearing. I couldn't think straight. I could hear you approaching, and I just wanted to get away, so I shifted and ran. I didn't even know at the time that I'd changed into a lion.

"It's why I couldn't trace you," he said, now standing. His face was looking up at me with more shock and slight admiration this time. "We ran all night, and we couldn't even find your scent. I never in a million years would have followed the scent of a lion."

Shifting back to my human form, I returned to the rock and sat. Following my lead, Kolter dropped down beside me. "I think this should stay between us for now, at least until we're back from Seoid and hopefully with some answers."

"I agree, but I still don't think the writer is my mother. She has never said she was Hadlick, and I would have remembered you. I know I would have. There isn't a lifetime I could have lived where I saw your face and forgot you."

"She wiped our memories." I pulled out the journal again and handed it to him. Reading to himself, he put his own pieces together. Looking back up at me, he shut the journal.

"Then I guess we're taking a little trip home." Standing up now, he reached for my hand to pull me toward him.

"You're not disgusted with me?" I asked him, eyes dropping to the floor.

"Look at me," he said, pulling my face back up so he could meet my eyes. "There is nothing you could do, no place you could go, no form you could shift to, that would make me disgusted with you. Ever, I need you to hear me when I say this. You will always be mine. In every form. If this comes to be true, and our blood is mixed, then it wasn't just coincidence that brought us together here, it was fate. Who would I be to stand in the way of fate?" He tilted my chin back and brought his lips to mine, kissing me softly before pulling away. "In every moment I've lived since we moved to Seoid, I've always felt like something was missing from me. My mind never seemed to be able to settle on what it could be. Truly, I don't need my mother's confirmation to say that what I'm feeling is right. You exist inside of me, and I'll never be disgusted with that."

My eyes welled with tears. How could I have been so stupid and wrong? How could I have looked at this man and thought for one moment he would hurt me? In that moment I knew, I was irrevocably in love with him.

Chapter Twenty-Two

Everelle

Getting permission for us to leave school for a three-day journey was a feat. It wasn't typically allowed, especially with the course exam needing to be run in a little more than a week. Somehow, the general felt forgiving, and we were awarded the time with the promise it was educational and we would return ready for whatever was to arise. The ominous implications from the commanding officer didn't sit well with me, but Kolter ensured me we would be ok. Victor and Assata agreed they would take over our respective positions within the pack while we were gone.

In my room, I was packing my bag with the essentials that I would need. It would be a day's journey back to Seoid on foot, running in shifted form. We hoped to find our answers quickly, and then we'd come right back.

I picked up the journal I'd come to rely on for answers. I realized I'd be meeting its author soon, and it felt all too surreal. Placing it in my bag, I noticed a crease on the page toward the back that I'd never noticed before.

I pulled it back out and opened the journal to adjust the page back, worried that I'd indirectly damaged the book when I'd placed it in my bag.

While doing so, it allowed me to examine the rest of the book a little more carefully. It was bound by soft black leather. The cover boasted an imprinted image of a rose and a delicate mountain stitched into the back. Flipping it back toward the front, I studied the rose again, noticing its line work more closely. I recognized it at once... It was the same rose that was inlaid in my corset. Moving the journal away from my chest, I looked down at my corset again. The roses were mirrored images. This couldn't be a coincidence. Swiftly, I placed the journal into my bag and headed out of the den into the clearing. Kolter and I agreed to meet just outside the ridge line.

Approaching him now, I could feel the electricity between us. Knowing what we'd done earlier, a blush crept across my cheeks as I stood next to him.

"Fix your face, princess." He didn't even turn towards me. "We have a long way to run, and I can't be distracted by the things I'd much rather be doing to you."

Heat fully inflamed my body now, but all I could do was nod and try to hide my desires for him. "I'll lead the way," he said and took off.

Following in stride toward Seoid, I felt like our answers were within reach. There was so much about me that now felt foreign. What was I? How did this happen? The only thing we could do was pray that I was correct about Kolter's mom being the author, and it would bring us clarity.

It was dawn before we approached the outskirts of Seoid. "You're sure she will be here?" I asked him. Seoid was not completely unlike Tuathanas. The low valley was nestled between three large ridgelines, offering a means of protection and camouflage. The mountain ranges ran almost a complete circle around the little village. The main difference between the two villages was that Seoid produced jewels and, more importantly, colorful rubix stones much like the one I'm wearing. The stones could be infused with flesh memories, or powers, or used for ceremonial purposes. While costly, they were also rare, and therefore, the military took special interest in the protection of Seoid and its people.

"Yeah, she's here. She won't leave them." He was referring to his father and brother, who were buried far beneath the surface of Seoid. They were memorialized in time with a stone plaque, awarded for their dedication to the service of Siochan. My heart ached for her. To go through life with your soul attached to another and have that person taken. It was too hard to imagine. Worse yet, to birth a child and have them leave this world before you...what could be more unbearable?

Walking in human form through the village, we were mindful about not creating too much noise. Most of the village hadn't yet risen with the sun, and it didn't seem right to rob them of their peaceful night's sleep.

"You know, I've always thought I'd come back here with the pack. Make a life for myself, find a mate among the villagers," he began, picking my fingers up and wrapping them around his. "I thought I'd go away to college, get the training and education they expected of me, and come home, placed on one of the military lines that served to protect Seoid. I never dreamed I'd be going to school as an alpha of a pack. The pack that's here, under my namesake, they are in limbo right now. They have to wait until I'm back home before they can even plan for a future, one I have to consent to. Could you even imagine? Having to be told to wait three years before being allowed to ask your alpha, whom you'd never met, if it was ok to be bonded with someone or to figure out what position they'd actually have once the alpha returned?"

"Isn't that exactly what you're doing?" I asked him, not sure he'd even seen the connection. "You were pulled from your home and told to attend Askari for three years. It didn't matter to them that you had other plans. The Sector planned for you the day your brother left this world. You didn't get a choice. I think that's what makes you a more profound alpha. The fact that you look at everyone else and their happiness before your own." I stopped there, turning him to face me, I wanted him to see my admiration for him.

"Take, for example, the pack positions in Askari. You knew Baldur and Lisbeth wouldn't be able to find another mate, knowing how deeply they felt for each other and that they'd bonded. You kept them together without persecution. You did it for the greater good of the pack. You knew Priya was so deeply smitten with Kentaro, and that he was too shy to start anything with her. You stepped in and made that pairing too. You see people, Kolter, not for just what their positions are, but for who they truly are inside. That's what will make you the best leader you can be."

He brought his hands up to cup my face. "You are the reason I even see them. You are so incredible. Thoughtful. Intelligent. You are everything I've ever dreamed to have and more." Knowing how he felt, it warmed my soul. "We're almost there." He placed a gentle kiss on my lips and brought his hands away from my face. I immediately was left with a lingering feeling of wishing he would have left his hands where they were.

We stepped up to an industrial-looking obsidian-colored home that I found charming and reminiscent of my own back in Tuathanas. He too had a swing on his front porch. Long stretches of wildflowers covered the yard in unkempt beds. Each one was bursting with varieties that I'd never seen. The stone walk up to the front door was lined with solar lights, brightening our path to the house.

Approaching the front door, he made for the knob, then second-guessed himself and pressed a finger to the bell. “Why not just go in? You live here,” I asked curiously.

“Not anymore. The day I shipped out to Askari, I knew it would be the last time I lived in her home,” he said, never taking his eye off the door. His words felt hollow.

The door cracked open slightly, then all at once a tall thin woman gasped. “Kolter! My boy. Oh, thank the heavens.” The woman threw her arms around Kolt with so much love it was hard not to feel homesick. “You scared me. The last time I got an unannounced visit, it was Askari officials coming to inform me of Kasen’s death. I’m so relieved.” She kissed him now, once on each cheek, and held her hands to his face. “How are you my boy? Have you eaten?”

Feeling like I was intruding on their moment, I tried backing away slightly, but his arm latched on to mine, preventing me from moving further. It was then that his mother’s eyes darted to mine, as if she hadn’t realized I’d been standing there.

Her eyes narrowed slightly and she cocked her head to the side. She studied me for a brief second, then her eyes connected with mine. I watched hers grow wide with recognition. “I know you...” Her eyes jumped from mine to Kolter’s and back. “Now I have a guess as to why you two are here. Please come in. Let’s make some breakfast, and then we will talk. It’ll be a long conversation, I’m sure.” She stepped back just inside the doorway and motioned for us to come inside.

Walking into his childhood home, my senses immediately found the scent of baked goods infiltrating my nose. Instantly my mouth began to water, and my stomach began to grumble in acknowledgment.

The scents of fresh cinnamon, nutmeg, and allspice mixed with coffee filled me with the warmth of memories from my childhood, relaxing me slightly after our long journey.

The home itself was quaint. Decorated sparsely, but filled with items that you could tell held memories. The front foyer had a simple but tasteful blue running rug that perfectly fit the distance between the front door and a set of stairs on the right-hand side. Immediately to the left sat an old wooden bench that looked as though it had been previously painted white but undergone years of use to put your shoes on and off as you came and went from the house. An old window, converted to a mirror, hung above it, bringing a rustic feel to the home. Passing through the foyer, we turned into the formal sitting room. The focal point of the room held a large white-stoned fireplace, it too had seen years of use and was missing paint. On the large oak mantel, in perfectly placed dainty golden frames, sat photos of Kolter and his two brothers, who I could only assume were Kasen and his younger brother Kameron. All three of them were beaming; their smiles and joyful poses flooded me with both happiness and turmoil. It must be so difficult for them to see memories like this.

Neatly in front of the fireplace sat two couches and a coffee table positioned facing one another. "You two can take a seat and make yourselves comfortable. I'm going to head to the kitchen and I'll be right back," Kolter's mom said. I looked at her fully for the first time and noticed she was stunning. She shared Kolter's complexion, though she had warm brown hair that was curly but well maintained. She was sporting a pair of soft flannel pajamas and a worn gray terrycloth robe. Mismatched fuzzy socks adorned her feet. She was radiant, and it made me understand now where Kolter got his features.

"Would you like some help?" I asked, genuinely wanting to assist her. "I don't mind at all."

"You're too kind, but I'll be fine. I'll be just a second. You two were up all night running, I assume. Take a rest," she said with a caring smile before turning to go through the formal dining room, which sat just a few steps from the sitting room we were in. The rooms were tall. Old crown molding and a beautiful golden chandelier, the kind that had all the glass jewels on it, hung centered in the room.

"Your home is amazing." I said to Kolter. He was standing by the mantel, holding a photograph of his mother and who I'd guess was his father. "Is that your dad?" I asked him as I approached him wrapping my arm around his waist as I tucked beneath his arm at his side.

"Yeah, that's him. He was an amazing man. I looked up to him so much," he began, not taking his eyes off the photo. "He always prioritized Kase, Kam, and me. He was never too busy to hunt or read to us. He taught me everything I know. I hope I turn out half as amazing as he was."

"Here we are. Come take a seat." Kolter's mom sang as she walked into the room carrying a tray brimming with coffee, assorted pastries, muffins, and bagels. "It's not much, but at least it'll keep you warm and fed."

"It's more than enough, ma'am," I reassured her, staring at the platter hungrily.

"Please call me, Lucianna," she said politely.

"Thank you so much for this, Lucianna. You've really outdone yourself."

"Anything for the two of you." She smiled sweetly. She poured the three of us coffee, and while we sipped it, she began again. "I have a few guesses as to why you're here. Kolter, I should have told you this story years ago, but I was too scared. Once I've told you, you'll understand, but my guilt isn't eased, rather, it's a parental burden. If you don't mind, I'll begin, and if you have questions, you can stop me at any time. Does that seem fair?"

"Yes, of course. I just wanted to ask quickly if you recognized this, and if so, I'd like to give it back to you." Reaching into my bag, I pulled out the journal I'd been reading for the last few months. "This is yours, correct?"

She took the journal and smiled softly. She held it delicately between her hands, then brought it to her chest. "Yes, it's mine. This was one of the hardest years of my life, and I just felt like writing down my thoughts and feelings would be helpful to what we were facing at the time. I'm not sure where you found it, but it was misplaced years ago." She was quiet for a moment while flipping through the pages. Once she'd perused it, she set it on the table and met my eyes.

"Nevertheless, I want to start by saying a little disclaimer. Nothing I tell you that was done, was done out of malicious intent. We were just young parents trying to do what we thought was best for our child and you. Can you understand that?" Her eyes were willful, and I couldn't speak. My own emotions threatened to spill over. Luckily, Kolter stepped in.

Kolter cleared his throat as he reached across the coffee table and grasped her hand in his. "Mom, you have nothing to apologize for. We aren't here for a blame game or out of spite. We just need help with figuring things out."

She smiled softly and nodded. "Well then, let's start at the very beginning then. The summer you turned six, you were in the woods with your brother. At the time, he had just made new friends in the pack, and older boys being what they were, bullied you rotten. They wouldn't let you play, and you'd spend most of the time crying on the couch. I felt so bad for you, but your father said boys needed to be tough and figure it out on their own. So, every day, heartbroken, I'd watch you run off into the woods, tagging along after Kasen, only to come home shortly thereafter, tears in your eyes, and slamming the front door, and you'd disappear into your room. Then, one day, that just stopped. I realized about midday that you hadn't returned yet, so I snuck out into the woods. I followed your scent and crept upon you on the side of the creek bed. Your laugh was infectious. Hiding behind a tree so you wouldn't see me, I watched you playing. You were so happy. At first I had no idea you were playing with anyone at all. I thought you were just imagining yourself with friends. However, a few moments later, a little girl popped up from under a fallen tree, and you shrieked, giggling loudly, so happy. She had tagged you or found you or something along those lines. The two of you then ran off in another direction out of sight. I didn't recognize the girl, or her scent, but I dismissed it at the time, seeing that it brought you happiness. It brought me so much joy that you'd found a friend," she said, smiled softly while recounting the memories.

"For weeks you'd get up early in the morning, race yourself through breakfast, and be out the door in a flash. Spending hours at a time in the woods with your new friend. I asked about you once." She paused, gesturing to me.

"I knew that day, my son had a crush on you. Oh, was he smitten. His little eyes lit up, and his face got so red when I asked him if he'd liked you."

"Oook, Mom, you can continue," Kolter said, slightly embarrassed.

"It was then that Kasen began to tease you back. 'K2's got a girlfriend, K2 likes a girllllll.' I still remember how heart-sick you looked as he teased you. You didn't let it faze you. You just continued to go play with the little girl." She paused for a moment; it was like she was bracing herself for whatever came next. Idly, she began to pick at the robe she was wearing, her eyes on her lap.

"Until one afternoon. You were out on the ridgeline, climbing the wall. I don't know what possessed you to do it, but you two decided to climb to the top as a race. Midway, Everelle, you slipped. You frantically began calling for Kolter to help, but being six, he didn't have enough muscle, and though he tried to grab your arms, you were just too heavy for him to hold. You slipped from his fingers, falling about forty feet onto the rocks below. I could hear Kolter screaming, even from here. It took me a moment to realize what was happening. He hadn't screamed out loud, but down the line in my mind. It was then I knew I had to expect the worst." Looking over to Kolter, she continued.

"I arrived at the scene at the same time as your father, Kolter. We saw what you'd done. You had bitten both of your arms until they bled and were dripping your blood into Everelle's open wounds and mouth. Something you'd seen me do previously when Kasen had run into the corner of the mantel and split his head open. You must have recognized even at your age that my blood healed your brother. Oh, Kolt, you were frantically begging her to be ok. Your father stepped in and wrapped Everelle in his jacket. Pressing her to his chest, he ran. He knew she needed to go home and seek medical attention. You just couldn't handle it. You shifted. Before my eyes, you shifted at six years old. This tiny wolf cub was at my feet, screaming inside and howling at the sky. Bucking your hind legs and kicking up leaves and twigs. I tried to calm you, but you wouldn't relax. You took off after your father; I had no other choice than to shift after you. We all raced in the direction of Everelle's farm.

Once we approached it, we watched as your father laid her softly on the ground on the edge of the clearing. Everelle, your father was out on the plow, and I could see in the distance your mother hanging clothes on the line. Looking down at you, I noticed your skin had already begun to heal. I recognized then that Kolter's blood had taken my pack's traits and saved your life. I knew you'd be ok in a matter of hours, but I didn't want to worry your family with our presence. Stepping just beyond the tree line, hovering out of sight, I whistled to get your father's attention. It worked because he raced over to the tree line where we had laid you on a bed of leaves. I watched your father stand over you. Noticing you were unconscious, he dropped down and touched your forehead. It was not until I watched him try to wake you up that I caught his scent and realized what he was... he was a lion. He frantically called for your mother, and she was beside you in seconds, holding you to her chest and crying. I wanted so badly to tell them what happened, that you'd fallen in an accident, but Kolter's father refused to let me. I watched your human mother and lion father hold you and cry. I don't honestly know how long we sat there waiting for you to wake up. It felt like an eternity, but you finally did, and they took you inside. Walking back to our home, Kolter, you were sluggish and started to run a fever, a blistering to-the-touch fever. I quickly got you in a cool bath and called our doctors. They all checked in on you, and I explained what had happened. They suggested we erase your memories. The less you knew, the less that would change. It made sense at the time, so I did. I erased your memories of each other. I'm not proud of it, but I thought it was what was best for both of you at the time."

"Wow...neither of my parents ever told me that they found me unconscious outside. They never told me I had a friend. I don't understand why they'd keep that from me. I never was even told my father was a lion! Why would they hide any of this from me?" I asked, more so to myself; I wasn't expecting an answer.

"My best guess is that when I finally approached them weeks later, they got scared. Your father has his own demons he faces."

"Have you ever researched what would happen to Ever after I gave her my blood?" Kolter piped in.

"I did," she said, sipping her coffee. She paused as if reflecting on what she wanted to say before she just came out with it. "If what I have learned is correct, Everelle, you now would be considered a biologically made Chosen by fate. You have a human mother, a lion father, and the blood of a wolf. For your own protection, I have never uttered my thoughts out loud. On this continent, the Chosen are not highly regarded. Headhunters seek monetary gain for turning in any nomadic Chosen that do come around. It would be in your best interest to keep to yourself what you are," she warned, squeezing my hand. I hadn't even noticed she'd picked it up, but here she was, holding the hand of a Chosen.

I didn't know what to feel. I had speculated I was a dual shifter, but hearing someone tell me I was one of the most dangerous Therianthrope, was one of the worst feelings and deepest fears. It was too much to handle. I began to rise, then sat back down quickly. I rose again and paced the room. "What am I supposed to do now? We have the course final to run in a few days. What if they know?"

"They won't know. You just need to be careful. Your line, the communication you have, can be heard and felt by any of the shifters if you allow it. *If* you want it to be heard. You alone are in power. You need to make sure no one in the lion's prides feels or hears you. If they do, they'll figure it out.

Oh my God. Folasade. She knows. Nalea must know.

"What? Ever, what are you talking about? How do they know?" Kolter was looking at me now with a mix of terror and anger.

"When I shifted, the first time, I heard Folasade's fear. I spoke to her down a line without thinking. I didn't know it was happening. I honestly didn't know it was a line or that it was possible. I thought we were talking out loud. I don't know what I thought at the time. Maybe I thought that all shifters spoke on the same line sometimes. I don't know. I didn't know what to think!" I was rambling and spiraling quickly.

"Ever, I'm going to need you to stay calm and look at me." Kolter was now standing in front of me, holding my hands in his. He brought them to my chest and put the rubix in my hands. "I'm going to need you to calm down so we can work through all of this. Why do you think Nalea knows you're a lion?"

"When we were sparing. I spoke to her. I taunted her and reprimanded her," I answered guiltily, my eyes dropping from his.

"No, babe, you didn't... I was there. The two of you were just..." he stopped talking then, realizing what I already knew. "I couldn't hear you, because you were speaking in lion's tongue."

"I didn't realize what was even happening. I hadn't truly understood until now that I was speaking down her line. I was in her head. There isn't any way she hadn't registered it. It's my fault. Ignorance isn't an excuse." He didn't get to excuse my recklessness. We needed to pray Nalea wouldn't have figured it out, or, worse, use it against me, against us. I fought my tears that were welling in my eyes. How could I have been so stupid? Flynn was absolutely right. I used the ignorance card and was so unbelievably sloppy with my powers. I put the entire pack at risk.

"You two need to be incredibly careful. Make sure you tell no one what you have figured out. Everelle, honey, look at me," Lucianna said, grabbing my hands from Kolter and locking eyes with me. "I'm going to help you the absolute best that I can. I'm sorry I've waited idly by for the last thirteen years, but I want you to know that I'm here now. I thought I was doing what was best for you both, and I understand now that it was wrong. I just prolonged the problem. I didn't fix it."

"This is not your fault or your problem to fix. I was the stupid one, not you. I'm going to fight this. I'm going to fight my own battles. No one is going to get hurt because of me."

"The fuck you are!" Kolter shouted. "We are in this together. You are not doing a damn thing without me."

"I can't risk putting you in danger. You've already saved my life once. I can't let you risk yours for me. You," I said to Lucianna, "can't risk another son. I will do the absolute best I can to practice and to lie low. Maybe we are giving them too much credit. Maybe they haven't even put it together. After all, neither has mentioned it."

"Let's hope for that, because I can't lose you, Everelle. I can't let you go." Kolter leaned forward and pressed his lips eagerly to mine. He pulled back and ran his thumbs over my cheeks, sweeping away tears I hadn't felt run. "I love you. There is nothing I won't do to keep you protected. I can't lose the one person I've given my soul to."

My heart burst, there on the sitting room floor of his childhood home. It burst into a million pieces. How could someone so perfect be falling for me? "I love you, too. So, so freaking much." I kissed him again. "I'm so sorry for everything foolish and reckless that I've done. All I've ever succeeded in was putting you into danger.

"I've said it once, and I'll say it as many times as it takes for you to listen. There is nothing you could ever do, no form you could ever take, that would make me not love you. You're mine, Everelle Marie. Mine. For the rest of your life."

"Let's hope it's a long one then, or you'll be widowed early," I said, chasing away the tension.

"Ok, you and Flynn... less time together from now on," Kolter said, eyes ablaze in passion, but grinning ear to ear.

"Speaking of Flynn, I feel like we should probably head back sooner than later. If anyone has caught on to what I am, I don't want them to take it out on the pack. They can't be put in jeopardy because of me."

"Agree on going back but disagree that you're putting our pack in jeopardy. We didn't ask for this, but we will fix it."

Goodbyes and hugs were short. Lucianna promised to deliver a note to my mother, and I promised to be smarter with my communication flaws down the lines. I was no longer going to speak into anyone's line. I would be smarter. I just pray that the Folasade and Nalea haven't put the clues together to my secret.

Chapter Twenty-Three

Everelle

Arriving back to the den in the next morning, we were exhausted. Kolter and I hadn't spoken most of the way back, and we hadn't slept in more than two days. However, a promise was made to our General Ulrich that we wouldn't be a hindrance, and we would rejoin the pack in whatever scheduled activity they were doing. A quick glance around the common room told us that the pack was out. Checking down my evergreen line, I saw Flynn sitting in Professor DeMarcus' classroom, and she was lecturing.

"Do we go in and interrupt them?" I asked Kolter, "Or do we risk it and take a much-needed nap?"

"I was thinking of something a little bit more fun," he said, making his way to me. He used one hand to raise my chin, my face reaching his. His other hand rested on the small of my back. Goosebumps immediately flooded my skin, and my breath caught in my throat. His lips were on mine in seconds. Soft at first, gently pressing against mine. I relaxed into him, feeling the bloom of heat beginning to creep down my chest and settling between my thighs.

His lips opened slightly, allowing his tongue to dart out and tickle my lips. I groaned. He deepened our kiss then, taking advantage of the moment. I gave a small gasp that he used as an opportunity to put his tongue fully into my mouth. He slid his fingers up into my hair, tugging slightly. My insides lit with fire. I was burning with desire, and all I could think was I wanted this man in every way I could have him.

He pulled away from me then; his glassy eyes fueled with an intensity that took my breath from me. He narrowed his eyes and crooked his fingers into a come-hither motion as he began walking backwards down the hall. I followed, like a sheep to slaughter, to what was for sure going to be the ruin of me in every way.

Coming together again outside his bedroom door, we kissed hungrily as he twisted the knob and opened it. We broke again, stepping inside. He shut the door, locking it, then stood with his back to it. Staring at me, his eyes darkened with desire, and his tongue escaped his mouth, and licked his bottom lip, and I'd never wanted to be that lip more in my entire life.

"Wait... are you sure you want to do this? Are you sure you still want me, knowing what I am? If you bond to me, you'll be signing your own death slip." I wasn't ashamed of who I was, but I knew if I'd been given the choice, I wouldn't have chosen this path. I didn't want to trap Kolter for eternity with his soul tied to a chosen.

"Everelle, I will tell you as many times as you need to hear it to let it fully sink in. You could take any shape, be any creature. You could start a damn rebellion and I'll be at your side. You will be the very bane of my existence. I will march to the front line of a war. I will never surrender or back down. I'll burn the entire continent of Siochan down to keep you safe. You will never find me ashamed of you."

Breathless, I swallowed hard as his words lingered in my ears, permanently changing the chemistry of my brain.

"Right, but it's against the rules, isn't it?" I felt so foolish for asking, but I wanted to keep us out of trouble and out of Pollsmoor. The General wasn't my biggest fan, and I had a sneaking suspicion that he would make our lives miserable if he found out. I watched Kolter slow, then he leaned against the dresser drawers and looked deep in thought.

"Everelle, I've waited thirteen years to see you again. You were once my best friend. Fate brought us back together, despite having our minds wiped, despite you not growing up with the knowledge of this place, of me, of what we are." He approached me then, kneeling before me and grasping my hands. My breath caught in my throat as I studied his features. "My heart has never been given. Have I been with other women, other wolves? Yes. I have. I know you're pure, so I won't ask you to do anything you don't want to do. I'm just telling you that if you ever doubt my feelings for you, I can assure you, you'd be wrong. Your doubts are wrong. Despite what the voices in that beautiful head try and tell you. Whether we bond or not. You will have my protection, and until I no longer can. I will guard you. I will support you. Until my last breath on this continent, God be my witness, I'll be yours, believe me, until I can't, I will." His eyes darted between mine, tears threatening to spill from them.

Any doubts I'd ever had were suddenly gone. He didn't care what I was. He didn't care that I was a liability. He just cared about me as me. "I want you. More than anything. You're all I think about, all I feel when you're in the room. When you're not there, I feel you down our line. You are the center of every desire I've ever had." I looked down at him then as he grinned. Kissing me delicately on the cheek as he stood up.

He began taking off his boots, one, then the other, and kicked them to the corner of the room. His shirt came next. Pulling it over his head, I was left in awe at the sight of him. His shoulders flexed, and his stomach muscles distracted me, as my eyes met with the v of his pelvis. I bit my bottom lip. "Like what you see, Ever?"

"Mhmm..." I moaned.

"Should I keep going?" he asked, unhooking his belt and pulling it from his pants.

"Please... please do."

"Do you still doubt my loyalty?" he asked, smirking as he then unbuttoned and unzipped his pants, slowly, watching me with sinful satisfaction as he did. In one smooth motion, he was standing before me, in all his wonderful glory. I sent a prayer up to God, asking how in the hell I got so lucky to have someone who looks like him love me?

"Not currently, check back in a few days... you'll always need to give me reassurance." I said, never taking my eyes off of him.

The grin on his face as he walked my way took my breath. He met me and slowly began walking me backwards until the back of my knees hit his bed. He dropped a long, hard kiss on my lips while running his fingers up my waist and onto my corset. "Oh, um, hold on, I have to untie it... uh, it's kind of tricky," I said, breaking free from his lips.

"If you don't think I know how to use my fingers for something as menial as untying a corset, you have got a world of surprises coming your way." He nudged my hands away from the twine that laced my corset. "I've got this." With almost no effort, my usually tight top was on the floor. My naked chest exposed, and the cool room brought my nipples into two hard peaks. He used the pads of his thumbs and index fingers to roll them, squeezing gently. The moan that escaped my body was almost too embarrassing. If not for the heat growing within my body and the feel of Kolter's lips beginning to trace my neck, I'd have run from the room.

Slowly, he made a trail with his kisses, down my throat over my rubix. He suddenly captured my nipple in his mouth, sucking and tugging on it as he rolled the other between his fingers. The pure ecstasy coursing through my body was enough to make me weak in the knees. Maybe he hadn't been lying when he said I would be limping after. He popped my nipple from his mouth with a devilish grin. "You want to limp, do you?"

I stuttered. "Stay-ayy out of my head." I demanded, my voice catching in my throat as he traced his fingers down my flat stomach until he met my pants. With one swift motion, my pants were unbuttoned and open. "Damn, you're good at that. Should I be concerned?" I teased him as he began to slide me out of them.

"Only if you're ever disappointed. Then you can be concerned that I didn't use my time before you wisely enough to learn how to please you." The deep tenor of his voice, so close to my center, immediately sent a wave of clenching tingles that made me squeeze my thighs to ease it.

We were both fully naked now, and gently he laid me down on his bed. He kissed me, deep and ravenous. Our tongues were playing their own version of war as he lay next to me, our mouths filled with hunger and lust. He nipped my lips, and then I caressed his tongue with mine. His fingers began to trace their way up my body, stopping short of my wet center. Teasingly, he began making circles from my knee up my inner thigh, stopping just short of my dripping core.

My body began to burn with anticipation and need so strong I felt I'd burst if he didn't touch me. I jerked my hips as he trailed further up, this time slipping his fingers through my opening and grazing his middle finger over my throbbing clit. The feeling of him was enough to send me screaming his name. He swallowed my gasps with his mouth, quieting me, as he pulled back again, teasing me until I began to whimper for him. Climbing on top of me then, he used his knees to separate my thighs. I could see his hard member ready. Achingly I wanted him. I wanted to feel every part of him.

"This is probably going to hurt, but I want you to know, it won't always be like that," he said, looking a little hesitant. "I also want you to know I've never taken anyone's virginity. I'm honored you're giving that to me." I read his face and saw how sincerely he meant it.

"You're welcome." I said softly, looking into his passion-fueled eyes. I'd underestimated the power this moment truly had for us. The reason I'd never gone to bed with someone was because it just never felt right. Sure, I wasn't as beautiful as most girls growing up, so when I'd been ridiculously accosted by boys, it just seemed like the right thing to do, turning them down, because I felt like they were only after one thing. Why allow a boy with no feelings or skills to take me where a man could, only better? Looking up into Kolter's eyes, I knew I had the latter.

"It's ok. I'm not scared...I just... I need you, please. Please, Kolter." I moved beneath him then, allowing for him to have better access. I dropped my hips so there was more leverage.

Slowly, he lowered himself on to me. His hard cock pressed against my center, heat filling me, lust and hunger consuming my every thought. Carefully, he pressed into me, little by little, slowly stretching my body to fit his. I gasped and felt entirely reawakened. The scorching of heat burning it's way across my body.

My entire body began to explode with a glowing intensity. Kolter hadn't just sheathed himself in me. It was like he completely changed my entire chemistry. I felt his blood racing through my veins. I felt as his breaths filled my lungs, and I could feel as my brain rewired to match his. I felt transformed. I felt reborn and awakened. I felt unstoppable. I watched his face as he slowed his movements and stared back at me. He looked at our arms, tangled together in a mixture of lust and pleasure, and back to meet my eyes. I could feel his confusion.

"Are you ok? Do you, do you feel this?" he asked me, confusion growing across his face.

"I don't want you to stop. Whatever you're doing, whatever you're feeling... I feel it too, and it's incredible. Is this bonding?" Part of me was embarrassed for asking questions right now, but he said he's done this before. I needed to know if this was natural.

"I've never... I've never felt someone like this. I've never felt so connected," he said, regaining his rhythm. "I think..." he stopped talking then. He grinned then and pushed further into me, and then I felt him at my virginity. Holding my breath, I stilled. "Baby, I'm going to need you to breathe through this, or it'll hurt," he warned.

I tried to listen and release my breath, but it built up again as he pressed against the door to my womanhood. Turning my attention away from it, he tweaked my nipple with one hand and brought his mouth to mine, deepening our kiss. He then thrust hard against me, and I felt as the burning tear and heat fill me all at once. He now had unlimited access to me. He pushed inside me further, stretching as he went. The burning sensation turned from painful to pleasure with each push forward. A few more slow pushes and he was now fully sheathed inside of me. Pausing, his eyes met mine with a passion I'd never seen. Slowly at first, he began to move, sliding in and out of me, gently. Each time he thrust back in, he stretched me a little more, the pain and pleasure that filled me continuing to build. The feeling like a soothing scratch on an itch only, more intense. I clawed at his back, gasping for breath; as a warm sensation began to build within me. My heart pounded as his thrusts in and out became firmer and quicker. "Oh my God, you feel so incredible. I've never felt this good before. God Ever, you're so damn tight. It's perfect. You're perfect." He moaned, and his eyes again met mine, blazing with desire.

I could feel my walls falling and the pressure inside me building at an intoxicatingly fast rate. I closed my eyes as he moved in and out of me, faster and faster, as if keeping rhythm with my heart. All at once there was a blinding explosion inside of me. The sheer power of my orgasm made me scream his name and claw his skin. I'd never felt that much euphoric pleasure. I knew then I'd become addicted. I now understood my pack mates desire to never leave their rooms.

Once I'd come, I didn't want to stop. I spread my legs wider and pushed my pelvis upward, giving him a deeper angle to continue. He thrust harder, and the sensation began to build deep inside of me again. The power of my last orgasm was still radiating through my body, and snowballed, beginning to fill me again. "Kolter!" I screamed as he brought me higher and higher.

"Go, baby, I'm going to need you to..." He couldn't even get the words out, his hot cum pushed into me, sending me into another round of dizzying bliss. I felt my body give out. My legs limp, my arms wrapped around him, and I went slack. I would never again ridicule Lisbeth and Baldur for never wanting to leave their rooms. I don't think I'd ever tire of the way he just rearranged the chemistry of my brain and body.

He collapsed beside me, using a tissue from his side table to clean himself. He was looking at me, proud as he ever had, and smitten. Once he'd finished cleaning up, he rolled over to me, wrapping his arms around my body and pulling me against his chest. Cuddled up, he threw the blanket over us, wrapping us in a cocoon of sex and exhaustion. In the comfort of his arms, I let sleep pull me under. The last thing I heard was his profession of love.

A few hours later, I stirred to noise in the hallway. Kolter's breaths were deep and rhythmic next to me, indicating he was still asleep. Careful not to move so as to not wake him, I took a mental inventory of my body. I was a little sore, but overall, I felt amazing, reborn, even. I was thankful I'd never given anyone the chance to ruin what we just did, with horrible results. I was confident ***no one could have ever done what he had.***

"You're right about that." His eyes were slowly opening; a light smile danced on his lips. "How was your nap?" he asked me, nuzzling my neck. I really needed to work on keeping the line to my thoughts closed down. Kolter seemed to have steady access to my thoughts, and if he felt them, all of my pack could, and that would be embarrassing.

Nestling against him, I breathed in his scent. It was intoxicating. "Wonderful, I had this dream that you and I had, *mated*." I gave a small laugh, and he captured it with his mouth. Kissing me deeply, he helped clear my mind and reignite a fiery burn inside of me.

"That was no dream, princess. That was real. Let's not joke about it. I promised you I was all in, and nothing will change that." He kissed me on my forehead and closed his eyes. "They're back... and trying to mind their business, but I can sense Flynn is going to break down the door if we don't come out soon."

"It's always Flynn," I chuckled, rolling over to get out of his bed. I didn't make it up before Kolter grabbed my arm and pulled me back to him.

"Ok, maybe we can go for round two quickly." We both laughed as he pulled the sheets around us and climbed on top of me.

The bliss was still lingering as we stepped into the hallway fully dressed twenty minutes later. I could hear the hushed voices from the common room. I looked up at Kolter, but he just looked amused and shrugged his shoulders.

Cautiously, I walked into the common room, and all heads whipped in our direction. "Well, it's about fucking time," Flynn teased, walking over and handing me a glass of champagne. "Maybe now you two will have your heads on straight, not your head on another head like the other day...in the woods...against a tree. If you catch my drift."

Oh my God, this was embarrassing.

"No, babe, what's embarrassing is you gave it to him, then said no for you? What kind of girl are you?" Flynn rolled his eyes and smirked, walking back across the room.

I loved to hate Flynn. He was the best big brother I never had. Maybe if he'd been there for me while growing up, my life wouldn't have taken the turn it had.

"You two slept through Professor DeMarcus' class. It's fine though. I don't think they know you're back yet," Priya started. "But we have Monaghan's course trial to run in fifteen minutes, so if I were you, I'd put the champagne down until later. He made a comment yesterday that this will prove to him which teams are ready and which ones need extended hours." She looked extremely nervous as she clutched Kentaro's hand. Meeting my eyes now, she just shrugged her shoulders.

"Listen up everyone," Kolter began, taking the attention of the room. "We have been practicing and going over maneuvers for six months. We knew from the beginning the course would be run at the end of August. I understand that the closer it gets, the more stress we feel. I just ask you to try your best to put that aside and remember how strong this pack is. As long as we go out there and you do your best, I don't care what place we come in. We are a well-oiled machine. We may not know where we will be hunting, but no matter which terrain, we will do great. Just keep motivated and keep yourselves alert."

The pack all nodded, looking around the room. My heart was pounding with the anticipation of the course trial. "You've gotten so much better, and we are so lucky to have you as our female alpha. It's been such an honor to be your friend," Priya said, hooking arms with me as we began our ascent out of the den. "Just stay focused on the task, and no matter what happens, you need to keep going." She smiled then and quickly added, "Also, don't get distracted about how hot he is." She winked, and her eyes directed me to Kolter. He was busy discussing tactics with Victor and Brandt, and I could see the seriousness on his face. Looking at him now, it was utterly amazing to me how beautiful one soul could be in all their forms. He was a threat to be reckoned with.

Chapter Twenty-Four

Everelle

Stepping out onto the course, we were in our formation, in line with the other packs and prides. Professor Monaghan stepped forward, raising a long tube to the side of his neck, allowing him to project his words to the masses. "Today is your first trial run of the course. You will begin by completing a timed five-mile run. The position you end in will put you in pairings with the next task. Any pack or pride that fails to complete this run in less than one hour will find themselves at a severe disadvantage." He scowled out at all of us now, as if challenging us to not make that time requirement. "Once you've crossed the finish line of your five-mile run, you will wait in the clearing for your next orders. Take a moment to organize yourselves. We begin in five minutes." I watched as Professor Monaghan dropped the tube from his throat and stepped back to discuss things with the other professors.

Looking over my pack, I noticed Priya was clutched to Kentaro's arm, trying to get his attention. I watched in silence as he looked down at her and nodded, as if understanding she needed a moment. Kentaro picked up his gaze and drew it to Kolter, throwing his thumb over his shoulder. Kolter nodded, and the pair stepped away for some privacy.

A few minutes later, we had all regathered at the top of the course trail. The air was electric, and a chorus of growls, pants, and snarls echoed out across the clearing. Professor Monaghan stepped forward and thrust his arms toward the sky. "On my command," Professor Monaghan said, then paused for a moment, fist held taut in the air, and he peered out at the restless crowd. With no warning, he quickly swung his arm down, bowing to us all. At once, a stampede of wolves and lions surged forward across the starting line. The trial had begun.

The thundering sound of a monstrous army attacked my ears, and for a moment, it became too overwhelming to zero in on just my pack's line. In confusion I began to stumble, while shaking my head, trying to rid myself of the assault that penetrated my mind. I frantically searched my mind for Kolter's royal blue path. Finding it, I heard him slow down and yell to me, *Ever, I'm going to need you to focus and get your ass moving. Respectfully, of course.*

I found his voice to be the anchor I needed. I adjusted my form and raced after Kolter and my pack. *That was embarrassing.* I glanced around and found other prides and packs were in formation, racing through the woods, over fallen limbs, and sliding across the stones. I pushed on, through the hordes of animals that didn't belong to my family. In the seconds it had taken me to push everyone else out, to focus on Kolter and our pack, they'd progressed almost a quarter of a mile ahead of me, and I wasn't going to allow myself to be the weak link, crossing the finish line later than they had. What kind of alpha was I being?

Turning a blind path through the ridge line, I caught my first visual of Lisbeth and Baldur. Steady and strong, they were the caboose of our pack, like Kolter and I. Their strides were a perfect match of fluidity and power. Pushing forward, I was gaining on them. Irritatingly to my left side, the Molti pride was in sync.

"Looks like you could use some work on how to stay with your pack, mutt." Neo grimaced at me. I turned my eyes back forward; I wasn't going to allow him to torment me. "If you were in my pride, you'd be buried by now; no one is allowed to anchor our progression."

Seeing that he wasn't getting a rise out of me, he pushed himself more, passing me along my left side, then quickly darting in front of my path. The ripple this caused came too quickly. I leaped to the right to avoid colliding with Neo and ran directly into Baraka, who was flanking him. A deep growl left his throat as he lunged back at me, barely missing my neck with his strong jaw, and clipping my cheek.

The pain didn't hit me at first. Pure adrenaline, which was coursing through my body, continued to burn my muscles and nerves; my body was pissed at me for several reasons.

Adjusting my stride, I skirted around the lions and surged forward, feeling them nipping at my hind legs as I ran. Again, just up ahead, I caught sight of Lisbeth and Baldur, their pace slowing minimally. I knew at this point they were slowing so I could regain my position among the pack. They were willing to forgo us crossing the line first in order to provide me protection.

My body was in protest, but I kept pushing forward, desperate to reach Kolter's side. We were about two miles in, and I was still about fifteen seconds behind them. Approaching a river bend that we normally would follow, I made the hasty decision to cross it and merge with my pack once they raced down the other side of the pass. Veering off course, I hit the water's edge with enough force to shower the shoreline with water. It was freezing, too cold for a midsummer river. The shock of it took my breath for a moment, and I gasped. My legs and paws froze, stiffening my joints as they met the hard bottom of the river. I didn't want this to be another bad decision, so I forced myself forward. Midway across the icy river, I felt a presence behind me; I was being followed. I didn't need to turn around to know Folasade was sprinting through the water, charging directly for me. If the temperature of the river bothered her, she showed no signs. Her advancing across the river sent a surge of adrenaline through my body. No one from my pack was out here. No one could save me now. Side-stepping some slippery river rock, I mistakenly dropped my paw directly into a hole in the riverbed beneath the surface of the water, loosening some rocks and shifting them to cover my paw, pinning it to the river's floor.

Oh no no no no no... This can't be happening. I yelled at myself, frantically pulling at my paw, ripping the fur and skin along my toes against the clamped rocks. Looking back up, I could see Folasade was at worst ten steps from me, crouching down into the river, locking her deadly eyes onto mine like I was the prey she'd been hunting. Closing my eyes, I made sure that the line to her was closed. I didn't want her to feel me or hear what I was thinking. I needed to get the hell out of there.

Frantically, I began shoving my other paw into the rocks and pulling back on my stuck paw. I begged the river to release me. As if it listened, the rocks began to tumble away, just enough for my paw to slip through and regain footing on the next bit of river floor. I heard it then, Folasade lunging at me, teeth clamped, with snarls emitting from her throat. Looking at her now, her eyes were deadly black, and panic filled my throat. As quickly as I could, I lunged to the right, nearly missing her body as she propelled in the direction I once was. I couldn't allow her to overtake me out here on the river, not when no one was here to witness it.

Looking back toward where she landed, I noticed she was completely submerged, falling into the hole that had previously taken hold of my paw. Counting silently, I began to panic with each number, my count rose. I waited on bated breath for her to resurface, but she didn't, and I became torn with the idea of leaving her to drown. Rage fueled me. I wasn't that person. I wasn't the type to leave someone hurt and in danger, no matter how much they wanted me dead.

I raced back toward her and dove beneath the surface of the cool running water. Swimming against the slightly rough current, I pushed weight behind my strokes. Visibility was poor as I kicked up dirt and sediment from the bottom of the river bed, but I finally approached her. Her fear-stricken face let me know immediately I'd made the right choice. As I'd suspected, she was pinned where I previously stood, and her body was too short to keep her head above the rushing water.

I began propelling myself forward, continuing to fight against the current, to reach the pile of rocks pinning her to the floor. My lungs began to burn with the lack of oxygen. I couldn't imagine Folasade. I needed to get her out. In one fell swoop I shoved them with my front paws, freeing her paw and allowing her to breach the surface of the water. She shifted back into human form, gasping as she took in breaths of air filling her lungs with oxygen and spitting out residual water. I pushed off the river's floor, exploding onto the water's surface, and began to make my way to the far side of the river. I took a second to look back toward her as I shook the icy water from my fur. She was standing in the river's middle, scowling at me, but her eyes no longer portrayed vengeance. I nodded to her, silently letting her know that it was ok. It was our secret.

I raced along the far edge of the forest as it reconvened with the packs and prides on the five-mile course. By the grace of God, I'd broken the forest line and met back with my pack, into the line as if I'd never left it.

"Why are you wet?" Kolter asked, looking at me with concern.

"It's a long story... just go. I'm sorry," I said, not allowing myself to look him in the face.

We continued to plunge forward as a pack now, crossing through the third and fourth miles with ease. The forest began thickening and the trail slimmed in an effort to tunnel us toward the finish line.

When we'd got to the rocky pass of the last quarter mile, I looked up and saw that the cliff sides stood towering above us about three stories high, enclosing us in. A sinking thought raced through my head that we could be trapped in this tunnel if someone had wanted to hurt us, but I didn't let it stay there.

In unison, stride for stride, our pack crossed the line at forty-eight minutes and sixteen seconds. We were the first pack, and the joy I felt was palpable.

Slowing down, we grouped together on the side of the forest clearing that acted as our holding area as we awaited further orders for part two of the course.

"What the hell was that, Everelle?" Nikita said, stopping in front of me. "What the hell happened back there? What, you go to pound town once and now suddenly you can't run?" She looked at me with disgust, then, doing a double take, she asked, "Why the fuck are you wet?"

Enough, Nikita. We finished, and we placed first. It's fine. Drop it, Kolter ordered through the line in his, I'm the alpha, don't fuck with me voice.

"Ok, fine. That's fine. Our female alpha decides to take a dip in the river, and it's alright? No questions asked. Sure, Flipper, you can stop mid-patrol to take a fucking swim! We got the hard stuff. No problem!" Nikita was more pissed than I've ever seen her, and she was always pissed.

"It wasn't like that!" I started in protest.

"It never is!" Nikita cracked back. "It's never your fault! I'm tired of you constantly making Highland Pack look like a fucking joke! Wake up already. This was supposed to be the easy part! A fucking run!! Something we do every damn day, and you still found a way to take a fucking bubble bath instead of sticking to the course. Then you wonder why no one can count on you." She was boiling mad, and I couldn't blame her. I was cooked. Deep fried.

"I..."

"Don't even start. You know what you can do from now on? You can show up, keep your fucking mouth closed, and follow directions with your head down. That's it!" Nikita lectured, standing inches from my face so that I'd get the memo loud and clear. "It's what he'd do to anyone else. The only difference is he wants to fuck you, so he can't ruffle your pretty little tail feathers."

She walked away toward Kolter now. "Peh... you said your brother was pussy-whipped... look in the fucking mirror. You're turning this pack into a joke." Looking around the pack, it was evident that they were all in agreement.

"It's not his fault...It was mine!" I cried out in defense for Kolter.

"Ever! I don't need your defending." I slammed my mouth shut, hot and angry. "I need you all to get your shit together. You think she's the liability? Maybe you should start taking looks in the mirrors when you're in the den. She's brand new! Brand new to shifting, and she was able to keep stride with the rest of you who've been at this for the better part of a decade!"

"Kolter?" a timid voice came from behind us.

"WHAT?!" he snapped, snarling as he turned around. Behind him, a re-shifted Folasade stood. Seeing her only intensified Kolter's anger. "What is it? We're in a pack meeting here. State your business, then get the fuck lost."

He was madder than I'd ever seen. If he were a cartoon, he would be one of those steam kettles that blow steam in all different directions, and I was the cause. It felt defeating. I was tired of never making the right choices. I suddenly longed for my mother's salon front window and a good book. I missed those easier days. This, this constant need to be four steps ahead was a nightmare.

"Well, I know who won't be getting a Christmas card, asshole." Folasade was no longer looking timid. "I came here to apologize to Everelle and thank her for saving my life. If we had played different roles, I would have stood idly by and watched you drown," she said as she turned towards me. "I came to offer a truce. You have my sincerest gratitude." Turning back to Kolter, she said, "But please, continue your ego-driven pep talk. It was riveting, truly motivational." She rolled her eyes at him, then turning back to me, her face warmed slightly with appreciation before turning in the direction of her pride.

"You're going to have to explain how Ms. Kitty from the city just walked over here with her tail between her legs and thanked you, because I'm damn sure that's never happened before. Lions hate us," Flynn said, wearing a look of pure bewilderment.

I breathed a deep sigh out, looking at them all. I knew they needed answers, but the idea that again I'd look like I wasn't putting my pack's interests first or that I was trying to skate around the fact that I'd failed again was pressing on my mind.

"I was trailing behind because at first the sounds of everyone stampeding toward a common goal and listening to..." *Shit... I can't tell them that I have lines to the lions as well...fuck.* "Everything... It threw me off. When I finally righted myself seconds later, I was already significantly behind you all. I tried my best to get back on track, but then Neo and Baraka put their two damn cents in and bit me, putting me further behind."

"They bit you?!" Kolter interrupted coming to examine my body. I slapped him away and scowled before continuing.

"I got frantic, and I became reckless again. I made a hasty decision to dart across the river and meet back up with you on the wayside when my foot got stuck in the riverbed. I was able to get myself free, but then Folasade saw me jet that way and followed. She got stuck in the same spot I had been, and I rescued her. She was too short to keep her head above water, and I knew that if I didn't step in, she would likely drown. I didn't want that on my conscience. So, I saved her. I stuck around just long enough to see her free and ran. That's when I came out of the wood line just as you all rounded the bend before the large field. That's why I'm wet." I looked around my pack now. Victor seemed pleased with my answer, but some of the girls still showed hatred, and Nikita just looked disgusted with me.

"Bitchhhhh, I would have let that cat drown, ok? Shit, she would still be there, leg all stuck, and I'd play stupid like oooh nooo... she's missing...

what??" Flynn said, miming the actions of a worried wolf. Kolter shot him a look, and he quickly adjusted his face. "I mean... good job, Everelle. Great example to set and all that positive shit I should say." He sighed and walked away to talk with Flavia.

"Well, I for one am proud of you. Not everyone..." Priya began, casting looks at Flynn, making him roll his eyes and throw his hands up, mouthing, "Whattttt?" "As I was saying, not everyone would have helped her, and it shows your maturity and that you're a bigger person."

"Who knows, you may have just created an alliance. Fantastic job, Ev," Lisbeth said, coming around now and giving me a side hug. "Also, I did try and slow us down a bit, but this ass hat wasn't having it." She rolled her eyes at Baldur.

"What? Me?!? I was just following the pack. Why do I have to be the ass hat?" Baldur asked worriedly.

"Because... you should be following your mate, not your pack." She rolled her eyes and grabbed his hand. "He's a slow learner."

"This changes nothing for me, nor my opinion of you and Kolter. I still find you reckless, and risking the lives of everyone in this pack can't be allowed. You two don't get the luxury as alphas to surrender to the feelings of just one another. You have to put your shit aside for the betterment of the pack," Nikita chimed in, her face still upturned in annoyance.

"It was the betterment of the pack. Like Lisbeth suggested, this could end up saving us in the long run. From now on, keep your damn mouth shut unless it's productive," Kolter barked at her, causing her to grimace and cower back. "You don't get to say every single feeling you have just because you used to be an alpha. You don't get the luxury of disrespecting Everelle because you can't get over your own jealousy and resentment. It's not her fault Kasen isn't here. The bottom line is, it's your fault, and the sooner you cut the bullshit, the sooner the pack can heal from it."

He overstepped. In that moment I saw a deep level of hatred fill Nikita's eyes. I didn't exactly know what happened to his brother, and to be honest, I don't think he really did either. There seemed to be deep-seated feelings here, and Nikita didn't deserve the lashing he just handed her.

"Congratulations, everyone!" boomed Professor Monaghan over the loudspeaker he held to his neck. "I'd like to take this moment and celebrate a few outstanding packs and prides who not only stayed together for the entirety of the course but also pushed themselves to a better finish time than previous attempts." My eyes shot across the groups toward Folasade's. Her eyes mimicked mine in worry that something bad would happen because of our grapple in the river.

"However, not all packs and prides get to celebrate this evening. Highland and Ade teams, please step forward." I gulped, catching eyes with Kolter. He looked stoic, never dropping his eyes from Professor Monaghan.

"It has come to our attention that while the trial was underway, a member of the Highland pack took a deviation from the course in an effort to cheat the length at which the course is run by an eighth of a mile. While this pack member was on this detour, a member of the Ade pride also deviated course and followed suit." Looking around, I could tell the forest was alive with whispers. Everyone was looking at our pack and pride, wondering what the hell had gone on out on the trail. "Because this is a direct violation of the course trial, we will be holding those two teams accountable. Their placements will drop to the bottom of the list. They will also be running the course again this evening until they can successfully complete it in sync and with a ten-minute shave off of their ending time from today."

"We need to shave ten minutes off the best time we've ever run? Son of a bitch!! Tell me again she's not a fucking liability, and you're not just as much of one!" Nikita snarled at Kolter.

"Let this be a lesson to all of you who may choose to deviate from the rules and regulations of this course. Due to the unforeseen nature of this course's completion, we will hold off on part two until tomorrow. Those not receiving consequences, please head back toward campus and your respective dens. That is all."

"Well fuck. We might as well grab a damn tent because we live on this course now. There is no fucking way we can shave ten minutes off of forty-eight minutes!" Brandt complained, kicking the rocks in front of him.

"Not with that attitude, we can't," Flavia retorted. "I, for one, think we can do it. Especially now that there aren't so many creatures running it and Everelle will stay with us this time. Let's just get this over with." She turned to start heading back to the start of the trail.

"Just a moment, ladies and gentlemen, just a few more words for both pack and pride." Professor Monaghan still stood on the wooden dais that housed the judges' panel for the course, grinning wickedly. "Come now, don't dilly dally. I have things to discuss before I depart." He waited momentarily while Ade pride and our pack both reconvened in front of the dais. "Ah, yes, good. While I have you, I wanted to expand on your consequence tonight. It appears as though while Everelle's motive for deviation from the course was superficial and ill thought out, Folasade's intentions were those of a more severely ill-intended outcome. It seems you two teams are the only ones on campus who can't stop fighting with each other. As such, we have devised a plan for you to truly have the desire to shave the time off." He turned his head and gestured toward the side of the dais and into the woods. Approaching us from the dense forest walked a pack of wolves and a pack of lions. Each group was made up of older men and women, thus equating to more power and strength. I gulped and held my breath as the smile widened across Monaghan's face. "Did you honestly think we'd let you off with such ease as to just improve your time? Oh, silly you... no, no. Instead of simply running, you will be evading tonight. You will start exactly thirty seconds ahead of your hunters. They have only one goal this evening. That's to destroy anyone they can reach."

I felt sick. My stomach turned inside out. I had a flash of Kasen, sitting in a similar experience. Forced to outrun his competition and not make it. With my jaw dropping, I looked at Nikita. She stood still, face paling by the second, and her eyes brimming with tears. I knew then that this is how Kasen was taken. I couldn't let them face this trial because of my reckless behavior. I stepped forward.

"Professor, I ask that you take my pack out of the running. It was my fault that I cut across the river. They had no idea what I was doing." Kolter reached for my arm to bring me back, but I shrugged him off. "What I mean to say is, I would rather face my consequences alone than risk their lives for my stupidity."

Professor Monaghan's face dipped lower. Without his expression faltering, he cleared his throat. "While noble your intentions may be, I alone dish out the consequences. While you may think you acted alone, you didn't. You have a direct wolf pack line. Your alpha and mates could see you and what you were doing. They chose to ignore you and allow you to follow your path without interference. They also left you, from what I'm told. Not very noble. Seems to me, you may have the only pure soul on your pack. Now, get back in line and prepare for your consequence."

Chapter Twenty-Five

Kolter

This wasn't going to end well. I already could feel Everelle panicking beside me. Nikita was far from willing to work as a team, and the others were sore and tired from running the first portion of the trial to their full ability. How could I have let this happen? I should have slowed during the trial when I knew she wasn't with us. I should have stopped us. No matter which position we ended in, anything would have been better than what we were doing right now. I was a fool for thinking I could run a successful pack. While I may be a Highland, I was acting like a joke, and now we would pay for it.

"Look, I know I've led you all like shit. No need to sugarcoat it. All I ask is that we stay together. At any point one of them could attack, and I'll be damned if my pack loses a member for something I've caused." Ever's eyes looked at me then, filled with shock and hurt. "I understand I've been a terrible leader, but that changes now. I will lead this pack, and I'll do so in a way I see fit. Despite what others may think, I'm not blind, and I refuse to accept that we're in this position because of her. Now, let's get up the trail, and when the horn sounds, we run like hell. No one looks back unless one of us falls. Is that understood?"

"Yes, sir," I heard in unison. That was by far the closest we've ever come to doing something as one. I'd make sure it wasn't our last. I couldn't stop the nagging feeling of guilt. The way Kolter took the blame for everything as if he was the sole person responsible for my actions made me feel defeated.

Stop, get it together, and stop playing the victim. I couldn't keep wallowing in self-deprecation; it was exactly how I kept finding myself locked into these situations. I heard Everelle say, but I wasn't going to correct her or beat her down. She knew she messed up, but where she was wrong was that it did fall back to me. If I can't keep my pack together, I'm doing something wrong.

We walked in silence, a mass of conflicts, toward the start of the trail. The sun was just beginning to set, and the odds of all of us living to see the morning unscathed were slim. I wasn't going to allow those slim odds to prosper. I was betting against the house. I was betting on our pack.

Once we got to the mouth of the trail, we lined up in running positions and waited in silence as the eerily serene night began to fall around us. I scanned our surroundings, my heart beginning to race with both adrenaline and the stress of the unknown. Approaching from the dark trail, my eyes closely followed the Pride of Ade as they made their way back to the line formation. They were stoic. It did not appear that Folasade got the same level of support that Everelle received. She was limping and already showing signs of weakness and disconnect. I thought back to what Everelle obviously left out of the retelling of what happened earlier. It seems Folasade went after her, and yet, Everelle still turned around and saved Folasade. It was both startling and impressive. I shook my head; I had no idea how I was going to survive her.

Professor Monaghan stepped out to the dais beside the mouth of the trail. He looked menacing, with his deep wide-set eyes and mouth turned into a snarl. "You will have no more than thirty-five minutes to complete this five-mile run. You will also be tasked with outrunning my assembled hunters.

If at any time, one catches you, you will end up in Pollsmoor for three days as additional punishment." The fuck that would happen. I won't let one of us end in Pollsmoor, especially not Everelle. We would make it to the end of the trail; there would be no mistaking it. I dropped my body down, crouching in position, a silent command that my pack follow suit. Around me, all of our eyes locked on Monaghan, jowls snapping and growls rumbling the ground's surface.

"Ladies, and gentlemen, take your positions." With that, he held his long arm in the air like he waited to be awarded a trophy, but it only made me think he looked stupid.

Remember, no one looks back. I said down the line, and as one, we lowered our bodies toward the ground, bracing ourselves. Once he dropped his arm to signal the start, all I saw was red. I burst from the starting line, making sure we were all in position as we began to thrust forward. I zoned out to the rhythm of our bodies pounding the gravel through the woods. The first obstacle in the course was a long skinny log that was used as a makeshift bridge over a canyon. It was only passable by one member of a team at a time. I made sure our pack made it there first. This allowed us to pull ahead of the pride and keep distance and bodies between us and the hunters. We continued to push forward. Mile one, down. Only four more to go. So far, so good.

The next mile began the winding portions of the trail. While racing downward, the trail tightly wove around a series of curved bends, creating in total seven 'S' formations. We as a group flew through the first two before I heard a sickening roar behind us. The hunters had caught one of the members of the pride. Knowing they weren't far behind us, I spoke down the line, *Push harder. They are gaining. Stay focused. So far, excellent job.*

I didn't speak to them in complete sentences for a multitude of reasons, the main being that no one wants to listen for words when they're deadly focused on the task at hand, and right now, that task was survival. I didn't think for one second the hunters would just innocently capture us and we'd walk to prison nice and neat. I knew they were here to shed blood, and I'd make damn sure they didn't shed ours.

Once we were done with obstacle two, mile marker two appeared ahead, signaling that we were beginning mile three, otherwise known as the rock scaling phase. This was a tough jaunt. It's where we typically struggled. It's why every morning I made them start and end our five-mile jaunts by climbing the exterior walls of the den. Just like this obstacle, those walls were made of obsidian, and the intricate lines formed in them created sometimes too smooth of a surface for our paws to fully grasp, causing slipping and missteps. I knew I could count on my pack to scale the wall with ease, and just hoped the pride behind us to falter. As they attempted to scale the wall, several lions slipped once or twice, allowing us to again take a sliver of forward progression unhindered by the hunters.

I was right. Halfway through the third mile, I again heard the roars of a lion most likely caught by a hunter. It was a daunting feeling knowing we were in a race to outrun masked killers, but it was practice for real life. At some point in our future, we would be tasked with a protection force and would have to do this very thing. I prayed we would succeed.

Coming out of mile three we were still running strong and fast and making excellent time. We just needed to pick up speed. The fourth mile was just a stretch of tall grass in a field. I knew this would make or break us. Though the area was wide-open without obstacles, the tall green and brown grass made it next to impossible to tell what direction we were headed in. It was also razor sharp. With each pass through, it would slice at us, sending trickles of blood over our bodies.

We forged on, faster and harder. We passed through the final stretch of grass and back through the forest tree line. The last mile was one of innate fear for Everelle. She didn't like seeing the tall walls surrounding us, tunneling us into the final finish line. I never bothered to give them much thought as we raced through them, but now I wish I'd paid better attention because we were headed directly into the tunnel, and it was pitch black. I could sense that we were all still together, but oddly, I couldn't pick up on a single threat behind us. Lion or hunter. I pushed on, funneling us closer to the final mile marker and finish line.

All at once, I was slammed on my shoulder by a falling rock, throwing me off balance while another smashed directly in front of my path. The raining of rocks sent me jumping at the wall, then back to the path to avoid it, watching down the line as the other pack mates did their best to avoid the treacherous obstacle. Pushing on, my only thoughts were getting us to that finish line.

My paws were mere feet from the finish line when I heard a loud, screeching howl and a sickening thud. I looked down my line and saw Priya pinned underneath a large fallen rock and Kentaro next to her, howling toward the moon, pain-stricken. I wanted to stop; I wanted to help her, but I knew in the best interest of the pack we had to keep going.

Everelle didn't feel the same. She turned abruptly at my side and raced back along the path to where Kentaro was howling. Rocks began to fall more quickly now, and the sounds of the approaching hunters approaching, were bludgeoning my brain. "Leave her! You have to leave her; there's nothing more you can do! Move! NOW!" I frantically shouted to them as I watched Nikita, Victor, Brandt, Assata, Flynn, Flavia, Lisbeth, and Baldur all passed over the finish line. Everyone but Kentaro and Everelle, who remained in place howling over Priya's lain body. "THEY'RE COMING. MOVE!" I shouted again to them down the line. They needed to leave her and go. I couldn't cross the finish line without Kentaro and Everelle.

I watched in slow motion as she relived a part of our past. Everelle shifted back into her human form despite the danger of the falling rocks and bit her arm hard enough to create a pool of blood at its surface. I watched in angst as she grabbed Priya's wounded head and began to squeeze her blood into the wound.

"You need to get the rock off of her," she screamed to Kentaro, breaking him from his spiraling and giving him something to focus on. I knew if I was going to get Everelle safely across this line, I needed to act fast. I raced back toward them in time to help Kentaro remove the boulder from Priya's mangled body. I thought I was going to throw my guts up, looking down at her. The air smelled thick with the metallic zing of blood. The rocks still pummeled the path, and the hunters were approaching us quickly. I knew we needed to get moving.

Everelle was still frantically trying to mix her blood with Priya's. I watched as she again bit her arm, this time placing it on her back where Priya had suffered a deep wound. She was sobbing, begging Priya to come back to her. My heart was breaking seeing Everelle and Kentaro spiral.

"Grab her," I barked at Kentaro, nodding toward Priya's body. Gingerly, I bent down and took Everelle into my mouth and allowed her to cling to my chest as we turned racing back toward the finish line. Kentaro with Priya on my heels.

Everelle was stronger than I was. She was physically and mentally stronger than all of us. She just didn't know it. The way this woman would literally throw herself under falling boulders to make sure her best friend didn't die on the field, proved it.

We raced across the line with six minutes and one less pack mate to spare. No one was speaking out of respect for Kentaro. He gently laid Priya on the ground in front of the pack, shaking as he dropped to his now human knees in front of her. Grasping her hand, he began screaming over and over, his broken heart on full display. His sunken eyes, rimmed in red, spilled liquid in waves. "I told you to go home. I told you to go," he repeated, burying his face into her chest.

Everelle was in hysterics. I could feel her blaming herself for Priya. She was manically repeating it was her fault in her mind. Reaching for her, I cupped her cheeks between the palms of my hands. "Look at me!" I shouted, waiting for her bloodshot eyes to meet mine. "This is not your fault!! You did all you could. You tried to save her. You are not to blame; do you understand me?" My eyes followed hers back to Priya's body, then to her arm, which was mangled from her bites. "This isn't your fault!"

I stepped back from her, tearing a piece of my linen undershirt off. I reached for Everelle's arm and began to gently wrap her wound, hoping it would allow her to heal faster.

"Everelle, you need to come back to me. Stop spiraling. It's not your fault." I soothed, trying to hold her gaze. Her eyes continuously found Priya's body while she sobbed.

Our pack paced back and forth, unwilling to speak. Professor Monaghan was nowhere in sight, and time stood still.

The Pride of Ade crossed the line, with three fewer members of their pride. The night was eerily silent. Only those with broken hearts could be heard. Their grief was palpable.

After what seemed like an eternity, Professor Monaghan stepped forward from the shadows and onto the dais. "We have experienced tragedy this evening in the form of a deceased cadet. This is a direct result of your own foolishness. Those at fault for tonight's re-run, understand her death is on your conscience. There is no worse punishment than that of death. May you learn your lessons the hard way and not repeat your mistakes." He stared out at the group of us, all taunting. He snapped his fingers then, signaling his men, and thrust them toward Priya's body.

"NOOOO! Stop!!!" Everelle shouted as she stepped forward to protect Priya's body. "You need to give her body back to her family. They need her to be buried with dignity." Her tears began flowing all over again as she and Kentaro held Priya's lifeless hands. "She's still warm. Get her to medical. Please, please try and save her. She's still warm!"

"Get back!! NOW!" bellowed Professor Monaghan. His anger was so visible the veins in his neck bulged, and his face turned the color of lava. "This is your fault, you foolish girl! You think you get to decide what happens to people here in Askari? You don't!! You are the reason this poor girl's family will never see her again! I hope your guilt keeps you up at night. NOW STEP BACK IN LINE!"

I reached forward, gathering Everelle in my arms and allowing her to bury her face into my chest to muffle her sobs. I'd never wanted to rip someone's throat out so much as I had these last few weeks. How these men could be so callously cruel bewildered me.

Five men stepped forward and gently picked up the remains of Priya and headed toward the trail back to campus.

Once the men were out of sight, the professor turned his venom back toward our pack. "Now, you will run the course again."

No. NO FUCKING WAY! Hatred, like I've never felt before, spewed from my mouth in the form of a growl so deep and low it could not be mistaken.

"Kolter, you would do best to keep your head. You never know when an apple may fall from your tree," Professor Monaghan mocked. "Now, I said, AGAIN!"

He would die. There would be no justice to our continent if he were allowed to live after what he had done tonight. For Priya, he would die at my hands.

We ran the trail eleven more times. We ran sixty-five miles total. Our bodies were shutting down; our thirst was long overdue. At the first light of morning, the professor let us leave. He made sure to let us know that this long night in no way exempted us from our classes in just a few short hours.

"I fucking hate him," Everelle barked as we crawled into our den. "I absolutely fucking hate him."

"The feeling is mutual," I acknowledged.

"Are we just supposed to leave her with them? Who is going to tell her parents? What will they tell them? What about her eight brothers?" Everelle became undone again, and I held her in my arms as we laid in my bed.

"I don't know," I whispered into her hair as I kissed the top of her head. "I don't know what happens now."

Chapter Twenty-Six

Everelle

Priya was gone, Kentaro was devastated, and I was filled with the worst kind of guilt imaginable. She was my best friend. The first person who made me feel seen. She took me under her wing before even knowing where I was going or if I would be in her pack. My heart hurt for her family. My heart hurt for Kentaro. My heart hurt for me. What's worse, before the course, she'd said it'd been an honor being my friend, as if she'd known she wasn't coming home. I caught the sob leaving my throat with her blanket. I was in her bed. At some point during the night, I'd left Kolter's embrace for Priya's scent on her sheets.

There was a knock on my bedroom door, and for once, I didn't feel like getting it. I didn't honestly care who was on the other side. It wasn't Priya, and nothing I did would bring her back. It was my fault.

The knocking came again; this time it was a little louder. "Ev, could you open up? I don't need you beating me to the punch. It's my job to blame you."

Fucking Flynn.

I rolled over and put my feet on the floor. Shuffling past my desk, I noticed the photo of Priya and me from the train that second day. She'd helped me get dressed and insisted we take a photo because I was hot. That was all it took; my eyes were again filled with tears. I took the photo and put it face down on the desk. I couldn't see her right now.

I ambled to the door against my will. Once open, I found Flynn with a cheeky smile on his face. He stepped in and shut the door behind him. "Ok, girly, let's get this over with."

"I can't do this with you right now," I said, backing away from him and heading to my bed. I wasn't in the mood for all of Flynn right now.

"Ouch...you'd think I'd be used to hearing things like that by now, but nope... it still stings." He made his way over to me, shaking his head with a small smirk. I crawled into my bed and curled over to the side, looking up at him. Flynn's face softened and he brushed my hair from my forehead. "I'm sorry, but I'm really going to need you to go easier on me. I'm sensitive after all." That was all it took.

I lost it then. He got me. He got me to laugh on the day my best friend died. It felt wrong. I was going to hell. May as well send my request to the Devil now.

"That's better. I can't have you already crying when I've come to scold you... It takes the enjoyment out of it. So, for me, could you pull yourself together?" he teased, while making himself comfortable on my bed.

"You can't do this. Stop trying to make me feel better when I'm the reason she's dead. It's my fault! If you think about it, I saved Folasade and killed Priya. I'm fucked up."

"What in the deep, dark, and dangerous kind of shit are you thinking?" Flynn looked genuinely concerned, and it made me feel worse. "That's a stretch, and you know it."

"It's true, if I'd been more like you, I'd have let the bitch die, then..." He needed to understand. He needed to know that I chose a pride member over my own best friend. I couldn't stomach the thought anymore. I felt sick.

"Let me stop you right there. One, you'll never be like me, but it's flattering you want to be. Two, Hun, even if you had left her to die, we'd still have had to run the course again. You had already diverted from the course at that point. Saving Folasade saved your heart another death to grieve. You would have beaten yourself up for both, instead of just Priya's." He was now lying on his side, facing me, his arm stretched under our heads to help hold them up. He reached for my other hand and squeezed it. "I'm sorry we, as a pack, give you so much shit. It's not fair. I get now why you do things. I saw it when you turned back for Kentaro after Priya passed. You care about people. You put everyone over yourself. I want you to know that is your best asset. You're not reckless, babe. You're human."

He was right. I was human. I felt deeply for people, wanting them to be ok over me. It's why they all believed we were on different wavelengths. Not one of them, Kolter included, had a human side to them. Yes, they could shift into a human by default, but they weren't one. My mother, she was a human. She fell for a lion. It's why there seemed to always be three sides to me. I was extremely sensitive and nurturing, my human side. Strong and fast, my wolf side; and extremely smart and prideful, my lion side. I was always going to be in constant conflict with one of my sides. I was a walking, talking mess.

"I just want you to know, I'll talk to the others. You don't have to explain yourself anymore. I am truly sorry we give you so much shit. You're still young in the shifting phase of your life. We should be giving you more grace than we do."

"It doesn't stop the fact that when pen hits paper, facts are facts. Priya is dead as a direct result of my reckless actions. I couldn't keep up with the pack, and therefore I tried to cheat my way back into formation."

"You didn't cheat. You thought logically, and to be fair, nowhere has it ever been said you can't make your own path on the trail. It doesn't say you have to follow those clear lines. I looked. I want them to pay for Priya's death. By class standards and rules, you didn't do a thing wrong."

If what he was saying was true and I truly didn't break any rules, I'd have Monaghan's job, or his head. He wouldn't walk out of this school with both.

My door opened then, and Kolter stepped in.

"Babe, do you even knock? We were in the middle of something here." Flynn mocked outrage.

Kolter stood in the doorway, one eyebrow raised. A small smirk formed on his face as he stepped in and sat at my desk.

"Oh, for fuck's sake, not like that. You think she'd settle for what I have to offer when she's seen what's under that hood?" Flynn scoffed.

"You didn't have to tell me that. I already knew." Kolter grinned.

"Well, ouch again. You know, this has been really fun, but I think for my own mental health, I should probably head out." He squeezed my hand before dropping it and climbing out of my bed. Once across the room, he sized Kolter up as he was walking by. "Hmmm, I don't see anything worth competing for."

"Flynn, get the fuck out," Kolter barked as he shoved him out the door. "Have a great night."

"Yeah yeah, go fuck yourself," he chirped back.

"Nope, that's what you'll be doing. Last I checked, Flavia is still holding out," Kolter's eyes gleamed with jest.

"Ooooh, another dagger to my chest, I don't know how I'll survive..." Flynn mocked getting stabbed in the chest, as he backed out of the door, letting Kolter slam it in his face.

It happened again. Thanks to my two favorite men, I was laughing again. The guilt was a little less severe, but nonetheless the tears were of happiness and not heartache.

"He brought up a good point," I said as Kolter climbed into my bed, where Flynn was just lying, wrinkling his nose at his lingering scent. "He said he checked everywhere in the class rules and protocols for the course, and nowhere did it say you have to stick to the path. It says you need to cross the finish line at the end of the five-mile trail, but it doesn't say how you have to get there. So, by default, me crossing the river to meet back up with the pack wasn't wrong or against any rules."

"I like the sounds of that, but it's implied. The rules imply that you must stay on the trail, and you cut the distance by an eighth of a mile that you wouldn't have been able to make up," Kolter began.

"Where? Where is the implication? Professor Monaghan has never once said, stay on the course, stay on the trail, nothing. He told us to cross the finish line at the end of the trail by the allotted time. Nowhere does it say, nor did he say, how we have to get there. I get the semantics of distance, but he killed Priya by forcing us to run that trail at night through the rock tunnel. That is on his conscience, not mine." As I said it, I lost steam. Who was I kidding? I'd still beat myself up every day until I died. I killed my best friend. That was on me.

"Ok, so what are you going to do about it? I'm assuming he couldn't care less. One dead cadet after his class makes no difference to him. To some he looks like a hero who is training us for anything. What will have an influence?"

"I don't know, but the General will be hearing from me," I said confidently.

"And what do you think will happen? Do you think he will just sit down with you and agree while you sip a cappuccino in his office? Everelle, look at me. These men, these leaders, they don't care about you or me. They care about the bottom line, and that's to put strong and like-minded individuals in power and on the front line for defensive measures." His eyes were burning with anger as he continued, "They couldn't have cared less that we lost a pack mate last night, or that three from a pride were sent to prison. To them, that means there is one less individual they need to pay to feed, clothe, and bathe, and in their eyes, she was weak if she died. That's what they'll tell her family. That she died in the line of service to the greater good of Siochan. I know because I've lived it twice. The only thing I care about is that neither your parents nor I are ever on the receiving end of that news about you."

Indignation fueled me, and I began to sit up. "Are you to lie here and say that what they have done to Priya is over? That we will just need to forget it and move on, as long as it's not you and I, who the fuck cares?" I was blinded by rage.

"No, Ever, I never said that. I said that's just how it is, not that I agreed with it. I've had to receive two of those calls now. Someone has stepped on our doorstep, rang our fucking bell, and said, 'we regret to inform you that your family member died in the line of duty, sworn protection to the continent.' Then they hug you and act as if giving you their bodies and a fucking stone slab engraved with their names somehow makes up for the years of memories that are now frozen in time. My dad, my brother, Priya, they don't get to make new ones! We no longer get new memories. There will never be another new adventure with them. They're gone." Kolter was spiraling. Fueled by anger and resentment, I wanted to reach out and hold him, to pull him closer and make the pain stop. I was afraid that the pain never would stop, it was locked in for life thanks to this fucking school. "When I say there is nothing we can do except be better today, I say it so that the shit out there, the deaths, hopefully won't happen again. I need you to be on top of your game. No matter what happens, stop losing perspective. It takes my mind from worrying about the pack to worrying about just you. Nikita is right. I need better priorities if I'm to lead a pack where no one else dies!"

The blow hurt just as bad as her death. Without saying it, he blamed me for her death. He blamed my recklessness and my human nature for Priya's death, and I couldn't unhear it.

"I think I'm going to ask you to leave," I said, my eyes locked on his.

"What? Why? Because I asked you to keep your head on?" Kolter asked me, confused.

"No, because you blame me for her death, and right now, I can't unhear that. I'm pissed and I'm hurt and I'm going to need you to leave." I began to get up from my bed and gesture him towards the door.

"Ev, stop. That's not what I'm saying." He was reaching for me. Trying to gaslight me into thinking he didn't just blame me for her death. I wouldn't allow myself to be blindsided in love. Reaching up around my neck, I took his rubix off and clasped it shut before returning it to him. "I don't need your calm. I think you need this more than I do. Now, please go. I'll be out for positions in a little bit." I knew that would hurt him and that I wasn't playing fair, but I didn't care. I could beat myself up for Priya's death. I could blame myself, but Kolter? He was supposed to have my back and help me through this. I was so disgusted I couldn't look at him.

He took the necklace into his hand and didn't speak. He just looked from it to my eyes and back. I could see that I'd wounded him, but he had hurt me in a much larger way. He wouldn't see me cry again.

"Ev, look, I'm..." he began, but I just put my hands up and closed my eyes. I didn't want to talk to him anymore. I wanted him to get the fuck out of my room.

Slowly he sat up and walked toward the door. "I'm sorry," he said. "Truly, I am."

The door closed and he was gone. After closing down the lines between us, I allowed myself to cry. Not just for Priya, but for me, for Kolter, and for every fucked-up thing this school had done to people.

An hour later, my tears were dry, and I was dressed and ready for day two of trials. Professor Monaghan wasn't going to succeed in killing me or my soul. I stepped into the common room, and the loss of Priya was evident. I hadn't realized until now that she was the first person whose eyes I searched for in every room. Now, those eyes would never share the room with me again.

"Today is aversion training. We drew aversion first," Kolter began, pacing back and forth in front of the mantle. "I'm not entirely sure what today brings, but please try and stay as levelheaded as possible. We need to be sure that above all else, we come back as one unit. If you need a moment to gather yourself while we are out there, tell someone. Don't fight your demons alone," he said genuinely. I watched his throat bob, fighting back emotion. "All I ask from you, is that you remain vigilant. We will try and keep our hiding spots to a fifteen-foot radius. That should allow us ample time to hide, but it also means we have each other's back quickly if one of us is found. If you have any thoughts or questions, now would be the time to ask them. When we're out there, I want to make sure we're a united force to be reckoned with. I want them to know Priya didn't pass in vain." Kolter finished by looking me in the eyes. He was speaking those words to me. She didn't die in vain. I got it, but I wasn't going to take his bullshit attempt at a peace offering. No one else had anything left to comment, so we headed out to the fields in silence.

As a pack, we arrived at the sparring field at the hottest part of the day. The sun was brutal, it's direct rays shone down due to the cloudless sky. Looking around me now, I noticed how much the hunter's toll last night had taken. I saw just how much of a toll this year had taken. Most of the packs or prides had lost at least one member. Why was I so self-absorbed as to not notice this until now? Every student on this field shared a common interest... grief. It was truly heartbreaking.

Professor Monaghan was accompanied today by three individuals I'd never seen. All were in militaristic-style mustard-gold uniforms. It led me to believe that they worked for the school or on the front lines. Neither was putting any faith in my heart that they could be trusted.

"Good afternoon, cadets!" he began. His smile today was wider than previous days. The sinking feeling in my gut told me this could only mean that whatever was planned wasn't one we were going to enjoy. At this point, I had the feeling that Professor Monaghan enjoyed torture disguised as education. "Today, you will either be working with Sergeant Stone or Captain Archibald as you complete the aversion or hunting trial runs of your final course. The position you take has already been decided for you and was dropped off this morning to your alpha or king. Please be advised, we wish no harm to any of you, but take heed in knowing the simplicity of rule following should be adhered to in order to maintain proper safety and protocol. If you are aversion trial running today, please make your way to Captain Archibald. If you are hunting, please see Sergeant Stone. They will set you up for your next task. At eighteen hundred hours we will reconvene here on the sparring field, and your scores will be adjusted to the scores from yesterday. Keep in mind that just because you had minor setbacks yesterday doesn't mean you can't squeeze ahead today. I look forward to watching your trial! Let's begin!"

As a pack, we headed over to Captain Archibald to prepare for aversion tactic trials. He was a gruff man, tall, with short buzzed blonde hair and dark eyes. He presented a 'no nonsense' kind of attitude, which resulted in me feeling little hope for a successful completion of today's trial.

"Step on over, fill in the circle... that's right, keep coming in," the captain hissed. Once all were settled in a circle, he stood front and center of it so he could easily walk around and see everyone, and we too could see and hear him clearly. "Today we will be honing our aversion skill tactics. In layman's terms, this means we're keeping away from the hunters. It's a tactic for when you choose to hide and wait." The captain emphasized his words similarly to the general, spit spewing from his lips. He stood erect and tall, making it a point to look into everyone's eyes as he walked around the circle. "As a pack or pride, you will enter the forest and will have until seventeen thirty to keep from being captured by the hunters. Succeed, and you will earn the winning points today. If you fail, and those hunting find you, you will lose points and score at the bottom of the group. Am I clear on your expectations?" he asked loudly.

"Yes sir." Everyone recited in unison.

"Excellent, then let's get you into the woods."

"Cadets who are averting, you will have exactly forty minutes to make yourselves scarce in the woods. The only rule you have is that you must stay on school-approved grounds. Do not extend your positions to outer territories. The bells will chime at seventeen thirty. Once rung, please find your respective packs or prides and make your way back to the sparring fields," Professor Monaghan projected from the dais. "Cadet's ready!" He thrust his arm in the air, holding it steady for a moment, then dropping it.

In seconds, we were off and rushing toward the forest line, outpacing the Mazza and Hadlick packs. As I leapt forward, it hit me suddenly. Why were just wolves averting? Opening the line I'd slammed shut this morning, I reached out to Kolter.

Why are only wolves averting? Something is up. I think we're being set up again. I looked around, anxiously scanning the woods. Watching as wolves disappeared among the trees, all racing in search of hiding or places to stake out.

I agree, Kolter, Something isn't right here, Nikita chimed in down the line. *What is going on?*

They didn't say anything when they dropped the card off today. It had one word on the index card, 'Avert.' I'm not sure what they're planning, but I agree. We've spent all year paired with a pride. Why not keep it that way?

I watched as Kolter began searching the area for any signs that something wasn't right. If he was worried, you'd never know. He was stoic, determined, and focused. I mimicked his actions, telling myself that he needed to lead the pack, and I needed to stay in my lane and with the pack. Above anything else, I wouldn't be the fucking liability today.

We'd been running just under an hour through a maze of trails, up rock walls and down, through rivers and across fields. At this point we were almost completely one hundred and eighty degrees from where we started. Kolter came to a cliff ledge, with a bunch of smaller hideaways hidden from view along the top of the ridge.

"There, we will stay tucked in those." Kolter gestured with his head toward the top of the rocky cliff. "I need you to stay in groups of two or three. No one is to be left alone, and no one is to make a noise. No matter what you hear or what you see, you are to stay put unless you hear from me. Are we clear?" The pack agreed with a decisive nod. "Then let's get up there. We have exactly three hours to wait this out. I'll stay down here until every one of you is fashioned in your crevices. Then I'll light the scent diffuser to clear our scent from the trail. Everelle, stay behind Kentaro until I get back."

As he departed from us, we all climbed the wall in human form, making sure not to shift again until we were safely inside the dark crevices.

Once in position at the topmost peak, I peered out over the edge to see if I could see Kolter. "You will need to stand behind me. Everelle, you're white, you'll reflect color when they look at the wall. Stay back down the cave there a little further." Kentaro nudged with his nose toward the back of the cave we'd entered.

He wasn't wrong, and although I'd rather search for Kolter, I did as was suggested and moved back, deeper into the cave.

"I don't blame you, you know. For Priya I mean." Kentaro said, quietly, his voice full of sadness.

"I know, but I do. I blame myself, as does Kolter. While it wasn't intentional, it still happened as a result of my poor choices. I wouldn't blame you if you did."

"She told me she felt she was going to die on the course. Right before we ran it the first time," he said now, looking down, shaking his head softly. What did he mean she knew? My head began to swirl. A brief memory of her last words to me replayed. Was she saying "goodbye," to me? Oh, I was going to be sick.

"She said she saw it happen. She saw everything. Down to the rock and you helping her. I just blew her off. I knew she had visions sometimes, but after the first race, when she was fine, I thought she had it wrong."

She saw it. Priya was a seer. This made so much sense. All the times she'd latch on to me with confidence. The reason she knew I was going to Askari on the platform. The reason she knew I was Highland before myself or Kolter. She was a seer. A seer that I'd given her my blood in an attempt to save. Throughout my spiraling thoughts I'd zoned out on Kentaro. I'd missed what he'd said. So, I simply nodded in agreement and waited patiently for him to speak again. My mind was still buzzing with this new information that was right in my face all along.

"I never got to tell her I loved her. I know that sounds so stupid, right? What I regret most was not telling her that I loved her." He shook his head as if in disbelief. "She told me last week, and I felt it too, but I wouldn't tell her. I made such a big thing in my head that I needed to tell her in a big way. It couldn't just come out after we'd been fucking. I needed her to know I honestly meant it. Now, she'll never know."

"She knew." I said looking at him now. "We talked about it, she knew. She said she'd seen that exact thing you'd planned in your mind. She knew exactly what you said. She told me. She told me she didn't care how you said it, just that she was just so lucky to have you. She wanted you to have your moment because it was important to you, but she'd seen it happen." I hinted toward Priya's powers. I wanted to see if he'd remark on it or connect the dots. If he did, he didn't make mention of it. He just continued looking grief-stricken. "She thanked Kolter that night too, you know, for position matching you. She was so unbelievably happy to have you as her mate, Kentaro. You made her feel so loved."

He was crying now. Not loudly or obscene, just a slow trickle of tears, silently sliding down his face as he looked out over the treetops. "I already miss her," he said then. "It hasn't even been a full fucking day, and I miss her. When do you think that stops?"

"I hope it doesn't. Wolves, I'm told, mate for life. Seems like even if you two hadn't officially bonded, she would have still considered you her mate, and she wanted nothing more," I said. Then, rethinking it, I added, "but I hope one day you can find someone else that makes you just as happy. She'd want that, you know? She wouldn't want you living out the rest of your days alone."

"We did officially bond," he said then quietly. "I know we aren't supposed to without Kolter's permission. It's frowned upon for cadets to bond officially because you never know the outcome of your life or path they'll assign, but we couldn't help it. One night one thing just led to another. It wasn't intentional.

I remember pacing the floor after we were finished, worried that Kolter was going to kill us. It was Priya who reminded me that he'd been fine with Lisbeth and Baldur, and that you two had..." He stopped now, almost embarrassed to say it in front of me. "Thank you for your kind words, but I won't be able to find another mate. We're soul-bound for eternity. I can still feel her, which to me is the craziest thing." He looked back at me now. "You know, you're much better to talk to than Flynn. God, he makes me want to punch a wall."

"Definitely," I agreed.

We sat in silence for a bit as per Kolter's instructions. After the better part of an hour, I began to worry about Kolter. He wasn't being picked up on the line, and I was beginning to get anxious when he finally crawled into the cave and stood behind Kentaro. The silver in his fur would be easily spotted amongst the black cave, like me. I realize he put us with Kentaro because he was the largest of them, aside from Kolter, and could help hide us behind his dark fur.

I motioned for him to look at me, screaming at him, *turn the line back on!* I rolled my eyes when he finally came back on.

Where the fuck were you? Why'd you turn the line off? You had me scared to death! I shouted at him.

That's funny, I thought you were still pissed at me... I was making sure the scent was scattered as far back as the river, so even if they crossed it, they wouldn't necessarily come here. He didn't meet my gaze. Instead, he kept his face forward, looking out at the treeline between Kentaro's legs.

It would have been nice to know that, so I didn't think we were sitting ducks with no damn alpha. I rolled my eyes even if he wouldn't see it.

I'm sorry, but why do you think I answer to you? He snapped his narrowed hurt-filled eyes to me now, a dark scowl on his face that took me aback.

Because I'm your pack's female alpha. It would have at least been nice to know where the fuck you were.

Shut up... Kolter said quickly, his head jerking back forward.

Don't tell me to shut up! I'll have you... He cut off my lashing.

Stop talking! Someone's out there! Kolter barked quietly at me.

I shut up. Right away I stiffened and shut up. Kolter lowered himself to the floor of the cave again, making sure he could still see out between Kentaro's legs.

I wanted to turn the line on for everyone, but it was too risky. We all needed to remain quiet and still.

Then, I heard the voices.

"There are so many lions out here today. Do you suppose we will see the white one we saw a few weeks ago?" It was the female from the woods. The one from weeks ago when I ran away. My breath caught in my throat, and I cowered lower.

"I doubt it. We should have tagged her when we had the chance. The Sector would have paid top dollar for her. Blah, the only ones we've seen today are brown and tan." I recognized his voice too. It was the smaller man who'd accompanied the woman in the forest. They were lion hunting?

"I'm glad we didn't tag her. She seemed lost to me, scared almost, like she woke up unaware of who she was."

"Who she was? What are you talking about Emory? Lions aren't people." The man was chuckling now.

"You mean to tell me you haven't heard about the shifters? Lions and wolves? Shifting? None of that rings a bell?" she countered him.

"Those are old wives' tales. No one has heard or seen a shifter in hundreds of years. Their species probably died out, if they existed at all."

"Oh no, Theo, they exist, and I wouldn't be too sure they aren't still around. I think the pretty white lion was one of them. She seemed too human to be a lion. I just hope she found what she was after," Emory said dreamily to Theo.

"I don't know, babe. You're such a dreamer." You could hear the smile on his face as he spoke.

Kolter looked at me then.

You?

Yes... I'm sorry, I said, my eyes drifting to the floor.

It's fine. They seem human, naive. You'll be alright. He gave me a thoughtful look then, and we continued to listen.

"I don't know, I heard that people once walked the continent and could change into all sorts of different things. Lions, tigers... wolves... you name it. I was told only those that were the most powerful were albino. All others were muted, but the white ones, and they were said to have no strikes against their power, which is why they're white. Almost like pure magic."

"Ok, Em, let's get you home. I think the heat is getting to you."

"Theo...."

"Excuse me, you two there, have you seen any wolves or anything out and about in these parts?"

I froze; it was Neo. I would recognize his voice anywhere. He was asking the people if they'd seen us.

Breathe babe. You're fine. Kolter said, placing his paw onto mine.

What do we do? My eyes darted from him to Kentaro, to the outside treetops. We could hear them; we just couldn't see them.

"No sir, I'm so sorry. You're the first person we've come across all day."

"Perhaps you heard me wrong. I didn't say people. I asked if you'd seen wolves."

There was an edge to his voice that made me uncomfortable. I suddenly felt fear tangibly prickling the fur down my spine. I was worried for the people down on the ground.

"No, again, we haven't. We've been out foraging for truffles. The woods have been quiet today."

Please don't find us, please don't find us, I thought, praying to God or Kasen or anyone to look out for our pack hiding in the wall above them.

"Alright, then, have a good day."

"You al..."

His voice dropped completely. Then I heard it. An earth-shattering scream pierced my brain. Something I'll never forget.

Then just as suddenly as it had erupted, it was gone. Nothing could be heard except a sickening thud as a body hit the ground.

"Sir, they're obviously not over here. I think we should run course back toward the fields. We have less than thirty before the bells toll, and we're no closer now to them than we were when we started."

"I just thought I felt them. I thought I felt...her."

"Who? Everelle? Again?" Baraka asked Neo.

"Yes! I swear to you, there's something off with that wolf. I know it. You mark my words, your highness, Everelle is not someone we want to be standing at the end of the year." Neo's warning gave me an instant chill. Trying to remain calm, I focused on my tangibles, wishing I'd had Kolter's rubix.

Kolter jerked in front of me as if punched; he slowly turned around, studying me in confusion. I swallowed and spoke down the line; *I didn't say anything! Did they hear me?*

No, no, that's not it. Never mind. They're leaving. We just need to lie low and still until the bells toll. I'll handle the threats from here on out. He won't get away with that. He said, turning his face back toward the front of the cave. Fear and anxiety began to bubble in my chest. If Neo was on to me, there was no telling who else was. I didn't need this kind of stress.

Ok, you just looked like you saw a ghost. That's all. I commented trying to ease my mind. The stress unwinding slowly.

No, nothing like that.

The three of us sat in silence waiting for the bells to toll. They should be ringing any moment. The sun was setting in the sky, creating a perfectly peaceful night. The stars were just making their way across the sky when the bells finally began to ring.

Stretching out in the cave, I yawned. We successfully evaded capture. Now we just needed to get back down and head back to the sparring fields. Kentaro was first to shift back into human form, leaving Kolter and me alone in the cave.

"I feel awful for that couple. They didn't deserve to die today."

"Not many people do. It's part of how this cruel continent operates." He gestured for me to go second down the face of the rock wall. Stepping to the mouth of the cave, I shifted back into my human form. Turning around to brace myself on the rocks and begin my descent, I noticed Kolter standing still, eyes wide, frozen in place. I scurried back up to meet him. "What? What's happened? Are you ok?!" I asked, taking inventory of his body to make sure he hadn't hurt himself.

"How did you do it?" he asked, voice shaking.

"Do what? What did I do wrong this time?" I asked, flabbergasted. "You're giving me a damn heart attack, Kolt."

"That," he said, not acknowledging my rambling, and began pointing at me. "How did you pull it from my pocket back there?"

"What are you talking about, Kolter! You're freaking me out; I didn't pull anything from you."

He stepped forward, and with timid hands, he grabbed the rubix, which until now, I hadn't realized I was wearing.

"I don't... I didn't realize..." I was now looking down at the rubix he held in his hand.

"What did you do, Everelle?" he demanded now, looking sterner.

"Hey, I didn't mean it! I just wished I hadn't given it back to you earlier when I was having an anxiety attack after Emory and Theo lost their lives. I don't know! I just wished for it!"

"You wished for my rubix back? Then it came back?" He asked, looking confused.

"I didn't mean it! I'm sorry!" I was pleading with him not to blame me for another thing. "I tried my damn hardest today. I followed all your fucking rules. I was quiet when you asked. I'm sorry! I just needed your comfort, that's all." I was spiraling now, sobbing.

His lips were on mine in a moment. He held me in his arms and kissed me tenderly. Pulling back, he cupped my face in between his hands. "Stop apologizing for things you didn't mean to happen. I'm not mad at you; I'm impressed by you."

"Oh..." I said, wiping the tears as they escaped my eyes. "Do you want it back? The rubix, I mean." After all, it was his. If he was upset I'd taken it, he could have it back.

"No, I don't want it back. I hated that you'd given it back in the first place. I just don't understand how it happened. But regardless, it is where it's supposed to be. Right next to your heart. A piece of me lives next to your heart. That's all I want."

"A piece of you lives in my heart. Your blood, remember?" I joked. I was trying to break the seriousness of the situation.

"Baby, stay the hell away from Flynn." He kissed my forehead then, and turned back to begin the descent down the cliff to our waiting pack below.

"What took you two so long?" Victor accosted me.

"They were probably taking advantage of the situation... moonlit cave, middle of the treetops, cool breeze, bow chicka wow wow."

"Shut up, Flynn," four people said in unison.

"Well, what the fuck! We stay alive tonight, and I can't make a single joke. You all could use a good romp in the sack," Flynn whined, rolling his eyes and crossing his arms over his chest.

Heading back toward the sparring field, the mood in the pack was peaceful. Surprising us all, tonight was a success. What started with tension and worry about the trial at hand ended with high spirits because we'd come so close to being discovered but were able to stay hidden.

As we approached the field, we could see it had been lit by torches, illuminating the entire area. Professor Monaghan, Captain Archibald, and Sergeant Stone were all waiting on the dais for us to return. We were the first pack to arrive. The only other team on the field was the Molti Pride.

"Hey man, great job. Wherever you were at, we didn't even catch your trail." Xolani said, clapping hands with Kolter and slapping his back. "Proud of you, man."

"Thanks, it was a group effort," Kolter said, humbly.

"Let's hope we can evade you all tomorrow. I scouted some pretty awesome places out there while we were searching."

For the next twenty minutes, packs and prides began filing in.

"Come now, let's not delay. Some of us have things to do tonight," Professor Monaghan said, obviously frustrated. "Alright, now that we are all here, congratulations seem to be in order for all wolf packs. You all successfully averted your hunters, and as such, you shall be rewarded with special dining menus hand-delivered to your dens this evening." He seemed less than thrilled to be announcing this, and collective cheers went up throughout the packs. "Prides, this evening you will be running drills until you can successfully find my men, who will hide themselves among the trees in the forest. Stepping out onto the field were the older wolves again. This time, I paid special attention to a female I hadn't seen yesterday. Her eyes were wider than the others, and she seemed to be looking around, unsure of how to take in where she was. Then she locked eyes with mine, and I felt a pull. It was similar to the pull on the line when we speak to one another, but less intense. I shook my head and looked at her again. Her eyes were swollen, sad, and lost. She then darted her eyes away, looking across my pack, then dropped them toward the ground. I'd never felt sorry for one of our mentors before, but I felt sorry for her. She clearly wasn't here on her own accord.

"If there are no further questions, you are all dismissed."

Chapter Twenty-Seven

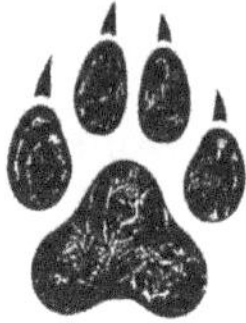

Everelle

Sometimes I wondered, when I was sitting alone, how I was chosen or destined by fate for this life. For over a week we had been sparring, running trials, averting, hunting, over and over again. Mentally, I was strong; physically, I was weakening.

The course was being run in two days, and I was feeling like I could just fall apart. I didn't know how I'd completed six months at this academy, but I had. Not all were lucky enough to say the same.

It was a cold, rainy, and miserable Saturday. They'd given us the weekend to rest with the warning that Monday morning, we'd begin the course in finality. It would presumably take all day. We'd never done all three parts in one day before, and I wasn't going to lie, I was nervous. Stretching my bones, I began to think about the nuances of my life.

It seemed like the more I was beginning to learn about myself, the less I truly knew who I was at all. Kolter and Lucianna were my only confidants. I'd lost my best friend before even having the chance to tell her what I was going through. Now I was trapped in a world I had no clue how to walk in.

I guess I could wonder if that's how my mother felt. She was married to a lion and birthed a lion child that decided to take wolf form. I wondered how much of this life she's even aware exists. If she had any knowledge about shifters. Lucianna had said she was ignorant to our customs and ways of life in shifting forms. I could only pray that was true.

On a campus with hundreds of people, I felt alone, and I knew in my heart it would only get worse with time.

As I began to walk toward my door, I was startled by a knock upon it. Clutching my chest, I opened it to find Flynn.

"Hey, you got a minute?" he asked meekly. He must have noted my worry because he then grinned and added, "Who did you think was there? The boogey man? You're in a den full of wolves and you're scared to answer your door?"

"Oh shut up," I said rolling my eyes and motioning for him to come inside. He looked every bit as nervous as I felt, and that wasn't typical of his personality. I knew whatever he was wrestling with, I'd need to take seriously.

"I'm not coming to you as my alpha. I'm coming to you with thoughts as a friend, needing to walk someone else through the madness in my brain, which is my disclaimer before we begin," he said, sitting in the chair at my desk now. I noticed he was sliding his hands up and down his thighs as he sat. Something was really bothering him.

"Of course, I'm here as your friend. To be honest, I'd be shocked if you did come to me needing advice from an alpha. I haven't exactly proven to be alpha material." It wasn't victimizing myself for sympathy, it was the raw truth. I was one step away from being Priya.

"Have you stopped to wonder why the lions continue to run the exact same hunt maneuvers, despite being 'punished' with an all-night constant relay of them?" Flynn looked at me now, curiosity curbing his expression. "Because, it seems to me, and I like to consider myself a smart individual, that if I were hunting for six hours and couldn't pick up on a single trace of a wolf, I'd change up the tactics, especially when I was called out in front of the whole brigade day after day and then punished for it. In the last week, each time we are averting, they haven't caught us... not once. We have run three different aversion techniques, and they've done zero to improve their hunts."

"I don't know, maybe they're just not taking it as seriously as we are?" I shrugged. I mean, we all know this isn't life or death. Everyone on the continent knows that wolves are the primary line of defense. What do lions really need practice for? Will there ever be a time when we don't have wolves fighting the battles of the continent?

"I really don't think that's it, Ever. I think they're studying us," Flynn said now, adjusting himself in the chair, making it creak as he leaned forward.

"Studying us? What are you getting at?" I was starting to get more nervous than I already was.

"I'm saying, I think the lions are studying what we do. Instead of hunting us, I think they are trying to map out where we go and what we're doing to see if we repeat any of the aversion techniques we had previously. Which we have. We've run a circuit. I think they know exactly where we will be Monday, and they'll be waiting for us to get there."

"What would be their purpose? Just for the satisfaction that they bested us? I mean really. What difference does it make to them what the hell we do?" I asked him, partly because I wanted to know if he had any answers and partly because I was nervous about what they'd be if he did.

"That I don't know. I think it would be in our best interest to deviate from any of the ways we've been averting before. Same with hunting. I think they've allowed themselves to be caught each time so they could see what we were doing and how. They're one of the smartest predators on the continent, and we've been treating them as if they're fools. I think it was the plan all along." What he was saying made complete sense, but at the same time, it lacked completeness.

“Who would voluntarily sign up to be punished every single day, just so they can do what? Best us on testing day? It doesn’t make sense. They’re weakening themselves if what you’re theorizing is correct.” I stood now from my bed. Walking to the door, I reached for it.

“Wait, I don’t know if we should tell Kolter until Monday... If what I think is true, we don’t need the prides having any warning that we’re on to them.” He met me at the door now and looked me in the eyes. “I can’t prove any of this, but what I fear is, if it’s true, they’ll be out for blood. I think the prides are humiliated that a brand-new wolf has bested them and sent a pride princess to prison. I think they’re taking things way more personal than they’re letting on. Lions are known for playing with their prey before slaughter. I worry this whole thing has been for play. Monday will be our slaughter.”

He left then, leaving me to grapple with the theories he just detonated like bombs in my brain. If the prides were in fact studying us and our patterns, what would the gain be? Shaking my head, I brought it to my hands. Wishing now, more than ever, that I’d known since birth what I was and could have had proper training.

The rest of the weekend we spent lying low, eating, and preparing for our final run. When the screech of my alarm clock rang out on Monday morning, I couldn’t help but feel like it came too quickly for my liking. Kolter was readying everyone in the common room about the course final today. With Flynn standing next to me, I urged him to say something. He blatantly ignored me. Turning to him now, I used my eyes to convey that he needed to say something. Again, he refused to open his mouth, pissing me off. We listened to more of Kolter’s briefing, and Flynn never once opened his mouth. “Ok, does anyone have any questions or concerns as to your positioning today?" Kolter asked, finishing up his debrief.

At this, I elbowed Flynn straight to the gut, hard, making a point to him and everyone that he had things the group needed to hear.

"Flynn? Everelle? Is something wrong?" Kolter asked, with concern.

"Oh. No. Well, yes. Flynn, why don't you take the lead on this one?" I said, daring him with my eyes to defy me again. I didn't give a shit. I was pulling rank, and he would obey. After all, it was his idea to wait until this morning.

"Ugh! Fine! Yes, I have a theory about the prides," Flynn started, stepping forward to stand beside Kolter at the head of the room. "I think we've been being played by them. To be honest, I'm wondering how the professors hadn't caught on."

"Flynn, what are you talking about? What do you mean we've been played?" Kolter asked, the concern rising in him.

"What I mean is that we're not giving enough credit to one of the smartest breeds of shifters. I know, stab to the ego, am I right?" Flynn chuckled then, but the attempt at a joke fell flat. "Tough crowd," he said, straightening up and getting serious. "I know biologically, wolves outpace lions on the intelligence scale, but you need to remember that a traditional wolf is also smaller, leaner, and less strong than a traditional lion."

"What are you getting at? We're not traditional animals. We already know that," Victor said, throwing his hands up as if to say, "who brought this guy?" and I could tell Flynn was beginning to spiral.

"What Flynn is trying to say is that traditionally speaking, wolves are more intelligent than lions... but we're dealing with shifting lions and shifting wolves. Shifting lions tend to outrank us with the depth of their intelligence. They have a habit of playing with their prey, leading them into a false sense of security or gain. Then once bored or once they've reached their desired purpose, they strike," I clarified for the group. All eyes were on me now as I looked over to Flynn. "The floor is yours."

"Thank you," he said to me and began again to address the group. "What I'm failing to explain in more layman's terms is that they haven't been averting or hunting us. They've been studying us avert and hunt them. They've been preparing their prides for whatever they think we'll do today, and we've made it easy for them. We've averted their capture in the same exact three ways, and we've never changed our hunting maneuvers because they've never shown a different strategy to averting or hunting themselves. Bottom line, I think we're walking straight into a trap. The why though, is still undetermined."

Watching the group now, you could see them all begin to put the puzzle pieces together, clicking one by one, silently. Then many people began talking all at once.

"So, what do we do now?" Assata asked Kolter.

"We need a different strategy, and we need one now," Nikita barked.

"How much time do we even have to try and make something new?" Lisbeth worried.

"We haven't even attempted a different plan!" Brandt shouted.

"SILENCE!!" boomed Kolter's voice. "Now, I can see how all of this seems feasible, but we don't even know that this is the case. I feel we should just stick to the plan. For six months we've outsmarted them all. I think we can last one more day."

"But doesn't that seem odd to you?! For six months they haven't changed their plans. They haven't altered their maneuvers. They have always gotten caught and punished. Why would they do that unless it was because they're studying us and preparing for the final?" I challenged him. Was it a good idea to challenge the alpha? Absolutely not. Did I care? Not in the slightest.

"I'm not going to alter plans and perfectly oiled maneuvers because you all came up with this theory today. It suddenly dawned on you right before the final? I think you're giving them entirely too much credit. We stick to the plans that have carried us this far, and that's final."

"I don't think you're giving them ENOUGH credit," Flynn said as his eyes bore heat into Kolter's.

"I think you're giving too much energy and thought into a class final. That's all this is. School. These aren't real scenarios. Stop stressing. If they 'best us' today, then you know what? Congrats to them. They put in some extraordinary work at making our packs look unprepared in school. Whoopee," Kolter said now, rotating his finger in the air and rolling his eyes, like he couldn't have cared any less. "Prepare to leave for the course trail in five minutes."

With that, the meeting was over, and my heart was worried about Flynn. "Hey, I'm glad you spoke up. Even if he doesn't see what we do, it doesn't mean it's not true. I believe in you, and I think we're making a big mistake if we don't alter the plans."

"Thanks... I'm worried too, but what can we do? He's not going to change. There's no point," Flynn said, defeated. I reached out and hugged him, silently praying we'd make it out of this final today, intact.

Twenty minutes later we entered the top of the trail to our final as a pack. I was still worrying about the pride's motives as we stepped into formation at the mouth of the trail.

Staring at the dais, Professor Monaghan was joined by General Ulrich and another man whose back was to me. He was also in mustard-yellow military style clothing, and his hair was kept shoulder length. They looked to be in a heated discussion, as evidenced by their faces turning the unfortunate shade of pink.

"Highland, you got a second?" It was Folasade, and she was accompanied by her dynamic duo again. Stepping forward, I met her first.

"Listen, you didn't hear this from me, but keep your eyes open out there. Things may have changed, and this time, never stop moving." She then turned her eyes to mine. "We're even. Whatever happens today, know that we're even from the river." With that, she and her friends turned and slinked back to their pride.

"Why would we ever stop moving during the race?" Brandt joked. "Man, these lions are on something today." He was laughing now. "What are we supposed to do? Stop and rest at the halfway mark?"

"Get your head on, Brandt. This isn't the time for any jokes; we don't need distractions," Nikita scolded.

The men on the stage were ready now, the microphones screeching as Professor Monaghan neared it and then tapped it. "Now that we're all here, I can be the first to welcome you all to your course final!" He paused, as if anticipating cheers or applause. None came. That must be embarrassing. "Well then, as you all know by now, your first task will be the five-mile run through the obstacles we've put together. Once you're successfully through, you'll immediately go into aversion if you are a member of a pack. The quicker you are through the run, the more time you have to avert the prides. Once all packs or prides have successfully finished the run portion of the trial, prides will be asked to wait forty minutes from the time the first pack sets out to avert." This caused a few gasps. We'd always been told we all would get forty minutes, and that it started after all teams crossed the line and rested. This was going to be tougher. If we weren't the first pack across the finish line, we would be shorted time and essentially have to run and hide much faster, giving us a disadvantage.

"After the allotted three hours of round two, a toll will ring out over the course, and you will then be forced to switch roles. Provided you haven't been captured, of course. If captured, you will be out. Your pack or pride will not be able to have you assist them in part three. If an entire pack or pride is captured, you fail this course, and consequently, will repeat it in an accelerated fashion, finishing in December. Does any cadet have anything to say or questions to have clarified?"

No one moved, no sound was heard. It was nine in the morning, and our bodies were already feeling as if we'd been awake for days. Anticipation was running through our veins like a raft on a raging river.

Kolter looked at us all now, down the line. I could feel him there, hovering. *You all will do great. Keep focused. Whatever you do, we stay in position. Everelle, remember trial day? All that chaos. It will be worse today. Keep your head on straight, you will not be falling behind this time. We have this. We don't get captured. We remain intact.*

Every one of us nodded. I began picking up my paws one at a time as I displaced my weight back and forth. The air was thick and heavy. The sun had barely risen, and it was already warm. It would certainly be a long day. I was thankful the running portion was in the morning. I couldn't even think about how awful it was going to be in a few more hours.

Looking around, I could see packs and prides, all lined up, raring to go. Blends of fur and pelt, muscle and tension, all brimming with anticipation of the final course. No team wanted to end in last; no one wanted to repeat this at an accelerated rate.

Looking forward, we could see the professor and general comparing maps and time schedules.

Finally, General Ulrich stepped to the podium. "It is with great esteem that I bid you good luck and safety on this course final. Remember all you've learned and all you've trained for and all your strengths. Remember your opponents' weaknesses and use them to your advantage. Is that not the lessons of war?" He looked like a snake then. His eyes gleamed with joy that we were about to be put to the test, one we hadn't noticed we'd been studying for, but Flynn did. Staring at Kolter now, as if boring a hole in his head, I wanted to convey to him that we needed to take Flynn's advice, but he was fixed on the General. There was no use in bringing it up again until we were crossing the finish line in leg one. If we crossed and I still felt like something was amiss, then I'd fight that battle. For now, like Kolter said, my head needed to be on straight.

"You will find the obstacles a little different as you head through the final. Whereas they are all the same idea, they may come at different times than previously encountered. After all, we can't give you the answers to the test, or what would we be testing you on? The ability to just retain knowledge isn't what you're tested on. It's the ability to learn from the knowledge we give that is most effective. Be safe, Cadets. On your marks." My breath caught in my throat. As we all crouched in unison, it was deafeningly quiet. "Get set," adjusting my weight, I heard the chorus of growls and roars mixing with the anticipation of the general's command. At that moment, his arm rose into the air. "GO!" and it swung back down with enough flair for the ages.

We were off, exploding over the starting line. This time, I was keeping pace with Kolter at the head of our pack. We barreled into the woods like a freight train at full speed, the woods racing by my vision in a blur. The gravel ground barely moved as we lightly raced across it. Our breathing all came out in rhythm as we set the pace for our five miles. The first twist came within mile one. Where previously sat a large fallen tree across the sixty-foot-wide canyon for us to cross, now sat a smaller, thinner log that looked much less sturdy than the old one.

Kolter was first to hit the log, and it groaned under his weight. "We're going to have to do this one at a time. I don't think it's strong enough for multiple wolves on it at once." He made quick work of the log and was pacing the other side watching as I began to make my journey over. Mid-way through, I noticed a large cracking sound coming from beneath me. "I think it's been hollowed out! Try not to jostle it in any way or it'll break." Quickly I made it to the other side. Behind me at an even faster rate, came Victor, Nikita, Flynn, and Flavia, none seemed to have an issue or worry that they were too heavy for the log.

“I think it’s moving. It seems to have slipped down the ridge from where you all started,” shouted Brandt. He was ready to cross the log, and as he stepped a paw on it, I noticed its weight moving.

Baldur, check to see if there is another log down the side of the ridge, and report back, Kolter barked down the line. Because of the speed at which we’d arrived at the log, other packs hadn’t made it to us until now.

“What’s going on, Highland?” Gunner from Hadlick asked as they began approaching.

“The log is smaller and less stable. The more weight that’s been run across it, the closer it is to sliding down the canyon. We don’t want a cadet on it when it gives way,” Kolter shouted across the sixty-foot crevice.

“Any other passes you think?” Gunner asked, looking around them all.

“I sent Baldur, but he hasn’t reported back yet,” Kolter acknowledged, also checking the area for where his pack mate had gone.

Mazza pack had now caught up and joined us at the log, along with Pride of Ade.

“What are we all waiting for?” Folasade growled deep in her throat, the agitation plain on her scowl.

“The log isn’t going to hold much longer; there are now a few wolves in search of another crossing.” Assata said.

“For fuck’s sake, move. They’re not going to put an impassable obstacle for us,” Neo said, jumping onto the log. Everyone watched in bated breath while he walked across the stump. It wasn’t until three quarters of the way across that it happened. Loud snaps were the first indication to all that this wasn’t going to end well for him. Neo froze in place; we could see him still his breathing and crouch down. It didn’t matter. The log split jaggedly down the side, creating a large enough break that the log snapped in two.

In slow motion we all watched in horror as Neo leapt from the spot he was in fifteen feet toward our side of the crevice. Kolter bolted forward to try and help grab him, but missed, and Neo hung from the rocky wall, sinking his nails into the rock and mud.

The roar Neo let out alerted all other prides that had reached the obstacle that this was planned. The professors planned for this to happen, and all eyes looked at Kolter before returning back to Neo. Kolter was trying to reach him, but there wasn't anything any of us could do. Watching Neo, his arms began trembling, and he looked panic-stricken.

"Shift back! It's the only way you stand a chance of making it out of there," Victor yelled. "You need to shift back so your hands can grab the wall better. Someone see if we can find him a stick or vine to grab on to!!"

We all began frantically searching, but Neo refused to shift. His pain-filled roars began to echo down the walls of the canyon. Baldur appeared now at my side. "There is a much smaller gap about two-thirds of a mile down the ridge. Wolves can easily make the leap, but I'm not sure about the prides, especially the smaller lions," he informed Kolter and me, his eyes then dropping to Neo.

"Neo!! You need to shift back! It's the only way!!" Victor was pleading with him, but Neo's stubbornness continued. He wouldn't shift. He tried again, leaping up the wall, but this time, he couldn't secure his claws back into the muddy rock wall. We all watched in horror as Neo fell deep into the canyon, roaring loudly, trembling my chest, and vibrating pieces of rock free from the wall. A sickeningly loud thud was heard, and the roaring was gone. All eyes shot up and looked at Kolter, almost looking for advice on what to do now.

"Baldur found a passable portion of the crevice about two thirds of a mile down. Let us show you, and we can work together to get everyone over. No one else will die today!" Nods and barks resounded across the mass of teams that were waiting to cross.

"Baldur, lead the way," Kolter demanded. "Follow us along the ridge."

Baldur raced down the ridge back toward where he'd just come. It was denser in this neck of the woods, well off the beaten path. Baldur led both sides to a crevice with about a twenty-five-foot gap across the canyon. We could see his slide marks from where he'd overshot his landing, letting us know it was possible.

"You're going to have to make a running leap to make it. I had about three feet of wiggle room, and I was fully sprinting. My best advice is don't look down," Baldur spoke to the group.

Assata backed up, and racing forward, she lunged into the air with grace and fluidity. She landed softly on the ground on our side of the canyon. She made it look easy, and I was impressed again by the strength of our pack. One by one, the rest of Highland were able to make the leap.

"We stay until the last cadet is over," Kolter barked with authority. We all stood motionless as we watched wolf after wolf cross the canyon. So far, the packs and prides had honored the order in which they'd arrived at the obstacle. It was a pleasant and unexpected feeling to witness honesty and integrity among rivals during a final exam.

Once all wolf packs were over, they too waited patiently. It was an unspoken decision that Highland would move first through the course. Out of respect to us for reaching the obstacle first and finding an alternative to the log, the wolves waited.

"Whenever you're ready, Prides. We will be here to help anyone who struggles to make it across," Kolter said.

"We don't need to be babysat. We can make it just fine. Go on ahead," Baraka roared. He paced for a moment, then ran back toward the thick forest before skidding to a stop and facing us. He was further back than any wolf previously had been. With an elongated roar, he pounced forward, surging toward the crevice. Watching in awe, I held my breath as Baraka leaped into the air, higher than I'd even thought he could. He landed gracefully directly in front of Kolter, as if to challenge his idea that the prides couldn't make it across.

"While your concern for us might be genuine, it's also disrespectful. I ask that you move on ahead. I'll keep our prides safe from here," Baraka sniped at Kolter before turning his back on him and facing the canyon.

"Everyone, you'll need to take about ten paces further than I did to get a true running start. Please take it easy, and if you feel you're not going to make it, don't attempt it. Try again. We don't need any more deaths today." Baraka was taking his rightful place as pride king, and it was mesmerizing to watch.

"You heard him. Let's clear out," Kolter addressed the packs beside him. "Get in formation and keep up." We then began our sprint back toward the trail. We'd already lost close to an hour with the detour and alternative obstacle, and who knew what else would be in store for us along this path? I also couldn't stop the emerging nagging that was eating at me. It was telling me that the tree was removed intentionally and that one of our pack members was the intended target. However, it was a pride member that took that bait instead. That could have potentially been our second pack member gone on this very course, and I was afraid to know what else was coming down the line today.

Stop worrying. It was coincidental. They had no way of knowing it would be our pack reaching the log first, Kolter said down the line.

I wanted to argue that in each trial run, we'd always been the first pack to make it to the log. Every time. While they may not have known for the fact that it would be us, there was an extremely high probability of it. Even if we weren't first to it, a broken log across the canyon would slow us down significantly.

We hit the trail within minutes of leaving the others at the side of the canyon and were back on track toward the next obstacle. The next task had always been the sharp turn assessment, making sure that all of us could adapt our running to a steeper, more directed attack. Approaching mile two, however, the formation wasn't there. Somehow the grounds had been shifted, as if we were running a different course.

Where is the turns assessment? It should be here, I asked Kolter down the line, worried that we had somehow run a different trail instead of the usual one.

It's probably been changed, as the first obstacle was. The professors probably changed the maneuverability of the trail. Keep focused. We will come to it when we come to it, Kolter told me, his eyes scanning the path ahead. *I want everyone to stay alert. We may be looking at another change to the course coming ahead, and*

I don't want any risks taken. They may try and take us out, but truly, only we can do that by rushing and not being prepared. Flynn, what do you have for me? Kolter asked down the line. As if he were manually dimming a light switch, all focus down the line turned off and only brightened over Flynn.

I'm still looking aerial. I can see the path from above looks like it used to, so we should be approaching the curves right about now... His words were cut off by the sickening thud of Kolter smacking into a tree, and I followed directly after. It knocked me for a loop and threw me over the edge of the trail. I was tumbling down the side of the cliff toward the next trail meeting. With each thrash forward, I smacked my head on a log or rock. I smashed through tree limbs and fallen leaves and finally halted on the gravel trail eighty feet below where I'd started. The wind was knocked out of me, and my vision was dizzying. I heard my name being shouted from down the line and above me on the trail.

I tried to stand, slowly bracing myself in case something was broken. This wouldn't be ideal for the rest of the final. It wasn't fair. Standing now, I shook my head to alleviate some of the ringing and refocus my vision. No one had reached me yet, but I could see them in my mind racing down the trail toward me. I gingerly took a step forward, testing out my limitations, and nothing appeared broken. It would be a hell of a night and week, though, because I was most certainly bruised and sprained.

Are you alright? shouted Kolter down the line. The pack was about ten yards from me now; Kolter had blood soaking his face and jowls as they approached. When he smacked into the invisible tree, he must have broken his nose.

I just got the wind knocked out of me and some bruised ribs. I'll survive. What about you? I asked, nodding at his face and crinkling my nose.

Nothing more than a flesh wound. You ok to race on? His eyes were still scanning my body, making me feel warm and tingly. That should definitely not be happening at a moment like this. Perhaps I'm broken after all.

His chuckles met my eyes. *You're not broken, just well loved.* He shook his head as everyone else caught up to us. *Let's keep going. They're relying on our sense of remembrance for the trail. We have to sense it, like in a pitch-black room. You need to close your eyes if it's easier. The trail is there; it's just camouflaged.*

"Alright, let's get going then," I barked.

We raced on, and I took his advice at some points and closed my eyes. We made the rest of the maneuverability assessment without injury or issues. My front and hind legs were sore, and the breaths I took were more shallow and rigid as my lungs couldn't expand at full capacity. It burned with each sudden intake, so I adjusted my breathing to a quicker pace. It would probably wreak havoc in my heart, but at least we were moving through the course and hadn't been outpaced by other packs or prides yet.

Reaching mile three, I anticipated the field crossing, but instead of a wide field filled with sharp grasses that tore at our skin, we found ourselves standing at a lake.

The lake was quiet and murky. The smell alone coming off it made me want to gag as the hot stench of decaying trees and alligator shit penetrated my deflated lungs. The water, if you could even call it that, was polluted with sickly green algae and lily pads. The Lord only knew what was living in it.

"What if it's just like the maneuverability task in mile two," began Assata. "What if it's actually the field disguised as the lake, and we're thinking too much into it?"

"We could only hope," Kentaro said, looking as repulsed as I felt about the voyage we'd soon be taking through the lake.

"Ugh, I'm going to need the world's longest and hottest shower after this. Damn it! I just washed this hair," Flavia whined.

"At least you're not white like Ever," Flynn retorted.

"Let's get moving. We can't stand around all day waiting for the lake to bite us, and we don't want other cadets catching up. We have to keep going," Kolter quipped. "You can shower tonight if we make it out of here in one piece." With that, he leaped forward, unconcerned if it was lake or grass that lay ahead.

Sadly, it was every bit a lake as it looked. Stepping into the lake, it was tepid bath water and felt grossly thick. The mud at the bottom of the lake squished between my toes and created a suction that required force to undo. This would make each step through the lake unbearable on my already sore and bruised muscles. The stench emitting from the lake was putrid. It was foul, but we kept moving forward. I could hear Lisbeth in the back of the pack gagging, causing Baldur to throw up as a direct result of her commotion. The worst part of it was the unknown about what was potentially lurking in the lake. It only pushed us forward faster, motivating us to keep focused on the end of the lake, and the start of mile four.

When we finally exited the water of the lake, it was only then that we noticed the sickening discovery. Most of us were covered from neck to paw in leaches. Large black, slippery blood-sucking leeches about three to four inches long.

"Oh my God, I'm going to burn myself alive," panicked Lisbeth. "Get these off of me, please, get them off, get them off!" She screeched as she began rolling around on the gravel.

"I think the only way would be if we were to shift back and burn them off, but that would waste so much time," Nikita wailed, obviously torn about keeping them on her body or removing them.

"Fuck it," Kentaro barked and began to bite the leaches off Nikita's back. He gripped one between his front teeth and yanked it, turning his head to spit it out. "Bite them off and let's go."

"I can't, I can't put those in my damn mouth!!" wailed Lisbeth. Someone else do this for me, please!"

"I got you babe. Just relax," Baldur said, coming to her and beginning to hunt for the leeches on her body.

"Turn around," barked Kolter, looking at me sternly. "No one else is putting their mouths onto your body, so turn around."

"Oh, ok," I stuttered as he brought his mouth to my neck, closing my eyes. I allowed the heat of his breath to warm my insides, causing me to slowly burn in my center.

"I'm going to need you to not do that if we have any hopes for finishing today. Stop. Doing. That." Kolter groaned gruffly in my ear. "Get them off me while I clear you, if it doesn't gross you out."

"It doesn't," I said curtly, slightly offended that he after all this time would associate me with a weaker member of the pack.

"I'm not trying to. You're right, you've come a long way," he said, picking up my thoughts down the line. "But there is no part of this that isn't revolting, so I apologize for assuming you'd think so too."

"You're forgiven," I said as I latched onto a slimy leathery leech between my teeth and spit it out.

It took us another half an hour to make sure we were all picked over. At this point we could see other packs forging through the water. We needed to get moving if we were going to make it to the finish of this part with a large enough lead to avert the prides.

"We ready?" Kolter asked, looking everyone over. "Let's get going. Only one more mile of this bullshit test, and we're on to averting. We can do this. Stay focused. Stay alert. If you sense anything falling, alert the rest of us and move. The quicker we run through the tunnel, the faster we're out of the tunnel."

We all gave a curt nod as we did a final shake off the remaining lake water embedded in our fur. I was with Nikita; as soon as this was over, I was taking a two-day shower. I felt putrid. On Kolter's signal, we formed and began the course again.

Racing toward the tunnel, the sky darkened ominously. I looked over my shoulders. We were all intact. Good, that's how it needed to be. Approaching the tunnel, I began to worry, my thoughts racing back to Priya. Wondering how Kentaro was handling it, wondering how any of us were going to be able to race past where her body once lied, paralyzed in time.

Unequivocally, we were a solid pack, but at our core, we were a mess of emotions, personalities, and histories. We were fractured. While we'd spent the better part of the year just trying to survive, we failed one important thing, bonding with one another. We truly didn't trust one another, and that was where the problem for the future tasks was going to show our cards.

Funneling through the tunnel, we each had different jobs. Flynn was tasked with the aerial view to catch something in his sights before it fell. I was tasked with the right side of the tunnel, and Kolter with the left, while Baldur made up the rear for any unforeseen attacks. Several others scanned each of the same areas as backups. We weren't going to let another one of our pack members die here. Progressing forward, we saw the light at the end of the tunnel, figuratively and literally. There was a light.

Has there always been a light? I asked down the line, to no one in particular.

No, I'm thinking it's part of dais the professors are on to rank our times and places. It's gloomier now than it was earlier. Maybe they need to see the dais, Brandt suggested.

Approaching the final leg of the five-mile run, we were subjected to the harsh reality that we weren't going to be met with joyful applause. Instead, we were bombarded with a blinding light that overrode our senses. We stumbled forward, running on instinct rather than sight.

"What the hell is this?" Kolter barked, turning his head away but trudging forward. "Flynn, what can you see above?"

"Nothing... I can't get a read about where we are. What is this shit?"

All at once, a thick smog came into the tunnel. If I thought it was hard to breathe before, this was taking the cake. It was so thick and dense that it felt tangible in my lungs. Coughing took over as we neared the end of the tunnel.

Stepping out and on to the field that housed the dais and finish line, we were ragged. Coughing and stumbling blindly. "In first place, for task one, we have Highland Pack!" boomed the voice of Professor Monaghan. If he was surprised or thrilled, his voice didn't indicate it. Instead, he seemed almost annoyed. "Don't stop, please head directly into your aversion test! You have three hours from this moment to stay averted from the Prides of Askari. We wish you luck! As always, stay within the borders of the school's grounds. If captured, a flare will be fired off, signaling your location, and you will be escorted back to the dais at the end of the trails, where you will await the remaining packs and prides left in the final exam. Let us hope that case doesn't happen.

Kolter continued forward, not stopping to even allow Professor Monaghan to finish speaking. We entered the heaviest portion of the forest, continuing forward in the direction of the outskirts where the caves were in the rock wall.

Kolter, I think we need to seriously consider diverting from anything we've previously done at this point. If the run was any indication as to how this final is being done, I think Flynn's theory that the prides were studying us may have been valid, Victor chimed in down the line.

I've thought of that too, but honestly I don't know where to go then. Does anyone have any reasonable suggestions? Kolter asked down the line as he continued to move us forward through the thicket.

This may seem crazy, but I have an idea. Kentaro came through the line. Kentaro rarely spoke. The pack was usually so overridden with Flynn and his jokes or Brandt and Victor bickering for the lead position in whatever we were doing, that when Kentaro did speak, he earned the silence so he could get his thoughts out.

What is it? Kolter asked, still leading us forward. *At this point, crazy sounds just fine to me.*

I think we need to go to Pollsmoor. No one would ever go there. No one would think of looking at the prison or its grounds. Hear me out, I think we can hide in the vaults there, Kentaro said hopefully.

Are you out of your mind?! You want us to waltz right up to Pollsmoor and ring the damn bell?! Nikita scoffed. *Then what? Ask to be booked?! You're out of your damn mind, Kentaro!*

I'm just saying, have you once even thought for a second of Pollsmoor as an option when we were out hunting for the lions? No, because who would?

He has a point...albeit it is a little troubling, but he has a point, Victor chimed in while at Kolter's and my backs as we continued to race forward toward the cliff wall.

I didn't know how I felt about going back to prison, but I had to admit, it was an obscure idea. So, obscure I think we could just pull it off. Looking toward Kolter, I could tell by the furrow in his brows that he was contemplating it.

Let's give it a shot, Kolter said, kicking us into high gear and rotating our direction toward Pollsmoor. It was about a three-mile run from where we were. *Let's try and get there and set before prides even finish the track of the five-mile.*

We raced in silence, the only sounds heard were the snapping of branches and the flutter of dried dead leaves that traversed the ground. I felt my lungs burn less with each intake of fresh air as we ran through the forest headed to the mammoth stone gates of Pollsmoor. My body was still so unbelievably sore that the thought of having a few hours to rest during aversion seemed like bliss.

Cresting the last hill, I saw the behemoth dark-stone fortress rising from the horizon ahead. It was spooky when you thought of it. What school also occupied a prison that the capital housed its criminals in, and regularly sent their students to be punished? The sight of it alone sent chills down my back and made my hairs stand on end.

That's the most depressing and terrifying thing I've witnessed today, Nikita gulped as we approached the large wooden bridge crossing the ravine that enclosed the prison. We could only hope this didn't go terribly wrong.

Chapter Twenty-Eight

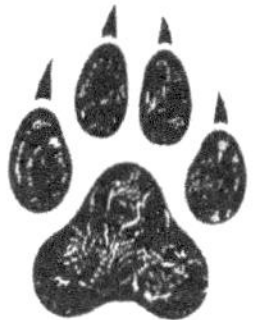

Everelle

Stepping up to the large wrought iron gate, Kolter shifted back to his human form. He grabbed ahold of the large knocker, which I was sure was more for show than formality, and knocked it against the aging stone wall of the fortress. We waited impatiently while a guard came from the top box above the door, slowly making his way down to the gate.

He was a burly man with a scruffy face, missing teeth, and pudge in his midsection. It seemed to me that he didn't have the most exciting job, and the care he took for himself was of equal importance.

"What do you scruffy mutts need? Can't you see we're working in here?" the gruff guard said as he tossed his thumb over his shoulder and spit black tar on to the ground at Kolter's feet.

"We'd hoped you'd be of assistance to us. We're in our final exam for aversion and thought that just inside the walls might be a good spot to hide from the hunters we're trying to outsmart. By any chance, could we hide here for another two and a half hours? That's max time. We promise not to be in your hair," Kolter asked him; hoping he'd let us in.

"Are you out of your mind? We're a prison, not an amusement park. Go on, get lost. You're wasting my time."

As the man turned and began to walk away, Kolter looked at me as if he had a plan, and I wasn't going to like it.

"Sir, wait!" The man turned and gave him a death glare, irritated that we weren't taking his answer and leaving.

"What part of no..."

"What if we agreed to be housed in the cells? Make it look like we were inmates for the time being. No harm, no foul, then when the bells toll in two and a half hours, you just take us out? Then you won't have to babysit us, and we're still hidden behind the walls. Seems like a fair deal to me. What do you say?"

We all waited now, my breath caught in my throat. I didn't like the idea of being locked away and without the ability to free ourselves at the end of the time. The time was ticking, and if this guard decided he didn't want to help us, we would be sitting ducks and back to square one. The odds of us finding somewhere else to go were minimal.

"Fine! But you must stay where I put ya and not annoy the inmates or guards at work. Also, you can't be shifted in here. Get back to your baseline."

"Deal! And should anyone comes asking for us, you'll tell them you never saw us, right?" Kolter asked him, brow arched, and a grin plastered his face.

"Now you'll be asking too much. What's in all this for me?" the guard asked, halting on opening the doors for us.

"I'll give you three hundred bits," Kolter said. "Take it or leave it."

The guards brows rose a bit as he swung his eyes over the pack of us. He let out a gruff cough and concluded, "Deal."

With the agreement set, the man pulled down on a large wooden wheel, which released the chains that held the large iron gate. Slowly, it began to clink as the chains wound upwards around the large wooden wheel, raising the iron gate. Once it was midway, we all shifted before walking across the old bridge and under the iron gate. When we were all in, the guard began the process of lowering the gate back down and securing the rigging with a steel spike. It was very medieval in its construction but obviously served its purpose.

The scent of rot filled my nose as we walked into the stone fortress. A sudden sense of déjà vu hit me, and all at once I began to get anxious and second-guess this entire plan. The thought of being locked away in a prison for the remainder of part two of our final seemed idiotic. We would voluntarily be locking ourselves behind bars with no means of escape to avert the prides hunting us.

I looked at Kolter, and he seemed to be entirely too onboard with this idea, making me even more nervous. The air was thick and humid as we continued our descent into the ground far below the fortress walls we'd walked in under. Through dimly lit corridors we walked through a maze of tunnels for the next twenty minutes.

Finally, we arrived in a large open room, three cells on each side. "You all can stay in here. If you annoy the guards, they may just put you in those." He gestured to the small dark cells around the room. “So, if I were you, I’d keep my mouth shut and just wait for me to come back.”

He turned then and left us, locking the door to the room after he’d closed us in. The room was relatively large. It had a monstrous slab of wood for a table large enough to seat eight, which made up the center of the room. The table was flanked with two long, short wooden benches down each side. Two of the walls housed iron-gated cells with one singular bed, a bucket for your business, and adorned with chains on the walls. The room was lit by a series of candles hovering just below the ceiling. All things considered, it wasn’t that bad of a place to avert the prides.

“Ok, well, it could be worse,” Flynn said, checking out the room as most of us made our way to the table. “I mean... it’s no Hog’s Head, but it’ll have to do.”

“I honestly don’t like being down here. We have no way of knowing where the prides are, where they’re looking, or if they’ve caught our scent. I think we should leave,” Flavia said, looking from me to Kolter.

“We’ll be alright. We just need to hang tight. Every one of us is going to smell like swamp ass thanks to the lake we all crossed. It kind of hinders the ability to be tracked. Another reason I think they put it there. I think they want us to be able to use other means to track,” Kolter answered, walking over to one of the benches and sitting down.

“We have about two more hours of aversion. Why don’t we use it and think of a plan for hunting the prides?” I suggested, as I gingerly sat down, holding my right side. My ribs were badly bruised from my fall earlier, and I was extremely sore in other places. “It’ll help us keep our minds off being locked in prison, and maybe it’ll make the time go faster.”

“Well,” Brandt started, clearing his throat. He was leaning up against one of the walls near the door that we’d been brought in, and he looked worn down. “The last two times we’ve run trial hunts, they’re either in a naturally made den, like a sitting duck, or they’re running loops to try and outrun us. Not entirely sure they’ll have a different approach today.” He sighed deeply as he made his way toward the table. “It just sucks. If Flynn’s right, maybe they’ve been playing us so that we don’t know what they’ll be doing or where they’ll go today. I mean seriously, nothing counts before today. All the effort we put into the last six months, doesn’t matter. I’m honestly glad He didn’t think of this before. We practically gave them our blueprint. We’d really be screwed if he hadn’t figured it out,” he said throwing a thumb at his twin.

“I wouldn’t go that far,” Kolter began. “Did we recycle ways to avert and hunt? Of course, but I wouldn’t say we gave them the blueprint to our pack. I think being here proves that we were willing to try anything new so they wouldn’t know what to think.”

“So what? They’ll be out there, hopefully just checking the same places we’ve been repeatedly, trying to track us, but they can’t because we reek of swamp shit? I have a feeling they know where we are. I don’t know why I think that, but I think they know, and we’re sitting ducks, literally sitting ducks in here. We can’t escape, can’t leave, can’t even see out to know if they’re on to us,” Assata said, and I felt every one of her thoughts. I too felt like we were just sitting waiting for the judge and jury to come in and throw us away. How would we get out of this now?

“Let’s hope for the best. It’s all we can do at this point. We’re here, and I don’t think Kentaro would have suggested it if he thought we’d be sitting ducks, right?” Victor chimed in.

“I mean, it’s just a place I thought of that I don’t think any of them would have used as an option,” Kentaro shrugged.

Suddenly a loud boom was heard above us. It was muffled through the floors of the prison, but we could still make out that it was in the distance, not loud enough to think that it was in the prison. We all looked up at each other, some with worried expressions, others looking to see if there was an explanation.

“What do you suppose that was?” Nikita asked Kolter.

“Maybe a flare? I’m wondering if someone was caught.” He shrugged.

"I don't like the sounds of this; I really think we need to go," Flavia now said, standing up. She began pacing the room, a nervous ball of energy.

"Babe, it's fine, we're going to be fine. This is the easiest we've ever had it while averting, and the best part is, we're protected from anything out there while we wait," Flynn assured her, running his hands up and down her arms. She leaned into him then, and my heart swelled. The comfort you get from your person was something I would never take for granted.

"Let's give it an hour, and then we'll make our way topside. Sound good to everyone?" Kolter asked the room. As his eyes met mine, he had a fierceness in them that was emphasized by the flickering candles.

For the next hour and a half, we all sat, chit-chatting about the last few months while we waited. The monotony only broke when a noise at the door we came in through, brought us all to attention. Kolter stood to meet whatever it was first, gripping a blade in his hand while standing between the table and the door.

I mimicked his motion and reached to my ribs for one of my daggers, my eyes never leaving the door as it unlocked and then swung into the room, bringing with it a dozen or so guards carrying batons and wearing smug faces. "Please, don't let us interrupt your midday debrief," one of the guards mocked.

"Actually, we were just going to ring one of you all. I believe we're ready to head out. The bells should be tolling soon, and we want to get a head start on the hunting portion," Kolter remarked. I felt the rest of the pack begin to stand now, behind Kolter and me. The tension filling the room became insufferable.

"You think we're going to let a pack of wolves leave our fortress freely?" one of the guards snickered, and the pit of my stomach dropped to the floor.

"She's being taken for questioning, and then we'll decide what will happen to the lot of you," he retorted, pointing his baton in my direction.

"Me? You want to take me for questioning? About what?" I asked, moving forward to stand next to Kolter. My shift made the pack step forward as well.

"You're not taking her anywhere, I can assure you of that," Kolter said, deepening his voice. His eyes narrowed while looking at the guards as he stepped in front of me, sliding me behind his back. Victor was next to take me and move me behind him, then Flynn, then Kentaro. I was moving down the line behind the men in our pack.

"You think you have the wits about you to stand up to a prison filled with guards? You waltzed into our house; you don't get to leave without paying the toll." He lunged then, directly for Kolter, and the gasps heard around the room flooded my ears. I watched in horror as the guards began to swarm the room. I knew we were in trouble, and there was very little we could do about it.

Kolter threw the first blade, and it embedded deep into a guard's chest, dropping him to his knees. His second move was to throw a punch, connecting solidly with another guard's jaw, throwing him back a few steps with the momentum of his swing.

I skirted the table to join the fight that was now in full swing. Running forward, I leaped off the table and threw my stiff leg into the back of a guard's neck, forcing him straight into the brick wall. He slammed with such force it knocked him out cold. For a moment I beamed, celebrating that it had actually worked and I could do something so badass. My celebration was cut short as two arms wrapped around my waist and hauled me off my feet. Reaching my hands back, I used my fingers to trace the guard's face, as he tossed his head sideways, carrying me in the direction of the door. I thrust the pads of my thumbs directly into his eyes with enough force that I'd hoped would blind the son of a bitch.

He yelped then, dropping me to the floor and reaching for his face. While he clutched his eyes, I grabbed my blade I'd put away, and with one fell swoop, I sliced through the tendon on the back side of the guard's knee. This would be a career-ending injury to him. Not fatal, but career-ending.

No sooner did I have that guard down, than I felt a tear across my thigh. It stung as nails dragged through my leather pants, ripping them open. I didn't even have time to process what had happened before the pain exploded to the back of my head and darkness came. I stole one last memory of the room, everyone fighting for their lives, before I faded out of consciousness.

Chapter Twenty-Nine

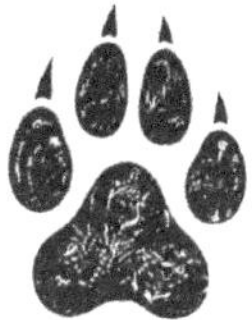

Kolter

I had my sights narrowed on to the two men from Everelle's beatings when she was previously tortured here. I wasn't going to let them leave this room alive. The others in the pack could take whatever guard they wanted, but those two assholes were mine. The guard had no idea, truly, who I was, but the look he gave to Everelle was enough to make my blood run magma hot.

Racing forward, I used my stiff arm to clothesline a guard, flipping him hard to the stone floor onto his back with a thud and groan. I didn't stop to care about that guard; my mind was steadily focused on the guards that beat Everelle.

I made it to him the first guard at the same moment I pulled a blade from my hip, grasping it tightly into my palm. He never even saw me coming, and the blade was licked carefully across his throat, slicing him deep enough that the waterfall of blood began to pour out, and his confused eyes met mine.

"That was for Everelle, you fucking piece of shit. May you die and your family never mourn the loss." I bent over and used his uniform to wipe his blood off my blade.

Turning my attention now to the other guard in the room the one who assaulted Everelle, I saw him fighting Victor. He was throwing punches like he was untrained and visiting a carnival, playing the game where you toss punches at a hovering bag to win a prize. Idiot.

I stalked my way across the room, eyes never leaving the man I wanted dead at my hands. Coming up to his back, I tapped his shoulder. When he turned around, I thrust my knife deep into his stomach, twisting it and retracting it back toward myself in a quick, fluid motion. His eyes drained before me as he dropped them to his waist. He then brought his hands to his stomach, as if he still wasn't registering what I'd done. Pulling his hands away, he saw the blood, then slowly, his eyes turned back to mine. The look of confusion wasn't hard to miss.

Inching my face closer to his, I stared into his soul. "That was for my mate. You don't deserve this lifetime, or another." I shoved him over then, slicing off the hand he'd used to touch what belonged to me. Once severed, I then kneeled to use his uniform to clean my knife.

Standing back up, I did a quick surveillance around the room, and I couldn't find Everelle. Guards lay all over the floor, and one in particular drew my attention because of the blade lodged in his chest. It was Everelle's dagger. She had killed someone, and the momentary pride that filled me was short-lived. I couldn't find her, my pack was fighting hard, but the one person who I needed to see wasn't here. Internally I began to check our line, and it was dead. Like a disconnected phone, I couldn't hear any of them.

It hit me then, like a ton of bricks. The prison must be fortified with magic. We wouldn't be able to shift in here or communicate. Anger fueled me, brimming to the surface with a hot molten sear. Wherever they took Everelle, they'd be sorry for it. I looked over at my pack and saw that they had each continuously fought their way to the door. Most of the guards were now either dead or unconscious on the floor. Baldur dropped the last of them to the floor, and we all took a moment to breathe.

Whistling, I caught everyone's attention. "They took Everelle. Where did they take her?" I barked, the irritation as much toward myself as them.

"I don't know! I didn't even see it happen." Nikita stood now, analyzing the floor; it was littered with guards' bodies. "We need to get her and get out of here."

Looking over, I watched a guard stirring on the floor. Flipping my knife in the air and catching it, I stepped over his comrades' bodies as I went. His eyes began to grow as I leaned over him; my blade pressed delicately against his throat. I watched as his adam s apple danced beneath the blade.

"I'm only going to give you one shot to save your own life. If you lie to me or fight, you will meet your maker in this very room. Do you understand?"

He nodded, closing his eyes, reopening them with wetness in the bloodshot whites.

"Where did they take Everelle?" I demanded, releasing a little pressure so he could speak.

"I...I don't know. I wasn't privy to the information that they divulged. I'm relatively new here." His eyes began darting around the room. He swallowed hard.

"Why did they want her?" I wasn't letting him off that easily. I needed answers, and he was the only person stirring right now to try and get them.

"They think she's a hybrid. They want to kill her. That's all I heard from them. I swear it. That's all I know."

"Who's they?" If the professors or guards were on to Everelle, this could present us with a world of problems.

"The lions... the lions are convinced she's a lion hybrid. They're obsessed with killing her for treason." He was still lying on the floor, scanning everyone's eyes above him. That made no sense. Why would the lions have any level of power over Pollsmoor?

"Why would the lions have any pull in here? The prison is run through the capital, not the school, is it not?" I asked more directly now, hoping he'd give me a real answer. Every minute we were in here was another she was out there with God knows who, being subjected to their viciousness.

He scoffed beneath me now, regaining some of his confidence. Big mistake. I pressed the blade harder into his throat again. I watched as his eyes got bigger, and he began to put weight into his body to get mine off his. I thrust the knife back down onto his neck, nicking the skin and popping the vein on his throat just enough to start a warm trickle of blood beading to the surface.

"OK OK! You really don't know?" He swallowed and closed his eyes. "The lions run this school. They run this prison. No one moves in this city without a lion's approval." He looked me dead in the eyes now. "All of them, professors, and the officials, they're all lions. They think she betrayed them, and they want her dead."

No. This couldn't be possible. Lions don't run the school or government, do they? Looking up, I connected eyes with Nikita, hers emitting the same confusion and anger that was already brewing in my mind.

"Where would they take her? Is there somewhere here that is another guard's favorite torture place? Perhaps a meeting room for the prime minister or the general?" I was grasping at straws and I knew it. I needed to have any indication of where they might take her.

"Yes, the general. He has an office upstairs, but I don't think they'd bring her there. You'd have better luck finding her in the stowaways. Those are the cells beneath the courtyard. It's where we hold inmates that haven't been processed. It allows for torture techniques to get inmates to talk before full processing. That way, if they've committed more crimes or serious offenses, we can add it to their registration."

The more the guard said, the more I wanted to end his life here and now. He'd been useful, however, so his life wasn't worth taking. Not when I'm sure there were far worse offenders inside these walls.

"Thank you, you've been helpful," I said, then used the hull of my knife in a downward blow directly onto his forehead, rendering him unconscious.

"Do you really think the school and government are all run by lions?" Brandt asked, stepping forward.

"It makes sense, doesn't it? Why do the professors never truly consequence the prides for poor averting or hunting? Why they took extreme measures to punish Everelle... I don't know what is happening here, but they won't get the chance to kill her. They'll lose their lives if that's what it takes."

"Fuck em," Flynn retorted. "Let's burn this whole prison down."

Chapter Thirty

Everelle

"EVERELLE!!!" screamed a booming voice. My eyes shot open, but the room didn't become clearer. The scent of decaying humid earth infiltrated my nostrils and stole what little breath I had. My heartbeat was rapidly increasing to an almost deadly rate, and every nerve felt as if it was on fire.

Rolling over, I felt the floor quickly, running my hands in sweeping motions across the stone. Heart pounding, I frantically crawled, making my way toward anything that I could use as a weapon or hiding spot.

"EVERELLE, YOU COME OUT RIGHT NOW!" The voice berated my head with its power, ricocheting off nearby walls as if it were tangible. I could feel the urgency, the pure hatred that its tone inflicted.

I had to get up; I had to clear my head of the disorienting room and focus. If I failed, I wouldn't be able to save them or myself. I couldn't lie here like a damn damsel in distress. It's not who I was, at least, that's what I liked to remind myself of. From what little I've learned about who I truly am, I know I don't end in this shit hole.

I began maneuvering around the room, urgently searching for some sort of escape. Something or someone was looking for me, and I had a sinking feeling it was to finish what it had started. Finally, after what seemed like an eternity, I felt it. My salvation. I had discovered a slit in the wall just slim enough for my fingers to slide through. I dragged them upwards until I met the ceiling. Finding nothing, I dragged them back down to waist level before I found what I was searching for, a latch. I removed my fingers and inserted them again blindly into the crevice just below where I had met the smooth metal and flicked my fingers upwards. I heard the snick of the latch at the same time the booming voice again echoed my name, taunting me to come out of hiding, as if I'd chosen to be here.

I knew I had just minutes to figure out where I was if I was going to save anyone and survive. I shoved the heavy stone door with what little energy I had left, gritting my teeth through the pain I felt. I found myself in a sunken hallway, dimly lit by flickering candles. I paused in the doorway, looking for movement in the flame, willing it to indicate a source of air travel. I looked to my right and saw a sliver of light beaming down from the ceiling at the end of the corridor, and I frantically made my way toward it. I felt a burning in my chest begin.

Subconsciously, I began to massage my sternum as I ran crouching up the dirt path. Come hell or high water, I was getting out of here, and no one else would suffer. The thought, however, was fleeting as I was immediately tossed into darkness. A moment later, I felt a hot, sticky rush of air blow past my face with incredible force. I was screwed, and nothing I did was going to fix it.

"I knew I'd find you down here," the gravelly voice came over my shoulder. A deep chuckle echoed down the hallway. I had no more time; I needed to get out of here. I forced myself forward, up the sloping pathway. At the top of the ramp, I threw myself into a large wooden trap door. I continuously pushed all my weight into the door, urging it to budge. *Why?* I thrust my shoulder onto the door. *Won't?* Thrust. *You?* Thrust. *BUDGE?!* One last thrust and the door flew open.

I scampered up the wall to the stone floor above and threw the hatch door closed, locking it into place.

Crouching down now, I noticed I was in the large courtyard of the prison. I needed to find my way to my pack and get out of here. Beneath me, I felt and heard whoever was chasing me begin to throw themselves at the door. I needed to get moving, but where? I concentrated down the line, but it was still not connecting. I was alone in my thoughts and had no clue where the rest of them were.

A quick scan of the courtyard provided me with twelve-foot walls surrounding the yard, breezeways running the tops of the walls, and tangled scraps of razor-sharp barbed wiring curling over the tops. The breezeways connected them to the other side of the wall. That wouldn't allow us any chance of escaping. I slinked against the far stone wall, hoping to remain out of sight as I continued scanning the area for a way back toward my pack downstairs.

Reminding myself to stay calm, I began slowly creeping down the dimly lit halls in the general direction of the dungeons. I was grateful that I'd paid attention as we were being led downstairs earlier today. I tucked the information away in case a problem arose, and would you look at that? One did. A very big problem. All I could hope for at this point was that my pack was unharmed and we'd get out of here. The uncertainty of the rest of the final was a problem for later.

Midway through the first hall I heard the loud shattering of wood. My heart froze in my chest. Whoever has been hunting me managed to get out of the tunnel beneath the floor of the courtyard. *Shit, shit, shit!* I needed to get downstairs. Scanning the hallway quickly, I found the entrance to the dungeons. Quietly I crept forward, trying not to alert anyone of my presence. I could hear guards loudly talking to one another in other rooms and inmates crying out in pain from below. I didn't want to be on the receiving end of those consequences, and I knew if I didn't hurry, I'd be receiving much worse.

My shoulder burned in agony, my head still radiated in pain, and my ribs still ached. I'd long given up hope that they'd allow for full expansion of my lungs. However, I used all my might to press against the door to the dungeons below. It was heavy and moaned loudly as it opened. One quick glance behind me proved that as of now, I was alone in the hallway. I quickly squeezed inside the small opening and slid the door back closed. Breathing out a sigh of relief, I held back a sob. I was tired, sore, alone, and something told me that it wasn't going to be over any time soon.

I just wish he were here. Oh Kolter... I heard it then, the commotion coming up the twisted stairwell.

Frantically I began to search for anywhere to go, but there was nowhere. I was trapped between the door I'd just come through and the bombarding stampede of guards I heard coming up the stairs. It was probably the guards from the room we'd been locked in, coming to alert everyone that we had attacked them. Quickly, I slid the door back open a little, looking back down the dark hall I'd just left. I couldn't see anyone, but I could still hear voices. Taking my chances with the hallway, I slid back out and quickly crept back toward the front entrance, beside the courtyard. I dipped inside the little storage room as the door to the dungeons slammed open.

"Be quiet! You want to alert everyone that we're here?" I heard the voice of Nikita, and my mind instantly flooded with relief.

I tossed caution to the wind and threw open the storage door and ran back into the hallway for a third time. As I rounded the corner, I saw my pack, filing into the hallway at the other end, and I stopped, collapsing to the floor in a fit of relief.

"Everelle!" Kolter's eyes met mine. Relief flooded his face as he raced down the hallway. "Are you alright?" He picked me up off the floor and held me to his chest. Once he released me, he frantically began to scan my body. Only spinning me back around to his chest when he was confident that I wasn't gravely injured. "You have no idea the amount of relief I have right now. I love you so much." His lips were on me in an instant, and I melted into him. The pent-up stress and agonizing worry all seemed to melt as his mouth greedily devoured mine.

"I hate to be that person, but we really have to keep moving. As romantic as all this shit is, it can wait until we're back in our den." Flynn rolled his eyes as we broke apart.

"I was just..." my words died on my lips as a loud burst of commotion erupted at the end of the hallway.

"There you are! Men, grab them all and take them to the dungeons. I want to have a word or two with Everelle," the general ordered. It wasn't until now that I realized his voice had been the voice in the dark hallway beneath the courtyard. He'd been taunting me. Grabbing my hand firmly, Kolter addressed General Ulrich.

"You won't be taking her anywhere. Neither will you be taking my pack. I alone determine what happens to them and where they go. If you think for one moment that any of us are going to be subjected to your traitorous actions, you have another thing coming."

"I applaud your courage, Mr. Highland." He began with a stiff chuckle as he walked the hallway slowly, stopping within a few feet of us. His guards began to fill the hallway, preventing us from escaping toward the front gates. "But you're again under the assumption that you make the rules here... I can assure you, you don't." Snapping his fingers, he pointed in our direction.

Kolter let out a low and long growl. "I wouldn't try anything foolish, son. You're liable to get yourself hurt, and you can't shift in here... the wards prevent wolves from shifting." The smug look on his face boiled my blood.

"Only wolves?" I asked with a sneer. It made the harsh reality that the school was being bought and paid for by the prides increasingly evident to me.

"Why of course, why would I need to protect myself against my own kind?" My eyes immediately turned to Victor. He hung his head in shame, as if this were a huge secret he'd been holding on to and now was embarrassed to be in the same hallway.

"Your own kind? Your son is a wolf, and you want to say your own kind would protect you? What message does it send to him and his pack?" I taunted. I honestly just wanted him to hang himself verbally. I wanted to see exactly how arrogantly he viewed himself compared to his constituents.

"He's my son, by namesake only. He lost the privileges to my kin the day he shifted wolf, like his bitch of a mother." The general snarled at me. "Any wolf is as good as kindling in my opinion. I run this school merely to watch as the wolves become weaker. We all know the lions are the more superior shifters. Why do you think we throw all of the packs on the front line? I assure you it's not because we find you stronger. Quite the opposite in fact. We get rid of you from our streets and keep the lions protected against the harsh realities that the chosen could come and hunt us. If they do... the wolves will take the first fall."

Kolter was radiating heat beside me, and the longer I heard this piece of shit speak, the angrier I became. I couldn't stand here and allow him to speak ill of my friends, of my family, hell, of his own flesh and blood that way. I'd been fighting the urge to shift from the moment the door downstairs burst open and the general's men funneled in. I couldn't take it anymore.

I felt myself growing before I even realized that I'd wanted to shift. Stepping forward, to protect my pack, I watched as each of the general's men's faces rose to find mine, their mouths agape and their eyes fueled with worry and stress.

"I knew it," the general celebrated, clapping as he smiled, "You just signed your execution papers, my dear. Guards, NOW!"

All at once, commotion exploded in the tunnel. The guards began to charge me with their batons held high. Stepping one giant white paw forward, I lowered my head to their level, roaring as fiercely as I could, saliva spraying them as they approached. I couldn't have cared less about the guards; it was Ulrich I wanted. Charging forward, I allowed the guards to pummel me with their batons. I already had broken bones, so at this point what were a few more? I could handle a few more. He was in my sights, fire burning behind his eyes.

I could hear my pack behind me, arguing with Kolter, asking him how long he'd known what I was and why we hadn't told them. That was a conversation for another day. Right now, I only had one thing on my mind. Reaching down, I still couldn't feel a line. It was frustrating, and I was torn between the idea of killing Ulrich directly in front of his son or taking him anywhere else.

Seeing that his guards had no effect on me, the general dipped between the columns, entering the courtyard beside the hallway. I too stepped between them, just as a massive iron rod landed hard over my shoulder blades, dropping me temporarily to the floor and flooding my senses with explosions of pain.

Rising, I stumbled forward and found the general, still unshifted, holding a massive iron stake he pulled off the wall.

"I'd put that down, if I were you," I growled at him. "What's the matter, General? Can you not shift in here?" I taunted him, and he looked at me with his eyes burning, narrowing them as he snarled.

"It's you that should worry, Ms. Monica. If I shift, you will be of no match to me. I'm simply narrowing the playing field. It's not a fun fight if you immediately dominate it. We like to play with our prey, or didn't you know that?" His laugh became wicked as he closed his eyes, shifting before me to a strong, blonde lion, the one I'd previously met during my first week here.

"It was you that day. In the forest, it was you that interrupted Folasade and punished her. Why?"

"Oh, you ignorant foot. I didn't punish her. I simply scolded her. You think we'd allow a pride princess to enter these horrific walls? No, she was reprimanded for engaging in a battle that wasn't hers to fight."

"You let me go. You made me think you were on my side... was that all for show?" I couldn't believe it. He was right, I was ignorant. How could I have been so foolish and naive?

"To be fair, I'd hoped you'd show your pride side, and we'd pull you from the pack, but alas, here we are. You've chosen to lie with dogs; you've ended up with fleas." He now paced toward me, stalking me and my movements as he came. "You're a beautiful lion. It's quite rare to have a white lion. Your father was wrong to keep you from us, don't you realize? He thought he could outrun this life." He wasn't even circling me. He just stood there pondering my lineage and spitting what he felt were facts. My father had nothing to do with why I'm here. "But I had to right what he had wronged. Why do you think you were summoned to Askari? That was my doing, of course." My stomach dropped to the floor. Was he right? Was my father running from this life in a way to prevent me from entering it? Did he feel like because I was a female, perhaps my place was better suited for home? Self-doubt began swirling in my head, and it was a struggle to break the cycle, to stop the thoughts from consuming me. I refocused on the general, sinking a little toward the stone floor to protect myself while baring my teeth.

"When those people in the forest talked about the white lion they'd seen, I knew you must have shifted. I knew what you had become. What you are. You're a hybrid. Second to The Chosen, you're even more of a risk to the prides of this continent. Hybrids, unless on our side, will be taken care of swiftly; it's law." He lunged now, swiftly swinging his large paws toward me. Fortunately for me, I was faster and able to sidestep his strike.

Again, he began to prattle on, as if this skewed lesson in history were somehow warranted. "My very own son is only alive because of who made him. It was an accident, you know? I didn't plan for him. I thought I'd go out for fun a few nights, and that would be the end of it. I had no way of knowing the bitch was too poor to afford the tonic required to prevent offspring. I nearly spit on her when she came to me months later, explaining what she was growing. It made me sick. The only reason he's not dead is because I'd be dead too. It's against the law to create hybrids. No matter who you are. Keep that in mind the next time you use your blood for the greater good of Highland Pack."

He came at me again, this time, nicking me on the side of my foreleg. It burned as his nails sunk in. However, I was quick. I was able to turn and strike him in the face with a hard swipe. I felt his skin rip under my nails, getting stuck in his soft tissue as I pulled my front paws back. Pulling back, he raised his paw to his face, touched his cheek, and looked at it. He was bleeding profusely from the giant wound he'd suffered. Grinning now, I beckoned him forward.

The blows became quicker now as we grappled. Blow for blow, we'd strike. He was tougher than Nalea, I'll give him that, but that didn't stop my assault. I traded a blow to his face, for his shot to my leg. He never quite reached my face. When I'd finally had enough of the smaller blows, I lunged for his hind leg as he was turning around. I sank my teeth deep into the muscle of his backside, dragging him to the floor, and slamming my paws into his underbelly, ripping him at the core, creating deep lacerations. He yelped and retracted again. I could see the worry in his eyes now as he stalked a little further out of reach. We mimicked each other, walking around in a circle, eyes never leaving the other. I could see he was bleeding profusely.

"You may want to call it and go seek medical," I scoffed. "I wouldn't want you to die on my account. Not when so many people would love the opportunity."

He lunged at me now, unbothered by his open wounds. I waited for my opportunity. I didn't want to let my fear cause me to act foolishly. I waited until he made his final leap at my body, but I leaped lower, grabbing his underside with my jowls, and slamming them shut. I heard his cries, and then his body slacked in my mouth. He lay unconscious now, his hot salty blood pouring down my face. I spit him out onto the stone floor of the courtyard. He could bleed out for all I cared.

Turning away, I searched for my pack. They'd been left in the hallway when I'd begun following General Ulrich, but as I turned around, I saw they'd been standing, watching us battle in utter silence. The shock and awe across their faces was enough to make my eyes finally release all the pent-up tears they'd been holding back.

"Wait!!!! Ever!" Kolter cried out. His eyes were as wide as saucers. I couldn't even register what he was saying before the blinding pain hit me like a wrecking ball.

Looking down, I'd been impaled with the iron spear that General Ulrich had hit me with earlier. The shock of the blow didn't register. The only thing that did was Kolter's anger boiling over. Then there was darkness, and I was being pulled under yet again.

Chapter Thirty-One

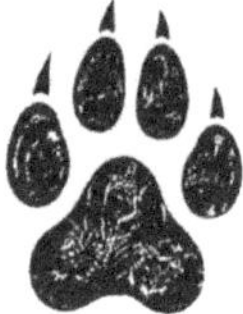

Kolter

I watched the life drain from her eyes in front of me. Time slowed down as I watched her be impaled by Ulrich, right in front of me, and there wasn't a damn thing I could do to fix it.

Time resumed, and I was racing toward her, catching her before she fell to the floor. She looked peaceful, almost serene, as I looked into her eyes while they closed. She went limp in my arms, and I screamed. I screamed for our pack members. I screamed for Ever and her broken soul. I screamed that I'd murder him myself. I screamed because if she died, I'd be alone for eternity. And then, I snapped. Pieces of me broke. I shifted there inside the walls of the fortress. I shifted and then dropped Everelle into Flynn's waiting arms. *Run, take her to medical.* I tried to say it, but it didn't seem like the words were coming out quite right. The shock on his face as he held her made the situation she was in all too real for me. Flynn simply nodded to me.

As if he understood what I needed, Victor stepped forward, addressing Flynn. "We're going to need you to get her out of here, and to medical. I'll be along in a second," he ordered. He stood in for me when my words failed. Flynn took off then, running while my very existence was dying in his arms.

I then turned my back on my pack and scanned the room for the bastard that took the only thing in this miserable world I cared about from me. He wouldn't leave this fucking room alive.

The coward was in the corner now, crawling toward the open doorway that led to the hallway. I took my time sauntering over to him. I wanted to make him pay for all he'd done to Everelle. I wanted to make him pay for the death of Priya and what he'd done to all of us under the guise of education. He needed to pay for the way he disregarded Victor so callously.

Reaching him, I brought my paw up and sunk my nails into his hind leg, dragging him backward as he roared in pain. I let go as we reached the middle of the courtyard. He snapped his jowls shut and threw his forelegs out in front of him, using what little strength he had to begin crawling again for his escape. I let him get to the edge of the courtyard before I pounced again, biting his back leg, and using all my force to throw him back toward the middle of the courtyard.

"Wha-What do you want with me?" the once-tough general blubbered in front of me. "Whatever it is, just fucking do it! Finish what she started. You know you want to." He blanched in pain again as he continued to crawl toward the exit of the square.

"I'm not done with you quite yet. First, I'm going to make you answer all my questions." I passed by him as he crawled, and I looked down at him as if he were nothing more than an ant on the sidewalk. "I want to know why you ordered for Everelle to come here in the first place. She never knew about any of us. She never knew about shifters. Why did you bring her into this world and then put her in Highland?"

He began coughing as he neared the end of the courtyard. He wasn't answering my questions. He didn't even acknowledge that he'd heard me. Again, I found myself sauntering over, slamming my nails directly into his hind quarter, and listening to the roar of pain he was emitting. I then slowly dragged him back toward the center of the room, dropping him like he was a useless throw rug.

"I asked you why you brought her here." I was growing angrier with each passing minute.

"Why the hell would it matter to you? You won her. Isn't that all that matters to you?" He stopped crawling now, defeated and accepting that he'd get nowhere. He turned and looked at me. For a brief moment he looked shocked, but the pain he must be feeling made him wince and close his eyes. When he reopened them, the look was that of pure agony. "She's powerful, the most powerful shifter we have seen in almost a century. I wanted her to train here. She needed to know her full potential. Then maybe she would have chosen to join her father's, MY pride. Instead, she fell, and you mixed your blood in hers, and look just how well that turned out for her."

"You thought she would choose to be a lion? Why?" I already knew she was powerful. I knew she had more depth than she was even aware of. I just needed to know what he knew.

"Of course! Most often, if given the choice, anyone would choose the more powerful route to success. Wouldn't you? If you knew that you'd be on the winning side of this war, wouldn't you choose it?" He was coughing again, blood splattering from his mouth onto the stone floor. He'd already painted most of the courtyard red with his blood. I didn't know how much more time he had left.

"No. I'd choose the right path. The moral path. Everelle would too. We don't choose to hate and use violence. It's apparent that that is a lion's trait," I quipped.

"Pah, you hardly know what a lion's side is. You will soon, but you don't know what we all go through. How we protect our prides. You'll see. They will replace me here, but the problem will always be there. Lions rule this continent. The sooner you come to terms with it, the better for you both." He was losing a lot of blood now. Looking around, I could see my pack waiting for me in the wings. Flynn and Victor had taken Everelle to medical, and the rest of the pack was just waiting for me to finish off the general so we could reunite with them.

"I hope that for your sake, you led your life how you wanted, because in the afterlife, you won't have as many options. I'm sure of that." I walked forward, pinning my paw against his throat.

"You'll never be more than you are, because you won't allow yourself to see your potential, you'll always hold Everelle back, and there will always be someone ready to take my place. Welcome... to... the war... Highland." He lay back then, closing his eyes, and I stole his last breath.

I'd make damn sure that Everelle never saw this side of war. She deserved to be protected and not deal with the stressors of political injustice.

Walking back, I shifted back to my human form to rejoin my pack.

"I didn't know you had that in you," Nikita said, solemnly. "We need to get out of here and back to the main campus. Someone has to inform the council of what happened here today and that the General is dead."

"First, I need to check on Ever." They all nodded in agreement, no one really looking me in the eyes. I gave one last glance back into the room that took everything from me before we headed toward the front gate.

The iron bars were up halfway again, signaling that they'd raced through without waiting for them to finish rising.

Stepping outside of the fortress, it was becoming dusk. We'd been locked away for hours, but that's not what surprised me. Standing alongside the tree line were all the packs and prides of Askari. They were bowing to us as we walked out and toward the path back towards the school. Baraka was the first to approach.

"I just wanted to say we heard about Everelle and what you all just went through. That was in no way related to us, nor was that something we stand behind. If there is anything you all need, please, let us know. You're always welcome in the Molti Pride." He bowed and I nodded in thanks.

Folasade, with the entire Ade pride beside her, bowed as well. "We also stand with your pack. I know we had a rough start, but we would never condone that level of violence and political bias in Ade. The Outlands will hear of this, and our assembly will head for the capital to speak of the injustice done here today."

"Thank you, Folasade. You will always be welcome by our pack."

The packs came next, with Mazza and Hadlick showing their support.

Lastly, my eyes met Professor DeMarcus. She was waiting patiently off to the side. "Kolter, I'd like to extend my deepest condolences. I know this is not how we as your professors wish to have you taught. Putting your lives at risk is never the answer. I will be addressing the school board and the assembly in the capital. If there is anything your pack needs, please don't hesitate to let me know. I'll do whatever is in my power to be at your service."

"I appreciate that, Professor. Right now, my only thoughts are getting to Everelle. I just pray Flynn and Victor made it in time." I checked down the line, but the three couldn't be felt, and it was bringing a lot of unnecessary stress to the pack.

Turning back to them, I addressed everyone, "The General has fallen, as a direct result of his cruel and unorthodox mindset. He challenged students to their death, and unfortunately for him, it led to his demise. If you all would excuse my pack, we'd like very much to see our mates." I then looked at my pack, eyes red, brimming with tears in most of them, and I nodded. I shifted back into my wolf form and raced towards our future. Or at least mine.

Chapter Thirty-Two

Everelle

Waking up in the medical wing of Askari was very disappointing. I thought that I'd had the upper hand, but apparently judging by the throbbing pain in my side, that wasn't the case. Slowly I began to stretch. I hadn't even opened my eyes, but the sunlight that was filling the room led me to believe I'd been here overnight.

Then Kolter's scent hit me, full-nose assault. The scent of him alone, not even the sight, did the most wonderful things to my body. I craved him as much as I'd craved air. This was a startling thought considering that just this past spring I had no idea he'd existed. I guess that isn't entirely true, though, is it? Lucianna did wonders to make sure we weren't at risk. For almost thirteen years she'd harbored our secret, and in six short months I ruined all the work she put in. My only hope is that she would forgive me and not blame me for the trouble we'd got ourselves into at my expense.

Cracking open my eyes, I looked around the small room. It was minimalist for sure. Monotone gradients of black to white. There was one single window above where my heart lay sleeping, crumpled up in a chair. I was thankful for him, even though I had no clue how my night ended with me in this bed. After falling onto the stones in front of the general, I knew in my heart he was the one who saved me.

Actually, that was me. Flynn walked into the room silently so as to not disturb Kolter. Making himself at home on the small bed I was in, his eyes met mine with unease and worry. "How is it, I rescued the fair maiden and got her to the medical unit within mere moments of her life being taken, and he gets the credit?" Flynn tucked a loose strand of my hair behind my ear. "How are you feeling?"

"About as well as a kabob?" I shrugged. He laughed now, too loudly, and Kolter began to stir.

"That's why he doesn't like me spending too much time with you, you know. Something about a bad influence and the inability to take things seriously?" He began to roll his eyes and mock Kolter. I had to admit it was exactly what I'd needed. Aside from each laugh splitting my insides.

"Well, damn, don't hurt yourself on my account, especially after I worked so hard to save you and all that." He was leaning me back now and tucking the sheets around my body.

"You may have saved her, but I avenged her," came a gruff, sleepy Kolter from the side of the bed. "Stop making her laugh. The medicine isn't instant. She has to regenerate enough tissue and muscle to fix the in and out he gave her." He was bending over now to kiss my head. "You need your rest; it's only been three days."

I was sitting up now, "Three days?!! I've been in here for three days?" I had so many questions and a million thoughts racing through my head all at once. Starting with the fact that he was still wearing his blood-soaked torn leathers. He clearly hadn't been home to shower. *How were the others? Is the general alive? Am I going to be a permanent inmate of Pollsmoor? Do the lions want me dead?*

"Woah woah woah, shhhh," Kolter began, brushing my hair away from my face.

"I think this may be where my best friend boundaries lie... Kolter, you can have our babbling kitty. I'll let everyone else know she's awake," Flynn said, playfully grimacing as he stood up to leave the room. "For what it's worth, your name is on everyone's lips, but I assure you, it's not with hate." With that, he left the room.

"What happened? Why have I been asleep for three days?" I asked cautiously.

"Well, Ulrich impaled you with an iron stake. It went completely through your midsection. Luckily, he somehow managed to miss every single organ when he did it. So, either his intention wasn't to kill you, or he had awful aim for a general."

"Had.. you said, 'had'. Does that mean he's dead?" I was sitting up again in bed, my heart racing, and my head beginning to feel dizzy.

"Yes, but you don't need to worry. The Assembly and the Sector are meeting to sort it all out. It doesn't bode well that a capital school has had several students perish and one get critically injured in such a short time."

"We need to get to that meeting; I need to get out of here. They'll need to understand that I'm not a threat to anyone." I frantically began pulling at the covers Flynn just tucked in, in an attempt to get up.

Kolter wasn't having it. He gently began pushing me back down in bed now. "The packs and prides have reached an agreement... No one will speak to what you are. If guards at the prison speak on your behalf, we've got a plan in place to say otherwise. No one is going to leak you to the capital. We have their word."

"How can we be so sure? This is my life in their hands. The same ones that tried to attack me in the woods alone, or cross a raging river to drown me... I don't know how you blindly put your faith in them." I was shaking with anxiety filled worry.

"They're also the same ones who left us clues toward the final, worked with us to pass the crevice, and stood outside the prison in a bowed formation as you were carried out, impaled by their general. He doesn't speak for them or their prides. You've also had pride security since you arrived here. No one has left you alone." Kolter said, giving my hand a tight squeeze. His warm eyes held gratitude and love.

"I don't understand. What changed their minds about me? I was a traitor to them."

"You're not just a powerful shifter, Ever, you're the one who's going to help bring back justice to the continent. You will forge an alliance and bring forward a wave of moral rule against those in office who seek only to dismantle and destroy the packs. You're a hero in our eyes," he was beaming with pride. I was a hero? Six months ago I was an invisible girl who read books in her mother's salon window... now I was a hero?

I couldn't wrap my head around any of this. I wasn't a hero, nor did I have the ability to change minds. I could barely keep mine straight. How was I going to help change the continent from those who sought to control it?

"The first thing we have to do is get you rested so you're able to get on your feet. For now, that is your only focus."

Nodding, I just escaped into my own head. I needed clarity, and I couldn't get that lying in this bed. The nurse came in the door at that moment, disrupting my thoughts, ending what we'd been discussing, and beginning the process of healing.

"Well, good morning, Ever! We've been waiting for you to wake up. How are you feeling?" She began checking my sides and humming to herself.

"Eh, I'm alright, sore mostly." I leaned back, closing my eyes.

"I could imagine so! You took a nasty little fall, didn't you?"

My eyes looked at Kolter, and he remained stoic. I grimaced while she worked on my sides.

"Now then, you'll have to have at least two more doses, and then I'm sure you'll be right as rain to go home tomorrow morning. How does that sound?" The Cailleach was looking at me now, eyes hopeful.

"That sounds great, thank you, for all your help. I appreciate this so much." The feelings were genuine. I couldn't imagine how I must have been when

I'd come into the medical unit three days prior. She raised a medicine cup to my lips and rested her fingers delicately on my chin. I drank from the vessel and immediately regretted it. It was the foulest, burning, thick liquid I'd ever consumed. A coughing fit awoke in me, causing blinding pain to my ribs and taking my breath away.

"There you are. Now, get some rest. Only one more dose of curefix to go!" she sang out as she left my side. She patted Kolter on the shoulder as she walked from the room.

"If the impaling didn't kill me, that shit will." I made a disgusted face that made Kolter laugh. "Go home. You need to shower. You're stinking up my clean air that is used to rebuild my lungs or some shit."

Laughing now, he got up and kissed me. I began to fade out, the medicine kicking in. "I love you." was the last thing I remembered hearing.

After being cleared to leave, the next morning, I found myself stepping into the brisk fall sun. It immediately put me at ease and made me feel like I wanted to run. "I'll race you back?" I challenged Kolter, grinning at him.

"As much fun as that sounds, I'd rather we take it easy on you. You've just healed from a major injury. I can't have you rupturing." He was no fun. We walked instead, slowly following the long path back through the woods to our obsidian-covered den.

When we entered the den, we could hear the gleeful chatter of my pack, and it warmed my soul. I turned the last bend, and it opened to the common room, filled with my pack mates and some pride members of Ade and Molti.

"The prodigy returns! Welcome home, love, how are you feeling?" Assata beamed with excitement as I walked through the archway. She motioned for me to take a seat. The room was filled with treats on every surface, soft music played from the record player on the side table, and everyone was bursting with happiness. Victor was the only one who was not gleeful, and my heart broke for him. At the end of the day, Ulrich was still his father. The sting of rejection and death was taking a toll.

Looking around the room, I could see the ding this year had taken on our pack and the prides. It was a wonder we had anything in us left to celebrate.

A chime rang out around the cavernous den, and we all looked up.

"Do we have a doorbell?" Nikita asked the group. "Since when do we have a damn doorbell?"

Getting up and following Kolter to the mouth of the den, I was a nervous ball of energy, built up from days locked in healing. "Who could be here that isn't already?" I asked him as we approached the cave's entrance.

Standing in the clearing of the forest just outside our den were none other than Professor DeMarcus, Professor Monaghan, the professor for wilderness survival Dr. Sanger, and a third male I'd yet to meet.

"Good afternoon, you two. It seems that most of the cadets across the campus can be found within your den's walls, so we brought the meeting to..." The man I'd never met had his eyes draw lines around our den as if being in its presence caused him stress. "Your humble abode. Could we by chance step inside for this conversation, or would you prefer everyone come out here?"

"Of course, come on in. Everyone is in the common room, so it's a little tight, but we should all fit just fine." Kolter said, holding his arm out and gesturing for them to start inside.

The appearance of school officials in a cadet's den was a serious occurrence. Walking into our common room, the mood in the room immediately shifted. Those who were once seated in joyful conversation now stood, stoic and unwavering.

"Please sit. Don't rise on our accounts. We come peacefully," Professor DeMarcus spoke calmly. She looked disheveled, worse than I'd ever seen her before. Her usual neatly curled hair was now frizzy and growing as if the leftover humidity from the summer days was penetrating her cuticles and wreaking havoc on her cortex. Shaking my head, I laughed at the observation. The usual mindless ramblings of my mother had stuck with me, and in this moment, I missed her.

"We come today to discuss the final course, your grades, and what to expect for the rest of the term. We will start with the biggest news first. As you may already know, General Ulrich is no longer with us, and therefore his seat as acting school general is vacant. The Capital has appointed Dr. Charles Hoboke for the temporary replacement in that position. He bears no militaristic nature and will be a much-needed relief to built-up tension and worries. He promises to be fair, unbiased, and nurturing, as his area of expertise happens to be youth psychology. Please offer a welcoming hand to Dr. Hoboke." She raised her hand to the man that accompanied them, and he gave a small bow and cleared his throat to address the room.

"I've been briefly filled in in regards to the activities that have happened as of late, and I assure you all, this will no longer be a school filled with threats of death and violence. It is my great pleasure to work with you all as you navigate this treacherous time of trauma and shifting. Please stop by my office at any time. It's an open door to you all."

My eyes met Kolter's from across the room. His thoughts mirrored mine. *Just have to trust him for now, you trust until they give you a reason not to.*

"Thank you, Dr. Hoboke. I'm sure the cadets will all take that offer should they need it. Next up, we have the results of your final course. Being that the second task of the final was interrupted due to imminent violence, we have decided as an academy to ask that you complete parts two and three again under the strict guidance of safety and supervision from Dr. Hoboke, Professor Monaghan, and myself. We understand this may not be the outcome you wanted, but we can promise you, there will be no further deterrents from the course that you'd previously run." Groans could be heard throughout the room. No one was in the mindset of running a course of aversion and hunting.

"If I may, Professor, with all due respect, Everelle is just coming off intense surgery. In case you all have forgotten, we were kidnapped and attacked, and she was impaled by the general of this academy. You can understand how the idea of retaking a final exam, which we in all actuality survived quite well, would be, at the minimum, mundane," Kolter interjected, his expression flat. You could read the anger written on the lines of his face.

"I'd have to agree, Professor. There have been more than enough maneuvers that you should be able to grade something for each pack or pride," Baraka added. "We have all lost someone while running these courses, and I think finding any cadet with the gusto to run it again after the tyranny we've been subjected to will be near impossible."

The room remained silent while the professors and Dr. Hoboke all convened in the hallway to discuss the running of the final.

"I don't think that they can rightfully ask us to run it again. Not after all we have been through," Assata said solemnly.

"We're a military academy. They're training us for battle, war, and protection. I wouldn't count your chickens. They'll most likely institute that we run it again out of fear that if we were to be given a pass, what's to stop next year from creating an issue that results in them getting a pass? We have to keep the mindset that we're running it again." Kolter spoke now, moving to me and wrapping his arms around my waist. I nudged him softly and rested my head on his shoulder. This wasn't going to be easy. The room was broken into small groups, all discussing the final. Feeling hopeless, I wished they'd just come to a decision already. Enough with the discussion.

"Can we have your attention, please?" While I'd been in self-wallowing, they'd returned. Professor DeMarcus looked pleased for the first time since she'd entered. "We've reached a decision." She began fiddling with one lone strand of her hair. "If this had been a true representation of your orders after school, which is what we are in fact preparing you for after all, you'd have been granted a reprieve from your assignments for the trials you suffered." The room buzzed now with excited chirps from the cadets. Kolter reached for my hand and gave me a squeeze. "However, we feel you should know that considering the circumstances you all will have to face once you're assigned orders, you won't be done fighting after one instance. Often, you'll be tasked with battling or protection daily. As a result, we've decided that you will take part two and three of your final again, but at a smaller scale." The room filled with unease and groaning.

Professor Monaghan stepped forward now, addressing the room. "You need to prepare yourself that in real life, when working for our government and military sectors, you will be tested far beyond your strengths and reach of mental exhaustion. We would be doing you no favors granting you a pass today. With that being said, please meet us at the sparring field in one hour. Your final exam will resume today," Professor Monaghan stated curtly.

After his words, they all bid farewell and left the den, leaving all the cadets speechless. "I get that if this had been 'real life' we wouldn't be offered a pass; however, come on! Everelle almost died out there. Neo and Priya did die. They want us to just perform as if nothing happened? It's not fair," Kentaro huffed.

"I figured this was going to happen. We can do it; we just need to keep our heads on and stay on the course. She said there would be no more deviations from the courses we'd previously run, and if that's the case, it should be relatively easy," Victor chimed in. "As long as we have no more unexpected instances of bullshit, we should be ok."

"Can I have everyone's attention for just a moment, please?" Xolani was addressing the room now, and everyone snapped their heads to give him respect and allow him the floor. "As the king of the Pride of Ade, I'd like to call into conversation the fact that we were asked as a pride to study you all year. We allowed you to think we were putting in full effort, but we weren't. We were following orders to hide in plain sight and give you the illusion that we were giving our best effort."

"I fucking knew it!!" hollered an enthusiastic Flynn. "I called that shit. You didn't have us fooled. It's why we ended up in prison. We knew you were up to something..." Flynn grinned in satisfaction. He was right. He had pegged them. If it hadn't been for him figuring it out, we may have found a worse fate.

"Yes, well, that's part of the problem, you see, we were tasked with hunting you down for real and turning you over to the guards in Pollsmoor. You were always meant to end up there. Now, when it comes to the final again, we just ask that you understand that we were coerced and had no say. We'd like to officially offer you a truce, and perhaps an alliance of sorts," he finished, looking ashamed that he even allowed his pride to be manipulated by the general in the first place.

"I get it. He was my dad, and I still felt like I was never good enough. You're forgiven by me anyway; I can't speak for my pack. I just know how he is and what lengths he can go to. I get it." Victor shrugged.

"We hold no grudges," Kolter said, reaching his hand out to Xolani and shaking it.

"Ever, I'm sorry for what we've put you through. You saved my life despite how I'd been treating you. I wish I'd learned quicker. All I can tell you is that in the future, you'll have me as an ally." Folasade stepped forward and reached out her hand; I took it and pulled her in for a hug. This girl needed love more than she let on.

Chapter Thirty-Three

Everelle

We all arrived as one to the sparring fields, none of us wanting to complete the final again, but there nonetheless. The two parts would be "smaller," Professor DeMarcus said. Let's hope it wasn't too strenuous and we could do the exam without any further issues.

"Thank you all for coming within the allotted time. I expect this will be quick, and we can begin the next portion of your studies on Monday." Professor Monaghan said, stepping forward on the makeshift dais they'd erected just for this occasion. "Due to recent events, we've decided as an educational body to minimize the final requirements, thus lessening the expectations and maneuvers. As such, we hope that you all will be willing to do well and participate to your fullest ability in the course final." He looked out at the group and nodded his head in the direction behind him. "In this final exam, you will spend exactly one hour averting, and one hour hunting. Due to your recent bonding experiences, we feel it's only fair that we use our own team of wolves and lions to help hunt and avert you. To the left..." He gestured to his right side to where the pack of wolves were standing from our previous trial runs. "You have our academy's very own wolf pack. The packs will have one hour to avert them. Your range of travel has shrunk, and you will have the left half of the school grounds. Prides, you will have the right side and will be hunted and hunt our Askari lions. After the one-hour mark, if you haven't been caught and brought back here, you will hear a toll. When it rings, you will immediately begin tracking and hunting our teams. Does everyone understand the tasks I've laid out?" Professor Monaghan looked around the groups and nodded before stepping back to his seat, and Dr. Hoboke stepped forward.

"Fear not, cadets. You will not be harmed during this final. I have personally walked the grounds and made sure no previous deviations are still active. You will also not be truly hunted and captured. Merely, they'll call out to you when you've been found. If at any point you find yourself feeling overwhelmed, hurt, or anxious, I ask that you simply return here to the dais, and we will end your exam and score you to that point. Your scores from part one of the exam are still here and will be added to your final score. No one fails today. Based on the scores from your first part and the curve we have added, no pack or pride will be given a failing grade. That will be worth celebrating!" He began to applaud us with a cheesy grin. I looked at Kolter, still unsure if he was trustworthy. Kolter nodded at me, his thoughts again mirroring mine, but he tried to keep a positive face for the pack. "Cadets! You have one hour! GO!!" He thrust his hands in the air, throwing a green flag. Before it had even hit the dais, we had shifted and were across the sparring fields, headed toward our spot on the rocky river walls.

Baldur, make sure you're releasing the scent blocker, I heard Kolter bark down the line as all of us were running in rhythm. It was one hour; how badly could this go? We'd already been promised a passing grade just for stepping on the field, and the promise that nothing ill would happen to us either was a little comforting. I wouldn't allow myself to relax, however, until we crossed the finish line, holding onto a wolf that we would have successfully hunted.

We reached the riverbank in record time. One by one we shifted and climbed the river wall and backed into the caves, out of sight. Baldur made quick work releasing the last of the scent blocker and climbed up into his cave. Kentaro shifted his body to block Kolter and me from view. This was very much reminiscent of earlier this year when we ran here for the trial. It had been the most successful aversion tactic we'd tried, so it was best to go with it for the final. Especially when we weren't being hunted by the lions who'd previously learned our routines.

Flynn, what do you see? Kolter asked down the line.

They're twelve kilometers to the west. So far, so good, boss.

Perfect. Let me know if anything changes. Everyone else, how are we doing?

Locked and secured here, Lisbeth rang.

Hidden, Flavia and Flynn confirmed.

Ditto, Brandt and Nikita said, from where they were hidden together.

Victor and Assata, how are you guys?

We're set. Rang their voices in unison, a slight smirk could be felt down the line.

Perfect. No one is to move without my permission, clear? Everyone nodded into the line. Silence took over.

Nearing the end of the hour, we heard it. The wolves were down below. *Flynn, I'm going to need an update, quickly,* Kolter stressed down the line.

There is only one wolf, the younger one from the last trial. I don't think she senses us. But she's stopped directly outside and is *looking up at the wall,* Flynn said. Eerily she didn't move. She sat there, waiting. Never moving a muscle. We could see her through Flynn's vision.

What is she doing?? Where is the rest of her pack? I asked down the line to no one in particular.

I miss you.

She's turning now! Running away. Ever... we miss you too? Flynn chuckled down the line. Kolter looked at me strangely. The only problem was, I didn't say it.

The bell tolled then, and we all jumped out of the river's wall, successfully averted.

Good job, guys! Flynn got in the air. Where are they? Kolter cheerfully rang out.

The lone wolf is leading us directly toward them. I'll keep her in our sight, and we should outpace her and find them. She's leading us dead center, headed west. Flynn responded.

Ok, let's pick up the pace, everyone. Let's catch us a wolf and get back to the sparring field. Kolter led the formations after the lone wolf. A little more bounce in our steps.

Everyone did just that. We locked in, going full speed and sprinting back toward the main school grounds. Rounding the last bend, we spotted the pack, grouped together around the canyon obstacle from the five-mile run. They seemed to be bickering about not being in agreement on their plan. Bad for them, perfect for us.

HOLD! Kolter said, slowing down and crouching behind some trees. *Blend and cover. I'm going to want Baldur, Lisbeth, Brandt, Flavia, and Kentaro to head East, rounding the pack five yards from center. Hold in the tree line and don't get seen. Stay upwind. Victor, Nikita, Flynn, and Assata, you head west. Ever and I will take the lead, dead center. Once in position, signal, and wait for my go,* Kolter ordered the pack.

Everyone broke into positions then, sauntering around the pack in the middle of the clearing, closing in on them without them even knowing we were here. *East is clear and in position. Holding.* Baldur's voice came down the line.

West is clear and in position. Waiting for the signal, Victor's voice came over the line.

Flynn, what's the read? Kolter asked, tossing his head at me and motioning me to begin walking forward with him.

We're still set. They seem to be fighting; none are paying attention or actively searching for us. Flynn's calm smooth voice came through the line. Hunting was one of the few times we ever saw him relax and take something seriously.

Alright, advance! Kolter barked across the line. In an instant we all moved.

In that moment we all burst through the tree line, surrounding the wolf pack and crouching low. The lone wolf from the riverbank looked wide-eyed and stepped a few steps backward. The leader of their pack grimaced. Shaking his head. He barked a few orders at his pack, and silently, they all turned and walked back toward the sparring fields. The lone wolf, bringing up the rear, hung her head in shame.

Does anyone find it odd how quickly that happened and that they just didn't seem fazed? I asked down the line as we walked the wolves back toward the professors.

They probably don't truly care too much about the exam. It's not like they're being graded on it, Victor retorted. The way the newest wolf looked so defeated and the frustration the alpha took on, I didn't get that vibe. At least our final was done, and we didn't have to worry about the hunting and averting maneuvers again until next year. It had me downright cheerful.

Stepping back onto the sparring fields, Professor DeMarcus was beaming. We were the first back, but over my shoulder I could see the Mazza pack headed our way, also having captured their wolves.

It took almost the full hour for every pack and pride to make it back to the field successfully, and we weren't at all disappointed. The air around us was lighter than it'd felt in months.

"It's with great pleasure that I announce our highest-marked cadets for this course final. Highland Pack, you have successfully crossed part one's finish line first. Averted capture on part two and successfully hunted and captured your prey in part three in less than eighteen minutes. With that in mind, you will each receive the highest scores! Congratulations!" Professor DeMarcus shouted. She continued with the scores that each pack and pride had received. However, my eyes kept jumping to the pack of wolves we had to hunt. There was something about the lone wolf that I couldn't figure out. She was sad, of course, but it wasn't just that. Perhaps it was simply that she wasn't given enough credit in her pack. I mean, she did find us, though she didn't act on it, during the averting portion of our exam.

"We will have a long weekend of rest and relaxation, and if you'd like, you may go in the city to partake in one of the finer establishments. Keep in mind you are a representative of Askari. Any negative behavior will be held to the highest standard of consequence. You are all dismissed! Have a great weekend!" Dr. Hoboke shouted gleefully.

Chapter Thirty-Four

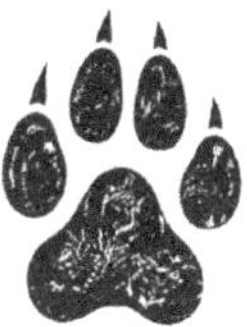

Everelle

The weekend was spent indoors, relaxing, resting, and participating in otherwise indecent activities. It was Monday morning, and we were lying in Kolter's bed. I nudged him. "Hey, we have to get up. We'll be late for Dr. Sanger's class." He yawned and threw his arm back over my waist, holding me to him while he nuzzled my neck. "Just five more minutes. They can wait five more minutes." Rolling my eyes, I laughed.

"No, I already gave you fifteen. Let's goooo." I was now shoving him off the side of the bed.

"Oh, it's like that now? You're done." He was jumping back on me now, tickling me and play-fighting me. "You think you're the boss of me?" he asked, between nibbles on my collarbone and tickles down my side.

"No, no, no, I don't! I don't! You win; you win!" I shouted between bursts of laughter erupting from my chest. He stilled now, hovering just above me, looking down, tracing my face with his eyes.

"You are the most beautiful woman I've ever laid eyes on. Truly." He bent then, kissing me softly. I melted into him. How could just a simple sentence, a small proclamation of beauty, steal my soul?

"We have. To. Go," I said between his kisses. "We've spent over six months here, and it hasn't been easy. Not in the slightest. I want to start this mini portion off on a good foot." Shoving him now, I was able to stand up and begin getting my leathers on. Other than to eat and shower, we hadn't left this room for the better part of the weekend, and if we didn't show ourselves soon, I'm sure they'd send in the cavalry.

With a deep sigh, he rose and began dressing. I watched in awe at the flex of his muscles across his back and the ridges of his shoulders. "Ever, fix your face, or we're never making it to Sanger's class." I hadn't realized I'd stopped dressing and stood there staring. If I were a man, without a doubt I'd be pitching a tent.

"Sorry, oof." I fell into the desk while putting my pants on. Bending over, I rubbed my thigh.

"Oh, fuck it," he said, throwing his shirt onto the bed and walking toward me. "If you're going to beg, I suppose we have time for a quickie." His grin spread devilishly across his face as he unzipped the very taut pants he just put on. My jaw dropped as I stood. "No, babe, no need to stand up." He put his finger in the air and motioned for me to turn around. He approached me then, sliding his hands over my waist and bare ass. He spanked me playfully while using his leg to spread mine. Dragging his hand up, he gently bent me over his desk and then ran his fingers lightly down my spine. The touch of his warm fingers sent my nerves on fire and goosebumps to flood my skin. "That's my good girl," he said, in his deep husky voice, immediately turning my core into a running faucet. He touched me then, sliding his fingers between my folds, directly into my wet sex. "You're so wet for me. Mmmmm," he moaned in my ear, turning me to putty in his hands.

My insides were ablaze, wanting him desperately, so I slowly arched my backside into him, nudging my ass against his raging hard on. "Someone's a little impatient, I see." He chuckled, running his right hand up my stomach and onto my freed breast. He aimlessly began tweaking my hard, peaked nipple, rolling it between the pad of his thumb and finger, while his other hand lined his hard cock up to my dripping core. Flicking downward and up as he did, he sent heatwaves crashing into my core. It was already bringing me to the height of my pleasure. With one fluid motion, he thrust inside of me, stretching me and erupting my orgasm. I screamed his name without warning. "You like that, do you?" he coaxed while kissing my shoulder blades. Both of his hands worked my nipples while he thrust in and out of me with such vigor, I didn't know how we'd survive. Already building toward another climax, I felt him getting harder and thrusting deeper into me. The pleasure was almost too much.

"You're going to need to go, baby, I'm almost..." We went together then, both of us reaching our climaxes and exploding in unison. Slowly, he thrust a few more times before pulling out of me. He kissed me gingerly on my neck and tweaked my nipple one more time for good measure before using a tissue to wipe whatever was left of our love off of him and pulling up his pants.

I was still bent over his desk, shaky legs and a hot core. "That's never going to get old, is it?" I asked, finally finding the strength to pull my pants up the rest of the way.

"God, I hope not. I love how you feel," he said, throwing his shirt on now, covering his chest, and grinning at me. "Get a move on Princess. You're making us late." He winked at me and headed toward the door. "I'll meet you out there; don't be too much longer."

"Yeah. Sure," I said, the leftover tingles still very much keeping me from moving too fast. He chuckled as he shut the door and left me with my thoughts to get ready.

Finally dressed and making sure I'd grabbed my bag, I left his room and headed for the common area.

"Well, I'll be. She is alive. I was worried he had you locked away and murdered by now. Ooh, Ever, you got something right here," Flynn said, motioning toward my bottom lip. I instinctively wiped my face, and he lost his mind laughing. "That was good, that was too good."

"Shut the hell up," Kolter said as he walked by, smacking a laughing Flynn in the back of the head with a pillow from the chair he was leaning against. "Go get laid yourself, why don't you?"

"Can't. You took the only good piece of ass in this group."

My eyes flicked to Flavia. "Don't look at me. I don't control him." She threw her hands up with a shrug.

Kolter's eyes looked like they'd murdered Flynn where he stood, but his eyes retracted from Flynn's and met mine. All the passion they previously held, now held built up frustration and irritation with Flynn instead. *Sorry about him.* I said down the line to Kolter, but if he heard me, he didn't act like it.

"Gear up, we're headed to Sanger's class. I want everyone to be ready and actively participating. The next three months should be relatively easy. Let's not find ourselves in another bad situation."

Walking into the forest, we were met by Dr. Sanger and a small group of men and women who flanked him. The outdoor classroom was set amphitheater-style, in a massive circle. All the packs and prides would have separate classroom instructions to make sure that they'd get the most of their education. However, today all packs and prides were together for orientation. "Good morning packs and prides, and welcome to this year's wilderness and abandonment survival course. I'll be your professor, Dr. Sanger. Alongside me are my colleagues, each specializing in a different technique you'll be using over the next three years." He clapped his hands together and held them chest level as he spoke. Dr. Sanger was a shorter, stout man with a protruding belly. He wore round glasses and had the makings of a goatee that hadn't quite grown in yet. He wore a beige plaid vest under an off-white tweed overcoat and off-white cotton dress slacks. He was not at all what I'd imagined our survival instructor to be.

"Allow me a moment to introduce them to you. First, as the instructor for shelter construction, I have Professor André. André, please step forward." Coming to the front of the dais was a middle-aged man, also wearing glasses and of average build. He kept his brown hair cut short and wore an off-white khaki uniform with a bright red ascot tied around his neck. "Hello all, I'm Professor André. I come to you with over eighteen years of experience in wilderness survival and habitable structures. This quarter, you will be taught by me about the proper construction of a shelter in whatever environment you may find yourself dropped into. We will create representations of those environments here on the dais, and we will reproduce those structures we have gone over here. That way, no matter where you're sent on assignment, if lost, you can always maintain a level of safety and survival. I'm looking forward to this quarter!" He seemed genuine and approachable. Both of those traits were welcome as we were running out of those whom we could trust.

"Thank you, André. Next up, we have Professor Johnson. She will be your herbologist and edible survival instructor in this class. Please join me in welcoming her to the dais." The groups clapped in welcome. She was tall, with luxurious, long platinum blonde hair. She wore a simple white pantsuit made of cotton, and an oversized hat adorned her head. Her pleasant aura immediately made her my new favorite teacher. Her smile beamed as she accepted our welcome and the welcome of Dr. Sanger.

"Hello! I'm so excited to be at Askari as your herbology teacher! I can't wait to walk through the different plants and foliage you can use at your will for survival in many different environments that you'll surely encounter throughout your life. I'll also be walking you through the dangerous ones too! What to expect while you're in the wilderness is vital to your survival, as much as a shelter, if not more so. We will begin each morning with a new herb or nutritional element and end each class with the plants to be aware of. I can't wait to help you with your journey here and in life! Life is just a success story in the garden of the continent. You were planted, and now, you're blooming. I can't wait to help you thrive!"

We all clapped for her. She made it seem like learning would be fun again, such a much-needed change of pace from what we've previously experienced.

"Thank you, everyone! Lastly, we have Professor Fabian. She will be your camouflage expert for this course! I'm so excited to have her as one of your survival experts. The art that she can truly make with her surroundings is absolutely befuddling." Called forward to the stage was a tall, lanky woman with jet black hair. She used way too much eyeliner, in my opinion, but it made her icy, electric orange eyes pop. She was tan-skinned and wore a simple black crop top and faded black camouflage cargo shorts, which, in my opinion, shouldn't be classified as shorts. The amount of skin she was showing in the classroom was mildly unprofessional, to say the least. She was toned, and the sheer volume of the muscles in her arms and legs made me envious. I wouldn't even consider discussing her abs that poked out below the top and above her low-rise shorts. "Remind me later to get back to the gym because damn..." I leaned into Flynn as I whispered.

"Honey, there is not any length of gym time you could complete that would make your scrawny little arms look like hers. God, she's stunning." He never took his eyes off her as he answered me.

"Alright, pick your jaw off the floor and wipe your drool," I said, rolling my eyes at him.

"Jealousy sucks, doesn't it?" he said, now meeting my eyes. The sinking feeling in the pit of my stomach forced my eyes forward. He could bother someone else with that bullshit.

"Hi everyone, I'm Professor Claire Fabian," she began.

"Yes, you are, honey," Flynn shouted, whistling at her.

"You're too kind, but I honestly don't care if you like me or not," Professor Fabian retorted to Flynn's cat calls.

"Eeee... Perhaps I romanticized too soon about that one." Flynn said, leaning to me, grimacing.

"I don't care if you think what I'm here to teach you is a waste of time, or if you men seem to think it's a 'girly class'." She threw her hands up, quoting and making a snarky face. It was evident that she was a hard ass and didn't care about any of us. "I'm here for one purpose, and that's teaching you how to blend in with your environments. I could lie to you and tell you all that you'll probably never use what I teach you this quarter, but what is the point of a lie? I've found myself on more than one occasion needing to blend in. More times than I care to admit. You all think that shifting alone will be enough to protect you, but if no one has told you yet, let me be the first to break your heart... Shifting doesn't make you invisible, and it won't save your life. Camouflage will and has."

"Tough lead," I said, leaning over to Flynn again.

"Shhh, my wife is on the dais." He was still leaning over, arm bent onto his knee, supporting his face, and locked in on every word Professor Fabian was saying.

"Good lord. Ok, Flynn." I got up then and switched seats, so I found myself next to Kolter and Victor. Flynn's chuckle followed me as I went.

"So, as we finish up this morning, I'd like to introduce myself to you. As I said, I'm Dr. Sanger. I'll be facilitating the courses and projecting them onto the stage. Once you've successfully completed your proper survival shelters or camouflaging or use of herbs and plants to make food, you will be tested out by Dr. Hoboke and me to ensure you've met your targets. Thank you all for being here and being so enthusiastic about this quarter's lessons! If there are no more questions, you will all be dismissed, and your schedules will be posted this evening. Enjoy your afternoons."

"What was that all about?" Kolter asked me as we were headed up the amphitheater stairs leading to the exit of the classroom.

"What was what?" I asked noncommittally, avoiding eye contact with him.

"What happened with Flynn? Why'd you get up and move over to us? Miss me that much?" His flirtation was falling flat because it reminded me again why I was irritated with Flynn.

"Because he makes too many jokes sometimes, and honestly it just wears on me. So, I figured I'd just join you." We entered the trail now back toward the den.

"You're sure?" He looked at me now, and the guilt crept up. I didn't want to worry him about things that meant nothing.

"Yep. I'm good." I grabbed his hand then as we walked back. "I'd really like to go and see our families soon. I know school is over in a few months, but I kind of miss my mom and dad, and I'd really like for you to meet them."

"You, Ms. Monica, would like me to meet your father?" Kolter quipped as he stopped on the trail and brought me to face him.

"Of course, why wouldn't I want you to meet them? We're pack bonded, aren't we? That must mean something, doesn't it?" I was confused. Why wouldn't he want to meet them?

"Ever, there are no two people on this continent I'd rather meet more. The two people who created you gave me you when they let you come to Askari... I owe them more than just a simple visit," he said, stealing my breath away from my chest.

"Do you think we should ask them about us? Do you think my mother knows what I am?" We were walking again, slowly.

"I think she may be as naive as you were. Your father, though, may struggle. He may have a hard time understanding why you're a wolf and not a lion."

"I am a lion, though. I may habitually shift as a wolf and may be part of your pack, but I am just as much a lion. I just wish I knew more about it. I wish he had told me."

"I'm sure he had every reason to hide that from you, and we will go get answers at the end of the term. It'll be here before you know it." He squeezed my hand as we continued to walk, nearing the den now. Out of habit, I squeezed three times.

"Why do you always do that?" He chuckled.

"Do what? What did I do?"

"You always squeeze me back three times. Always. Every time. I picked up on it a while ago and have just been tucking it away to ask. You never falter. It's always three." He brought my knuckles to his lips and kissed them.

"Oh, it's silly. Don't worry about it." I shied away from him, pulling my hands back to my sides.

"I'm serious, what is it? I think it's cute! Don't go." He was following me now. I wasn't going to get away without telling him. Ugh, this was embarrassing.

"It means," I said, taking his hand and placing it in mine and squeezing. "I... Love... You. Three times, and I love you too, four times." It's just something my mom and I do. I guess I'm just used to saying how I feel through squeezes."

"That is probably the nicest thing I've ever heard. Thank you for telling me." Kolter's grin was infectious.

I smiled at him. I did though... I loved him. More than I loved myself. Despite him being pre-bonded to me, despite our blood being mixed, despite our minds being wiped. I have loved him for a very long time. It's most likely why I'd never dated anyone nor bothered to really be with anyone. I knew someone better was waiting for me.

The next morning, we were sitting in Professor Johnson's herbology class, and she had begun her course, listing ten plants we could eat while stranded in the forest. Her list included things like dandelions, cattails, clovers, sheep sorrel, and a few others.

"Yeah, ok. But are there any that aren't a flower or leaf? There have to be berries, right?" Brandt asked her.

"Yes, of course there are berries, but could you do me a favor? Hold on for one second." She took the time to look for two pictures in her folder on the desk while she held her finger up to him. "Ah, yes, here they are." She placed both photos against her chest, holding them up. "Do me and the rest of the class a favor, and show me which is a blueberry and which is a deadly nightshade."

"Oh, well, you see..." he was stuttering and at a loss for words.

"I'm not trying to trick you; I'm trying to give you a realistic example of why eating berries while walking through the forest would be a bad idea unless you're more than one hundred percent sure you've got what you think you do in your hand." She dropped the picture on the left, leaving only the one on the right. "Atropa Belladonna, otherwise known as deadly nightshade, is in most forests, along banks of water, in shrubs and looks damn near identical to blueberries. However, those berries contain a mixture of tropane alkaloids that affect the nervous system. Within minutes, typically, someone who has ingested the berries will begin sweating, vomiting, and have difficulty breathing. Then comes the confusion and hallucinations before it brings you to your death. This isn't meant to scare you, but to inform you that these are some trying times, and just racing for any berry while stranded in the forest is libel to have some serious effects."

"Ok, I think I'll be good with the flowers," Brandt said, making Professor Johnson chuckle.

"I'm not saying you can't eat berries in the wild. I'd just rather you do so after I've taught you. Keep in mind that now that you carry the knowledge and I teach you the exact ways to know which is which, if you came across the nightshade, it doesn't mean you couldn't use it to your advantage if needed. Food for thought, use it as you wish."

A few hours later, we found ourselves on the dais, surrounded by twigs and mud. Structural survival with Professor André was equally informative. Learning how to create a habitable structure in the forest with the use of mud, branches, and pine needles wasn't a first for me, but to some it was a struggle. Once instructed, the nine of us got to work to build the structure. It was slow going at first, but we ladies got the men lugging all the materials in the forest, while we made cement out of mud and water to secure the sticks and logs together. About an hour later, we had a good semblance of a structure going, and we were very pleased with it.

"Excellent work, Highland! That looks like it'll dry quite nicely. We'll leave it for today, and then tomorrow we can add on to the walls and create your roofing. Great job!" He patted the men on the back, and we all stood back and looked at the small structure in front of us. Was it our den? No, not in the slightest, but would it work in a pinch if left stranded? Absolutely yes, it would.

"Everelle, could you by chance stay behind? I'd like a moment," Dr. Sanger asked as he wiped his hands from the mud he'd had on them. Nodding yes, I locked eyes with Kolter, letting him know I'd be ok.

"I'll be just up the hill. Let me know if you need anything." He gave me a quick kiss on the forehead and proceeded up the hill.

"Thank you for staying back. I won't keep you long. I just wanted to know if you've let anyone in on your abilities yet?" Not entirely sure what he was getting at, I decided to air on the side of caution.

"I'm not sure I entirely know what you mean, sir." I adjusted myself so I was sitting across from him.

"I'm talking about your abilities. It could be anything, like for example, the ability to make things happen at your will. Have you honestly never realized that you could control things around you simply by just willing it to be so?"

"I think that's just my rubix," I said, pulling Kolter's necklace out of my shirt and holding it up for him to see.

"Yes, while I'm sure that's a very sentimental piece of rock... I'm not sure you're giving yourself enough credit. I'd like you to also know I'm not in the business of divulging secrets of those I educate to those who wouldn't have their best interests at heart. I know you've only known me a short time, and I'd be naive to think that you'd be willing to give up all your talents to me. Trust is earned. Just know that I'm here if you'd like to practice and work on honing your powers."

"With all due respect, sir, whatever you think I have, I'm flattered, but I don't have extra powers. I'm average for my breed."

"Your breed, yes... you're referring to yourself as a hybrid, are you not? You are doing well hiding that you can double-shift. No one has caught on to it that I'm aware of other than, of course, the cadets. If your educators are aware, none are saying as such. Let me take a stab. Father's a wolf? Mother, a lion? You're able to choose because both parents offered a significant balance of power, and neither would back down, thus making you a super hybrid? I'm impressed. Again, your secrets aren't mine to share. Yours are safe. Unlike the others, I imagine your powers will save this continent. I'm not in the business of killing off brilliance, and you'd be hard pressed to find anyone on the continent who doesn't hold a seat in government office who would sentence you to slaughter. You're an asset. I'd love to have you fighting on our side."

"I'm not sure I follow Dr." What was he saying? Was there a rebellion? Were we amid another overthrow?

"I'm saying that there are armies that fight for justice for all shifters. This continent has been run by only one set of shifters, and change is needed to regain a balance of control. You would be a huge asset to that fight." He began collecting his paperwork on the desk and placing it in his briefcase. "There is a reason I came to accept the position here at Askari and brought my own valued colleagues. I assure you, monetary gain wasn't the reason. You are something our rebellion is looking to collect. Give yourself time to think about it. First thing's first, we need to teach you to see your full potential in the safety of someone who understands you. Second would be to hone those skills, and lastly, would be to help join the rebellion to fight this war that is brewing beyond the borders of the capital. If any of this is something you're willing to do, I'm here, as are my colleagues. They've been handpicked by me from our rebellion."

"And my pack? What's to happen to them if I choose this?" Kolter... I couldn't do anything without him.

"Would you believe me if I told you most of your pack is aware of you and your alpha's true powers? They'll follow you. Think about my offering. I'll see you tomorrow." All I could do was nod and watch as he headed out of the classroom.

Was I truly an instrumental part that could help fuel a rebellion? I had no idea there was even a rebellion to begin with. This was too much.

"You ok? Everelle?" Kolter was approaching me now. He needed to know what was happening, but I couldn't imagine not telling Flynn or the others as well. They all deserved a right to know what they were harboring with me.

"I'm needed for the rebellion. There's a war brewing outside the walls of the capital. Wolves are gearing up for a fight against the government because of the injustice in political structure. It's been led by a lion shifter for far too long. It's 1286 all over again."

"I'd love to say I'm surprised about the rebellion, but honestly, there's been injustice for a long time, and the grumblings have been getting louder over the last few years. What does he want with Highland?"

"He says that he knows I'm a hybrid. However, he hasn't figured it out completely, and I didn't correct him. The less that's known, the better. He also said I have powers, that when I will for something to happen, I can make it so. I'm not sure I buy what he's selling in that regard. I blamed it on your rubix."

Kolter looked frozen, staring off in space; his eyes slowly met mine. "I don't think it's the rubix, I don't know why I never put it together. Ever, you do have powers. I don't know the full extent. We'd have to talk to my mom again, but I think you can siphon the powers of the wolf packs. Remember when we were in the caves, you'd wished for my rubix, and it appeared around your neck? I think you did that. I think you called for it, and it happened. Hadlick wolves can't do that, nor can Highland. Highland wolves," he reminded me, "have strength and sight. It's why Flynn is so invaluable. We can project our vision both down the line and above. You already know that Hadlick wolves are able to cure those that are wounded, but to my knowledge, neither Hadlick nor Highland wolves can call for things." He looked so lost in thought that I felt guilty for bringing him this much confusion. I got up and walked to him, trying to comfort and still his spiraling.

"I'm not sure why you're able to will things to yourself, perhaps the lions do have powers they've kept hidden after all." He was relaxing now, slowing the running of newfound scenarios though his head. "Did he say he'd help you with developing the skills?"

"Yes. He said he would help me unlock all my potential and that he wasn't in the business of discussing my secrets. He understood that trust was earned and not automatic, so he would work with me when I was ready." I was watching Kolter still pace and brought my arms up to stop him. "I think before we do anything, we need to have a conversation with the pack. They're just as much part of this as we are. I think it's only fair that they're given the chance to have a say."

He nodded now. "That's fair. Let's go. I'll call the meeting."

Chapter Thirty-Five

Everelle

Everyone was huddled up now, sitting around the fireplace that Kolter and I now stood in front of. Victor was the first to speak. "So, he wants to help you gain more strength with your powers and also wants us to help join the rebellion against the capital...which also happens to include this school...where he works and we attend?" He was looking both confused and unsure if he'd got it right.

"Yes. Essentially. Kolter seems to think my powers, so to speak, come from the Hadlick blood he gave me." I shrugged.

"Wait a damn minute. What do you mean Kolter gave you Hadlick blood? You're gonna need to run that back slower for all of us who have no fucking clue what you're talking about," Flynn said, angrily.

"That's the second part of this conversation," I said, looking at the floor, unsure if I could look at my pack while I betrayed them. I knew once they learned the truth about me, it would change their loyalty, because they'd assume mine would change on them. "I'm not biologically a wolf from birth...

I'm the opposite. My father is a lion. I have the blood of a lion. However, Kolter and I have had a past long before this school. We met in childhood, and we were unaware of it until recently. We used to play, and long story short, I got severely hurt, and he gave me his blood. It healed me, but it also changed me biologically. His mother wiped our memories for fear that I would be killed, and now you're caught up." I picked up my eyes and looked at Flynn. His eyes were filled with a mixture of anger and hurt.

"He didn't just change you biologically," Nikita said now, looking at both Kolter and me, with angst. "You changed him too."

"So, you manipulated and lied to us. Great. Whatever Everelle. You're always doing the most. Why can't anything with you ever be black and white? You're so morally gray you may as well exist in the twilight!" Flynn was spiraling, standing now with his arms crossed and his face filled with hurt.

"Now just hold on, Flynn. That's not fair. You need to remember she is new to this entire lifestyle. She is traveling through it as best she can, and to be fair, her life has almost ended twice since she's arrived here. No one is very trustworthy... Her best friend died. Cut her some slack and stop taking everything so personally," Brandt cut in.

"Thank you, Brandt. Yes, Flynn, I may not be making the best choices, but I'm trying my best, and I'm working with what I have. I'm sorry I didn't tell the pack from the start. That won't happen again. To be honest, I was more worried about your protection from knowing this than holding it from you out of spite. I can't help that this is what I am or that I'm ignorant of most of these lifestyles. But I'm trying."

"Flynn, stop being a bitch just to be one. She owes you nothing. She's the alpha, not the other way around. Calm yourself down," Nikita butted in.

"Where do we go from here? I guess since it's decided for us that we have a pack with a hybrid couple. What happens now?" Flynn said, exacerbated, crossing his leg over the chair's arm and throwing back a shot of whiskey.

"That's part two... Dr. Sanger is working with a rebellion that is brewing outside the capital walls. The injustice of shifters has always been evident.

The time has come when our families want to fight for our rights. He wants to train Everelle and have us join the rebellion." Kolter addressed the room now, sternly, his voice gruff and full of confidence. "I won't force anyone to join a fight they don't want to be part of. I will take your feelings into consideration. I know that I will go wherever Everelle goes. I won't surrender her and I won't retreat from a fight. However, I'll make sure we all have a voice. You can trust me, especially when there is no one left to trust."

"You don't even have to ask. I'm with you. No matter what it takes," Victor said, standing to shake Kolter's hand.

"Me too. I'm in this." Nikita stood.

"You already know we've got you." Baldur stood, holding his hand out to Lisbeth.

The room followed suit. Everyone was standing now, looking down at Flynn. He remained sitting, looking like the wind had left his sails.

"I'm in, but on one condition," he began.

"What's that?" Kolter asked, smirking.

"We tell them...it's time," Flynn said, looking at the group.

"Tell who what?" I asked, looking at the rest of them. "What are you talking about?"

"Nikita, you promised you'd be the one to do it, the floor is yours." Flynn stepped forward, handing her a glass of whiskey.

"Can someone please just tell us what the fuck is going on?" Kolter barked.

"You're a fucking hybrid too!" Her eyes were filled with defeat. "When you shifted in Pollsmoor. You didn't shift into a wolf like we allowed you to believe. You shifted into a massive silver lion, Kolter. How could you not see that if your blood changed her, hers could change you too?" Nikita's voice came through hot and visceral.

I felt like someone knocked the wind out of my chest. Kolter looked paralyzed.

"We wanted to tell you, but with everything going on and the issues with Everelle healing and becoming a martyr, we just figured we'd keep it muted until we had to face it," Nikita said now, reaching for Kolter. "We don't think less of you. You're still our alpha."

"I'm so sorry. I can't believe I never put the pieces together. How can I fix this?" Kolter stuttered, looking at his pack.

"You don't need to fix anything. You didn't do anything wrong. You're still the same Kolt, just more powerful, bro." Brandt said, stepping forward, squeezing Kolter's shoulder. "We have your back."

"So, what do we do from here?" I asked now, breaking the silence that filled the room.

"We need to stop lying to each other. Omissions are betrayals. You want us to work as one? Treat us like we have a fucking voice. Not omitting important information, disguising it as protection. I know what I signed up for. You don't need to protect me from a fight." Flynn cut in.

"That's fair. Done." Kolter slapped his hand to Flynn's and hugged him.

"Also, if it's not too much to ask... can I get her? Maybe then I'll have some kick-ass powers too," Flynn then said mischievously, pointing in my direction. The punch directly to his face caught him off guard. "God damn it, Kolter! I just grew that fucking tooth back!! Son of a bitch!" Flynn cried out as he spit his tooth into his palm, accompanied by some blood.

Kolter stood, looking like the fires in hell existed behind his eyes. Shaking out his hand, he approached Flynn. "She's not up for negotiating. She's mine. No matter what form she takes, no matter what power she has, no matter where she goes. She's always going to be mine. Enough of the peacocking bullshit."

He walked toward me now, grabbing my hand and leading me to his room. The door slammed to emphasize his point.

Chapter Thirty-Six

Everelle

Days later, once the dust had settled, we all came to terms with our new reality. I was standing in the amphitheater for my first session with Dr. Sanger. I waited for everyone except Kolter to leave the outdoor classroom.

"Eradicate," Dr. Sanger said, while waving his hand in the air. I looked around in confusion.

"What was that?" I asked as he prepared a row of objects across his desk.

"I was eliminating everyone from the area and creating a temporary wall so no one could stumble upon us for our session.

"I need to tell you something, Professor." I began timidly.

He looked at me concerned, and it further amplified my anxiety. "Kolter needs to be trained too... that's why he's here." I looked at the professor now, worried I'd divulged too much.

"I assumed as much. Now, I'd like you, Everelle, to focus on the objects in front of me." He was now gesturing toward a yellow tennis ball, a glass of water, a book, and a pen. "I'd like you to select one and will it to come to you."

Looking at the objects, I just selected the first one in line and settled my gaze. Looking at the yellow tennis ball, I asked it to come to me. "Come," I said, holding out my hand. Nothing happened. I shook out my hands then and stood closer to the table. "Come!" I shouted at the ball, and it again refused to budge. I looked at Dr. Sanger, then I swiveled to Kolter. Neither offered a piece of advice.

Frustrated now, I looked at the ball and yelled. "COME!" The ball mocked me by staying in place. "What am I doing wrong?" I asked Dr. Sanger.

"Perhaps you're not truly willing for it to join you. Have you had an experience before of getting something to come to you?"

"Yes," I said, grasping my rubix and thinking back to the cave.

"How did you feel at that moment? How did it happen for you then?" He sat behind his desk and propped his feet up. The arrogance of his statement, essentially telling me we'd be here a while, fueled me with anger.

"I felt anxious and nervous. I wanted the rubix back that I'd stupidly given to Kolter." I felt myself release some of the frustration now, and remembering the feeling of the cave brought back the nervousness and the sounds of the couple getting murdered.

"Ok, good. Feel that and ask the ball again."

Closing my eyes, I held my hand out in front of me and thought back to the moment that they were murdered and the fear and anxiety I felt. I then clearly begged for the ball to come to me, to help ease my worries. It took a moment before I realized the ball had made it into my hand. Opening my eyes, I looked at my hand, rotating the soft fuzzy ball, and my smile grew.

"Excellent! Now, try again, this time with the glass of water."

Closing my eyes, I again asked for the water to come to me. Immediately, I was met with a soaking. I opened my eyes in frustration again. "Seriously!" I yelled, spitting out water and wiping my face.

"Don't yell at me! I haven't moved. What did you ask for?" Dr. Sanger asked.

"Oh... I asked for the water. I didn't ask for the glass."

"Quite right. It seems you'll need to learn to be more specific."

For the next two hours we worked on willing things to come to me. I got into a rhythm where I was able to keep my eyes open and get something to come within the first few tries of asking. Kolter sat quietly throughout the process.

"I have to say, I don't believe I have this particular power. I can't say I remember a time that I willed for something to happen and it did. I also tried silently several times to will one of the objects to come to me, but none did."

"It's alright. I figured as much. You two, while connected, aren't a clone of one another. You have similar attributes, but in the risk of sounding incestuous, you're like siblings, not identical twins."

Kolter looked at me now, trying to keep a straight face, since I could tell I was making a face of disgust.

"You've done great today, Everelle. Keep practicing for the next few days. Then we will work on how to put things back," Dr. Sanger said, proudly beaming.

"I'll be able to put things back?" I asked, in shock.

"You should be able to. What you can receive, you should be able to give. You have a world of possibilities that you need to be open to. We will continue working with your powers, the same for you, Kolter."

"Maybe it's my ego swinging, but how do I know that this isn't just a result of you empowering me?"

"I'm flattered, but even I can't gift you powers you don't already possess. Have a good night, Everelle." He walked out of the classroom then.

"I have to say, I'm seriously impressed and proud of you," Kolter said, reaching in to pull me close. "Let's go. The pack will be wondering where we are."

Chapter Thirty-Seven

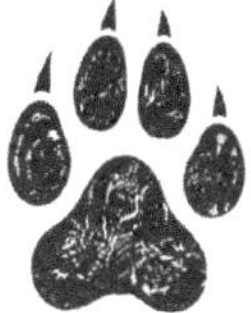

Kolter

Dr. Sanger had turned out to be a huge asset to our pack. Through the individual sessions I'd attended with Everelle, I'd realized I do, in fact, have a power. Recalling six weeks ago, I thought of how it all started.

"Kolter, I want you to try and think hard about your life. Has there ever been anything you can think of that you were able to do that others weren't? It could be the simplest of things that you'd never thought twice about," Dr. Sanger prodded, while leaving me with a little nugget of self-reflection.

"I can't think of anything. I'm sorry," I said, fueled with frustration. Why was this so difficult? If Everelle had given me anything aside from her ability to be a hybrid, I was missing it.

"It's ok, Kolter, you don't have to have the answers today. I just want you to be thinking about your life as a whole. We will reconvene tomorrow, same time. You two are excused," Dr. Sanger said, adjusting his tie, as he began packing up his things.

Everelle and I left his outdoor classroom and headed back toward the den after our sessions. She was beaming because for the first time, she'd successfully willed things to her without closing her eyes and with minimal effort. While she was thrilled, I continued to be fueled with self-doubt.

"Ugh, I just don't understand why I can't think of anything!" I snarled, stopping Everelle in her tracks. She looked perplexed, and I felt even more guilty. Bending over, I picked up a rock and threw it, ricocheting it off some nearby trees.

I wish I could help him. I'm such an asshole! No wonder he's pissed. I'm over her bragging and celebrating my accomplishments, and he has yet to find his. I'm the worst girlfriend ever.

"No, you're not; it's not your fault," I said, picking up another rock and putting my entire force behind the throw. It made it three trees further this time. "Maybe I should check with my mom. She would know if I had some powers I wasn't supposed to, wouldn't she?" I turned to look at Everelle, and she had a look of bewilderment on her face.

"What? Do you hear someone?" I began frantically scanning the area, looking for threats.

"No! It's nothing like that," she said, shaking her head, a small smile growing across her face. She ran toward me then, leaping into my arms, wrapping her legs around my waist. "Kolt! Do you know what you just did?" she asked, her grin so wide I worried she'd rip the corners of her mouth.

"Judging by this position, I'd say my aim was a turn-on?" I asked her, comically. When she didn't say anything, I took the conversation more serious. "Obviously not? What is it?" I asked, returning her smile if not for the simple reason that hers was infectious.

"Babe! You read my mind!" she shouted, excitedly. "I wasn't sharing my thoughts with you, nor have I opened my line yet from Dr. Sanger's session. You knew what I said though, anyway. Do you know what this means?" she asked me. She was so excited she was bouncing in my arms for emphasis.

"Care to fill me in on your thoughts?" I asked her, clearly not following what she was saying.

Oh my God, this man. I swear you're not stupid...

She looked at me now, rolling her wide eyes, and it clicked. All those times when I'd first met her and no one could hear her or feel her. I could. All the times when my pack mates were having intimate moments or insecurities, the reason I'd known was because I could read their minds. It had nothing to do with the line at all. They couldn't shut me out. Everelle had been the only person to ever successfully close her door to me. I gently put her down now and took a step back.

Years of memories flooded my mind, moments when I was privy to my mother's intimate sorrows of my brother's and father's deaths. Moments when the pack experienced their highest points and their lowest failures. Moments when I'm sure they'd not want someone knowing what they'd felt, I knew. I knew, against their will, because there wasn't a part of them they could keep hidden from me. It felt too real, too overwhelming.

"Kolt? Are you ok?" Everelle asked me worriedly. I knew she was worried because she was spiraling again in her mind... where I lived rent-free, and she hadn't invited me to be there.

"We need to go back to Dr. Sanger. He needs to help me," I announced, not looking toward her. Catatonic, I began retracing our steps toward the classroom we'd just left.

By the grace of God, Dr. Sanger was still there. I watched in slow motion, not saying a word as Everelle frantically filled him in, looking at me now. She pierced my soul with those same eyes that just moments ago had been celebrating. They were worried now, wet with tears on the verge of escape.

"Kolter," Dr. Sanger broke my trance from watching Everelle. "If you can hear me, I'm going to give you something to help. I'm going to ask that you drink it. I think you're in shock and experiencing mental overload. We need to get you to calm down." Dr. Sanger was now reaching into his briefcase, pulling out a small blue vial of liquid. "Kolter, can you hear me?"

I couldn't process anything that was happening. My mind saw it all, but my mouth couldn't communicate. I just kept reliving moments from my past, precious intimate moments when I shouldn't have known things, but I did. Memories that weren't supposed to be mine now haunted me.

"How do I turn it off?" was all I could think to ask him. I took the bottle of liquid and brought it to my lips. Praying, I wasn't the monster I began to fear I was.

"I know someone who can help you, Kolter. I'm going to need you to trust me, and I need to know that I can trust you, also. Can you do that?" Dr. Sanger asked as I drank the liquid. I nodded in reply.

"Professor André can assist you in this particular department. He shares this gift, but Kolter, it is extremely important that you do not mention this to anyone. Shifters with your gift are extremely lethal to the Sector. They will collect you and force you to do their bidding. If you refuse, they will most likely kill you for fear of what you could use against them. Do you understand what I'm telling you?" he asked me, calmly.

I could only nod. Slowly my brain began to unwind, relaxing itself, as if using a garden hose on a fire, slowly putting it out. I sat in the chair in front of Dr. Sanger's desk and waited for the liquid he'd given me to finish its job.

Everelle and Dr. Sanger were in a quiet discussion, and I slowly began to fade out. Blinking, I saw them talking. My eyes closed, and there was darkness. My eyes, heavy now, rose ever so slightly, and Ever and Dr. Sanger appeared again, approaching me. My eyes became too heavy. I couldn't keep them open. Darkness.

When I opened my eyes again, I was back in my bed in the den. My heart was lying beside me fast asleep. Looking toward my desk, I saw the clock read four thirty. Based on the fact that our sessions started at five in the afternoon, it was pretty safe to say it was early morning.

I relived the realizations that came to me after Everelle figured out my powers. It didn't have to be a bad gift. Now that I knew I was privy to intimate things at any given time, I could just choose to not read them. Couldn't I? Visions from earlier came back, haunting me all over again. I shook my head, desperate for them to leave me.

We would have a session with Professor André later this afternoon. I'd get my questions and worries answered then.

Looking down, I saw Everelle, sleeping peacefully, and my heart settled. My feelings surged with a new sense of hope and purpose. I'd promised her I'd be her protector with my mind, but I had no idea I was also the reason hers wasn't safe.

I scooted closer to her, wrapping my arms around her thin waist and kissing her head. I let sleep pull me under, if for no other reason than to quiet my spiraling mind.

Chapter Thirty-Eight

Everelle

After we'd learned Kolter could enter minds, he began working exclusively with Professor André while I'd met with Dr. Sanger.

In hindsight, we should have known much sooner about Kolter's power based on the amount he was always milling around in my head. He'd worked tirelessly to be able to lock himself out of everyone's minds, because once he'd learned he could enter them, it was as if the doors that housed everyone's deepest thoughts and secrets were wide open. Kolter was powerful, probably one of the most powerful hybrids on the continent, Professor André had said. He was able to reach inside someone's mind without even trying. No matter how many wards Professor André put up, Kolter always penetrated his mind. No matter how hard we all fought to keep him out, Kolter could enter our minds. Because he'd been doing it for years, without knowing, he had developed the skill so fluidly that he didn't even have to look at someone to read their mind. Professor André's sessions were spent teaching Kolter how to stay out of people's minds. It seemed that was harder for him to control.

With Kolter being as trustworthy as he was, he wanted everyone to still have their privacy.

In the six weeks it'd been since we'd begun our private lessons, we'd managed to be able to utilize our powers to our will. It was exciting to know we'd have a real future with new skills.

We as a pack were also making progress in survival structures and herbology. This week I had been able to use the mud from the forest to blend myself seamlessly with a pine tree. Classes and cadets both seemed much calmer.

"Alright guys, this was an excellent last class! Break is here this weekend. You'll have your respite for the next three months before we reconvene. Please try not to forget everything you've learned. I'd strongly encourage you to study. Take time in the forest and other areas on the continent and challenge yourselves with the skills we've learned here this quarter. You never truly know when you'll find yourself needing to use them," Dr. Sanger said as he dismissed us.

"Everelle, Kolter, please stay behind. We'd like to discuss something with the both of you," Professor Johnson said as the pack gathered up their things, celebrating that we'd be leaving tonight to head home.

"How can we help you guys?" I asked, once everyone but Kolter and I had left the room.

"We mostly just wanted to see if you'd given any more thought into joining the rebellion. We'd love to have you both come out to Draiocht over break and see the headquarters and continue your private lessons. There are also more of us who can assist you in ways you've not yet discovered," Dr. Johnson said as she packed up her belongings.

"I did have the chance to talk it over with my pack. We are all on board to join the rebellion. I can see to it that we give you some time over break so you can show us what you're working on and how we can be of assistance." I reached for Kolter's hand as I spoke.

"We're definitely looking forward to assisting in any way we can, Professor," Kolter added.

"Perfect. That's what I like to hear. Your pack has done phenomenally this quarter; I anticipate that you'll have no problem at all joining forces with our men and women already on the ground. There will be rebellion houses and meetings within your respective villages. Please try and attend one meeting a week. The mass meeting is every Sunday afternoon at four. We connect every village to one large virtual meeting, and everyone can give updates and critical information. It's imperative that you attend that meeting, if possible. Introduce yourselves to the members of the rebellion there. It's been such a pleasure this quarter. I'll see you over break then." She hugged me and shook Kolter's hand before leaving the classroom.

Slowly we made our way back to the den. It was mostly quiet.

"Do you know where you'll go? Are you going to Tuathanas with me or back to Seoid?" I asked, trying desperately not to sound like a pathetic girlfriend who couldn't stand to be away from her boyfriend.

"So, you're my girlfriend again now?" He joked, pulling me closer as we walked.

"I mean... I'd hope so?"

"Babe, you're not getting rid of me so easily. I never thought otherwise. But to answer your question, I figured I'd get off the train at Tuathanas with you," he said, tightening his grip on my hand. Although there is a rule for boarding the train at certain stops, the Sector doesn't care where you go when you leave on break, so they don't keep track. "I'd like to meet your family and stay for a few days. I do have to go home to check in on Mom, but maybe you could come? She'd love to see you, and you could meet Kameron. He comes back with us next year, and I worry that it'll change the dynamics in the pack. Victor knows that bylaws of the pack indicate Kameron would be my beta, but you also know that I run it how I see fit. I can't imagine myself using Kameron as my beta when I've had such a good rapport with Victor."

"I'm sorry the responsibility is on you to decide. It can't be easy to make that choice. I know whatever choice you do make, you'll make it with logic and reason. I support you," I said as we entered the den.

"There you two are!" Nikita hissed. The train leaves in fifteen minutes. I want to go home, sooo can you get your shit together for once in your life?" She pushed past us then, headed for the exit of the den.

"I'm already packed. I can meet you back here in five minutes or less," I said as he kissed my forehead.

"Perfect. Meet you here."

Walking into my room I stopped and took it in for one more time. This school, while strenuous, has made me such a different person. The person who slept in this bed that first night is not the same one who slept in Kolter's last night. Picking up my bag off the desk, I noticed it was quiet in the hallways. Everyone must have gone up to the train. I sighed a deep breath as I turned to leave the last room my best friend had ever slept in, one we stayed up way too late gossiping and dreaming in. I turned around, and my heart broke all over. With tears in my eyes, I closed the door for the last time. I sighed deeply as I started down the hallway to meet Kolter.

Later, after we boarded the train home, I noted there was a buzz of excitement. Most of the cadets were eager to get home and celebrate the holidays.

Much like the first time I rode the train, everyone was calling dibs on rooms, and the thought immediately hit me. Priya wouldn't be here this time. I wasn't sharing a room with her. Walking toward the sleeping quarters, Kolter rested his hand gently on my back. "I thought it would be kind of fun to room together on the way home. Is that too presumptuous?" he asked, kissing my shoulder.

"No, that's fine. I'm ok with that." The tears in my eyes brimmed.

"You alright? he asked, sensing me as I opened the room I'd stayed in previously.

"Priya," was all I could muster. Crossing the room, I fell onto the bed.

"Oh, Ever, I'm so sorry. This can't be easy for you. I'm so sorry. What do you need?" He was putting our bags away while I lay in the center of the bed looking toward the ceiling that was transfigured into a starry night sky.

"Nothing. I think I'm just going to soak in the tub. I've dreamed about it since I saw it and never got to use it."

He came over to me then. "I think that is the perfect plan." He grabbed my left foot then, raising it off the bed and placing it directly on his chest, making quick work of his fingers on the laces. My boot was now on the floor. He repeated the process with the right and then pulled me to my feet.

Dragging me into the bathroom, he leaned over and started the deep golden tub, the steam rising in minutes. I watched him with curiosity as he walked to the closet, removing a lavender-scented bath bomb, lavender soaking salts, and bubbles. With precision, he scooped out the salts, sprinkling them in the tub, immediately giving the room the euphoric scent of relaxation. He then dropped the ball in the water, and it began to fizz, spinning repeatedly around the tub. Once he'd doctored up the water, he rose to me.

Delicately, he untied my leather ropes that held my corset closed. When the last tie broke free, my corset fell in two, dropping to the floor. The cool air immediately hardened my nipples and cascaded a coat of goosebumps down my body. Without taking his eyes from mine, he glided his fingers across my waistband and popped the button while delicately running his hands down to my hips and slipping my pants down my thighs as he kissed my stomach. I stepped from my pants, now completely naked. The lurch of the train beginning to roll down the tracks forced me into his arms. Raising my face to his, he softly put his lips to mine, kissing away my sadness.

"Why don't you soak? I'll go grab you a dinner tray and a drink, and we can spend the night in bed, just relaxing."

"That sounds perfect." He took my hand and helped me gingerly step into the tub. The heat from the water felt good, rising over my sore and taught muscles and joints.

I watched him leave then, and I put my head back against the tub, dreamily going in and out of consciousness. Drifting my pain away.

He was back then, in what felt like minutes, but the water had gone cold. Instead of getting out, I simply flicked the hot water back on. "How are you feeling?" he asked, coming over to bring me a drink.

"Better, thank you." I smiled at him as he sat on the tub's edge. Grinning now, I asked him, "What are you doing?" Self-conscience taking over, I brought my arms up to wrap across my torso.

"Stop doing that." He reached into the tub and pulled my hands away, exposing my nakedness below the water. His fingers lingered now, running slow circles over my stomach. "You're absolutely beautiful; don't ever be self-conscious for me to see you." He continued to run his fingers over my body delicately. Absently, a moan left my lips as I tilted my head back. He then reached over and turned off the knob to the tub and resumed his stroking. With each pass, he got slightly lower until he was just above my folds. I arched my back then, relishing in his touch.

"You want to know my fantasy?" he asked while teasing the folds of my center.

"Mhmm," I moaned, not opening my eyes.

"This," he said as he slid his two fingers between the folds of my lips and slowly rubbed my clit in circles. The pressure and warmth were intoxicating. He'd just started, and I was already moving my body to match what he was doing. All at once, he began slipping his fingers inside of me; the pressure was building, and I shot my eyes open. His eyes were burning with desire, and he was now leaning further into the tub as he rubbed me, sliding in and out.

With his other hand, he used his fingers to roll my nipple, squeezing it as I thrust onto his fingers. "Oh my God, Kolter," I moaned loudly.

"Yes, baby? Something wrong?" he teased, stopping what he was doing and waiting for my answer.

"No, don't, don't stop!" I was now fully thrusting my pelvis, riding his fingers, water splashing from the sides of the tub with the momentum of my body.

"That's my good girl. Cum for me," he purred, his voice deep and husky. It was laced with desire.

The pressure built until it erupted with screams of his name and the heat bursting between my thighs. I threw my head back, breathing erratically.

In one smooth motion he was pulling me into a towel, fervently kissing me, and walking me gently to the side of the bathroom wall. When had his pants come undone? Did I do that?

Pushing me against the wall, he wrapped my legs around his waist, his mouth catching my gasp as he didn't hesitate, thrusting deeply into me with his extremely hard cock. Again, he thrust, the wall molding digging into my back as he rammed me harder, the pain mixing with sheer pleasure and burning me.

He came then, violently. Kissing me softly as he thrust a few more times, slowing down. "That has been my dream ever since I saw you step out of this room in your leathers for the first time." Gently, he put me down to the floor.

"Well...that was a fantasy I fully support practicing." I collapsed to the floor; my legs were too weak to hold me up.

"Anytime, babe. Anytime." He scooped me up then, taking me to bed.

The next three days were spent eating, reading, and meeting with the pack. The nights, though, were filled with shower sex, bathtub sex, bed sex, and wall sex. The train held no place we didn't break in, including the gangway on the very front car of the train.

On the morning of the third day, we pulled back into the same train station we left nine months ago. "You sure you're ready for this?" I asked as he carried our bags through the train station lobby.

"Of course I'm ready. I'm more than ready to meet the people who made my best friend."

My smile widened. He truly knew how to melt me.

"Babe, fix your face. We don't have the time or place to fulfill what I'd want to do to you if you keep looking at me like that."

I chuckled as we stepped into the sun and toward the parking lot. We never told my parents we were coming, so we'd have to take a bus. "Sorry, I forgot to warn them. They didn't know to come grab us."

"It's fine. I just hope they're ready to know you're dating someone, and a wolf at that," Kolter said, as if being a wolf was somehow a downgrade.

The bus ride was uneventful and quick, dropping us off directly in front of the same white house with its missing shutters. Stepping on to the porch, I took a note from Kolter's playbook and rang the bell. It was odd but felt like the right thing to do.

I watched my mother's smiling face open the door wide, and then upon seeing us, her smile dropped. "Ummm, Kalvin? Honey? You might want to come here for this..."

Looking at Kolter, I grabbed his hand and swallowed. All I could do was wish that all of my questions would be answered, as if finishing the puzzle on my first year as an Askari Military Academy cadet. Grinning at him, I realized the girl I was when I last stood on this porch was long gone. The girl I am now would never be the same.

Chapter Thirty-Nine

When I first broached the subject of writing a book, it was while in bed next to my husband. As an avid reader, he's notorious for having to tell me to put the book away and turn out the light. Usually, it would entail a sigh or a plea for one more chapter. That night, he asked me to put the book down and turn out the light, and I did. He knew something was off. Asking me if everything was alright, I just replied, "this book just isn't doing it for me." When you pick up this specific author, you expect this specific story line, as that is what the author has been known for their entire existence. It wasn't that at all. So, I simply said, "I wish I could write a book."

My husband looked at me with the most confidence I'd ever seen and responded, "You could. I'm sure you could. What would you write about?" For the next hour or longer, I can't recall, we dove into this world. The very world you just left. He helped pick out characters, and helped develop my plot, both of our minds working as one. It was amazing. I was inspired.

The next day, I asked him if I could get an iPad to begin writing, because I was serious about writing the story we'd come up with. I'd been at work all day, and all I could think about was getting my story, our story, "on paper." He did one better. I had a laptop by the end of the day.

This man allowed me peace, quiet, space, and picked up the slack for two weeks and one day while I holed myself up in our bed. Yes, my bed. This story was written from the soft cocoon of my very bed that the idea first took hold. My husband was patient, kind, and excited. Never before had he been a reader, but when I told him I'd written more chapters, he quickly would come running and gobble up the story, in his words, "as if watching a TV series." He'd been so impressed by me. I'll never get over the feeling that bloomed in my chest. I knew if this series came to fruition, it was all because of him. My real-life Kolter.

I'd like to acknowledge all of my coworkers, clients, and friends who had to withstand my constant chirping about this book. Allowing me the space to take time away from the chair so I could dedicate the time to it that it deserved. I'd love to send a shout-out to a few clients in particular that read it along with my husband and continued to ask for more, because they were enthralled. Your devotion and support, both in the chair, and for this book, means so much.

To the friends, Shannon, Natalie, Kayla, Mike, Mariah, and Ashley, who mean more to me than the term "friend" could define. You have indirectly become characters; my subtle nod to you. Though we may not see each other every day, I still love you. I miss you. The best way I could honor you was to create a character in your image, for you. Just know, though the image may not resemble you, your personality rings through in the characters. I couldn't have done that without you all being so invested in our lives.

To my long-lost friend and editor. We used to know each other on so much more of an intimate level, and, through the years, lost contact. However, you've never stopped being part of my life. I like to think of it as kismet that I reached out to you when this process began. I don't think this book could have been what it is without your support, work, dedication, and encouragement.

You have been nothing short of amazing. I can't wait to see where we take The Shattered Crown Series next.

To my readers, the dreamers, and the idealists. This one is for you. Know you're never too old, never too young, never too busy, or too poor to start a new dream. Use your talent for what God intended. If you think you can do it, my advice is DO IT!

Chapter Forty

Crystal Bittel is the author of *The Shattered Crown Series*, with *The Pack* as its captivating debut novel. A wife and devoted mother of three daughters, she draws daily inspiration from the love, strength, and imagination that fill her home.

Originally from Syracuse, New York, she has been an avid reader for as long as she can remember, always finding comfort and adventure within the pages of a good book. Her passion for storytelling began during her college years at SUNY Oswego, where she first discovered the power of weaving emotion, fantasy, and romance into unforgettable worlds.

A lover of escapism, Mrs. Bittel writes for readers who crave immersive fantasy, fierce loyalty, and stories that offer a magical refuge from the realities of everyday life. Through her richly imagined worlds, she invites readers to lose themselves in adventure, love, and destiny.

www.ingramcontent.com/pod-product-compliance
Ingram Content Group UK Ltd.
Pitfield, Milton Keynes, MK11 3LW, UK
UKHW022028190726
13853UKWH00005B/2161

9 798994 790502